Women Don't Need to Write

Women Don't Need to Write

Raquel Puig Zaldívar

Arte Público Press
Houston, Texas
1998

This volume is made possible through grants from the National Endowment for the Arts (a federal agency), Andrew W. Mellon Foundation, the Lila Wallace-Reader's Digest Fund and the City of Houston through The Cultural Arts Council of Houston, Harris County.

Recovering the past, creating the future

Arte Público Press
University of Houston
Houston, Texas 77204-2090

Cover illustration and design by James F. Brisson

Puig Zaldívar, Raquel.
    Women don't need to write / by Raquel Puig Zaldívar.
    p.   cm.
    ISBN 1-55885-257-3 (trade pbk. : alk. paper)
    1. Cuban Americans — Florida —Miami —Fiction. I. Title.
PS3566.U35W6 1998
813'.54—dc21   98-28335
                                                         CIP

♾ The paper used in this publication meets the requirements of the American National Standard for Information Sciences—Permanence of Paper for Printed Library Materials, ANSI Z39.48-1984.

8 9 0 1 2 3 4 5 6 7   10 9 8 7 6 5 4 3 2 1

Prologue

They chose Sunday on purpose. It was a day for outings, for pic-
nics, for excursions to the countryside. Fidel Castro himself said that
national tourism was of the utmost importance. Who would suspect
anything if they went to Las Villas for the day? It could not be early in
the morning; they had to take Juan Andres and me to church. They
would then have lunch, and after leaving the boy and me at the apartment, they would pick up the others and head for their destination.

Norma had believed in the justice of their cause; Andres had
agreed to store and transport weapons for the counter-revolution
because of his wife's blind faith in the movement. Neither knew that I
was aware of their plan. She was fully convinced that a just cause could
only bring about success; he had doubts when he remembered that the
trunk of the car was full of ammunition, medicines, and uniforms for
the rebels. I could tell. A militiaman could stop them any minute, and
then all of them—his son and me included—would land in jail. The
mission of supplying stores and ammunition had been entrusted to others; however, three of them had sought asylum in foreign embassies
while the fourth one had been arrested in Caibarien and charged with
distributing subversive literature. I just listened while I sewed, and they
spoke freely, thinking I couldn't understand. Andres, Norma, his wife,
and another couple would have to do it; they were all that remained of
their group. Talking about the trip, Andres' voice echoed his desperation.

"Norma, you've got to swear that this will be the first and last time
we'll get directly involved. It's too risky; think of the boy. Maybe in
trying to help, we'll be destroying ourselves and, what's even worse,
destroying him," he told her quietly in the car.

"All right, darling, all right. There'll be no more direct involvement. I agreed to do it this time because it was absolutely necessary. All
connections with the fighters up in the hills have disappeared, and
we've got to get these things to those brave men in the front. In the
future they'll be supplied a different way, I promise you," she answered
in earnest.

The noise from the engine could have kept their son, Juan Andres
and me from hearing their conversation, but I was so anxious about my
son's safety that I could feel Norma tremble in her speech. Then, she
turned around and began tickling Juan Andres.

"What have you got to say, *cielo*?"

"Mama, let's go to the movies, please."

"Not today, son, we'll go some other day."

"*¡Diablos, mami!*" he exclaimed, disappointed. "Papa, talk to her. Couldn't we go to the movies just for a while?"

"Your mother is right; it can't be."

"Well, tell the teacher not to come tomorrow."

"What did you say, boy?" Norma tried unsuccessfully to seem angry, but only managed to sound surprised.

"Mama, you think I'm still a baby. *Abuelita* and I get bored at home. Why can't we go for a drive with you today? It's Sunday!"

"It's too far where we're going," There was worry in Norma's voice again.

"Oh, I want to go, I want to, please," he begged.

"Impossible."

"Don't insist, Juan Andres. It just can't be. We'll take you some other day, but today it's out of the question."

Convinced, the boy sat back on his seat and cuddled close to me.

It was past one-thirty when they left us—the boy and me—and picked up Hilda and Polito Cruz. He was an attorney, she, a physical education teacher. Not until those hudlums came for us did I get any idea of what had happened. I didn't know that was the last time I would ever see Norma and my son driving together. Silly of me not to realize I, Rosa Garach, almost eighty years old, was facing the end of an era . . . once more.

Andres was driving with extreme caution, trying to avoid any minor traffic violation that might attract some policeman's attention. Inside the smoke-filled car, no one spoke. They were to drive down the Central Highway to Sancti Spiritus; then they would take a secondary road to Manacas. An old man with crutches would be waiting for them at the entrance to the town and would lead them to the meeting place. A truck, painted in a threatening shade of olive—military fatigue—green, overtook them. Its speed shook their car, and interrupted Norma's thoughts.

"Beasts!" she blurted.

"They're criminals. I can't imagine why people accept them. Have you read the newspapers lately? They're a laugh, I tell you. A few weeks ago, I read that the government had taken over CMQ because the management of the station was hostile to his employees. When they phrase it that way, people are glad to see those things happen."

"Norma and I have talked about it many times. They even come up with names to deliberately confuse the issue. For example: 'The Ministry of Recovery of Ill-Gotten Properties.' A gem, isn't it?"

"Remember Andres? Just the other day we read the government had expropriated three sugar mills because its owners allegedly used devious means to enrich themselves unlawfully under Batista's protection."

"We've got to get rid of the revolution by December," Norma sighed.

"This is not as easy as you think, Norma. Look, six months ago we tried to murder Fidel, and the attempt was spoiled when I fell from a high cement wall and ended up with a broken hip," Polito said.

"All cannot go wrong. These people up in Escambray are fighting well; they're fully devoted to the cause, and they won't stop until they overthrow the government."

"Unless they get stopped first, that is."

"Don't be such a pessimist, Andres. Do you remember how you used to tell me the revolution could not succeed, that there was no way of overthrowing Batista? Well, we did. Too bad we were mistaken."

"It was different then, Norma. The people rejected him, and it was just a matter of dealing with his army and police. Now, hundreds . . . thousands," he corrected himself, "are shouting 'Fidel, Fidel.' What do you intend to do about them?"

"One's got to be positive. As soon as they all see the lies hidden under those beards and olive green fatigues, they'll ask for his head. Mark my words."

They arrived in Sancti Spiritus, a colonial city in the Las Villas province, shortly after seven o'clock. A sign "Manacas," told them to turn right. Andres slowed down; the road was full of potholes. Somehow, his heart seemed to have stopped beating and started shaking. His mind, rebelling against the body and the space around it, went back to Havana, in a forlorn attempt to be with Juan Andres, his son, but the incipient, Las Villas night fell threateningly, only partially overcome by the car's headlights. It was October, 1959. The rolled-up windows kept out the damp, cool Cuban countryside. Suddenly, Andres, Norma, and their friends looked ludicrous in their city clothes; their excuse for being there—that they were on a picnic—rang hollow.

"If we bump into a militiaman, and he asks us what we are doing here, what will we tell him? Andres asked.

"Don't worry, we won't." Norma's optimism was boundless. "This is a small country town, they need no militiamen here, you'll see. How much farther is it?"

"Look, people, if things get tough and they stop us, we'll tell them that we've come to help the revolution stamp out illiteracy. That's kind of popular these days; what do you say?"

"Keep your eyes on the road; we're almost there. Somebody is supposed to be waiting for us, right?"

A few minutes later, they saw a man with crutches standing by the roadside. Nemesio Peña was his name. The oldest resident of Manacas, he said from the outset. Of course, he knew where to take them! There were so many nuts loose out there that somebody had to keep his head on, never mind that he was more than eighty years old!

"Not even in Manacas can we trust anybody any longer! But, like I've always said, when you get something for nothing, you'd better watch out. In the end, they'll wind up taking something even bigger away from you. Land Reform! I won't fall for that story!"

For the first time since leaving Havana, Andres smiled as he listened to the old man with earth-colored hands and almost no teeth. He wondered if the man could read.

Nemesio explained that they would have to drive across town and then, after leaving Manacas, turn to the right and drive a short distance. Then, they would have to leave the car and proceed on foot.

"Should we leave the car alone?"

"Lady, I don't know about that. Nemesio is at your service; I'm here to guide you and help you, but the car can't go into the bush country, impossible."

"I don't mean that. Shouldn't somebody stay in the car, just in case?"

"I agree with you, Norma," said Polito. "If they get their hands on the car we'll be in serious trouble."

"Why don't you stay, Andres?" Norma suggested.

"Good idea, Norma. We'll unload the stuff, receive our instructions, and get out of here. You stay here, Andres, and be ready to take off as soon as we return."

"No, Norma, you stay, and I'll go with you two and Nemesio. I can't just sit here and think . . . well, if anything happens, I'd rather it happen to me."

"The one staying in the car will be in a more dangerous situation. Besides, Andres, your leg . . ."

Other arguments failed to convince him; but he had to bow to the powerful logic of this last one. It was true; his gait was unstable, his leg . . . It was difficult to walk . . . impossible to run.

"Oh, all right; I'll stay! But if you . . ." Andres didn't finish the sentence and dismissed any additional comment on the matter. "You'd better hurry," he added.

"Don't you worry, sir. I know the back country as if it was mine. I've lived here all my life," Nemesio reassured him.

Despite the foreboding the night instilled in their souls, they were happy to get off the car. It was cool and slightly damp and the air smelled of Cuba, with a vibrant wet and fertile sweetness.

"My house is over yonder; your friends are waiting for you there. Leave the crates here; the ladies shouldn't be carrying them. The others will come and pick them up as they've done before."

Norma walked up to her husband. She smiled to conceal her fears.

"Come, now, why the sad face? I promise I'll never ask you to do this again. We'll be finished in less than an hour; we'll be home by dawn."

"I'll change the expression on my face when all of you come back safe and sound," he answered. She reached up on her toes to kiss him. "Norma! Norma! Why are we doing this? Why are we sacrificing so much?" he whispered in her ear.

"The cause is worth it, Andres. We're doing it for Cuba."

2 6

It must have been when it happened that I could sense that something was amiss. For several months, Juan Andres had been bouncing from house to house; today at Asuncion's, tomorrow at Milagros', or perhaps Carolina's or Lucia's. Andres would call on the phone instead of coming to see me. No, I did not ignore what was happening. At any rate, they needed me, an old woman in her seventies. The boy especially did, and after Milagros and Natalia left, I announced her intention of spending some time at my eldest son's apartment.

Juan Andres was eleven years old, but he was not going to school at the time. He was on vacation in August; when September came, Norma refused to send him back to school. She argued that the Communists had taken over. Instead, she engaged the services of an English instructor and a mathematics teacher who came to the house three times a week.

"Let's see, Miss Rosa, are you ready for your class today?" Juan Andres was a most imaginative boy. In just seconds, he could transport us to marvelous worlds, ready to tackle great feats with us as the main characters. That October evening, we were playing school.

"Yes sir," I know I answered, sitting at the table surrounded by papers and pencils. He was wearing a pair of trousers that belonged to his father and carried a globe under his arm.

"Take your pencil, please," he instructed me, knowing I had never learned to read and write. "We will first try to write your name. R is a pretty sort of a letter, actually. A stick and then a loop."

I was dying to learn, and he could tell. His attitude filled me with affection. He placed his arm on my own, and I remember I looked at the two skins, next to each other, realizing that those innocent but skillful fingers were an extension of my own, already cumbersome and rough. Overwhelmed by the miracle of generations I found it hard to concentrate on my task: R-O-S-A G-A-R-A-C-H.

"*¡Caramba, Abuelita!*" The boy jumped, forgetting his professional airs. His "eyeglasses" fell under the table.

The clock in the hallway chimed. It was eleven-thirty, the magic hour at the Garach home, when learned professors returned to their status as children, and pupils became *Abuelita* once again. It was bedtime.

"Ah, it's too early. Mama and Papa aren't even here yet!" he complained.

"Come, Juan Andres. Your mother always says you must go to bed at ten, and it's eleven-thirty. I pamper you too much; your father and mother wouldn't like it if they knew."

Juan Andres looked at me with mischief in his eyes and sat on my knees.

"You, gypsy, you. You really know how to butter me up! All right, we'll go to bed together."

We were headed for the bedroom when the doorbell rang. More than a call it was a warning, but I was perhaps too old to tell. Juan Andres ran towards the foyer.

"It must be mama and papa! It must be them! Quick, *Abuelita*, come!"

"Wait, child, Juan Andres! Don't open the door, sweetheart, your parents wouldn't ring the doorbell; they have a key!"

I was too late. The boy had opened the door and immediately recoiled and ran to seek protection in my arms. The machine guns and the olive green fatigues clashed violently with the youth of the three beardless militiamen standing in the doorway.

"May I help you!" I should have sounded firmer, but I had never seen a gun so threateningly close.

"Is this the home of Andres and Norma Garach?" The voice of the militiaman told me he was really still a boy.

"It is. What can I do for you?"

"Look, ma'am, we've got orders to take this child with us." He pulled a piece of paper from his pocked and despite the dim light, read out the name: "Juan Andres Garach."

"There must be some mistake. It's bedtime and a young boy shouldn't be out in the street at this time of the night. It's not good for him, the poor thing."

"I'm sorry, ma'am, but we have to obey our orders. The boy's mother has been arrested for high treason and for aiding and abetting counterrevolutionary elements." He hesitated a few seconds. "What do you think, Luis?"

"Hey, man, grab the kid and let's beat it. It's not for us to argue with the major." The youngest of the three soldiers remained silent.

"I'm sorry, lady, but we have to take the boy, by force if necessary. We've got to obey the revolution. Kid, come here!" Juan Andres violently shook off the militiaman's hand.

"All right, the two of us will go," I said trying to take off my apron quickly.

"*Abuelita*, don't let them take me away, *Abuelita*, please!" Juan Andres whimpered as he clung to me.

"We'll both go, sir," I repeated.

"You better stay, *Abuelita*. The barracks are no place for old people."

"Or children either!" I shouted angrily, pushing Juan Andres behind me. The militiaman walked up to us, grabbed my grandson by the arms and dragged him towards the elevator.

"Let's go, Luis." The second militiaman shoved me aside and tried to close the door.

As if activated by an electric charge, I flung the door open and ran towards the elevator. My boy's screams gave me powers I thought I had lost years before.

"Holy Madonna de l'Avella! Don't take him away, for God's sake!"

By the time the metal door closed and the boy's screams became fainter, and I couldn't speak. I hastened down the steps, clutching the handrail. One, another, why couldn't I go any faster?

"Help!" Didn't people hear me? "Help!" I shouted again.

No one heard my screams. The ground floor was deserted. The elevator, its door wide open, seemed to be mocking my slow steps. That night I remembered that despair felt cold. I didn't hear any loud thumping inside my chest like I had years before when fate or Juan Garach had taken Lucas, Fermin or Pepet from my side. That night my heart must have left my body and run after Juan Andres.

"The barracks are no place for old women," they yelled. Would they be the place for worn out hearts?

Of the three men, the one who was blonde, corpulent, with strong arms brought the strongest pounding to my temples. With the same strength that Juan Garach had once possessed, he picked up Juan Andres as any of us would pick up a paper bag, and threw the boy onto the back seat. That might, that strength, that raw violence . . . It was enough to take me back fifty years. I blinked, trying to get reality straight, but my desperate mind did not help. Whether in Tirig or in Havana, I found myself wishing, as I had often wished before, that I could at once conquer my helplessness, rise above it, put up a fight and win. No one should have been able to take another child from my side, but they had. The car's motor sounded farther and farther away, so I embraced the door frame of the building's main entrance and screamed my sorrow into the darkness where no one dared respond. That night I found out I had no tears left, so with a tearless grimace of grief, I waited for dawn at the foot of the stairs, once again frustrated and alone.

PART I

Chapter 1

In the spring of 1900, Juan Garach greeted the new century by getting married. He and Rosa met for the first time two years before. Juan, a heavy-set, energetic man, arrived unexpectedly at a *masia*, a big farmhouse, near Cati in the province of Castellon. He went to sell some sheep to old Fermin, who—so he had been told—was ready to buy them.

"I lost money on that sale," Juan added whenever he spoke of that transaction. Fermin's daughter had black, thick braids that graced her neck and made him forget the fair price of the sheep. On that day, Fermin got a flock of sheep for less than what he expected, and Juan Garach found Rosa the woman who eventually became his wife.

Juan's parents, his brother and sister attended the wedding at Cati and decided to stay overnight with Rosa's father. The newlyweds took advantage of the occasion to return by themselves to what would be their home from then on: the Masia Morellana.

Rosa looked at her husband tenderly; smiling, she asked herself if he would always love her and whether or not she would make him a good wife. Discreetly, she clasped her hands and prayed to the Madonna of l'Avella to bestow upon them many strong children and a long life. The donkey she was riding perked up his ears often, as if trying to hear her thoughts.

Juan, in his new *espardenas*—peasant's canvas shoes—effortlessly climbed the steep pathway and became part of the landscape, like the boulders and shrubs that lined the road. He reached the top of the mountain and looked around well pleased. The sides of the hills, like numerous green waves, rose up in a myriad of hues from the meadow itself sheltering a white, stone house.

The young woman,not really following the landscape which unfolded before her eyes, just looked at her husband, softly embracing him with her glance. Juan was content; the wind and sunlight toyed with his blond hair; his cheeks were red from exertion, and the narrow and eloquent line of his lips managed to convey a wordless feeling of satisfaction.

"Rosa, all you see from here is ours," he whispered reverently to her.

Smiling, she came out of her daydream and took a deep breath, as if wishing to become one with the view her husband was pointing out to her.

"What will I do?"

"Like my mother and my sister, you'll help with the land and look after the house . . . and me."

He said the last few words close to her ear, wanting his voice to penetrate deeply. Rosa shuddered when she felt her husband's warmth so close to her, his hand resting on her waist. They came down the hill lost in each other's arms.

"What are you doing?" she asked shyly.

"I want to see your braids loose," he demanded.

Rosa's shy, downward glance gave her an expression of purity. Her braids, undone, revealed a thick mane of black hair which Juan admired. Her shiny hair remained in rings and curls around his fingers, softly caressing his skin. Rosa blushed; her lower lip quivered, and it seemed as though she would cry for no apparent reason. Her husband held her tightly and, losing himself in the black sea of her hair, said to her:

"Rosa, I love you; come closer."

Seconds later, the timid donkey stopped grazing and looked at Juan and his wife running downhill. He hastened to follow them and reached his pen barely in time, as the door was being closed. They had ample reason to feel tired; the journey had lasted four hours; the animal, after reaching his destination, collapsed. Juan and Rosa laughed; they seemed to have recently awakened and to have found something so marvelous that all they wanted was to smile and look at each other.

"How many children are we going to have?" he asked his wife as they ate bread and sausages and drank a glass of wine.

"Many, and all of them blond like you!"

"We'll have six boys and one girl. The girl will look just like her mother, and the boys will be strong and active, so that they can do great things in the world."

"Yes, in this world you have shown me today. What did you ask the Madonna when the priest blessed us?"

"I asked her for many children . . . and much money."

"I asked for health, healthy children and someone who will teach me how to read and write. Do you know how?"

"Of course, but why do you want to learn?"

"I want to be able to sign my name, to write letters to my father and to read his. Besides, if you should ever go away from me, I would want to understand what you tell me on paper."

She had never confessed this wish to anyone; she felt that by sharing her secret with him, the bond between them had grown stronger.

"Women don't need to write, and anyway I'm never going to leave you. " He told her as he got up from the chair and caressed her shoulders. After a long kiss, uninterrupted by solitude, they climbed the stairs with their arms around each other's waist and lost themselves in the inviting darkness.

Chapter 2

Juan lied when he said he would not leave Rosa alone. Once every two weeks, he went to Tirig to sell the family's surplus honey, wool, or vegetables. That would take him almost seven days, and Rosa found it hard to forget her husband's absence.

Juan was the only member of the family who could sell. He was engaging and outgoing, capable of wresting quickly the darkest secret from the most tight-lipped person. He knew his customers' needs and strove to meet them, always at a fair price, as he assured them. Every time he arrived in Tirig with his three donkeys laden with merchandise, the town awakened.

"El Morellano is here; El Morellano has arrived!"

He would be invited to the tavern and there, between sips, Juan would make his sales. If he had wanted, Juan would have had his business concluded within two days, but he instinctively wanted to learn about the world beyond La Morellana. He would sit and listen without drinking much.

"Did you know that Pablito, Pablo Charral's son, has been sent to America?" announced Policarpo Borrell, Tirig's teacher.

"My brother-in-law tells me that there's gold in the streets there," admitted Don Sotero, the baker, whose flour sprinkled fingers resembled bread dough.

"¡Collons! If there was gold in the streets, everybody would go there," said Erasmo, the tavern keeper, he never stopped moving, serving drinks from one end of the counter to the other.

"It's hot as hell over there, I heard it said."

"Besides, what could we do in America?"

For Juan and his friends, America was the New World.

"What could we do? I'd rather stay here . . ."

"If I had the money, I would go right away," Juan confessed.

"Fourteen days on a boat. Who could stand it?"

"We should have kept Cuba; if Estados Unidos hadn't intervened, why, with a truly Spanish country in America we could all go there. Hey, Erasmo, let me have another glass of wine; I'm running dry!" Candido shouted out.

"You're right," Erasmo said as he filled up the glass, "that man Sagasta has no shame. He's made a shambles of the empire."

"Have you heard that there's trouble in Barcelona? I found out in Vinaroz last week; the workers want more pay," Don Policarpo said before leaving. He liked to talk but felt more at ease in the school than at the tavern.

"And who pays us? There's no way to understand this crazy world." Juan always had the last word where money was concerned.

The group dissolved, but some remained behind.

"It would be better to go, Candido, to America. I'd make myself a bag of gold and would come back a rich man. I'd open a grocery story back home and leave the farm to live like kings."

"It's a very big risk, Juan," his friend cautioned him. "What if you don't do well?"

"It's not that. There's mother, father, my brother and sister who only know how to plough the fields and tend the goats. They would starve if I left them . . . But, I know my children will do it; they'll go without fear. I'll stay here until they come back with the gold. That's how it'll be; everything will be better then; everything will be better."

"Juan, Juan, it isn't as easy as people say."

Chapter 3

"I don't know what's the matter; three and a half months have gone by and still they don't talk to me of having children!
Who's ever heard of that? I got married and my Juan was born nine months later. You tell me, why isn't that first grandchild on its way yet?" Vicenta, Juan's mother, wondered outloud. Her short, rounded figure hinted of many children and many worries.

"Calm down, mother; you'll have grandchildren. Rosa is healthy and so is Juan. Remember that God has a lot to do with it," answered Juan's sister, Socorro.

"Let her be, daughter; you know how impatient your mother is. As if things could be rushed. Let's see, if you plant wheat, don't you have to wait for months before the grain is golden?" Lucas face, constantly hidden under a cloud of cigarette smoke, was filled with lines of time that defied description.

"That's true, Lucas, but what has it got to do with my grandchildren?"

"Well, let time take its course, and you'll find yourself with a string of little ones."

"Hush, father, Rosa's coming!" warned Socorro.

Rosa's tall figure was approaching the door with a basket of lettuce on her head. She wore a blue skirt with small pink flowers, the same material as the scarf tied around her neck. She was wearing her hair in the usual fashion: braided and knotted behind her head. Juan wanted her black hair to be his alone and had forbidden her to wear it loose. She had pulled up the sleeves of the blouse; with one arm she was carrying a pitcher of water, while with the other she carried some wood they would need for dinner. She walked into the room, and the five Garachs who awaited her looked at her waist.

"See?" Vicenta whispered to Socorro. "She's thinner than when she first came. They'll never give me any grandchildren."

"Sssshhh!" said the girl impatiently, "Hush, mother."

Quicker than any of them thought, October twenty-eight arrived. All the townspeople would come: Candido, Balbina, Aunt Mari Pepa, Socorro's godmother, her husband, their three children, and a nephew from Albocacer. Quico, old Lucas' godson, would also attend; he was the messenger for the entire town of Tirig. Fermin, Rosa's father, would be traveling from Cati.

La Morellana had been in a festive mood for a week before the slaughtering of the pig. The women would end their chores in the fields early, so that they could come home and look after the details for the occasion.

"Rosita, it's three o'clock already. Aren't you getting dressed yet?" Socorro's excitement would not let her sleep.

Rosa blinked several times while gathering her hair to one side of her face.

"It's still a while before they get here, right? Juan told me that they would arrive around five." She looked at Socorro from head to toe and smiled. "And you're all dressed up already?"

"I'm afraid that they'll get here and find us all asleep. What then? Everything would have to be cancelled, because there wouldn't be enough time to kill the pig and all if we don't start early." Socorro shrugged her shoulders, not knowing what to say.

Moved more by her sister-in-law's enthusiasm than by the occasion itself, Rosa got dressed, and the two of them went down to the kitchen.

While Socorro spoke, Rosa got up and walked to the table to pick up some figs; she had not braided her hair yet and looked younger than usual. Her skirt and blouse were white—the same one she had worn on her wedding day—and accentuated her pallor. Before she got to the table, she collapsed.

"What's the matter with you? What's wrong? You're very pale; did you trip?"

Rosa shook her head; with Socorro's help she got up and sat on the chair. Frightened, the poor Socorro stroked her sister-in-law's head. Eventually, Rosa regained her strength and said:

"No, it was nothing. It's very early, and I haven't eaten anything, that's all. Please, don't tell anyone of this. It's not important and would spoil the party. I beg you to say nothing; I'm all right now."

"As soon as my brother Juan comes, we'll have to tell him how you feel."

"I don't want you to tell anyone, Socorro."

"Very well, very well, but if it should happen again . . ."

"Don't be frightened, Socorro," Rosa whispered. "This can't be anything serious. Sit down, listen to me."

Socorro's eyes were sad and fearful.

"I think I know what's the matter with me. This isn't the first time. Yesterday morning, at the garden, I had to sit down not to fall. I've heard that these things happen when a woman is going to have a child. I think that's what it is."

Socorro looked at her sister-in-law as if she were a prodigy, as though Rosa had achieved something that had never been accomplished before. Her face, lit by an expression of childish inexperience, drew close to Rosa's. Socorro kissed her.

"I don't want you to say anything. I'm not sure yet, and I wouldn't want to give false hopes. If strange things like this occur to me again, then we'll tell them what happened."

Chapter 4

Eight hands held the four legs of the hapless pig grunting and squalling for its life; it was six o'clock in the morning, and the sun, still half asleep, could not make up its mind whether to let its light shine on the front yard at La Morellana. All eyes were fixed on the knife and its victim. Vicenta and Mari Pepa held a huge kettle under the pig, to gather the blood that would later be turned into sausages; Socorro, Rosa, and Balbina looked on holding one another, moved by the animal's suffering.

Although she was diligently working and talking to Socorro, Rosa again felt nauseous. She thought of her husband. Would he like the news? Vicenta certainly would; she would be overjoyed. How would she tell them she was expecting a child?

Absorbed in her own thoughts and with the pig's gut already washed out, Rosa attempted to get up to hang it to dry. Her legs gave way under her and she felt herself sinking to the ground. Unable to utter a sound, she collapsed behind Socorro. The girl was so buried in her own thoughts that she did not hear her sister-in-law fall; the rest of the family was so occupied with its activities that no one heard Rosa's body fall to the floor. Only Pedro saw her and ran yelling.

"Rosa has fainted!"

All turned around looking for her; Pedro and Socorro propped her up, and then Juan came running. In a matter of seconds, Rosa had recovered and felt very happy to find her husband looking at her so intently.

"How are you feeling? What's wrong with you?"

"Suddenly I lost consciousness and fell. It isn't the first time it's happened."

"What? We'll have to go to town and see the doctor."

"Look, Juan, I think I'm expecting a child," she blurted out.

"A child? Who told you?"

"No one. I've suspected it for a month and a half, but I was afraid it might not be true, that's why I didn't tell you. Now, I think it is true."

"A son!" he said perplexed. "When?"

"If it takes nine months, I suppose it will be for May or June."

"A child!" Juan ran to the window and shouted: "Candidooo! Come up here." He turned back to his wife who didn't quite understand why Candido was needed. "You explain everything to him; he knows about medicine; let's see what he tells us."

Candido confirmed the news. It was a child: fainting spells, a weak stomach, total exhaustion that not even rest would cure.

"You can't feel it yet, but there is a child there," Candido said pointing to her stomach. Rosa, pale and fragile, looked with awe at the direction Candido pointed.

"We have to announce it to the family," Juan said.

Rosa did not wish to go downstairs; she preferred to stay in bed until she felt better. Followed by Candido, Juan raced downstairs, reached the front door and let out a shout:

"Guess what, folks? I'm going to have a son."

Everybody gave his or her opinion on the news. Juan was overwhelmed by the congratulations he received, and, even more enthusiastically than before, family and guests returned to the activities of the outing. The women exchanged triumphant glances; the predictions they made while Rosa was still on the ground had come true. Mari Pepa's children joined in the merry making, not fully aware of what it was all about. The eldest boy imitated the grownups by jumping and screaming joyfully. Only after a while when, exhausted, he sat on an enormous boulder, he asked himself: "Why is having a son so important?"

Chapter 5

"Rosa is having labor pains, and you must go and tell Aunt Patrocinia to come."

Lucas, Rosa's father-in-law, had to wake up Pedro, his younger son, and send him for the midwife.

The young man dressed in a hurry and set out for town, still eating some bread and sausages Lucas had fixed for him. He had not even seen his mother that morning; Vicenta had not moved from Rosa's bed-side. She knew what had to be done at deliveries but no risk should be taken; it would be better if Aunt Patrocinia, Tirig's official midwife, would come to deliver the first Garach grandchild.

The hills, dusty and full of rocks, covered the landscape from La Morellana to Tirig, ondulating almost to eternity. The three and one-half hour walk had never seemed so long to Pedro. He looked almost biblical in his peasant simplicity, canvas shoes, a rough, sack-cloth jacket, and staff in hand.

Juan was not home that evening; he had supposed that Rosa would not be due for another week or two and had gone to Cati to sell some goats. He had promised his wife that he would come back with Fermin so that the old man would be at hand for the birth of the baby. Juan would return on the evening of the thirtieth of May; thus, in the small hours of the twenty-ninth, Pedro had to set out in haste for Tirig, covering the mountain pathways on foot.

Aunt Patrocinia always slept close to the door of her house; those nights when she figured that her services could be requested, she would sleep fully dressed. One could say that the good woman had become a midwife because of her vast experience; after all, she had had sixteen children.

During her first fifteen years of marriage, she had thirteen children; she was beginning to feel somewhat relieved, and then she had twins; two years later, she welcomed a last child. When speaking of such a portent of fertility, the entire town would say that God sent her sixteen children. Patrocinia seriously doubted that the Almighty would have played so many tricks on her and rather believed that it was her husband who was responsible.

Following the saying that "God helps those who help themselves," Patrocinia steadfastly refused to share her husband's bed. It was around this time that the town's midwife died, and women began to call Patrocinia. With her ample experience and jovial temperament, she was a great help to them; almost without realizing it, she replaced the old midwife and began to receive small sums of money which helped her husband meet the dire need of sixteen mouths.

By 1901, Patrocinia had already been a midwife for twenty years. Her entire figure resembled the circle, from her face to her feet. Her complexion was ruddy; her countenance happy; she was alert, amiable, and sure of herself, one of those persons whose personality exudes the certainty of being able to solve any problem. Every time she was called to perform her duties she would grab a basket with the necessary equipment and would hurry wherever she was needed.

Pedro arrived in Tirig close to five o'clock in the morning and Patrocinia, warned perhaps by a sixth sense, awaited him. She took a kerchief, tied it to her head, donned a gray shawl she had been given as a gift following a particularly hard delivery, and rang a bell loudly; that was her way of letting her daughters know that she was off to work.

"How long does a delivery last?" Pedro asked once they were under way.

"Well, it depends. Some are over in an hour; others take up to twenty. My last one was very quick; it turned out that . . ."
The woman's explanations were very elaborate, and she proved to Pedro that, as far as that topic was concerned, she could talk forever.

Two and a half hours after having left Tirig, they were able to distinguish La Morellana from atop a hill. Pedro could not withstand it any longer and began to run; the midwife, under the impression that it was some sort of game in which she had to participate, followed him, trotting as quickly as her weight would allow. If apples had lips and smiled, they would resemble Aunt Patrocinia's face after the lively race.

The house was solemn; no one at the stables, no one in the kitchen; at last, the door to the stairs leading up to the bedrooms flung open, and Vicenta appeared.

"I have a grandson. I had to deliver him myself with the help of Zacarias and Lucas. Zacarias has seen so many sheep give birth that, well, at least he has some experience. Lucas is very brave and has seen me give birth four times. The three of us did it; I think that everything went as well as possible," she said hurriedly by way of an apology.

"How's Rosa?" Pedro asked.

"Sleeping like a queen. The girl is strong; she didn't falter for one minute; too bad her husband wasn't here to see her."

"And the baby?" Patrocinia interrupted.

"I washed him, put a belt around him for his navel, and he's asleep next to Rosa."

"*Mare de Deu!* Your mother has turned out to be a really fine midwife."

Chapter 6

"Socorro!" Juan awoke the fields around La Morellana at noon on May thirtieth. He ran from the hill which lead to the house followed by a flock of goats he was bringing home. "Socorro!"

"Juan! My brother; it's here, it's here!" she yelled waving at him in the distance.

"What do you mean it's here? What's here?" He could hardly hear his sister, for the wind and the noise of the goats on the run was distracting.

"You're a father already. Rosa had a son yesterday." Socorro put both her hands around her lips and tried yelling to her brother that way.

"A son?" he asked in disbelief. The goats, the wind, it all seemed to stop for Juan that very second. A son.

"What did you expect? Your wife was pregnant, wasn't she?" Socorro laughed watching her brother's reaction.

Juan took off the kerchief he wore tied to his neck, and by way of celebration, threw it in the air and ran to the house. His mother saw him and took him in her arms.

"Have they told you yet?" Vicenta trembled at the sight of her grown son crying, took him by the shoulders and gave him a kiss.

"Yes. Are they upstairs?"

"In your room. Both of them are doing well, thank God," she whispered smiling, holding him lovingly by the shoulders.

Juan, still shaking, raced to the door. He had gained much weight and was not as nimble as he used to be; he had to wait a while before climbing the stairs. Finally, he got to the upper floor of the house. The noise disturbed Rosa who instinctively held the baby close to her for protection. When she saw him standing on the threshold, she proudly held up the baby, as if offering a precious and unexpected gift.

"My son!" he said gravely, looking at the baby with devotion. His first impulse was to take him in his arms, but the warm fragility of the tiny body frightened him, and he merely stared at the child, examining him in detail, searching for some resemblance to himself in those eyes, in that nose, in that blond fuzz crowning his head.

The newborn was a Garach from head to toe; he had the family imprint in every feature, and this pleased his father's vanity very much. Suddenly, the baby rebelled against such scrutiny and began to cry loudly.

"What's wrong with him?"

"He's hungry. It's nothing."

"What will we call him?"

"Andres."

"Andres?"

"Yes, my mother's name was Andrea."

"I see. He's a strong baby, isn't he?"

"Yes, very. He drinks milk from Zacarias' best goat. We mix it with water and he leaves no trace of it. We are waiting until I have milk so I can nurse him."

"Your father came with me."

"Bring him up, Juan; I'm dying to see him."

Chapter 7

Aunt Patrocinia decided to stay at La Morellana until Rosa started nursing her son. Although the baby seemed satisfied with goat's milk mixed with water, such a situation could not last indefinitely.

"Andres needs a woman's milk, otherwise he'll grow up to be a sickly child and a weakling," Patrocinia told Vicenta in confidence.

On June second, four days after the birth of the baby, nothing had changed. The child cried disconsolately, apparently not satisfied with the nourishment his mother gave him. Before returning to town, the midwife informed Rosa of her opinion.

"If you want your son to grow up to be a healthy boy, you'll have to take him to a wet nurse," she said looking at Rosa in the eyes.

"Take him to her? Wouldn't there be some nurses who could come here to La Morellana?" she asked anxiously.

"It's possible, but she would have to come with her entire family, and the expense would be great.

"What do you think, mother?" Rosa asked Vicenta hopefully.

"I don't know, Rosa. We live far from everything. Taking the child to a wet nurse would mean that you wouldn't see him every day, and that's painful."

"What does a woman do when she can't feed her son?" Rosa bowed her head in shame.

"On the other hand," Vicenta continued, overlooking the young woman's embarrassment, "we can't afford to bring a wet nurse here now. The vegetable garden hasn't been as productive this year as in the past, and you know that Juan had to sell some male goats to build up our funds again" she closed her eyes in thoughtful meditation. Then, she called, "Socorro, call Juan."

"What are you doing, mother?" Rosa turned pale with anxiety.

"He is the one who will have to make the final decision, Rosa." With that simple announcement, the three women left the room, and Rosa was left alone to worry about Juan's reaction to what she thought a most unusual predicament.

"Andresito," she said as she looked at the baby. "Will I be able to part from you? I love you so. It's so beautiful to hold you in my arms, to look after you."

Juan was rather worried by his wife's dry breasts. His peasant mind could not understand Rosa's inability to nurse his son. One couldn't trust women; if they did one thing right, they would eventually do four wrong. They were only good to . . . Socorro's voice interrupted his thoughts.

"Juan, Rosa is calling you; she has to talk to you."

Ill humored, he went to the room where the young mother rested with the baby in her arms and was not moved any more.

"What's the matter with you?" he asked dryly with no trace of compassion in his voice.

"We have a problem, Juan. We must come to a decision."

"You're the one who has a problem. I already did what I had to do and gave you a son. What else do you want? It's you who has to do your duty now, but I can see that you're not even good for that."

"It's not my fault, Juan; I squeeze my breasts; I have the baby suck, but there's no milk!" she replied, setting the baby next to her so that the increased tempo of her heart would not awaken him.

"*Recollons*, don't you contradict me!" the violence in his father's voice made the infant shiver. Juan then lifted his arm, and slapped Rosa's cheek, making her turn first pale and then red as panic. Rosa did not cry.

Having physically vented his fury on his wife, Juan felt relieved; he felt superior and freed from all responsibility. And yet, he was unable to look at Rosa in the face that afternoon; unconsciously, he knew that a corner of that blue stare could reproach his behavior and give him away before his own conscience.

"What does Aunt Patrocinia say?"

Rosa had not regained her voice after the blow. She wanted to speak but could not. Finally, she struggled and answered.

"We have to take him to a wet nurse for three months. Perhaps we could bring one here . . ."

"Don't even mention bringing anybody here!" he said abruptly. "Money is scarce. Besides, if you can't be a mother to your child, as nature demands it, what do you want to have him near for? Patrocinia and I will take him away tomorrow, and that'll be the end of that."

His cutting tone closed the subject, and Rosa could say no more on the matter; she would have to be separated from her son. Juan closed the door behind him, leaving Rosa to her thoughts.

Juan did not approach Rosa's bed that night, although it was never clear whether it was out of contempt or out of respect. Rosa, in turn, opened her windows to penetrate the cool and pleasant darkness of the Valencian sky. She picked up her sleeping child all cuddled up in his blankets and sat quietly with him in her arms pretending to read the stars.

The sun came up on June third. Rosa got up, dressed herself and bundled up the baby in the blankets her mother-in-law had knitted for him; she went downstairs and placed the baby in Vicenta's arms.

"Look, mother, I'm leaving him with you. I'd die if I had to see him go. I'm now going to the fields to plant or to gather something. By nightfall I'll be too tired to miss him, and perhaps that way I'll be able to bear this separation better. Tell Aunt Patrocinia to take very good care of him for me, to . . . well, you'll know what to tell her better than me."

Vicenta was at a loss for words faced with her daughter-in-law's anguish.

"Child! You can't work in the fields today. It's not right. It isn't a week yet since Andresito was born, and you could hurt yourself."

"It would be even worse staying here; I'm sure my sorrow would be too hard to bear. Andres needs me, and I must take care of myself for him."

The young woman was crying; Vicenta, trying to hold the baby with one arm and give Rosa some food with the other, did not quite succeed in doing either.

"Rosa, take this bread and these salted sardines; they'll nourish you. Take some figs and an orange. You have to eat, my child."

Rosa put everything into a small basket, tied the kerchief to her head and went out. It was a proven fact that, in difficult times, Rosa craved for fresh air and sunlight to gain strength; she would have gone mad if she had stayed in that house.

That morning she plucked the weeds from the almond trees with unusual strength; not once did she lift up her head. She trusted the earth, and it was from it that she drew courage. If she had looked towards the *masia*, she would have seen Aunt Patrocinia's round hips weighing heavily upon Caliqueno, the donkey. She was carrying in her arms a small bundle named Andres Garach. Perhaps sensing his mother's suffering, the baby cried bitterly. Juan was pulling them up hill, and before long, they were completely out of sight.

The farewell over, Socorro ran to her sister-in-law. Rosa looked up when she saw the girl standing in front of her. She answered the mute question Rosa's eyes were asking with just one phrase: "They're gone."

Juan returned a week later with news that Andresito was doing well. He had gotten along fine with the wet nurse, and she had agreed to a good price. Rosa was upstairs in her bed, already asleep.

Juan climbed the stairs quietly. He believed Rosa could be waiting awake.

"Who is it?" she asked when she heard the bedroom door open.

"Me, Juan."

No other words were spoken that night. She wanted to avoid another unpleasant scene; he was tired and anxious to be with his wife. He undressed quickly and got under the covers with Rosa. Soon he was caressing her, and she, submissive and obedient, unhappily let him pierce the depth of her motherhood. She felt relief rather than pleasure when she watched him breathe rhythmically in his sleep.

Chapter 8

Two months later, toward the end of August, the baby had been away for so long that all the Garachs unanimously insisted that the child should come back.

"Juan, August is about to end, and Andres has been with the nurse for three months. Couldn't we bring him home soon?" Rosa had learned that, in order to get the right answers from her husband, it was best to approach him in front of the entire family. "I need to see him; besides, the *masia* needs the joy a child brings."

"It's true, Juan. Andres needs to be baptized and made a good Christian," Vicenta insisted.

"Yes, I had already thought of that; we'll go to get him in a few days, maybe this Sunday. We'll bring him home," he answered.

That afternoon, when she went to draw water from the well, Rosa ran into Zacarias. The old shepherd looked as he always did, like some saint who had escaped from heaven.

"How are you doing today, Zacarias?"

"Doing well, Rosita. What do you know about little Andres?" Despite the fact that he had only one tooth, the shepherd wore a constant smile.

"I've got a surprise for you; Juan says we'll bring him home on Sunday," Rosa knew the old man would be happy at the news.

"Praised be St. Andrew! I knew he would listen to my prayers. Andresito must have grown a lot; he must at least be this big by now," with his cane he indicated the baby's size.

"Not that big, Zacarias. He's only three months old," the smiling mother replied.

"Well, almost, almost; the boy will take after his father and will be tall and strong. I can't forget that he was born on May 29, the feast day of St. Mary Magdalene, yes sir!" Zacarias knew the days of the month by the feast days of the saints, not by their numbers. "I really love that boy, you know, Rosita? I was the first person to welcome him into this world. Miss Vicenta called me to help her out on account that Miss Patrocinia hadn't arrived yet and since I've been birthing sheep all my life, why . . . Well, he isn't the first baby I've delivered; I also delivered mine, may the Lord have them in heaven. But, of course, Andresito is the youngest; will you let me see him when he comes home?"

"Why, sure! A tiny piece of my son is yours, because you helped him into this world. God willing, you'll hold him in your arms on Sunday."

Chapter 9

Andres arrived none too soon to satisfy the need for joy of all the tenants of La Morellana. Rosa spent the day caring for her son while the rest of the family went about its business as usual. However, when the day's work was done, the young couple's bedroom turned into the focal point of the entire house. The child would then be placed on his parents' bed, and the family would talk to him, change his diapers, play with him, and even feed him whenever he cried to be fed.

"How did Andresito sleep?" Vicenta asked as soon as she saw her son downstairs.

"Not too well; he and Rosa spent the night pacing the room. They're asleep now."

"Juan, have you given any thought to the matter of the christening? That boy has to be baptized soon."

"Yes, mother; I had already thought about that. I think I'll go to Tirig Saturday afternoon and make all the arrangements. Then you all go on Sunday, and we'll baptize Andres."

"And the godparents?"

"Candido and Balbina."

"How did Andresito spend the night?" Lucas asked as he walked into the kitchen.

"Not too well," Vicenta answered. "Maybe he misses the old place. He's resting now with his mother."

"How did Andresito spend the night?" Socorro asked. Juan and Vicenta exchanged glances.

"I'd better go; as soon as someone sees me, all they do is ask me about Andresito."

"The boy's fine, dear; he's resting with his mother," Vicenta answered.

On Saturday, Rosa and Andresito went to see Juan off to the hill at the head of the road to Tirig. Everything appeared to have subsided between husband and wife. She held Juan by the arm, and he carried Andresito. They were talking to one another while the child looked about with natural curiosity.

"You haven't told me at what time we'll baptize him."

"You leave here early in the morning, and as soon as you get to Tirig, we'll baptize the child."

"Listen, Juan, before I forget," Rosa said casually, "you'd better be thinking about other godparents."

"Here, you take Andres now; here's where I have to leave you." Juan kissed the child; Rosa held him in her arms and kissed her husband. "What did you say, woman? You want other godparents? What's wrong with Candido and Balbina?"

"They're fine for Andres, but we can't always have the same one."

"What are you saying, Rosa?"

"Silly, that in a few months we'll have to go back to Tirig for another christening."

"Are you expecting?"

"I could almost swear it; I have the symptoms I had last year when I was pregnant with Andresito."

Juan held his wife and son tightly in his arms.

"Do you suppose you can get back to the *masia* by yourself?"

"Of course, don't worry. I'll see you tomorrow."

Chapter 10

The Garachs left La Morellana at sunrise. Andres cried almost all the way to Tirig; he had experienced many changes during the week. Judging from his crying, he was complaining for all of them at once. Sitting on a stone fence, at the entrance to town, two men impatiently waited for the party from the Masia Morellana. When they became visible, Rosa and Vicenta made out Juan's stocky figure. The distance between them drew shorter; they finally met. Juan went straight to his son.

"What do you think of my Andres? You can see he's going to be a strong lad, don't you agree?"

"He's going to be strong and a good singer, too. Listen to him," the baby had been frightened by his father's exuberance and was crying loudly.

"What's the matter with him?" he asked impatiently.

"Nothing, Juan. The trip made him nervous, that's all. Give him time to calm down, and he'll be all right."

Andres recognized his mother's voice, whispering in his ear. His crying soon changed into sobs that eventually vanished amidst sighs. The baptismal party went then to Candido's barber shop where the rest of their friends had gathered.

"Where is that godson of mine? I'm dying to meet him. Where is he? Where is he?" Balbina drew aside the curtain that covered the door to the establishment. She was ecstatic.

"The boy's in a bad mood today," warned Vicenta. "The trip was too long, and he's upset."

"It isn't that, mother; the poor boy is hungry," Rosa objected.

"Come to my room, Rosa, so you can feed him better there."

"Francisquito!" Mari Pepa yelled as she ran towards her youngest son who was attempting to shave with Candido's blade. "This boy can only think of mischief."

"Well, the priest is waiting for us," Balbina said out loud after Andresito had been fed.

"Let his godmother carry the child, right?" Juan said looking at Rosa.

"Of course. Here, Balbina, carry him like this, propped up against your shoulder so he won't complain."

"I'm not used to this business of holding babies."

"It's not a matter of being used to it; you just hold him tightly around his back, and everything will be all right."

Candido and his wife proudly headed the baptismal procession. They were followed by Rosa holding Juan by the arm; Vicenta, Socorro, and Valentin. Mari Pepa was last in line endeavoring to keep some semblance of order in her brood. As they arrived at the church, she cut short with a slap her youngest's intentions of pulling the tail of a mule tied to a nearby post.

"Don't you see she can kick you? Get away from there!"

The cool air of the church and Father Pratt's peaceful voice calmed down, at least temporarily, even the most mischievous spirits. Andres' countenance was peace itself; he did not notice the water splashed on his head or the salt placed on his lips. Once the ceremony had concluded, all those present prayed on their knees for the new Christian.

The children were the first to leave the church. Excitedly, they were leading the way to the barbershop. They returned through the same street they had followed to go to church and there, still tied to the post, they found the same mule that had caught Francisquito's eye. As the group got closer to the animal, the boy hid behind his mother. He intended to pull that irresistible tail. Balbina still carried Andres in her arms and walked behind Mari Pepa. They went past the mule; nobody was able to prevent what presently happened.

Francisquito pulled on the tail; the hapless mule, not being a party to the intended fun, got ready to repel her assailant with a series of savage kicks. Mari Pepa, alerted by a scream, dragged her son out of harm. Candido, realizing that Balbina and Andresito would be the target of the mule's fury, pushed them aside. Balbina lost her balance and fell to the ground sideways.

Rosa saw her son and her friend stumble. Quickly she picked up the boy who had already begun to wail loudly. She felt the small head and saw that there was no blood, just a scratch above the right ear.

"Juan, there is something wrong with the baby's head."

"Try to calm him down, Rosa; that's the first thing you must do. Let's go home, let's go," Candido ordered, alarmed.

Vicenta, distressed, cried in her husband's arms; Socorro was so frightened she was unable to move. A repentant Francisquito wailed as he clung to his mother's legs.

Chapter 11

When he fell with Balbina, Andres' head struck a boulder; after the blow, the child cried incessantly for over an hour. Rosa did not cease to kiss him, cuddle him, and walk him around the room to calm his down. It was to no avail. Candido knew enough medicine to realize that a blow of such intensity to a baby's head could have serious consequences.

Don Gabriel, the doctor, arrived immediately to examine the boy. He was a very serious man, with dark glasses and hands so thick that one would almost think nature had padded them especially so as not to harm anyone. For the time being, the child was in no immediate danger, but it was too early for a definite prognosis. Only time would reveal the consequences of such a blow. At least two years would have to go by; if the child did not develop like others of his age, then he would have to be taken to the city for tests. Would the child suffer from mental retardation? It was too soon to tell. All that could be done was to wait and have faith, great faith.

Juan and Rosa sat on the bed after Don Gabriel left; Rosa cried in silence. Juan was also upset, but in his case he was more angry than sorry.

"There's no doubt that this child has brought us nothing but grief," he said at last. "From the day he was born he's been nothing but trouble for everybody else."

"How can you blame him, Juan? Look at him; he's a helpless baby who needs us."

"I curse the day he was born. I hope the next one is not like him."

Rosa decided not to talk any more about the situation. She wrapped the baby in a blanket and held him close to her breast. Grateful, or perhaps simply curious, the boy touched his mother's face with his right hand.

All the excitement of the morning had vanished by the time the Garachs returned to La Morellana. The child was calm in Rosa's arms, but Juan was not at his best. It was obvious that he was in a rage; he looked much older because of it. In times such as this, it was better to leave him alone; he was utterly incapable of logical thought. Vicenta leaned on Lucas' arm; the old couple was as downcast as Rosa.

Chapter 12

No one suspected at Andresito's Baptism that his mother was already expecting a second child. Rosa believed the baby was not due until the end of May, but her stomach had grown so large that Vicenta and Juan decided to bring Aunt Patrocinia on May 10th. The experienced midwife was only too happy to oblige them; she had been needing a rest for a while, and a few days at La Morellana would do wonders for her. Her arrival in the *masia* lifted everyone's spirits.

"Vicenta, you've got a darling grandson; you've got one, maybe two, on the way have you realized that?"

"Why do you say two?"

"Haven't you noticed Rosa's belly? A child, no matter how big, can't make her stomach that large. Haven't you felt it? There are two heads and four legs there; don't you say anything to her, she may get scared, but trust my experience, I assure you that in less than twenty days, you'll have three grandchildren instead of one."

"Oh, my God! I'm going to tell Zacarias right away that we will be needing one more cradle, so he can start working on it."

"Forget about the cradle now; for the time being Rosa shouldn't know what's in stock for her. Once they're born, the two of them will be small enough to fit in one cradle, and there'll be plenty of time later on to make another."

"Rosa is a very stubborn girl. I asked her to move Andresito to my room. In spite of his handicap, he's a very active boy. She refuses to part from him. She says there's room enough in her bedroom for all of them."

"Too bad about poor Andresito; he's so cute."

"Just like my Juan when he was the same age. It really isn't too much of a defect, but it bothers his father. Whatever the boy does upsets him; I think he's ashamed the boy is lame. There's no end to worrying about one's children, I tell you, Patrocinia."

"Come, come. Look at me. I've got so many I have their names written down in a book. Sometimes a year goes by, and I don't hear from one of them. And then, just as my heart is about to break with grief, he shows up, and everything goes back to normal. My children are scattered all over the world, and I have given up hope of having them gathered around me. The best thing to do in these cases is to smile; there's no other way." And thus having concluded her little speech, the old midwife laughed noisily.

Three days later, Aunt Patrocinia ran downhill carrying Andresito in her arms. She kept putting her hands over her eyebrows, to help her make out Vicenta among the field hands.

"Vincentaaa!" she yelled when she finally saw her. "Vincentaa!"

"Sentaaa!" Andresito repeated, waving his good hand.

"Come, woman, Rosa's gone into labor already!"

Nervously wiping her hands on her apron, she went up to the *masia* as fast as her legs would take her. Rosa had her very worried. The girl had been in bed for four days and had secretly told her that she expected to die in childbirth. Vicenta had tried to dissuade her, but she could not help a feeling of foreboding.

That evening, the chores at La Morellana ended earlier than usual; everybody was anxious to hear about Rosa, and they forgave each other for the work they left undone. By six-thirty there was still no news. The pains had become increasingly frequent. Andres, frightened by his mother's screams, went outside with his grandmother.

Night fell, and nobody thought of dinner. Lucas was still and serious like a marble statue sitting at the foot of the stairs. He smoked his cigarette slowly, and if it were possible to read people's thoughts, a prayer would have been found that day engraved in his. Pedro and Zacarias were seated a few steps higher, while Juan walked incessantly up and down in front of the bedroom door. None of them uttered a sound. Zacarias was carving a sheep from a piece of wood for the Garach child about to be born. The old man asked himself why, at crucial moments such as these, humans were so much like animals.

"Vicentaaa! I need you!" Patrocinia's voice was heard among Rosa's moans.

"Mother! Go up quick; they need you!" Pedro said.

Pale and anguished, she tore up the stairs, leaving the boy with his grandfather. Mary, Help of Christians, Saint Barbara, please protect her; let it just be one child; two would be too much for Rosa. She crossed herself and, without saying a word, opened the bedroom door. A few moments later, a loud, piercing cry was heard.

"A boy! A boy!" Aunt Patrocinia was heard to exclaim behind the door.

Juan looked at his family with proud, burning eyes and said:

"Let's celebrate; let's drink some wine."

They went down into the kitchen, happy and relieved, shaking hands and pattering each other on the back as if, in some ineffable way, each of them had had something to do with the blessed event.

"Here's to the child's health!" Juan toasted after pouring everyone some wine.

"And to his mother!" Lucas chorused.

"To his father, huh?" Juan added.

"May there be many more."

Then, Rosa resumed her loud groaning.

"What's the matter with that woman? She's already given birth to the child . . ." Her cries persisted.

Fearful of what may be happening upstairs, they peered into the stairwell. They were ashamed of themselves for celebrating so prematurely, but they were afraid to go up and ask. Something wrong must have happened, or Rosa would not moan so after child birth. Nobody could even begin to guess the truth until half an hour later, when Patrocinia opened the door and announced in an even firmer tone:

"Another boy!"

The Garachs looked at one another, unable to believe their ears. Nothing like that had ever happened in the family. Juan was getting ready to go upstairs when suddenly he fainted. The men gathered around him trying to make him come to; the babies' cries filtered through the walls and filled the lower level of the house. Lucas did not stop repeating:

"Godammit! Twins!"

"Godammit! Twins!" Andresito echoed as he freed himself from his grandfather and crawled about the dirt floor examining shoes here and there and getting up whenever he found something to lean against. It was quite evident that he was lame; when he stood up, only the tip of his left foot touched the floor; he was unable to stretch his left arm fully. Nevertheless, he overcame his handicaps without much effort.

Andres had astonishingly understood his mother's tenderness, Zacarias' affection, his grandparents' compassion, and his father's contempt. His tiny intellect had catalogued all of them already.

PART II

I, Rosa Garach, see it now; with eyes that can hardly thread a needle, I see it all so well, better than I ever did back then. Andres did not have a chance with his father since Juan Garach thought his children had to be perfect. Andresito reminded Juan that his wishes were not the law, and, from the day of the accident, foolish Juan failed to see any relevance in the little boy's existence.

I was too young yet to realize the goings on in that truly enigmatic men of men, my husband. I think then I still loved him. Despite the occasional blows that left marks on my cheeks for weeks; despite the disdain he showed for Andres; despite the poor attitude, brief conversation and almost complete lack of spirit, I still loved him. It was love filled with hope and forgiveness. I thought, somehow, as he mellowed with age, he would change and make our union pleasant. I was sure that when he measured Andres' intelligence, sensitivity and keen perceptiveness against a small limp, he would honor his first born and find a place in his heart for him. It was this youthful certainty that helped me love him deeply and sincerely, enough to share his bed, enough to seek his support, enough to give him still more children, enough even to forget my desire to read and write . . . at least for a while.

Chapter 13

No sooner had the sheep been sheared than Juan left for Tirig to sell the wool. Rosa trembled at the thought of her husband's return; five years of disappointment had changed anticipation to fear. She felt invariably relieved whenever Juan had to go to town to sell the products of the *masia*.

"Lucas, Fermin, Andres. Uncle Pedro is ready now for your lesson." Rosa still wore her thick braids rolled up at the nape and a white apron around her hips. She looked at her three children proudly, sure that there could be no prettier sight in the world. Zacarias had given them a lamb to play, and the mischievous boys were chasing it. Lucas and Fermin, the twins, were up in front; Andres hobbled behind them, with persevering but hesitant steps. The eldest child was extremely sensitive; any argument or unpleasantness affected him deeply. He had blonde hair and big black eyes. On the other hand, Lucas and Fermin were of darker complexion and had blue eyes. Lucas, a plump, willful child, did not hesitate to slap his brothers whenever he deemed it necessary. Fermin was patient beyond his short years; he lacked Andres' delicate beauty and Lucas' strength of character, but he loved to talk and would relate in full detail the adventures of the day. Oftentimes, his mother would tactfully ask him to let his brothers speak; Fermin could talk straight until bedtime.

"Lucas! Fermin!" Rosa called out.

The baby was barely two and a half. He had been named Juan Jose, after his father, but in order not to confuse him with El Morellano, everybody called him Pepet. Rosa had more than enough with her first three sons, but she had been delivered of a fourth on February 6, 1909. He was a lively and playful child, one of those beings capable of solving seemingly insoluble difficulties with just a smile. It was only on special occasions that he was allowed to play with his older brothers. If Pepet's natural intelligence were to be coupled with the lessons learned from the other children, the situation at the Garach household would become intolerable.

The Garach children wrote their ABCs on some white papers they were given especially to practice. At the beginning of the class they made many mistakes; their eyes went after the patch of light shining through the kitchen door into the dining room. Little by little, somewhere between the "B" and the "U," Pedro grabbed his nephews' attention and succeeded in planting some seeds in those fertile minds.

They were having their third lesson that evening. Fermin and Lucas were fidgeting; Andres, on the other hand, seemed to hang on to every word coming from his teacher's lips. Rosa had just returned the lamb to Zacarias when she saw her husband approaching the house.

"Juan, Juan!" she yelled, waving her arms to call his attention. Pepet jumped for joy, making strange welcoming sounds at the sight of his father. With that enthusiasm typical of children, Pepet threw himself into his father's arms. Juan was in good spirits; he had sold all the wool and was bringing home some ropes, rice, a spade, green vegetables, and clothes for the children.

"Where are the others?"

"Learning their lessons with Pedro."

"Lessons? How long have they been taking lessons?"

"Your mother suggested it a few days ago; Pedro agreed, and . . ."

"Doesn't Pepet want to learn?" he asked looking at his youngest son. When he heard his name mentioned, Pepet replied in his own gibberish moving his parents to laughter.

"I want them to learn. They must know a lot to get ahead in life."

"Juan, don't you think we should leave the *masia*?"

"I've thought about it, Rosa. I wouldn't want to bury the children here like I was. There are more things to do in Tirig; there's even a teacher."

"I'd like to live there so they can go to school!"

"I know; I've been trying to make a go of it for some time, but it isn't easy. We're no longer just the two of us; it's six of us now, and we can't live on just any old thing."

Rosa liked to talk to her husband when he was in an affable and understanding mood; if only he were like that all the time! Past events had taught her that his positive disposition was rather short lived. The three of them went inside the house and

gathered around the table with Pedro and the three boys. Lucas and Vicenta were standing behind the children.

"Is Andres taking lessons, too?" Juan's voice disconcerted them all.

"How did it go, son?" Vicenta asked carefully. "I'm so glad you got back in time for supper! Are you all right?"

"Fine, mother, but why do you have Andres taking lessons?" He insisted; his temper was growing short.

"Leave the boy alone, Juan." the woman said sternly. She wasn't intimidated by her son's unreasonable fury. "He's a child like any other, and he must learn too."

"What's new with Candido?" Old Lucas, the diplomat, butted in. Juan ignored them both.

"Pedro," he ordered, "I don't want you to waste your time on Andres. He's not like the others; he's not normal. The twins must learn, but don't you pay attention to Andres. He's not worth the trouble of teaching him to read and write. As of tomorrow, the lessons will be only for Fermin and Lucas, Andres won't be learning."

"Juan, for God's sake, don't talk like that. Remember that he's your son, your first son; let him learn in peace." Rosa could not believe what she had just heard.

"Of course, he's my son, and that's precisely why I know what's good for him. Andres will help Zacarias with the sheep; he won't be able to do anything else. Lucas and Fermin must continue their lessons with Pedro; they'll need them."

Vicenta was standing right behind her grandson and squeezed his shoulders, as if to ask him not to suffer. The boy was petrified; he did not drop the pencil or even move. He stared sadly into the room while two silent tears ran down his cheeks. Rosa looked impotently at Vicenta; the old woman kept asking herself how she had raised such a son, at times so lovable, at times so hateful.

"What did you bring me, father? What did you bring me?" Lucas demanded, taking advantage of the situation to escape from his chair.

The group broke up, and the women got back to fixing dinner; out of the corner of her eyes, Rosa looked at Andres, still motionless in his chair. Fermin also seemed glued to his seat and his forehead denoted a deep worry; he had understood his father's insensitive blunder and wished to make amends for it with some childlike tactic. He let his index and middle fingers gallop across the table towards Andres' hand which was still holding the pencil. Fermin's two little fingers touched his brother's, and Andres looked at him. With the discretion all children seem to have when not wishing to be caught in the act, he pointed towards the door, tacitly inviting his brother to go out. Andresito wiped the tears off his cheeks and, holding his brother's hand, headed out into the vanishing daylight.

Chapter 14

Andres always wanted to work in the fields like his two brothers, but he had to be content with the life of a shepherd. His father did not want him to do anything else. El Morellano did not even wish to lay eyes upon his son, and he sent him to the only place where he would be away from him all day.

If one looked at the hills surrounding La Morellana, one would see the old bent silhouette of an old man followed by the delicate figure of a limping child close behind. Andres liked his job right away; all the six-year-old sought was love, and Zacarias gave him plenty.

"You know, Uncle Zacarias, all shepherds have a staff and . . ."

"What? You want one?" The old man smiled at having guessed the child's desire. Andres said no more and bashfully assented. "Let's look for a stick today, and in no time, I'll carve you a staff."

The bent stick Zacarias made for him was useful in many ways: it helped him climb the sides of the hills and also assisted him when his handicap became more of a drawback.

On sunny afternoons, Rosa would look out one of the windows facing the back of La Morellana, and she would see her son's golden head, and Zacarias' white, approaching. One late afternoon, Rosa greeted the pair with more joy than usual.

"Mother, mother!" the boy yelled as soon as he saw her.

"How's my eldest son doing? Tell me, Zacarias, has he behaved himself?"

"Rosita, I do believe that, without him, half the flock would have disappeared by now."

Andres almost burst with pride at the old man's report.

"I have one big favor to ask of you, Zacarias," Rosa said confidentially. "It's about Andres' lessons. You know that Juan . . . well, he has a bad temper. Sometimes he's too strict . . ."

Zacarias nodded.

"What can I do?"

"Do you know how to read and write?"

"Well, yes," he answered.

"Vicenta and I were thinking that, since you spend most of the day together, sometimes sitting under a tree, on the meadows, watching the sheep graze . . . what I mean is that, if you two can agree on it, maybe Andresito could practice out there with you and learn how to make his letters and write words and read them in a book and things like that . . . do you know what I mean?"

"I don't know much about letters and numbers, but if you want me to teach Andresito what I know, I'll be very pleased to do it."

"That's what we had figured," she said.

"Well, Rosita, we'll get started tomorrow. Provided, of course, that my partner here is willing."

The boy looked at his old friend and his mother with his enormous black eyes and flashed a grateful smile; his expression was eloquent proof that Vicenta's idea had been an extraordinary one.

Vicenta and Rosa were thankful that Juan retired early that evening. The children, exhausted after a hard day's work, fell soundly asleep after dinner. The two women were left alone in the kitchen, except for Lucas, who never asked questions. Their task was an easy one and before midnight three small knapsacks lay ready on the table. Rosa and her mother-in-law retired to their rooms, and all the lights went out at La Morellana except for one candlestick: Zacarias, sitting on his bed and leaning on a table he had improvised with some boards, unctuously practiced his ABCs with a broken pencil and a used piece of paper.

Chapter 15

Summers frightened Vicenta. They had been robbed one summer; at the end of a summer Balbina had fallen down with Andresito. She believed that the excessive sunlight altered the destinies of the Garach household and all through June, July, and August, Vicenta watched for some inevitable calamity. Perhaps she was not unduly surprised when, after one June dinner, peace left La Morellana once more.

"I tell you, father, it's not for me. It's for the children. It's for their sake that I want to leave La Morellana." Juan's expression was more serious than usual, almost solemn.

"But, haven't you got food on the table and a roof over your heads? Aren't you happy with us?" Old Lucas, almost pleading, sensed the impending change.

"It's not a matter of being happy or of having food on the table. Of course, we're better off here, with you all, than in any other place . . ."

"Then, why do you want to leave?"

"I already told you once, father. The boys need to go to school; they've got to get an education to succeed in life." What to Juan seemed so simple made Lucas's eyebrows curl and his head shake from left to right in disbelief.

"Succeed?" Lucas asked confused.

"There's a whole world beyond La Morellana, beyond Tirig. It's a world that's waiting for them, and they've got to be ready for it." Juan saw it clearly.

"But you've got everything you need here at the *masia*. Why, this year even the crops promise to be better than ever," Lucas complained.

"True. But I want more and better things for them."

"I don't understand you, son; honestly, I don't."

"Let them be, Lucas; don't you see they're young, and you're not? For you, La Morellana is the center of the world. Young people have a whole life ahead of them, and our young ones have outgrown the *masia*."

"Mother is right, father. Besides, Tirig is not that far away."

"Son, you're the life of this house; if you leave us, I don't know what will become of the *masia*, of the fields, of us." They had never seen Lucas so depressed. Juan's news meant a personal tragedy for the old man; Vicenta realized it when she noticed her husband's slouched shoulders and his hands lying motionless on the table.

"Pedro is also smart, father; he'll help you; he won't let the land go untended. With me in Tirig, I'll sell the wool; I'll buy all the bucks you need; everything will be almost the same, you'll see."

Juan managed to convince Lucas with unusual tenderness. He was truly sorry; he detested the very thought of hurting his father, but he had to be firm. His children had to get ahead in the world; there was no future for them at La Morellana.

Old Lucas did not want to go out of the house that Monday in August when Juan, his wife and their children left La Morellana. The sight of a couple, four children, one donkey, and a mule cart making their way up the mountain only to vanish behind it, would have been too much for him to bear. Pedro had disappeared, and only Zacarias was left to watch them go slowly uphill and to wave at the four boys. Since early in the morning the old shepherd had been helping them get their belongings in the cart. It was only towards the end that they saw him pull out a handkerchief and dry out his tears.

"Have a good trip . . . Children, behave. Don't cry at night, Pepet! Andresito, be good, be strong. Rosita, thank you for everything!" He shouted things out to them from the bottom of his soul until the cart disappeared from sight behind the mountain.

"Where are we going?" Lucas' demanding voice broke the silence.

"To Tirig," answered Juan.

"What is Tirig, anyway?" Lucas' curiosity was not satisfied.

"A town," said Rosa softly.

"And why do they call it a town?" Fermin asked.

"Because a lot of people live there."

"Is it like the *masia*?"

"No, it's many houses, one next to the other."

"And why aren't Grandpa and *Abuelita* coming?"

"Because they have to look after the *masia*."

"What will we do in town?"

"You'll go to school, you'll work in the fields, and you'll help your father and me," said Rosa.

Satisfied for the time being, they left their parents alone. The journey was long, and their short legs could not keep pace with Juan's or

Rosa's. One by one, they climbed into the cart where they soon fell asleep rocked by the rhythmic movement of the wheels. They realized they had arrived when they heard Rosa's voice asking them to be careful getting out of the vehicle. All four of them watched in fearful amazement as their father opened the enormous wooden door of the house on Charco Street.

Although it was noon, the house reeked of darkness, and they were more alarmed than joyful at the sight of it. Only Rosa crossed the threshold. She was truly moved; she carried a crucifix in her hands, and the first things she did was feel the walls until she found a nail from which to hang it. Having done this, she bowed her head in prayer. Later she explained to the children that she had thanked God for finally getting them home.

PART III

I was not completely a woman when I married Juan. Used to obeying my father, I came to obey a strange man who asked for my hand in marriage. I made so many promises to him at the altar. All of them I kept faithfully, with a sense of duty. So when the verbal offenses began, I erased these with a sigh. There was no way to react even to the physical hurt, his hand against my skin, a slap, raw pain. I had sworn obedience, and I did not rebel.

Tirig gave me the opportunity to develop the woman that lay inside me, though. When I entered the house on Charco Street, I knew that from those rooms, I would see some of the most crucial moments in my life as a mother. Perhaps that was why, when I arrived at our new home, I touched the tiles, the kitchen cupboards, with religiosity, almost wondering what was awaiting me that those walls would witness.

At the house on Charco Street everyone grew, including me. I would stand up to Juan, at times. I see now that I could never do what I really wanted, but, back then, I always thought I could, that if I really wished to, I could do my will. I felt powerful just thinking I could stand up to Juan and win. That thought alone gave me strength to face what lay before me.

Chapter 16

"Godfather Candido will take us today to meet the teacher," Rosa told her boys one September morning.

"Me too? Me too?" Pepet asked, hanging on to his mother's skirt.

"You must become big, like Andres. Hey, don't get dirty. Hold hands, and we'll go out and get your godfather first."

"Will Godfather Candido come with us?" Fermin asked.

"Yes, son; he knows where the teacher lives."

"Francisquito told me that Don Poli gives you a stiff punishment if you don't have your homework ready."

Rosa Garach smiled and walked happily through town with her four children. Her cheeks had a deep glow, the kind that surfaces from inner joy; her step was firm. As a mother, she had never felt as important, for she was going to enroll her children in school for the first time. Pepet walked behind her, holding Andres' hand; Lucas and Fermin, also holding hands, closed the family procession.

"Godfather!" the four cried in unison when they reached the barber shop.

"Coming!" he called from behind the curtain. "How are my boys? Who wants a piece of candy?"

"Me!" They surrounded him, waiting for the promised sweets.

"Listen, Candido," Rosa said as they got under way, "how long has Don Policarpo been the town's schoolteacher?"

"It's been about twenty years since he did it."

"Did what?"

"Turned his stable into a school."

"You mean to tell me that that huge house next to the school is his?"

"Don Policarpo is a real fine man; he doesn't show off his wealth. I still remember when I was a child how he used to go around town to find what the poor needed. On the next day, with his mother's help, behind her father's back, he would send a servant with a basket of food, clothing, or medicine. When he turned thirteen, his father sent him to Valencia to study. He returned to Tirig several years later with his degree and married to Carmelita."

"Was it then that he opened the school?"

"His father died in 1892. Shortly after his death, Policarpo sold almost everything he had, keeping only what he needed to support his family comfortably. He leased out his lands, and finished by turning the stable into a school. Soon, he had as many students as I have customers."

Candido had to cut short his story, for they had arrived in front of the school: a building with two heavy wooden doors that attested to its old age.

"May we come in, Don Policarpo?" Candido said as he put his head through the curtain covering the doorway.

The teacher looked up and winced to bring back his eyeglasses to their proper place.

"Don Candido, welcome! It's a pleasure to see you."

Trying to get up from his chair, his seemingly endless legs could not free themselves from the confines of the desk. Finally, he stood and walked towards the barber; affectionately he shook his hand.

"What brings you here, Don Candido?"

"Nothing, Don Policarpo. I've come to introduce you to my godson and his family; they've just moved to Tirig from La Morellana, where they used to live."

"Oh, the Garachs, right?"

"Yes, this is their mother, Rosa Garach."

"It's a pleasure to have you among us," Policarpo said as he bowed. The four boys watched him in fear. Pepet was so impressed that he hid behind his brother Andres. Straight and motionless, the other three boys kept their heads stiffly towards the front, looking up as high as they could without moving.

"This is Andres, my godson," he said stroking the oldest boy's blond hair. "These are the twins, Fermin and Lucas; and this is Pepet, the baby; he's still too young to come."

"Quite a handsome constellation you have, ma'am," he said admiringly. The boys didn't dare bat an eyelid.

"Thank you, Don Policarpo," she said rather moved, "do you suppose they can come to your school?"

"Of course; you'll see how fast they're going to learn. One can see they're intelligent children. Bring them here Monday at eight o'clock, huh?" He said as he ruffled Lucas' curly hair; the boy, frightened, squeezed Fermin's hand.

"I would like to ask you, professor . . . we need a vegetable garden, Juan, my husband, went back to the *masia* to bring the rest of our things. When he returns, he wants to rent some land to plant our vegetables."

"I'll see what I can do, and I'll let you know in a few days; I'm sure I've got something available."

"Well, Don Policarpo, please give my regards to Carmelita."

"Thank you, I will. Good-bye, Mrs. Garach; so long, children."

For Rosa, life seemed to be showing some sort of order until Juan arrived with his demands.

"Rosaaaa! Rosaaa! I'm home, woman; come down. Rosaaaa!" Half a dozen legs rushed to the stairs.

"I go first . . ." Lucas said.

"No, it's my turn," argued Fermin.

"Move over." The fight for first place made the boys frantic.

"Pepet down; Pepet down," even the little one complained.

The three boys, tied into a knot, vied for their moment of glory.

"I've told you it's my turn." Lucas hit Fermin with all his might, making him lose his balance. The boy fell down and made room for his brother to get through; Pepet began to cry.

"What happened? Was it you, Fermin?"

"No, Lucas knocked both of us down; he's already downstairs."

"Hey, let's all go, come! Andres! Andreees! Come, your father's home!"

The whole family welcomed El Morellano who was waiting for his brood sitting at the head of the table.

"How's Grandpa?"

"Everybody's just fine; Grandpa Fermin, from Cati, is there now. Your three grandparents will come down on Sunday to see you all."

"How's Zacarias, father?" Andres dared ask.

"The old man isn't too well. For a week now he hasn't been able to get up. He's very tired. He's old, you know. But, what's new around here?"

"We've been to school," Lucas announced.

"We'll start our lessons on Monday," Fermin added, "the teacher's name is Policarpo. He's a giant!"

"Did you ask him about the vegetable garden, Rosa?"

"Yes, he says he'll let us know soon."

"Good. We'll have to assign chores. From now on, each one of you will have responsibilities. Andres, you'll take the sheep out to graze each morning; Fermin and Lucas will look after the garden with you, Rosa."

"Pepet?" The little boy asked from behind his mother's legs.

"Pepet will help his mother and will eat a lot to grow fast."

"Juan, remember that they're starting school on Monday," Rosa reminded him.

"There's time for everything. The garden can be cared for after school."

"And the sheep?" She was thinking of Andres.

"No, not the sheep; they'll have to graze from early morning 'till afternoon." Andres looked at his mother with disappointment in his black eyes; taking advantage of Juan's involvement with the other children, Rosa motioned him to be quiet and began to set the table for dinner.

Chapter 17

"Candido, Balbina," Rosa protested looking at the barber and his wife, "what Juan is doing with Andres is a crying shame. It isn't the poor boy's fault; there's always something good for the other three but for Andres . . . nothing, except to look after the sheep. It isn't fair. I wish you could have seen his face, the poor thing. I thought all his tears would pour out at once, and all I could say was: 'Go, go, son; go at once so your father won't be angry.' I should have sent him to Don Policarpo like the other two. What should I do, Candido? This can't go on. Why doesn't Juan love that boy like the rest?"

"Come, come, Rosita; calm down. Despair never resulted in anything positive."

"I know, Candido, but there's nothing else to do. I've approached Juan in all possible ways; he doesn't want him to go to school. He says Andresito is an invalid and that's it."

"That's not true. He's a smart boy. But . . . we'll have to do things in a different way. Let's see. What is Juan planning to do for a living now that you left La Morellana?"

"He plans to slaughter sheep and sell the meat. They've also talked to him about the fairs at Jativa, where he could buy many animals and then sell them for a profit around here. For the time being, though, he'll stay here, to get the vegetable garden going."

"Very well, then, I'll ask him to send Andres to me in the afternoons; I'll tell him that I need the boy to help me around the barber shop."

"And then?"

"We'll see about the rest. I'll talk to Policarpo."

"What could he do?"

"We'll see. Right now, hold your tongue. If Juan should find out that we're going against his wishes . . ."

"Nobody will know, I give you my word," Rosa said firmly.

It was no secret in Tirig that Erasmo was an artist among tavern keepers. He would open the bottles and pour the liquor moving his hand and arm with the grace and skill of a Flamenco dancer. From dusk until the small hours of the morning, Erasmo soothed thirsty throats, listening in silence and smiling without showing the teeth hidden behind his thick, black mustache.

"I knew that Pablito Charral wouldn't last too long over there in America," said one of the customers. America meant any of the Latin American countries.

"What do you mean 'wouldn't last'? It's been over five years since the boy left."

"Haven't you heard, Juan? He came back from Vinaroz this afternoon, riding on Quico's cart."

"How can that be?" said Don Sotero. "Pablito?"

"In person! He's so scrawny you would think he walked all the way from America."

"Haven't you heard there's an ocean in between? Or do you think that they have taken the Castellon highway all the way to America?" The irony of the comment drew peals of laughter from those presents.

"Hush, man; if I were so stupid, you wouldn't have found out the news."

"Don't get upset, now; is the boy here on a holiday?"

"Like hell he is! He's come back for good to live in town again."

"How embarrassing for his father," Juan remarked.

"I heard he was fired from his job."

"I say, there must be ways to make a living in Cuba."

"Of course, Juan, but making a living in a foreign country is harder."

"You've got to persevere, whether in Cuba or in Madrid."

"Shut up, Juan; that's some mean country, Cuba. I've seen the boy; he wilted in the heat."

"It there's a will, heat won't stand in the way," El Morellano repeated. "One needs courage to make it in this world. Those who are born without courage would have been better off not having been born. Just wait until my boys . . ."

"Hey, hold your horses, Juan; it's too early to tell about your kids."

"Yes, the oldest one is nine."

"Eight, but he doesn't count. I'm talking about the others. You'll see how right I am. My boys, they'll grow up to be powerful gentlemen."

"I say, he thinks he can tell the future."

"Hush, Sotero; we don't want a stupid fight here."

Chapter 18

Lucas refused to do his mother's bidding with an obstinacy that frightened Rosa. This time he refused to take the sheep out to graze; it was July and that Don Policarpo had decreed a vacation until September; Andres was sick in bed, unable to do his assigned chore.

"No, no, no. I won't take the sheep out to graze; my father didn't tell me to."

"But I'm telling you, Lucas. I'm your mother. I can't go because today is Saturday, and I have to bake bread. Fermin is working in the garden and Pepet is still too small. You're a young man already, and you must help me."

"No, no. That's a sissy's job; I won't do it. I won't."

"Lucas, so help me . . . I'll punish you if you keep on saying no. I'm your mother; you've got to do as I say."

"If you force me . . . I'll tell father that Andres knows how to read on account that he's learning behind his back."

"Lucas! How dare you!" Rosa had never vented her anger like she did that day when she slapped her son across the face.

She took Andres' staff and pressed it into the hands of her defiant son. She pierced him with a stare more intimidating than any words. Then, she let the animals loose, and the boy, humiliated by his mother's reaction, could do nothing but guide them towards the countryside.

Andres had been ill for a week, since his grandparents came to Tirig and announced Zacarias' death. That same day, the boy ran a temperature; Candido prescribed soaking his feet in hot water. Rosa diligently followed the treatment every day for two hours. To no avail; Andres just lay in bed, pale and with dark circles under his eyes. He was too weak even to talk to his mother.

Aunt Patrocinia came and assured Rosa that it was nothing but indigestion; a good rubbing on the belly with oil, and the child would be fine. Nobody realized that the boy was simply frightened. His mother had explained to him that Zacarias was in heaven. That was the reason why they had dug a hole in the ground and buried him. They covered him with dirt, so he could go to heaven. In the ground like the seeds, but he would never grow back; his mother had made that quite clear. And the spirit? Where was old Zacarias' strong spirit? Concentrated terror had caused the fever. Two weeks later, Andres got up from his sick bed, healthier and less of a child.

Chapter 19

A pair of small, innocent hands, a child's hands, climbed up the splendid white tile shelves. Higher; just a little higher. Oh! Only he knew what was hidden under that small cup which was turned upside down. He hid his money there. Reaching up on the tip of his toes, Pepet took out a few coins from his hiding place, replaced the cup in its position and came down just in time to hear his mother and brothers entering the dining room.

La Morellana was far from the child's mind. He was barely six years old. It seemed to him that his entire life had unfolded in that house with shelves in the kitchen, tiled walls, and a heavily carved door: the house on Charco Street. Two years before, Juan had managed to sell forty hogs he had bought in San Mateo and had been able to move his family into what he termed the best house in town.

"Open your hands, mother! Open your hands!" Rosa thought it was some sort of game and stretched out her hands, so agile and well acquainted with the transparency of the water. The boy placed his fist over them; opening his fingers, he let the coins he had just taken from under the cup fall into Rosa's palms.

"For saffron. Didn't you say this morning that you needed saffron?"

"What a thoughtful son I have! He really looks after his mother! Thank you, Pepet!"

The youngest Garach felt, at age six, almost as big as his father. His two older brothers looked at him astounded, unable to understand where he had gotten what, to them, seemed a considerable amount of money.

"When will father and Lucas come back?"

"They've been gone for almost two weeks; I don't think it will be too long."

"Lucas must have played some sort of trick to get to go. I saw father wink at him so he would take the longer stick," Pepet commented ill-humoredly. To avoid rivalries, Juan made each son take a straw from a bundle he held in his hand. The one who picked the longest would travel with him that day.

"Don't say things like that, son."

"Do you know what Don Poli says?" Andres interrupted.

"Basilio, Erasmo's son, has left for Vinaroz."

"How did you know, Fermin?"

"Quico arrived three days ago with the news that the owner of this grocery store in Vinaroz needed help. Erasmo heard of it and suggested his son for the job."

"Where is Vinaroz?"

"Too far for you, Pepet."

"If they asked me, I would've gone," Fermin remarked.

"Me too; and, you know what? Vinaroz is by the sea," Andres added as if it were some valuable piece of news.

"What's the sea, mother?"

"Your father told me once, Pepet. Do you remember that big stretch of land with no houses as you leave Tirig for La Morellana? Well, the sea is like that, only it's water instead of land."

"Like the wash fountain?"

"No, Don Poli says that it's much bigger than a wash fountain," replied Andres.

"All right, all right; enough! Don Poli is waiting for you, and he'll be angry if you're late."

"Mother, I can't take care of the sheep this afternoon; Godfather Candido needs me at the barber shop after school," when his father was away, Andres went to school with his brothers.

"Who'll go, then? Today I have to bake the bread, and Fermin has to help me. Pepet will go." Rosa said, fixing her eyes on the boy and expecting a reaction. The child opened his eyes.

"Mother, tomorrow is the feast of the Immaculate Conception!"

"So? What has that got to do with the sheep?"

"There'll be a big celebration tomorrow."

"So?"

"Godfather promised . . ." He would have to give it all away.

"What did he promise you, Pepet?"

The boy sighed.

"He promised to roast them for me if I . . ."

"Pepet?"

"If I run some errands for him this afternoon; he can't do them himself."

"But son, why do you want roasted peanuts?"

"To sell them, mother."

"Sell them?"

"At the fair. To build up the savings I put under the cup!" Very much against his will he had to explain everything to the last detail.

"The flock comes first, Pepet. If then, you want to take care of your peanuts, that's your business."

"Mother . . ." he started to say, downcast.

"Off to school! Go!"

The rays of the early sun shone on the children walking to school. Pepet resembled the leader of an important parade who had forgotten his baton; he walked ahead of his brothers with his head high and a confident step. His corduroy pants—hand-me-downs from Lucas—were too long for him, and their friction against the dirt road left puffs of dust in the child's wake. He was blond like Andres, but was not interested in studying; he loved the hustle of the streets. Despite his age, he had kept the china cup on top of the kitchen shelves full of coins since he had begun his life as a businessman, less than a year before.

Chapter 20

Sotero Pellicer, the town's baker, was not unduly surprised when the curtains that kept the flies out of his bakery were suddenly parted by a whirlwind. Pepet had made his entry. The face of the portly old bachelor beamed with a frank and warm smile. Sotero claimed to see God every day in his bread and in children's faces. He welcomed Pepet with a loud, guttural laugh that could be heard several houses down the block.

"Have you come to run those errands we talked about?"

"Well, you see, Don Sotero, I'll have to do that later on, because my mother's asked me . . . well, since my father isn't here and my brother Lucas went with him, and Godfather Candido asked Andres to help him, and Fermin has to help mother on account that she's put on weight, and she can't bring the bread basket by herself . . ."

"Come to the point. Is anything the matter with your mother?"

"No; not with my mother. It's the sheep; there's nobody home to take them out to graze and my mother . . ."

"Good boys must always do as their mothers tell them," Don Sotero interrupted.

"Right. That's why I can't run your errands until I'm done with the sheep. It'll only be a few hours, and I'll be back soon. Will you roast my peanuts for me anyway?"

"Yes, bring 'em before you leave with the sheep, and they'll be ready. Is that new brother of yours due soon?" Sotero did not have enough to occupy his mind; therefore, he was keen on finding out what happened in town and passing on that knowledge afterwards.

"Mother says he is, but . . ." Pepet was not too clear on new brothers, and how they came into the world; he decided to shut up and leave as soon as possible. "I'll come back soon." Staff in hand, whistling a happy tune, Pepet and his sheep left for the meadows behind the house.

Chapter 21

There was only one bicycle in Tirig; bicycle owners, therefore, were extremely popular among the child population. It was the feast day of the Immaculate Conception, and Lucas was proudly showing off his new acquisition. As a part of one of his father's sales, he was granted permission to exchange a mule for a bicycle that had caught his fancy. He enjoyed its speed and, in true character, refused to share it with anyone, not even with his brothers.

Fermin begged him for a ride, but to no avail. He would only allow them to look at the bicycle without as much as touching it. Pepet was so immersed in his sales that he only thought of his brother when Lucas rode pompously by. Andres didn't even bother to think about Lucas' bicycle. As soon as he saw it, he realized his feet would never reach the pedal; besides, his mind was on more important matters.

His mother had looked somewhat different to him that morning. She had turned pale and had taken her hands to her stomach several times, obviously in pain. Andres remembered Pepet's birth back in La Morellana. The noises coming from the fair were distant; the Garach home was very still, and all that could be heard were Andres' worries, Fermin's disappointment at the selfishness of his twin brother, or the crackling of a board, contracting in the icy December evening.

Juan stuck his head out of the heavy carved door which led to the bedrooms. His eyes collided with Andres'.

"Are your brothers around?"

"They must be at the fair; I haven't seen them in a while."

"Haven't you gone?"

"No. Is mother all right?"

"Yes, she's fine, but go and fetch Lucas or Fermin and tell them to go and bring Aunt Patrocinia; we'll be needing her soon."

"I'll go. Lucas is riding his bike and Fermin . . ."

Fermin had been sitting on the other side of the curtain which covered the doorway. When he heard his name, he jumped up.

"Here I am!"

Juan turned his attention to Fermin and said:

"Go, Fermin; tell Aunt Patrocinia that your mother is ready."

Andres set out with such celerity that Fermin had to run to catch up with him. The older brother's face revealed his worry. Don Poli had explained it to him: that business of having babies was no child's play. Some women even died from it!

"Don't walk so fast, Andres; mother will be all right. What's the matter with you?" Andres didn't know what to say, so he just kept walking.

"Don't you think I don't know what's happening? There's another kid on the way. Remember the day we saw don Erasmo's wife, just as fat, and how she went on and had a baby just like that? It'll be the same thing like with Don Poli's goat. The kid comes and all it did was suck and suck milk . . . It was a cute kid; do you remember it, Andres?"

The old midwife was in the town square, in front of the church. Surrounded by Tirig's women folk, she was telling stories of her six-teen treasures, as she called her children. Andres and Fermin didn't have to say anything; Patrocinia immediately realized that Rosa need-ed her.

Pepet saw his brothers from afar and went to talk to them.

"Have you seen Lucas on that thing? He won't let anybody, not even me, touch it, or ride on it!"

"Go, Pepet; we're in a hurry!" Andres replied.

"Is Aunt Patrocinia going to see mother?"

"That's right; she's got a bellyache," Patrocinia explained.

"Oh!" he said in a daze. His sharp black eyes looked at both his brothers, and without asking for more explanations, he went back to the fair. He remembered what Aniceto had told him. His mother had a baby inside of her; it was hard to imagine how it breathed. The music com-ing from Don Sotero's accordion dispelled any doubts that the fledgling salesman may have had about the mystery of birth.

Many of Tirig's residents ended the evening's festivities in front of Juan and Rosa's home. Candido, Balbina, Quico, Erasmo's wife, Don Sotero, Aunt Patrocinia's two daughters, Don Poli, and his wife await-ed the good news with suitable impatience.

Lucas, tired of showing off his bicycle, put it away in the rear of the house. More weary than solemn, he awaited the news next to Fermin. Andres overcame his fears and chose to sit by his father, next to the door of the bedroom where his mother was.

Nobody noticed the absence of the fourth Garach boy. Pepet reached the end of the fair thoroughly exhausted. He had sold his entire stock and carried in one of his pockets what he felt sure was quite a fortune. On the church steps, he fell asleep leaning his head forward against the basket between his legs. A dog, seeking warmth, went up to him and lay by his side. The boy suddenly opened his eyes.

Realizing that the streets were deserted, he ran home. It was very late, and he was surprised that his mother had not gone out to look for him, as she had done in the past. He was glad; he would be able to go in the house unnoticed and would hide his coins under the cup.

As he turned to Charco Street, he saw neighbors coming and going excitedly. The boy drew the curtains and saw his father and his brother Andres pouring wine and laughing. He tried to slip past them, but Andres saw him and rushed to him with open arms.

"Pepet, we have a sister!"

"Sister?" he repeated scratching his head.

"She's with mother. Would you like to see her?"

Without waiting for an answer, Andres steered the little businessman towards the bedroom.

"Don't make any noise; the two of them are asleep," he warned.

Aunt Patrocinia was sitting in the small living room at the head of the stairs holding a rosary in her hands. The child peered inside the bedroom and by the pale candlelight was able to make out a small bundle of blankets and a pinkish little face. Andres pushed him to get closer, but Pepet refused shaking his head and leaving the room.

"Will the girl talk?" he asked frowning.

"Not today or tomorrow, when she grows up."

"She wasn't moving."

"She's asleep."

"She must be exhausted, don't you think? Coming out through the belly button must have been rough. She's a big girl!" he remarked. The boy remembered when once, trying to evade his mother's eye, he had tried to go out through the window of the stable and had gotten stuck. He imagined the baby girl in a similar predicament and could well understand why she was asleep.

"What's her name?" he asked undressing for bed.

"Who?" Andres said tired and confused.

"The sister's."

"I don't know."

"Could I show her to Aniceto tomorrow?"

Pepet didn't hear an answer this time. He fell asleep with a smile in his lips; never again would he be the youngest in the family.

Chapter 22

The twins went upstairs unnoticed by the guests. They didn't fall asleep right away; Lucas kept on talking and Fermin, patient like a child wise beyond his years, listened to him and soothed him.

"It's a baby sister and we must love her very much. *¡Collons!* You should consider yourself lucky. Not everyone has a sister!" he whispered to Lucas.

"I wish she hadn't come. All mother thinks about is having kids for us to support. No way! We'll all be in a fine mess; one more mouth to feed, and we . . . working for nothing."

"Hush, Lucas. Aunt Patrocinia may hear and tell mother."

"Let her; I don't care, I'm going away soon. Let her have more and more kids; let's see if she can manage without us. If I didn't collect the money for the horses father sells; if you didn't look after the vegetable garden; if Andres didn't take care of the sheep . . . even Pepet runs errands to bring home some money. Let her have more kids! I won't stay here to watch."

"You'd better not let mother hear you; she'll be very upset."

"I don't care; I'll go anyway."

"Where will you go?"

"To America."

"What happened to Pablito Charral will happen to you! That land is too far away; besides, the heat . . ."

"That guy Charral is a coward and a sissy. I'm a man; I'm eleven years old, and I'm not afraid."

"I'm also eleven, eh?"

"I've traveled with father," he boasted.

"It's all the same. Here we work for the family; we eat what mother cooks for us, and she doesn't remind you of it. You shouldn't say those things about her."

"I'll make money for me, not for her!"

Fermin decided to say no more. He had to rest; in the morning he would have to work twice as hard doing his mother's chores and his own. He smiled pleased. His baby sister was so cuddly, so pretty. Despite Lucas' acid remarks, he realized that already he loved her.

Chapter 23

August 1914. Europe was under the flames of war, but only remote blazes reached Tirig through the pages of the Castellon newspaper. Two items of news did stir the town: the death of Cirilo, one of Aunt Patrocinia's sons, and the return of Basilio, Erasmo's son.

"He died of women's disease," Aunt Mari Pepa confirmed the news in the public wash fountain. "They said his hair and teeth fell out. He came back to town, to die in peace." The place, which was crawling with women doing the laundry, turned as still as a cemetery.

"Poor thing!" Balbina sighed breaking the silence.

"Aunt Patrocinia is broken-hearted," Rosa said.

"She'll cheer up when somebody calls her to deliver a baby." The women, baskets in hand, stood motionless with their glances on the ground.

"Her grandson Basilio is also back from Vinaroz. He says he doesn't like the city, and prefers helping his father here in town. These boys from town can't get used to life in the city."

"Where's Lucia, Rosa?" Balbina offered a sign of relief.

"Fermin took her to the vegetable garden. She'll be there 'till I'm done with the wash, because he . . ."

"It's true; the girl can't stay still for too long."

The three older boys had already stopped attending Don Poli's school. Only Pepet went every day; Andres still borrowed a book once in a while.

At supper time, the seven Garachs gathered around the wooded table to eat and share each other's company.

"Father," Fermin said suddenly. "Did you know that Basilio has returned from Vinaroz?"

"Who's Basilio?"

"Erasmo's son; the one who left a year ago, don't you remember?"

"Oh, yes."

"He used to work for Alejo Querol; a big place, from what I hear. A bank and a grocery store, a big place he says," the boy repeated nervously.

They realized that Fermin was about to ask for something. Pepet ceased to speak and looked at his father and brother as one answered the other. Rosa listened attentively feigning indifference.

"Father, Quico says that they're looking for somebody to take Basilio's place, at least for the time being . . ."

"I'd like to go, father. Just to try it out. The money would come in handy, and I could send most of it to you."

"We'll go to Vinaroz in three days, and we'll see if you're right for the job."

The answer was totally unexpected; Fermin smiled gratefully, and his brothers sighed with relief that their father had not vetoed the idea.

"How many days to Vinaroz?" Rosa asked.

"Less than one if we don't make any stops."

"His clothes will have to be marked, won't they?"

"Not yet, Rosa. First we've got to see if they'll take him. Then, we'll come back for his things, and you can get the clothes ready. He will have to take enough for a year; he won't be able to come home often. If he wants to do his job well, he must mind the store every day. I'm warning you, Fermin, if you go, you can't do what Basilio did. A son of Juan, El Morellano, has to be courageous and hard working! I won't stand for less. You know what I always say: one needs courage to make it in this world. Those who are born without courage would have been better off not having been born!"

All four boys felt a gripping chill go up their spines; their father had placed a heavy burden on their shoulders. "Those born without courage would have been better off not having been born." Each repeated the words mentally. The moment grew solemn; not even Pepet dared speak. One by one, they got up from the table to help their mother with the dishes. Juan stayed at the table figuring out expenses, payments, and collections. His sons went upstairs, anxious to talk to Fermin, the hero of the moment.

"Don't you worry about the vegetable garden, I'll take care of it. I'll bring the vegetables home the way you always do," Andres promised.

"What are you going to do with so much money?" Pepet asked.

"It won't be that much. I'll send father most of it."

"Bah!" Lucas said disdainfully, "When I leave, it'll be for America."

"We'll go too, but when the time is right. Meantime, I'll get plenty of practice here, see?"

When the boys heard their father's steps coming upstairs, they ran for their beds. It was past midnight when Rosa finished ironing. Although nothing was farther from her mind than the idea of rest, she went upstairs and entered the children's room. Her white apron seemed to light up the darkness. She approached each of them, looked at them for a few seconds and kissed them on their foreheads. When she reached Fermin, the boy was still awake. Moved by his mother's expression of love, he stretched out his arms from under the covers and hugged her.

"Never be afraid to come back. This will always be your home," she whispered in his ear.

That night, Rosa could not sleep. She realized that her children were slipping away, and she could do nothing about it. Then she remembered something she had heard at the wash fountain days before. Erasmo, the bartender had made it known to the whole town that on his last visit to Castellon he had bought a new contraption. Look through the lens, cover your head with a black cloth to turn out the light, and a bright flash and a loud boom would produce a picture, excellent quality work, to keep for years of memories. Rosa had seen some already: Patrocinia and part of her brood; Candido and Balbina; Don Poli and his wife. All sitting areas in Tirig's homes displayed one. Rosa had a premonition that night that the world as she knew it was quickly coming to an end with Fermin's departure. At dawn, before anyone woke up, she ran to Erasmo's to ask for a special favor. Erasmo, after working late the night before, was sleepy and tired when he opened the door to Rosa thinking it was an emergency.

"Don Erasmo, I've never asked for anything like this before, but you must shoot us, all together," she asked hurriedly.

"Shoot you?" This woman had to be mad.

"With that thing you keep in the back that puts people's faces on cardboard for us to keep forever," she pleaded.

"Ah, a picture!" Erasmo exclaimed relieved.

"Yes, one of those, of my whole family."

"It's early, Rosa. We could do it in the afternoon, you know."

"Fermin is leaving this morning, after that, my family will not be together again. It has to be now, Erasmo," she explained with urgency.

"I'll get ready and you bring them over."

Lucia was still asleep in her arms when Rosa rushed back to Charco Street and to her own home, walked up the stairs, woke everyone up, and made breakfast. Nobody was to leave until they went to Erasmo's . . . together. During her children's long absence, Rosa would look at that picture often and would consider it quite an accomplishment.

Chapter 24

Fermin Garach came back to town the following year wearing a new beret and the same old corduroy pants he had worn a year before when he left for Vinaroz. Pepet was the first to hear the news, and he ran to tell his mother. Together, mother and son left the house with Lucia. As they passed Andres, they broke the news to him, and the three made haste, turned the corner on Charco Street, and saw Fermin approaching.

As if by mute agreement, they transformed the unspoken words into glances and embraces. They had so much to say, but their hearts, beating fast with excitement, spoke eloquently enough. The boy, changed after a year of hardships, was instantly surrounded by a compact ring of love and laughter.

Fermin had one week to spend with his family; he brought his mother a bunch of bananas and his sister a doll; that was all that his meager earnings could afford. But he came full of stories—fictional or real—in which he, Fermin, had been the protagonist.

"Yes, I've seen the sea. I've even gone swimming in it."

"Heavens, son. Don't be so reckless!"

"It's nothing, mother; someday I'll take you to see it too."

"What color is the water?" Pepet asked.

"Some days it's blue; others, it's green. It's like a huge field of water. Sometimes it's angry, and then it beats against the rocks; it has even swallowed whole ships full of people!"

"Holy Madonna of l'Avella! You go swimming there?"

"That hardly ever happens," he said reassuringly.

"Could we all go there someday and find the sea, like Fermin?"

"There's too many of us; how could we all go?"

"Then, I'll go alone!"

"Pepet!"

"Didn't you tell him about the job at the print shop, mother?"

"Your father thought it better to wait; Pepet is still too young," Rosa said by way of an excuse.

Daniel del Mas needed a boy like Pepet to work in his print shop, and the news quickly filled with expectation the Garach household.

The boy barely succeeded in controlling his nerves. Rosa felt the inevitable would happen.

"If his brother lives in the same city, I can't see why the boy shouldn't go. He's already nine. You'll go, Pepet; you'll go. There's nothing else to say on the matter," Juan said later, ending the discussion.

It was settled; Pepet would leave with Fermin and his father on Sunday morning. He would have to have enough clothes to last him a year.

Rosa shuddered holding Lucia tightly against her; at least she had a daughter who wouldn't roam God's good earth. She thought of Cirilo; he had been a grown man and yet, he couldn't help himself and had gotten really sick. How could her sons, still children, care for themselves?

When the house grew quiet, Rosa still toiled in the kitchen immersed in her thoughts; her hands, covered with flour, kneaded the dough soon to become bread. That night she felt very lonely. No one shared her worries. Her children were so young; they spoke with such innocence. They hadn't grown a beard yet, but Juan thought they could already go far away, with no one to guide them, with no family to protect them. How would she hear from them? She couldn't even read. This made Rosa wish she were someone else. She crossed herself and continued kneading the dough.

Later on that night, the door leading to the bedrooms opened slowly and the dark, lively black eyes of her youngest son glistened as they came to rest on her.

"What are you doing up so late, Pepet?"

"I closed my eyes but couldn't go to sleep. The others are already asleep. Will you be long?"

"I only have to break apart the loaves and put them in the basket; I'll do the rest tomorrow. Will you hand me that basket, son?" Rosa had been holding back her tears all evening, but somehow, the boy's tousled hair, his innocent hands made her cry.

"Mother, are you so sad because I'm leaving?"

"Pepet, do you know what you mean to me? My youngest son; the one who makes me smile; the one who helps me so much. Why do you want to leave so soon?"

"I'm already nine years old, mother. I want to go so that I can become a man fast and help you and Lucia and everybody else."

"Son, we don't lack anything; we live pretty well. What else do we need? You'll become a man in due time, I know."

"Yes, but I think you work too hard. I've never seen you rest. Don Poli's wife calls on other ladies and does embroidery in the afternoons. You've barely finished baking the bread when it's time for you to get our clothes ready for the next day."

"Well, that's my life; I have to take good care of all of you. Don Poli's wife has no children. I'm lucky to have you all."

"I want to start working, so you can rest more."

"Who's told you all those things, son?"

"Well, Aniceto went to Castellon and in just a few months he's been able to send his mother some money; why Aunt Mari Pepa told me the other day he had even sent her a bottle of cologne with Quico, the messenger."

"Aniceto's mother has no husband; that's why the boy had to leave home so soon. Besides, he's a little older than you. I've got your father. Come here, son," she said smiling.

The boy sat on Rosa's lap, leaned his blonde head against his mother and held her tightly.

"My son, my Pepet, I don't want any of those things you've been telling me about. I want you and your brothers, and I don't want anything bad to happen to you all. I won't mind if you leave when you're grown men."

"Father never seems to do well in business. We must also help him." The boy squeezed his mother and yawned.

"You've a lot to learn before you grow to be a fine, decent man, my son. You haven't even made your First Communion yet; time flies and before you notice, you'll be old enough to do all those things you're telling me." Rosa spoke without looking at the boy's face; rhythmically, she caressed his blonde hair resting against her shoulder. In a few minutes, Pepet found in his mother's arms the sleep that had eluded him in bed. His eyelids closed over his eyes, and his dark eyelashes, at last still, gave his face a peaceful expression.

"You know, son, you're a child for only a few years of your life; then you grow, and your childhood leaves you forever. Don't rush things because you can't go back. I don't know if you understand me now but, some day . . ."

Her eyes looked down and noticed Pepet's peaceful slumber. She smiled, held him even closer against her chest and then carried him in her arms to his bed, next to Andres. "So this is the one who already wants to be a man," she thought as she looked tenderly at the small boy curled up between the sheets.

Chapter 25

Eight months after Pepet left for Vinaroz, Lucas Garach and his father were climbing the path up the hill before reaching San Mateo, the last stop on the way to Tirig. The boy thought the moment appropriate to break the news to his father: a group of thirteen young men would be leaving for Barcelona at the end of the month, bound for America. The uncle of one of them lived in Havana and worked in a brewery; he would get them a place to stay.

"Hummm," Juan had said. "You can go, but I can't help you much on your trip."

Lucas was set to go, regardless of the circumstances. So, one Thursday, late in January, he bade his family and his town farewell. After a short while on the road, he felt transformed into a man.

Juan, after all, had given him six hundred *pesetas* before he left. Damn! Lucas didn't remember ever having so much money in his hands all at once. Rosa had sewn it to a belt around the boy's waist. "Beware of the women's disease; be careful, son; may God bless you," Rosa had exclaimed. Bah! Nonsense! One should never pay much attention to women, his father had told him.

He arrived in Vinaroz in the afternoon; the stores were still open and full of customers. Lucas got off his bicycle and began to walk led by a single, overriding desire; he had to buy a hat. In Barcelona and in Bilbao, where he had traveled with his father so many times, men wore hats. The first act of his recently attained independence was to buy himself one.

Looking at his feet, he paused for a moment before making an equally crucial decision. A suit. He needed a suit and a hat. On his way to the store, Lucas arrived at the conclusion that both items were not only necessary but, in fact, indispensable. In less than thirty minutes, a good portion of the six hundred *pesetas* had found their way into other pockets. Lucas' old rags—until recently his Sunday clothes—were thrown into the knapsack tied to the seat of the bicycle.

Lucas Garach—citizen of Tirig suddenly changed into an international traveler sent by the Garach family to an alligator-shaped island in the Caribbean—arrived at night at Don Alejo Querol's store where Fermin worked.

"What's that you're wearing? *¡Collons!*" One could tell Fermin was impressed.

"Can't you see it? I've bought myself a suit."

"But, are you leaving already? From where?"

"From Barcelona," he said proudly, "the ship sets sail the day after tomorrow, and a group of thirteen men, all from this area, will be leaving tomorrow."

"How's mother? Pepet and I will be going to Tirig in a few days."

"I know; father told me, that's why I'm here." The twins looked at each other's face; they were no longer identical. "I want you to keep my bicycle."

"For good?"

"When I come back, I'll have plenty of money; in which case, I will no longer need it."

"I don't know why you're in such a hurry to go so far away. Look, I'm doing all right here. Don Alejo is a good man and pays me well; in a few years' time . . ."

"You'll be just the same, father says so. If you don't go out to look for a better future, you'll be here 'till your hair turns white. Father wants us to bring plenty of money; we'll open up a business like this, only that it'll be our own. Don't you understand?"

"Father and you alone?"

"All of us together, of course, except Andres. He's a cripple."

"He is not," Fermin shot back. Lucas ignored his anger.

"Father will buy a farm."

"A farm?" The voice came from the door; it was Pepet. A friend had told him of his brother's arrival. "I came running; are you leaving? Where are you going?" The boy was bubbling with enthusiasm, although he did not stop scratching his head.

"Not now, Pepet; come, stop jumping and listen. Go on, Lucas."

"Father wants to buy a farm around here, near the coast. We'll grow the produce we'll sell later at the store and get double profit on everything."

"When will we buy the business?"

"What business?"

"Hush, Pepet!"

"We'll buy the business with the money we'll bring from America."

"Are we leaving for America already? Now? So soon?"

The twins looked at each other and couldn't help smiling at their younger brother's seemingly inexhaustible energy.

"You two, Fermin and you, will go later on. I'm leaving the day after tomorrow; I'll get myself a job and save to send you your boat fares."

"When are you leaving?"

"I'll spend the night here with you, Fermin; I'll go early tomorrow morning. It's several hours to Barcelona."

"Can I sleep here, too? The place where I live smells bad, it's dirty; Don Daniel doesn't tell his wife to wash the sheets."

"Just a few days, Pepet, and we'll be back in Tirig. There's no room for all three of us, but come, have a bite to eat before you leave."

Eating and talking as they sat on the bed, the three boys forgot the impending trip. The pale light from the lamp post on the corner let them know that it was time to say good-bye. Pepet stood before his brother, looked at him, and smiled.

"You don't look like you with that hat. Does everybody wear a hat in America?"

"All men do; I've seen them in Barcelona."

The eleven year old boy, with his *espardenas* and corduroy pants, looked even more like a child next to his brother. His blonde hair was in total disarray, for he constantly scratched his head.

"Listen," he said, obviously anxious to put an end to the embarrassing farewell, "do you know if they've got lice over in America?"

Chapter 26

Each time Rosa saw Quico come through the curtain on the doorway and utter his customary greeting, she shuddered and prayed to the Holy Madonna de l'Avella. The town's messenger always brought news of jobs for her children. One night early in May, as they were about to sit at the table for dinner, it happened once more.

"Come in, Quico; don't stand there by the door, come on in. Would you like to join us? Come," Juan invited him.

"I'm leaving already; I've just come from Castellon, and it was a long trip. I want to rest, but first I wanted to let you know that this man, Hipolito Blanch, in Castellon, needs a boy as soon as possible."

"A boy for what?" Pepet interrupted. Despite his unpleasant experience in Vinaroz, the boy was ready to leave again.

"Don Hipolito has had a pharmacy for many years; he now needs a messenger boy to make deliveries."

"Does he pay well?"

"Twenty-five *pesetas* plus room, board, and laundry."

"What are this people like?" Pepet wondered aloud.

"Don Hipolito and his family are among the most respected people in Castellon. The back of his store is as clean and neat as any private home. Don Hipolito and his family live upstairs."

"When would they want the boy?" asked Juan.

"The sooner the better."

"When are you going back to Castellon, Quico?"

"I'm leaving tomorrow for San Mateo; I'll come back and then I'll leave again for Castellon."

"Pepet, what do you say, son? I'm leaving tomorrow for Barcelona, and I'll look up Don Hipolito Blanch in Castellon on my way there. I'll square things out with him and by the time you get there, everything will be taken care of. Thank you, Quico."

"Good night; enjoy your dinner. See you soon, Pepet." Quico said good-bye by installments, bowing deeply with each phrase. In spite of her concern over Pepet, Rosa had to smile at the awkwardness of the messenger's farewell.

"Will you really go to Castellon?" Andres asked his brother that night as they counted the wooden beams on the ceiling above their bed.

"You heard father. I'll go with Quico in a few days."

"Do you suppose Lucas is already in America?"

"He left over one month ago, but it isn't like going to Castellon. You have to cross an ocean, and that's no joke, you know what I mean? If you'd seen the sea you'd know what I'm talking about."

"Haven't I told you what I plan to do, Pepet?"

"Do when?"

"One of these days, maybe after you're gone. I'll go to Vinaroz with Fermin. I've spoken to Don Poli, and he agrees with me; we need learning tools here in Tirig—pencils, erasers, rulers, papers, reading books. There aren't any newspapers either, except for the ones Godfather brings every three of four months. Don Poli's told me that if I go and bring those things, he won't have to go himself; the two of us can then sell them. I think I can make myself some money; I know about those things, you know."

"I remember Don Poli used to teach you. How will you go? Vinaroz is far away. How will you make it with your bad leg, Andres?"

"I'll go with Quico in his cart; we'll split the profits."

Rosa appeared in the doorway.

"What are you doing talking in the dark at this time of night?" Rosa stood at the doorway and smiled.

"We're men talking business, mother; there's a lot to talk at this time," Pepet said, feeling proud of himself.

"What business could you possibly talk about? You're still children," she came closer to the boys and sat at the edge of the bed.

"No, mother; we're grown up, we're men," Pepet answered with authority. "Look, Andres plans to buy and sell papers and pencils."

"And you, little one, are you planning on leaving again?"

"You'll see, mother, I'll have you living like a queen in no time."

"Well, are you too grown up for a kiss and my blessing?" As she leaned over her son's bed, one of her braids came loose and stroked Pepet's face.

"Remember, mother? When I was little I liked to feel your braids; they're still special, nobody else's got them."

Rosa laughed to herself.

"Hey, you, sweet-talker, go to sleep. May God bless both of you."

Chapter 27

"Push, Andres; the mules can't pull all this load, and we'll wind up at the bottom of the hill. Push hard, like this."

Quico and Andres were on their way back from Vinaroz after a visit they had planned a few days earlier. Away from home, the eldest Garach son felt stronger and more independent; he could have almost sworn that he did not limp as much as before, and that he could stretch out his arm farther.

"Gooooo, Quico, shove; we're almost at the top of the hill and from there on it'll be easy."

"Go, Preciosa; go, Calita; go my pretty mules, don't quit now! After this hill we'll be home, and then we'll all rest," Quico shouted at them, almost breathless.

Andres would have never thought himself capable of pushing a fully loaded cart, but his first trip away from Tirig taught him that he was able to do many more things than he had ever dreamed possible. Don Poli had lent him the money for the first purchase; Andres was afraid that if his father found out about his budding commercial venture, he would veto it. The school became his headquarters. Don Policarpo welcomed him warmly; he had set aside a shelf for all the merchandise Andres had brought, and thanks to the teacher's interest, the boy sold most of it in just two weeks.

"They told me at the tavern that Andres went with Quico to Vinaroz to get I don't know what. Is that true?" Juan was furious.

"That's right, Juan," Rosa acknowledged cautiously. "He told me before he went; you weren't here."

"What did he go there for?"

"I don't understand those things too well; the boy wants to sell books, pencils, things like that. Since he knows Don Policarpo, who's a good man, and he's taken a liking to Andres . . . Well, you see . . ." Rosa toyed with her apron fearful of the anger that was building up on her husband's brow.

"Who gave him permission to go?"

"Well, Juan, the boy's almost a man. He is also entitled to try to get ahead in life as best he can, the poor thing."

"Shut up; nobody asked you for your opinion. He shouldn't have gone without my permission, without talking to me first. Who gives orders in this house? Huh? Who gives the orders?"

Neither La Morellana nor the house on Charco Street had ever heard Rosa raise her voice. This time, however, she turned red with anger and, getting up from her chair, she walked to the other side of the table where she imagined herself more protected.

"Andres has to live," she said with determination. "Don't you ever get tired of putting him down, of calling him useless and good for nothing? My son's a good boy, hear me well, and he's entitled to live and make a man of himself, just like the others. His arm and his leg wouldn't have mattered if you had given him some of the love you reserved exclusively for his three brothers."

"I'll forbid him to go out; he's got to look after the vegetable garden."

"You'll do no such thing. I'll take care of the garden. We'll all pitch in and get things done. But you leave my Andres alone; don't you dare touch him, or I don't know what I may do."

Juan's eyes looked at her amazed. Never, in seventeen years of marriage, had he seen her like that, challenging him in his own home. He stood before her, bursting with the anger that had built up inside of him since he heard the news at the tavern. Rosa provoked him even further with her attitude. She remained impassive as he unleashed his fury and hit her savagely on her cheek. Never had his wife seemed more defenseless. Once, twice, and Rosa did not flinch. Faced with his wife's indifference, Juan stormed out of the house.

Andres drew the curtain that covered the front door; he had witnessed the unpleasant scene. Rosa was moved to tears by the expression of grief in the young man's eyes.

"Don't be hard on him, son. In his own way, he loves you, too. He really does. He's your father, son, that is sacred. Don't be too hard on him. Don't look at me like that, Andres." It was then that Rosa realized that the time had come for Andres to leave and find peace on his own.

The next morning, Rosa was again surprised. Don Sotero, the baker, was the one who received the mail for the whole town. No sooner did she enter his shop to have him bake her bread, that he presented her with a letter.

"For me?" Rosa asked surprised. No one had ever written to her.

"It says it right there," Sotero said with pride, "Señora Rosa Garach," he smiled watching her freeze looking at the letter in disbelief. "Don't just stand there, doña Rosa, give me your bread then go and read it. It's from America."

With the letter in her hands, Rosa rushed to Candido's barber shop. Women don't need to write, women don't need to write, she repeated to herself what she had heard Juan say so many times. Look at what happened. The woman who didn't need to write couldn't read her son's letter. She looked at the envelope in her hand, and tears ran down her cheeks.

"Candido!" she called softly at the entrance to the barber shop.

"Rosita! Come in, make yourself at home. Balbinaaaaa!" He yelled enthusiastically.

"It's this letter. I'm sure it's from one of the boys, and I can't . . ."

"Here, there's no need to cry; this is a joyful moment, and we'll enjoy it together, all three of us."

By then, Balbina had already joined them and quietly, the two women listened to what Candido was about to say.

For my family, Mother
    It's late at night and I feel like talking to you all, but we're far away—fifteen days and a sea as big as Tirig, San Mateo and La Morellana and all the land between covered with blue, salty water. The trip in the steamship Cadiz of the Pinillos Company went well with the 600 *pesetas* father gave me I bought myself a suit, a pair of shoes, and a hat because nobody was wearing *espardenas*, that's all right for around town, but for voyages and important things like that those clothes are no good and after buying all of that I just had enough money left for the fare. On board the ship I worked in the kitchen, peeling potatoes and cleaning and I already became a businessman selling in third class the leftover food from first class and so I gathered enough *pesetas* to buy an accordion and a tambourine at our first stop in Cadiz. My friends Rosendo and Bonifacio and me spent the trip from Cadiz to Cuba playing for the passengers. The others in our group did nothing but miss their families and feel sorry for themselves, but we worked hard and made enough money to pay the pesetas that they call *pesos* here that kept us from Triscornia, that's the place where they take foreigners who don't have money to pay their way into the country. Since the others didn't have any *pesos* to pay with, we let them have the money little by little we were all able to

leave without having to go through Triscornia, although we couldn't stay together, there were too many of us and we went our separate ways. I went with Rosendo and Bonifacio to the house of this Valencian guy. They began to work in grocery stores which is what I like but I'm working in a factory. A huge warehouse where they make iron, I work by the furnace heating up rivets, it's hard work and when I gather enough money to change to a grocery store I will, but I want to save enough for me and to send Fermin and Pepet enough *pesos* to buy their fares and come here because the sooner the three of us are here the better it'll be and the sooner we'll be able to gather money to go back home and open our business and I'll be writing soon again, a kiss for little Lucia and one for mother and one for father and say hello to everybody in town for me because the town is good because in big cities like Havana you only know the people you live with.

Lucas Garach
April, 1917

Rosa looked at her son's handwriting with a stronger than ever wish that she could read it. However, she was calmer, and as the letter ended, she smiled.

Chapter 28

When Juan realized that letters from Lucas could be coming regularly, he never went back to the house without checking with Don Sotero first. That's why, six months later, when Lucas wrote his second later, he realized he had raised his son well.

"Where's Rosa?" It was March, 1918, and Juan's joy was contagious as he entered the house on Charco Street waving a piece of paper in his hand.

"She's gone over to Don Sotero's to take the bread and the cake for him to bake for Sunday."

"I see. I just came from there." Then he hesitated. "I'll go get her." He dashed out again.

Socorro, who was now living with Juan, Rosa and Lucia, didn't show the slightest interest in the news that excited her brother so, but a few minutes later, when she saw Rosa's alarmed face in the doorway, she knew that something unusual had happened.

"What's wrong, why are you so pale?" Socorro asked, concerned.

"Juan just told me that Lucas, my son, has written again. He's sent the money for Fermin and Pepet to go to Cuba with him. Juan's going to get the boys tomorrow and within a few days, they're going to America," she sighed. "Fermin's already sixteen, but Pepet is also going; he's only eleven and he's going away, all by himself, on such a long trip, across the sea . . . Holy Madonna de l'Avella . . ." Socorro had never seen Rosa cry with such sorrow. "Why can't I ever have things the way I want them? Why must I lose my children?"

"Don't worry, Rosa; God will be with them. Fermin is a very sensible boy, and he'll take good care of his brother; don't worry; it's all part of growing up. Nothing will happen."

"May the Lord hear you; so many children and they're going away all of them; they're going away, and I might never see them again. Can't even read their letters!"

Rosa's frustration, which knew no bounds, lasted until the day of the boys' departure. Folding clothes gave her time to think. With every fold of the clothes she packed a caress, a "God bless you," a "Don't forget." She prayed that the separation not be final, that she may see them again some day. Holy Madonna de l'Avella, don't let them forget their home; let them come back to see her, to see all of them, don't let them get lost in the world the way others had.

"May I come in?" Fermin tapped on the door. Right away, he was sorry he had interrupted his mother; he would have preferred to study her features carefully and engrave them in his mind to remember her until they should meet again. She was sitting down on the bed, slightly bent forward, dressed in black—in mourning for Grandmother Vicenta and Grandfather Lucas who had died—and her white apron contrasted sharply with the dark hue of her clothes. Fermin had never seen his mother more beautiful.

"Come in, son; you can always come in. Here I am, getting everything ready for tomorrow. You're leaving, aren't you?"

"Right. We're going with Quico in his cart as far as Vinaroz, and there we'll take the train to Santander."

"That's far, son; you'll take good care of your brother, won't you? He's still so little; he shouldn't be going away yet. But, that's the way your father thinks, and there's no use trying to change his mind."

"Don't worry, mother; we'll be all right. We'll be back in a few years. To do the things we want to do, we've got to struggle hard now. That's why we're going to Cuba."

"My son, all I want is to see you all well and healthy."

Rosa spoke looking at her hands which did not stop folding clothes. Fermin saw that, as she spoke, tears ran serenely down her cheeks. The young man held her by the shoulders and made her stand up; he was already taller than she was. In an effort to choke the urge to weep that overcame her, Rosa buried her face in her son's shoulder.

"May Our Lord be always with you."

"Mother," he said running his hands over her head, "don't cry; we'll be back."

The farewell on the next day was made less painful by Pepet's excitement; the boy did not stand still for a minute. Their father had bought each a suit, a hat, and a suitcase; they knew from Lucas' letter that that was the correct travel attire. Pepet was showing off to the neighbors. The hat, despite the fact that it was the smallest possible size, was rather big on him and came down over his forehead almost covering his eyes. Rosa tried to correct that by tying a handkerchief around the boy's head to keep the hat in place.

Around ten in the morning Quico came to tell them that he was ready to go, and that they should go to where he had his cart. The whole town had heard that the Garach boys were leaving, and many of their friends came to see them off and wish them well. Candido, of course, was the first to arrive at the house on Charco Street with two bottles of cough syrup, just in case they might need it during the trip. Balbina had embroidered a handkerchief for each boy. Don Sotero brought them bread; Don Policarpo, some figs. Erasmo, the bartender, came expressly to congratulate Juan: having three sons in America was quite an accomplishment. Aunt Patrocinia, somewhat older and worn out, kissed and hugged them with such feeling that she knocked off Pepet's hat. The scrawny boy immediately reached his head to take of the handkerchief he wore underneath the hat to make it fit better. The house was not large enough for so many guests. Rosa was busy slicing ham and serving wine and no one, except Juan, saw the boys slip out and go to Quico's cart.

The wheels that took them away from Tirig forever started to turn slowly. Fermin rode in silence; Quico, used to the trip, hummed a country tune to the step of the mules; Pepet first looked here and there as if he had never travelled that road before. Eventually, the excitement of the last two days took its toll, and he lay down, intending to catch up on the sleep he had missed the past two nights.

"Can you both hear me?" he asked suddenly.

"Yes, Pepet; what is it?" Fermin answered.

"Well, since we're leaving for Cuba and all, I think I'm turning into a man, isn't that right?"

"Of course!" they answered and laughed.

"Well, from now on my name will be Jose, Jose Garach. Pepet is for children, and when I meet new people and I tell them my name's Pepet, they'll treat me like a child, and that can't be. So, you know, from now on I'm officially a man," he said forgetting he was but eleven years old, "and my name is Jose Garach, not Pepet."

Fermin and Quico exchanged amused glances and managed to control their laughter.

"Very well, Pepet; it'll be as you say," Fermin said.

A few moments later, they had to pick up Pepet's hat, which the wind had blown away and thrown next to some bushes by the roadside.

PART IV

It was about this time that every morning I used to have a special dream. I saw myself standing at my window in the house on the Calle del Charco. It was the window that faced the pasture land where my Andres and sometimes my Pepet would take the sheep to graze. In my dream, I could see more than just the sheep and the pasture. I saw only water at first; it was liquid blue, and it moved like the leaves of the trees during autumn. At the other end of this sea, I could see a patch of land, shaped like an alligator, and it had three boys standing on it waving at me. They were my boys.

It was a powerful dream, that dream. It woke me up while my eyes were still closed, and it made me stand up from my bed, open the window and wave restlessly to the fantasy I had created on the outside. I often woke up to find myself waving at the wind, all alone; Juan, asleep in bed, snored peacefully, never noticing my anguish. No one ever knew how the wetness of sweat and the depth of the sobs choked my hopes. Only I knew of this dream and its restless awakenings; only I felt with anguish the distance that separated my three small boys from me. I couldn't write or talk to them then. The best I could do was pray, and pray I did, every morning, waving good-bye to that imaginary, alligator-shaped bit of land that lay far, beyond my window. Now, you know about this too.

Chapter 29

After finishing school at Don Poli's one Thursday afternoon, weeks after her brother's departure, Lucia went to the town's wash fountain to help her mother do the laundry. Rosa saw her coming and smiled as she did every time she looked at her daughter. For her, the girl was like a miracle; so many boys scattered throughout the world, some perhaps bobbing up and down on the high seas, but she still had her Lucia to give some sense to her life, to make her feel like a mother.

"How was your day today, dear?"

"Marisol told me father arrived," Lucia answered curtly.

"Why, if your father's home . . ."

"Give me what you want me to carry, and I'll run home."

"No need to rush; your father won't be leaving again soon."

"He must know about the school by now; he told me before he left that he'd bring me news about the school."

"What about school?" Intrigued by her daughter's comments, Rosa began placing the clothes she had just rinsed inside the basket.

"A nun's school near Vinaroz, where the rich girls from the coast go."

"Child, you dream these things, and then you believe them to be real. Here, take one side of the basket; I'll take the other, and we'll carry this home between the two of us."

Rosa looked younger than her years with her sleeves rolled up, her hair covered by a scarf her son Andres had sent her and her face red from work and sunlight.

"Father!" Lucia shouted when she saw him, running to Juan and leaving her mother to hold the basket.

"Hello, Juan, how did it go?" Rosa asked her husband.

"Not bad; I collected on those horses I sold, and I've seen a farm near Benicarlo that I really like. With the boys gone and all, this might be a good time to buy it."

"Buy it? With what? Have we got the money for that?"

"Well, actually we don't, but we can get it. If we sold the animals at La Morellana . . ."

"Juan, I've never known you to give much thought to what can't be," Rosa looked at her husband in disbelief.

"You're right; I never have. But this can be. I've already given a down payment on the farm, and the two of us will be leaving soon, Rosa," he stared coldly outside.

"Well, the three of us, you mean. I don't suppose you're planning to leave Lucia in Tirig; she's coming with us isn't she?" Rosa was trying to catch Juan's glance, but he persisted in his stare.

"Lucia won't be staying in Tirig. I have big plans for her. She'll be able to go to a good school to learn what her brothers couldn't learn. When the boys come back, she'll be a well educated young lady, with plenty of business know-how, you'll see. Won't you, my girl? Lucia and I are leaving next week for Vinaroz. I've already made arrangements at this nuns' boarding school to have her admitted to learn all the things a well-to-do young lady should know."

"Juan! How could you take the girl so far away?" Rosa stood up, outraged.

"Mother, don't say no, please. Father says that in those places they teach the girls to embroider, and they read a lot and make their First Communion and things like that."

"Yes, dear, all that's fine, but you're still a child," Rosa almost begged her daughter's approval.

"Selfishness won't help your children's future. If I'd been selfish, the others wouldn't have gone away," Juan replied.

"Precisely. The others were boys and although it broke my heart to see them go, I didn't object; I prepared their things and saw them off. But now you're talking about my daughter, a girl, an innocent thing who won't have us by her side when she needs us."

"Mother!"

"*¡Recollons!* Enough of this. In this house, you do as I say, Rosa, and don't you ever forget it or . . ." Juan leaped to his feet and moved towards his wife. Rosa was not challenging him; her face tinted with sorrow, tears runing down her cheeks. She stared at him, miserable in her own impotence.

"I'm not afraid of you; you can't hurt me any more. First you took all my sons away; now, it's the girl. There's nothing I can do; I know that. It'll be as you say, but don't threaten me, Juan, no matter how many times you strike me, nothing you do can hurt me more than what you have already done. I am free of you."

El Morellano didn't know whether to strike her or not. This time he let his arms fall next to his body, shouted "*¡Recollons!*" once more and stormed out of the house, wild with fury. Lucia remained silent by the table. Rosa went upstairs holding the basket in her arms. No one saw her come down again that evening.

Chapter 30

Health reasons forced Lucas to give up his job with American Steel. In just four months he had lost his eyebrows, and his arms felt like coals. And yet, he did not give in until weeks later, when a red-hot rivet fell on him. There was no alternative then; he had to leave that job and find a new one.

The ward at the Quinta Covadonga, the hospital where he was admitted, had a row of beds on either side. It was painted white, but it had turned to a dirty shade of gray that made one feel like running away. Father Paz convinced him to stay. The priest had come to see him earlier, but Lucas had been asleep; he wanted to know if he could be of any help. The boy told him he was from Valencia and had come to Cuba a year before; he was waiting for his two brothers, and his entire capital amounted to three hundred *pesos*.

A job? Why, sure, Lucas Garach could do anything well. He knew about animals, about groceries, about tomatoes, lettuce, peppers, and all those things. He used to buy and sell with his father around town. Father Paz understood; no need to despair; God never abandons His children. Lucas, however, needed tangible evidence. He was not disappointed, though. It so happened that the good priest knew this gentleman, Lopez was his name, who owned a grocery story and needed a lad to help him. He would talk to the man. Perhaps he would be working by the time his brothers arrived.

Back in Spain, while the transatlantic liner was still in port, Pepet Garach became a fearless explorer of the unknown. There were many secrets on board that floating universe. It was inevitable that the boy should have reacted with excitement at the sight of the first bunker or the round little portholes which reminded him of numerous navels. He had never seen anything as large as the ballroom and nothing quite as hostile as the indifferent glances of a group of ladies with mink wraps.

"Listen, Fermin," he whispered to his brother, "that lady over there is looking at me as if I still had lice. Why?"

"Hush, Pepet; I think we're in the wrong place."

"If she knew that I made three goals, and that in Castellon I was the team's best runner, I bet you she'd look at me different."

"Hush, Pepet. Let's go before they kick us out of the ship. Come."

On the second night on board, Pepet's curiosity vanished, and the boy went to bed much earlier than usual. He complained that the ship was turning at the same rate as his stomach. Fermin, quite frightened, did not know whose help to ask when, after two days, his brother still had not touched any food. Finally, he gathered enough courage to march into the galley and got the cooks to let him have some broth twice a day. He would bring the big, smoking cup into the cabin and, after adding garlic and bread to it, he would attempt to feed his brother.

For the young boy, the ship never stopped turning. One afternoon, after Pepet finished his frugal meal, Fermin looked under the bunker for the suitcase where they kept their clothes and money. It was not in its usual place. The young man lay on the floor and searched frantically. It was no use. The suitcase was gone.

"Pepet! Where did you put the suitcase?" The boy did not answer. "Pepet!"

"What?" he answered.

"The suitcase, where is it?"

"I haven't seen it; with all this damn turning around I can't even sit up straight."

"It isn't here. Where could it be?"

"Who's going to take it? It's ours."

"You talk like a baby, Pepet. That's precisely the problem: it may have been stolen."

"Stolen? With money and everything?"

No one was able, or willing, to help Fermin. One suitcase, yes, sir. There was money in it, the passports, and some clothes mother had initialed. That didn't matter? Oh, somebody must have taken it while Pepet was asleep.

The captain promised to send Lucas a telegram; they would not need anything else until he met them at the San Francisco Pier in Havana.

"Pepet." Fermin had his mother's black eyes and seemed to have inherited her worry and her caring.

"Fermin, I don't want any more broth or nothing." The boy could hardly open his eyes, his hands lying limp by his side. "Listen, do people die of seasickness?"

"Hush. All we need is for you to start talking about dying. We've got to get to Cuba. Here, drink your broth," the older one insisted.

"Fermin, don't let them throw me into the sea. Did you know that there are fish big enough to swallow a man?" Pepet's thin hand tried to touch his brother's.

"You swallow your soup and quit talking nonsense," said Fermin taking the hand that was looking for some security.

"Fermin."

"Yes, Pepet, what is it?"

"I'm scared; don't go away. I'm scared to be alone, Fermin."

Fermin could not leave his brother's bedside until it was time to go ashore. They looked as if they had walked from the house on Charco Street. Pepet was pale, emaciated and had lost his hat; Fermin, bags under his eyes from not sleeping well, was not wearing his suit; it had been stolen. With hesitant steps he led his brother by the hand.

"I beg your pardon, sir. Passports? No, we don't . . . He's my brother, and he hasn't got one either . . . They stole them from us, you see? . . . No, we don't have any money either . . . We've come to join our brother; he lives here in this town . . . No, I don't see him out there, no. He must have come, but I don't see him . . . You've got to take us some place else you say? . . . Garach, sir. Fermin and Juan Jose Garach. Spaniards, yes, from Castellon de la Plana. Where are you taking us? Triscornia? And how will my brother Lucas know that we're there? . . . Juan Jose Garach, eleven years old . . . Oh, everybody who arrives like this, with no money and no family, goes there. Forty days? Fermin Garach, sir, sixteen years old . . . Pepet, why are you crying now?"

"They're taking us to jail," he whimpered, "can't you see that this man looks like a policeman?"

"It's not jail, I tell you. And didn't you tell me you were a man already? Men don't cry, Pepet. Hush! Yes, this is the first time we come to a place like this, sir. He will be quiet in a minute. He's been ill, sir, you know? Please, excuse him."

Chapter 31

Lucas did get that job at Don Isidro's and, since his address had changed, he only received his brothers' telegram three days after the ship had put into Havana harbor. The owner of the boarding house where he used to live brought him the news to the store on the corner of Chaple and Armonia Streets.

One afternoon, he told Don Isidro that his brothers had arrived from Spain three days before. The telegram said that somebody stole their suitcase, and they don't have a cent. Triscornia, that's where they had to be. Don Isidro had guessed right.

"Let's do this: this afternoon I have to go out to get some merchandise for the store. If you'd like, I can go get them and bring them home to you."

"Oh, would you? And I'll take them later to Safon's; he's the Valencian I stayed with when I arrived."

"Fine, we'll do it like that, then. I'll go pick them up."

Triscornia was neither hell nor heaven. Pepet stopped crying; seasickness and the ship became part of the past. The present became a loaf of Cuban bread and a slab of guava paste somebody gave them as a gift.

"What would you call guava, Fermin?"

"It's some sort of sweet stuff, don't you see?"

"If mother could see this!" he said licking his lips. "It's delicious; I like it better than sardines, and that's saying a lot because I really love sardines."

"You can't compare them, Pepet. This is sweet, syrupy, I don't know . . . anyway, we'll be able to eat all the guava we want; it seems it is a common thing here."

"Well, and why do you suppose there are so many dark people in this country? Didn't you see them when we left the ship? They were really black. Could it be the heat that makes them that way?"

"These blacks come from Africa and that's why they're like that."

"Doesn't it ever come off?"

"Pepet, don't be silly!"

"How would you know?" he replied defensively.

A voice interrupted their conversation.

"Fermin Garach, Juan Jose Garach. Fermin Garach, Juan Jose Garach. Somebody's waiting for you at the entrance desk. Somebody is waiting for you at the entrance desk. Fermin and Juan Jose Garach."

"Hell, that must be Lucas that came to pick us up. Listen, Fermin."

"Let's go," the older boy wasn't quite sure of what was in store for them. "Swallow, you can't show up with your mouth full of guava."

"Look, Fermin. There's a man waiting for us over there, and he's got one of those blacks with him." The boy would have given anything to have seen Lucas instead.

Chapter 32

"That's why I couldn't go to meet you. I left the hospital a week ago, when they took care of my burns. You can't imagine what that place was like; a huge warehouse, and I worked indoors. Since I was the last man hired, they gave me the job closest to the furnace, the worst one. I made some *pesetas*, but . . ."

"What do they call them here? *Pesos*?"

"That's right; I earned a few *pesos* and soon I'll be able to send father some money."

"Listen, Lucas, what really scared me was that black man who went to pick us up with Don Isidro. *¡Recollons!* I thought it was you and that something had happened to you, because, as I was telling Fermin, I think that's the heat that . . ."

"Hush, Pepet. Listen, Lucas, what are we going to do now?"

"Don Isidro's told me they're looking for a responsible boy at El Aguila, on the corner of Aguila and Neptuno, in Old Havana. It's some ways from here, but if they hire you, they'll give you room and board. It's a good place, and you'll be lucky to land a job there."

"Is there room for the two of us?" Pepet, with a hopeful expression in his eyes, sat up.

"No, just for one. But the two of you should go and let them pick whoever they want."

"They'll choose Fermin," Pepet said downcast. "He even looks like a man already. Look at him, he started shaving even, and I still look like a boy." He touched his face, hoping to feel the beard that had not yet arrived.

"We are the way we are, Pepet. Don't worry, you'll get a job, too," Fermin said, taking pity on his younger brother.

"Precisely. Father Paz, this priest I met at the hospital, has taken a liking to me, and he told me of this bakery where they need a boy to take care of the cleaning."

"Will they take me?"

"I don't see why not. We'll go there tomorrow afternoon."

"In the morning I'll go with Fermin to see about that other job."

"Wait till you see the girls in this town," Lucas said changing the subject to one evidently more appealing.

"Have you met many?"

"Not at the factory, but now, at the store, girls come from all over the neighborhood buying things. There's this one, Cachita is her name; she's the maid at Doña Alicia's house. She's really nice; she dances when she walks and has got tits out to here . . . I'm not kidding, they're all hers, too; nothing fake. Since it's so hot over here, women wear less clothes, and you can see more, just wait!"

Pepet dozed off almost immediately; the conversation no longer interested him. Fermin and Lucas, heedless to the time, continued talking until the small hours of the morning and by the time Lucas returned to Don Isidro's grocery it was time to begin another day's work.

Chapter 33

Isidro Lopez, Lucas' employer, and his fiancee Alicia were married one Sunday afternoon, almost six months after the arrival of the Garach brothers. The groom was not a wealthy man; everything he had, he had earned by working day and night, Sundays and holidays. Thanks to his tireless efforts, he had been able to buy a well-stocked grocery store and save a small capital. The wedding celebration was one of the best El Cerro neighborhood had seen in many years. Isidro invited Lucas to the party; the boy was a good worker. On his wedding day, Isidro closed the store.

A rather large group gathered at Alicia's house. Lucas had never been to a party like this; he felt happy and somewhat dazzled by the large number of guests, the cider, and Cachita's hips, which swung rhythmically as if to please the men in the group.

"When will you be done tonight?" he dared ask her once when the girl passed by.

"Oh, who knows? I'll be here a while yet; this looks like it's a long party, but I'll have to go home sometime I guess," Cachita's skin shone under a thin layer of sweat. Her blouse was off the shoulders; this made her neckline even more enticing to Lucas.

"And where do you go out from?"

"Why, through the back door," she said freezing him with her stare.

"Lucas Garach, come here a moment, will you?" Isidro was calling him.

"Look, I want to introduce you to my wife Alicia and to her sisters. You've been working with me for some months now, and you haven't met them yet. This is Lourdes, Magda, Emilia, Carmen, and Carolina, the youngest." All the girls greeted him and after the customary pleasantries, they each went their own ways, some in a group, others escorted by admiring young men. Only Carolina remained; the silence was embarrassing.

"It's a very nice party, don't you think?" Lucas tried to make small talk.

"Yes, it is!" The girl looked at the ceiling, as if hoping to find there the inspiration to carry on the conversation. "Isidro has told me a lot about you. He says you were in the hospital with burns."

The young girl chose the right topic; Lucas could talk at great length on the subject of his burns. Carolina wasn't pretty, but her features were elegant, and her eyes had a lovely blue-green hue. Her main asset was that she listened enraptured to everything the young Valencian had to say.

The rest of the evening passed quickly. The guests said their good-byes one by one and the newlyweds took advantage of a lull in the party to leave. Their honeymoon would last a week and during that time Lucas and Gerardo Santiesteban, Don Isidro's closest friend and associate, would mind the store.

"It's been a pleasure," Carolina said to him when almost everyone had left, and Lucas was getting ready to do likewise, "we hope that, why, you'll come back again; consider this your house."

"It's been a real pleasure to meet you, Carmen."

"Carmen is my sister; I'm Carolina."

"Pardon me, Carolina, I didn't mean to . . ."

"Don't worry. Good-bye."

Lucas was left with the impression that the girl would not want to see him again. It was unforgivable to mistake a girl's name after spending an entire evening talking to her. He wiped the perspiration off his forehead with a handkerchief and instinctively looked for Cachita. The girl, still strutting, was picking up glasses and dishes. Lucas said good-night to Carolina's mother and went out; he was extremely nervous. Although he had spent the evening talking to Carolina, Cachita was the one who really caught his eye. He went around the block to make time and returned to the corner of the house, so that he could watch the lively girl without being seen.

Almost an hour later, as he leaned half asleep against a lamp post, Lucas saw Cachita. The girl was not yet seventeen; her skin was cinnamon color; her curly hair covered her shoulders; her bare arms and lower neck glistened with July perspiration. She was holding in her hands a dish with party leftovers, covered with a napkin, and she almost dropped it when Lucas startled her.

"May I see you home, gorgeous?"

"God, you scared the living lights out of me, man. Well, I don't think that gorgeous bit fits us mulatto girls," she said turning on her charm and forgetting her surprise. "We may be shapely, full of soul, and things like that, but gorgeous is for white girls only."

"If you asked me, I'd say it fits you best of all."

"You don't say, and I wouldn't even know why," she said feigning innocence.

"You've got everything; those eyes, that mouth, the way you walk, your waist," he said putting his arm around her, "that's what I like most."

"Watch it! I may be easy to talk to, but I don't fool around like that. I'm a decent girl, and don't you forget it," she said forcing Lucas to take his hands off her hips.

She meant every word she said. Cachita allowed Lucas to go only as far as she wished, and that wasn't very far at all. They talked and perhaps he stole a kiss or two, but that was all; she would not let him go any further. One night, when things seemed to be getting out of hand, Cachita laid down the law.

"Look, man, the thing is that, maybe because of the way we look or God knows what, we seem to be something we're not. There are so many dark girls like myself around, single and with three or four really cute kids. Well, not me, no, señor. I'm looking to get married, and there ain't gonna be nothing, till I sign the wedding papers."

Lucas was not put off by the warning. Secretly, so that nobody would learn of his relationship with Cachita, he would meet her every night and walk her home. She would only allow him to look at her and put his arm around her waist; for the time being, that was enough for Lucas.

Chapter 34

Gerardo Santiesteban was a frequent visitor at Isidro's store. The two men were partners, and there was always some business to transact or some decision to make. It was thus that he met Lucas and asked him for help.

"Do you know a boy like you, who can do things around the store; wait on customers and the like? He shouldn't be too old. Under twenty, I'd say."

"Would twelve be too young?"

"Not if he's good."

"When do you need him?"

"Today, if you can get him."

"I've got a brother, Jose's his name; he arrived from Spain a few months ago. He's twelve but looks older and has been working since he was nine; he's always done quite well, and if you teach him, you've got yourself a good helper."

"That sounds good. Take him by the store when you get a chance, and we'll see if he works out."

"Thank you, Don Gerardo," Lucas smiled imagining Jose's joy.

That night Lucas ran to get his brother and took him to sleep with him in his bunker in the back room of Don Isidro's store. Poor Jose had been working at a bakery in Luyano since he arrived, and he was not happy. They didn't give him enough to eat, but despite the lack of food, the boy had put on some weight and had also grown. He looked healthier than when he stepped off the ship, and his personality was the same, happy and in the best disposition. He could hardly wait to go to his new job. Perhaps it would be there that he would make his fortune; he had discovered that they had lied to him when they said that there was plenty of money everywhere in Cuba.

"Look at me," he said to Lucas that evening. "I've been working for months, and I can fit all my savings in a handkerchief. I had to buy some clothes and food; those people really thought that I could feed myself on the smell of flour."

"You'll do well, now. Look, every month I save a little more. The way I figure it, in three years I'll have enough to buy my own store. But one needs to work hard and learn to do things right, otherwise, they'd fire you."

"The same way you learned and Fermin learned, I will learn, too. The three of us are brothers and we'll learn very quickly, isn't that so?"

Lucas smiled at his brother's comment and ran his fingers through the boy's hair.

"Fermin's already got the money ready to send Andres," Pepet went on, "besides, have you seen the clothes he's got?"

"Bah," he replied visibly upset, "he works at El Aguila; that's a classy store, not a neighborhood market like this."

"My brother Fermin's moving up in the world!"

"I'll prosper too, don't you worry; I'll prosper, too."

As it invariably happened whenever something truly important was about to occur, Pepet was not able to sleep a wink. He imagined Don Gerardo and the store, and the things he would have to do there and how well everything would work out. Lying next to Lucas, he smiled in anticipation of his success.

Before dawn, as Gerardo Santiesteban was preparing to open his store, the two Garach brothers made their entry. Gerardo was stocking some sardine cans on the shelf behind the counter when Lucas went in with Pepet.

"I came to bring you my brother as I promised you, Don Gerardo. This is Jose Garach."

Pepet was proud to hear his grown-up name.

"Where is he? I can't see him," Don Gerardo answered amused. The counter was a little high and the owner, crouching behind it, could not even see the head of the would-be store clerk.

"Here I am," the boy said, fearing that he might be turned down because of his height. "I'm only twelve years old, and I've still got a lot to grow; this problem with my height will take care of itself in a matter of weeks and in the meantime, a wooden crate will do quite nicely."

The owner was very favorably impressed by the way the boy handled himself. Pepet's blonde hair was wet and parted to the side; his bright, black eyes looked at Don Gerardo in awe.

"You'll do, son; of course, you'll do," he answered. "Thank you, Lucas. Leave your brother here; I think we're going to become good friends."

"So long, sir, and thanks for everything."

"You're welcome," he answered, and immediately turned his attention to the new clerk.

There would be much to do that day. Gerardo had to go out to purchase some merchandise. He told the boy the prices of the most common foodstuffs and provided him with a wooden crate so that he could transact business over the counter. The other employee would arrive at six. Gerardo would then leave and Pepet, finally turned to Jose, would prove how efficiently he could carry out his employer's orders.

"Everything clear?"

"Yes, sir."

Quickly, Gerardo gave Jose a tour of the store and explained to him the most important aspects of the daily routine.

"Do you know how to cook?" he asked once the tour was over.

"Yes, sir," the boy lied, afraid of saying no to something and being fired without being given a chance.

"Fine; I'll be back around one; you'll have some rice, eggs, and fried sausage ready by then. Justino, the other clerk, must not leave the counter for one minute.

"Yes, sir."

"Did you understand everything? Is there anything you'd like to ask me?"

"Where's the bathroom? I've got to—"

"Yes, I know." The man kept a serious face, although he felt like laughing. "Go straight down to the end of the hall, and then turn left."

Everything went as planned; Gerardo left, and the boy stayed alone with Justino, waiting on the customers as best he could. He asked anything that he didn't know, and things went smoothly until he had to face the harsh reality of lunch. He had said he knew how to cook. A fine mess he had gotten himself into! How could he possibly do it? He had never cooked in his life. He didn't even know how to boil potatoes; they would fire him for sure. Rice, no less! Leaning on the counter, his hands holding up his sagging chin, Pepet looked at the floor feeling sorry for himself.

"Could I have a beer, boy? I'm stifling in this heat." The customer's voice shook him back into his senses.

"Yes, sir," he answered sadly, fetching the beer and pouring it into a tall glass.

"It'll be ten cents," he said when he was done.

"You're not from here, are you?" Pepet shook his head negatively. "Where do you come from?"

"I'm Valencian, from Tirig, in the province of Castellon."

"I'll be! Well, I'm also from Valencia," the man said cheerfully as he drank his beer. "Have you been here long?"

"I've been in Cuba for a little less than a year, but this is my first day in this store."

"And what's the matter, man? Why the sad face?"

"They're going to fire me as soon as the owner gets back."

"So soon? What have you done?"

"Well, actually, it's what I haven't done. I told Don Gerardo I knew how to cook, and I lied. He's told me to make him some fried eggs and sausages with rice, and I don't know how. So, you see," he said looking at the clock on the wall, "it's already past eleven and nothing." The boy was about to cry.

"Don't get like that. Let's see. Do as I tell you and you'll see how everything will come out all right. Get some water boiling in a kettle."

With his usual diligence, the boy approached the stove and, following the man's instructions, had the rice cooking in less than half an hour. The sausages were already fried by then, sliced open as the man had suggested.

"The secret to frying eggs is to have plenty of oil in the pan and to pick them up with the skimmer."

"Which one is the skimmer?" Pepet shouted.

"The one with all the holes for the grease to flow through."

All the customers gathered around the man with the beer and joined in a lively discussion over the merits and advantages of the different methods of frying eggs.

"Well, I've got to get going. Listen, partner, you cook the rice over low heat until the grain opens; low heat, that's very important. Keep the lid on at all times, and make sure it doesn't burn. Once it's done, all you have to do to keep it hot is to keep the lid on the kettle."

"Don't break the eggs directly over the frying pan; put them on a plate first, so they don't burst," said a lady from the other end of the counter.

Pepet was red in the face from running from the counter to the hot rice kettle. Gerardo, always prompt, arrived in the store with a bag over his shoulder and another in his hands. He gave both bags to Justino over the counter and . . .

"Jose, did you do what I asked? Is lunch ready?"

"Yes, sir," he replied with a broad smile.

After seeing what the boy had fixed and listening to Justino's praise, Gerardo put his hand on Pepet's shoulder and said:

"You'll be all right, son. If you're honest, you are welcome to stay with me for as long as you wish."

Chapter 35

Visiting hours were not over yet when Juan slammed the main door of the Trinitarian Sisters' boarding school one Sunday afternoon. Neither the walk back to Benicarlo, nor the cool breezes blowing in from the Mediterranean succeeded in dispelling the anger he had felt when Lucia told him of her absurd ideas. He might as well not have had any children, or have supported them, or have spent a fortune in the nuns' school. Damn nuns!

"I let her stay there one more night because she had to gather her things, but the girl's coming back here tomorrow." He grumbled when he got home. And having said this to his wife, he undressed, got in bed and pulled the covers over his head. Rosa followed him into the bedroom, trying to find out the reason behind Juan's anger.

"All right, but what's happened? Why are you like this?"

"I don't want to talk about it now."

"But, Lucia is my daughter; is anything the matter with her? Is she sick? Have they mistreated her?"

"We'd be much better off if that were the case."

"What are you saying? Have you gone mad, Juan?"

"She's barely fourteen; she can't wash herself behind the ears yet, and she's already telling me what she wants to do."

"What does she want to do?"

"Your daughter has asked me for my permission to enter the convent, to become a nun. Would you believe it?"

"Ah," was all Rosa could utter; she was really taken aback by the unexpected news.

"A nun, no less! As if I hadn't sacrificed myself all of my life for their sake. To break all the plans one has for one's children to go and lock herself among four walls and light candles and mumble silly prayers! All my plans gone down the drain."

"Juan, how can you say that? Holy Madonna de l'Avella, forgive him. Juan, you don't know what you're saying."

Rosa would have liked to say that at times like these a mother's love and advice were needed. She did not blame the girl, she blamed her father, but it was not wise to contradict Juan when he was angry, so she decided to say nothing and left the room.

Lucia returned an extremely quiet and introverted girl. She was highly suspicious of everything and everyone and spent her days praying, reading, embroidering, or studying and refused to help her mother with her chores. Five years of separation from her family had completely isolated her, and Rosa suffered because of her daughter's absolute lack of affection.

Once the almost total silence of the first few days began to wear off, Lucia would talk to her father but only when Rosa was not around.

"It was mother, wasn't it?" the girl asked one day in an accusing tone.

"No, dear; neither one of us wanted you to enter the convent." Juan always concealed his anger from the girl.

"I know it was her. She didn't want me to go to the nuns' school and learn, or do you think I've forgotten that? She was the one who told you to take me out of the convent; she doesn't want anything good for me."

"Don't be so harsh on your mother. Things are not . . . they aren't the way you see them." Juan knew no way to correct the girl's warped vision of things.

"Won't I go to school anymore? I was going to ninth grade. I like to go to school. Can't I go back?"

"There's no high school here in Benicarlo, but we'll have to think of something. I'm the first to insist that you get an education and learn all those things nobody in the family ever learned, but . . ." He fell silent for a few moments. "Listen, I heard at the tavern that this professor had opened his own academy at home for boys and girls who want to go to high school."

"Well, will you talk to him? Do you promise me you will?"

"Yes, child, yes. That's the way I like to see you, happy."

"Don't say anything to Mother, so she won't say no to the idea. Promise me you won't say anything to her."

"Your mother loves you."

"That's what she says, but I know it isn't true. She loves the boys, but not me. Remember, Father, how she cried when Andres left for Cuba in January? Have you seen how she gets whenever we receive a letter from Cuba? Things aren't the same with me; she wouldn't even go and visit me when I was in school." Juan apparently had never told the young girl the truth.

Chapter 36

On July 24, 1924, a week before Lucas and Carolina's engagement, Cachita left the household she had served since she had been almost a child.

"You know, Miss Maria," she told the girl's mother, "I've found this other house to work at; they pay more and even though I've been real happy with you all, and you have always been real nice to me; I'm going to change jobs. It's good for me, see?" No one could realize that Cachita was lying. The young woman glowed with the warmth of a new life.

"We wish you luck, Cachita. I love you very much, almost as one of my own family, and I'm sorry to see you go. Maybe if some day our financial condition improves, you'll come back to us," Miss Maria could not help but smile at the girl whose transformation to womanhood she had witnessed. Cachita had worked for the Alvarez family since she was twelve, and in five months she would turn nineteen.

"Right away, Miss Maria. Come, let me give you a kiss."

Cachita was sincere; seven years of kindness and affection were not easily forgotten. Now, decency precluded her from being more open with Mrs. Alvarez; that was all.

A month before, she found out she was pregnant. The baby was due in about six months. Actually, it had not been her idea. She continued to dream of a good husband, her own home, even if it had to be just a room in the tenement house where she lived. Together; she would cook, wash, and iron for him; she would treat him like a king; she would bear him children . . . "I don't know what it is about us mulatto girls that we don't inspire the word *marriage*," she often reproached herself, looking in the mirror at her dark skin, curly hair, and protruding stomach.

Lucas had beseiged her. In absolute secrecy, the young man had insisted for three years and finally had found in Cachita the reward for his persistence.

"It was only last year that he finally won," she confided to her neighbor Domitila as soon as she learned of her condition. "It was when my aunt died; he didn't even show up at the wake. He told me he was working. The first night after we buried the old lady, he came around saying he was sorry for my aunt's death. Sorry my foot! He wanted to have me one way or another. I fought him off; don't you think I let him have his way easy; no sir," she said as she shook her head to emphasize the point she was making. "I struggled as much as I could but, imagine, one is human, after all. He started to say sweet things to me, to touch me here and kiss me there and . . . what can I say? It was really super, and all my plans to wear him down and march him down the aisle disappeared in one minute."

Cachita's bedroom became their nightly meeting place. He no longer waited for her at the corner of the Alvarez house; he waited for Cachita inside her room, and all the hapless girl could do was love him.

At the same time, Lucas continued to visit Carolina's house. Isidro had asked him to go and chat with the girl once in a while. Eventually, Lucas was granted official admittance into the house, and he was smart and resolute enough to face anything. On visiting nights, he would leave Carolina's house and make straight for Cachita's.

"It's not that I don't like Carolina," he said one day to Jose, who, at seventeen, worshipped his brother, "the girl isn't exactly pretty, but she's so sweet, so patient that I can't help but like her. She's got beautiful eyes and, besides, she adapts herself to me, you know? She doesn't say much, whatever I say is all right with her. But Cachita is something else; that girl can run circles around Carolina."

"Which one are you going to marry?"

"No doubt about it, Carolina," he said somewhat cynically. "Don Isidro has led me to believe that if I formalize my relationship with his sister-in-law, he'll sell me at a very good price the grocery store he and Don Gerardo own. And you know that's a deal you can't beat; the store is very well located, and the price he's promised me can't be topped."

"What about Cachita?"

"It took me years to convince Cachita, but convince her I did, and she's now having fun just like me. I don't have to spend too much on her; all I have to do is keep her satisfied . . . you know what I mean? There'll be no problem with Carolina; she doesn't have to find out."

"You'd better watch out, Lucas; you can get yourself into a heap of trouble that way."

"Don't be so old-fashioned, Jose; I can't believe it! It's me who should be lecturing you! Holy Moses! I've got only two women. There are guys around who have a different chick every week. So . . ."

At twenty-six, Lucas Garach had attained most of the things he had set out to achieve. In July, not long after having asked for Carolina's hand in marriage, Isidro and Gerardo sold him the grocery store and purchased a larger one. He felt tempted to break with Carolina after the deal had been closed, but he gave up the idea: it would create too many enemies, and both Isidro and Gerardo were highly respected in the community where Lucas would have to operate. He would keep the two women; something was bound to happen in due course, and there was no reason to worry. The news Cachita had in store for him, however, somewhat dampened his optimism.

"Look, honey," she began to say one evening.

"Come here, beautiful," he cut her short in his usual imperious tone. Her condition made the girl more attractive. Her breasts were turgid; her hips, wider. "Come close, I've been thinking about you all day long, thinking of holding you in my arms, of seeing your bare back, of letting your hair loose," as he spoke he took off the girl's clothes that fell into a pile at their feet. She looked at him lovingly. Lucas was ecstatic, standing next to her with his hands on her bare hips.

"Quit that, honey," she finally blurted out as she ran away from him and put on a robe. "Today we've got to talk a little; this can't wait no more."

"What's the matter? You don't feel well?" Lucas could not imagine what was on Cachita's mind. And, in point of fact, he could not have cared less.

"Hey, do you see anything different about me?" she said.

"So, that's it; you want me to tell you you're beautiful. Don't you know it? You're prettier than ever. Is that what's worrying you?"

"Look, pal, we've got this problem we have to solve. We've got a bun in the oven."

"A what?"

"Well, what's so strange about it? Don't you think that kind of thing don't happen? That's the most natural thing in the world; a year's gone by and . . . well, that's the way it is. In six months you'll be a father. I think it's your first child, right?"

"You can't have that child. Not right now, can't happen," he said as if thinking out loud.

"What are you saying?" Cachita asked in disbelief, "I may love you and all, but the man has not been born who can tell me when I can or can't have a child. Set that straight in your mind," she warned.

After a few seconds, Lucas blanched and sat on a chair to keep from falling to the floor. When he regained his composure, he managed to say:

"You know I can't marry you. Just a few days ago, Carolina and I were engaged and, as a matter of fact, we'll be married in six months."

"Nothing could be farthest from my mind than to hurt Miss Carolina; she's always been real nice to me. But my baby's here," she said pointing to her womb, "and something's got to be done."

"Then, the story about you job in Vedado wasn't true?"

"Right. I had to leave Miss Carolina's house because very soon people'll be able to notice my problem, and it's downright immoral to find myself like this because of Miss Carolina's future husband. In spite of everything, I'm still a decent girl. I may be your lover or what-not, mulatto and all, but I do know what's right and wrong."

"Listen, Cachita, if you're only two months along . . ." Lucas said, softening his voice to find a way out of his predicament.

"Three and a half, the doctor told me."

"Well, even if it's three and a half, there's still time. You can have an abortion." He said it quickly, not wishing to hear himself. Suddenly, he thought of his mother.

Cachita shook her head.

"No way. Forget it. You're dead wrong if you think I'm going to get myself in that kind of a mess. This baby growing in here will see the light of day in six months, and you'd better be ready to receive him, buster, 'cause he's your kid, too. If you were man to have me, you have to be man enough to face the consequences."

Cachita's voice was firm in a way Lucas had never heard before. However, life and the advice of her friend Domitila, an old and wise woman, had taught the girl the advantages of blowing hot and cold. She had barely finished speaking when she began to take off her robe, moving slowly towards Lucas as only she knew how. Cachita's body could make him forget anything, including the mess he had created.

"You're not only a rascal but a shithead, too." Fermin had mastered the art of plain talking. He became very upset when, two days before the wedding, Lucas told him about Cachita. "I can't believe that you did that to a poor girl you never intended to marry."

"If I had known this, I wouldn't have said anything to you. I told you so you'd help me, not to hear your criticism."

"What do you want me to do? You needed no help to get yourself into this muddle," he replied sarcastically.

"Carolina and I have a party tomorrow; we're getting married the day after, and then we're going to Pinar del Rio on our honeymoon. Gerardo has said it's fine for Jose to stay at my store," and he emphasized the positive; for an instant, everything he had done seemed right to him. "Cachita is about ready to have the baby, and she hasn't got a single soul. I have enough brothers to share, and I've given her your name and address so she can contact you when the time comes so you can help her."

"You're shameless, Lucas," he protested. "I shouldn't pay any attention to you, but I feel sorry for that poor girl who's going to have your child. What do you plan to say to that other poor girl who's going to be your wife?"

"She doesn't have to find out. I'm asking you for help, but that doesn't give you the right to poke your nose into my business."

"What will happen when the baby's born?"

"Nothing. I'll acknowledge it when the time comes. What else do you want me to do? Marry both?" he retorted cynically.

"Don't you wish! Look, get the hell out of here before I let you have it."

"Come on, Fermin, don't get like that. It's me who's your brother, remember? It's not Cachita. The baby shall be a Garach. I'm asking you to help me if anything happens while I'm away; if it happens after I come back, I'll take care of everything."

Chapter 37

Andres arrived in Cuba in January 1925, just in time for Lucas and Carolina's wedding. Fermin went to meet him at the pier, and it was hard for the two brothers to recognize each other. Fermin had left Spain at seventeen, a thin boy about to become a man. Andres had been taller, perhaps, but still far from being the man he would become.

Andres could not help but think that Cuba had done wonders for his brother: heavy set and dressed in the latest fashion, Fermin reminded him of a movie star. He was surprised not to see his other two brothers, and he immediately inquired after them.

"Hey, Pepet has become Jose, and he's almost eighteen. He couldn't come because he had to stay and mind Lucas' store. Lucas got his own store and everything."

"And where's Lucas?"

"He's getting married tomorrow, and he's at a party they're giving for him and his future wife."

"Mother doesn't know anything about this."

"She must know it by now. I wrote to her, but the letter must have arrived after you had already left. The bad thing about it is that Lucas is about to become a father, but the bride's not the one who's pregnant; it's another girl."

"Another?"

"Let me try to explain it to you." Fermin proceeded to inform Andres of all the details in the life of his twin brother. The eldest of the Garachs listened in silence.

"Having a child is a serious business," he finally said.

"I'd say it is, but as far as our brother is concerned, it's an everyday thing. And don't you dare say anything to him; he'll tell you to mind your own business. We have to be ready because any moment now, Cachita will be bringing into the world the first of the third generation of Garachs."

"When are we going to see Pepet?" Andres asked. "I really want to see the kid again."

"We'll go early tomorrow morning. I've asked my boss for two days off, and he's agreed."

"You know you talk more like a Cuban than like a Valencian."

"I don't know why. My heart still lives at La Morellana. Remember?" The two brothers smiled as they reminisced about their past. Fermin interrupted their reverie to tell Andres where he could leave his things until he found a job and a place of his own.

The evening was far from over when Fermin and Andres finally ended their conversation and went to sleep. Around midnight, Jesusito, Domitila's grandson, went to get them with the news that Cachita had gone into labor. The two brothers dressed quickly and got under way; Cachita lived rather far, and it would take them a while to get there.

Jesusito did not stop talking for a minute until they arrived. By that time, the entire tenement house was already up, milling about Cachita's door.

"Here comes the baby's father," someone said.

"He ain't the father," replied one of the women. "I saw that no good Spaniard tonight, cool as a cucumber, at a party at the Alvarez's on Esperanza and Moreno streets. Tomorrow he's getting married to the youngest of the Alvarez girls. That was the house where Cachita worked for so many years. And, would you believe it? Here's this poor girl, having his baby, and he's having a good time at a party."

"Let me tell you, I wouldn't mind being in her shoes. As long as someone pays for my room and board, like that Spaniard pays for Cachita's, I wouldn't mind having a kid every year."

"It takes balls to do what this Spaniard has done," disagreed a woman in her seventies, who sat on a chair by the door. "They've come here to have a fuckin' good time, make money, and nothin' else."

Fermin and Andres did not want to go in without finding out what was happening inside. They joined in the anticipation and excitement always associated with the birth of a baby. The central courtyard at the *solar* where Cachita lived was bustling with excitement. One of the neighbors had unearthed a bottle of *sidra*—effervescent apple cider— and was serving it in expresso coffee cups which each neighbor brought for the toast. The women paced from one end of the open hall-way to the other nervously while the children all wanted to peek inside Cachita's window. Cachita had promised herself not to scream like she had heard others in the *solar* do so many times, so all those waiting could only guess the events going on inside the room until the piercing cry of a newly born baby was greeted with sighs of relief from the crowd.

"At last, poor thing; it's over."

"I wonder what it was. I hope it's a girl, so she can keep her mother company."

"Yes, and so when she grows up, another of the Spaniards can do the same thing to her; is that what you want? I hope it's a boy; at least that way . . ." Before the old woman in the chair was able to finish her statement, Domitila opened the door and announced:

"It's a boy."

"*¡Al niño!*" yelled the man serving the cider, raising his cup.

"*¡A Cachita Montero!*" answered one of the women.

Amidst whistles and applause, Fermin thought it proper to identify himself and explain to the woman the reason why he and Andres were there.

"Yes, sonny. You're the brother of that . . . I'm glad you came. Cachita was countin' on you, but I didn't pay any attention to her; labor pains make you talk nonsense. Come here, sonny, take a look at your nephew. I haven't seen a baby boy as cute as him, since my grandson Jesusito was born, may St. Barbara keep him."

When she saw Andres also moving towards the door, Domitila asked suspiciously.

"And who's this man? I don't think he's got any business being here."

"He's my brother, ma'am; Lucas' brother, too."

"Sorry, sonny, but this world is so treacherous and evil, a woman just can't trust nobody." Andres, somewhat confused by the old woman's peculiar pattern of speech, managed to smile and nod. Inside the room, the midwife was washing the baby while Jesusito stared at Cachita.

"You think she's breathing? Take a good look, *Abuela*, is Cachita breathing?" From her bed, the young mother, her eyes still closed, smiled at the boy's concern.

"Sonny, leave Cachita alone; stop buggin' her. Move over and let these gentlemen get close to the bed so she can see them. Cachita, baby, these are the brothers you were waiting for."

Andres, as sentimental as ever, felt his heart sink. The poor thing, so young, so pretty, and alone with her son. Fermin and he leaned over the bed and when Cachita opened her eyes, it was Andres whom she saw first.

"Fermin?" she asked.

"No, Cachita; I'm Andres. I'm also Lucas' brother; I'm the oldest." She looked at him puzzled. "I arrived yesterday from Spain. This is Fermin, next to me. You have a very pretty baby; you can rest now," he lied to make her happy, for he had not seen the baby yet. The young woman was breathless, soaked in sweat, batting her eyelids, Andres thought, to ward off her sadness so as not to disturb the profound joy the new life brought her.

"The name," she said, again looking at Andres.

"What name?"

"His father's name; what's his father's name?"

"The father is Lucas Garach," Fermin answered awkwardly.

"Lucas' father; Lucas' father's name," Cachita insisted.

"Oh, my father's . . . His name is Juan, Juan Garach."

"Then, my son's name will also be Juan," and with a faint smile on her lips, she closed her eyes.

Chapter 38

Andres began to work as a sales clerk at the Caribe bookstore, on the corner of Infanta and San Rafael streets, not too far from the University of Havana. He found the job by pure chance. His three brothers were in the grocery business. He would have been able to find employment through any of them, but he decided that it would be better to look for something within the field he already knew. Helped by some of Pepet's and Fermin's friends, he made a list of all the bookstores and stationery shops in town and as luck would have it, one of them needed a clerk; the previous one had died of old age. When Andres had been at his job for barely two months, he was fully abreast of the most important political and intellectual developments in the island.

"The guy may have been elected by the people, but he sure looks like a dictator, Pepet," he told his brother one evening as they walked to Arena Cristal to see Kid Chocolate fight.

"Look, Andres, I don't know much about those things and, frankly, I couldn't care less. People who get into politics don't get anything good out of it. Half of them wind up either in jail or in the cemetery, and those are two places I don't care to know."

"Well, but you're interested in making money, aren't you? You even want to buy a grocery store when you get a chance, just like Lucas did and Fermin's about to do."

"Right you are. But what's that go to do with politics? In the end, it's money that matters."

"Well, I'll have you know that if this man Machado keeps things going the way they are, pretty soon there won't be money to buy anything; the country will be bankrupt. And then, you won't be able to make money, or buy a store or anything."

"As I said, I don't see what one thing's got to do with the other."

"I'll give you an example. Haven't you heard what happened to the Canarians?"

"I heard something about that in the market, but I didn't pay much attention, and I missed out on it. What happened? Look . . ." he said, casting suspicious glances in all directions, "Keep it down; you'll never know who's who in this place, and you can get yourself into a lot of trouble. Watch what you say."

"Rumor has it, that a group of Canarians, led by one Rosales, kidnapped Colonel Enrique Piña in Camaguey. The boss, you know who I mean?" Pepet nodded affirmatively, knowing it was President Machado, "had to pay fifty thousand *pesos* as ransom. And after that, more than one-hundred of those people have 'committed suicide' or have been 'shot while attempting to escape.'"

"They could have really committed suicide, couldn't they?"

"Jose, it isn't that simple. They were rubbed out, and many others are liable to follow them unless this man steps down."

"Shut up. If they hear you, it's you who's going to be stepping down. In the cemetery."

"You see what I mean? That," and he stressed the point, "is precisely what's happening."

Andres, challenged by political upheaval, was never afraid of possible consequences.

Chapter 39

When Juan Garach talked about his sons' returning with enough money to open a business, he never took into account how long it would take for his dream to come true. The first few years after he bought the farm, El Morellano would spend long hours sowing, tending the fields, irrigating whenever there was drought. That was back before the 1920s. Three years went by without setbacks; the farm enabled him to meet all his expenses and even make a small profit. Things changed in 1929: the boys' return seemed more and more remote; time passed, and he had no news from them. Juan lost interest; he would spend more hours at the cafe than at the farm.

By the time Lucas married Carolina, Rosa began to do the sowing. Every morning, she would tie her two braids—not so thick anymore and certainly not as black—above her neck; she would wipe her face with a wet cloth and, nibbling on a piece of bread and sardines or whatever else was available, she would go across town to the farm.

For four years she planted, cared for, harvested, and sold the crops with little help from her husband and absolutely none from her daughter. Her sole concern was to keep her family from going under; she had to keep it afloat until her sons returned. Nothing seemed right to Juan; he didn't make the slightest effort to see the brighter side of life and, of course, his wife was to blame for every bad thing that happened. Rosa was able to keep her sanity during those long years of neglect by learning to hear Juan but not listening to him, by not letting his stream of verbal abuse touch her soul.

"Look, Rosa, would you come in for a second?" a neighbor asked her one late afternoon.

"Is anything the matter?" Rosa eyebrows questioned her friend's evident worry.

"No, nothing's the matter with me. Listen, Rosa, you're a good woman, and I don't know how to say what I've got to say to you, but I don't think you deserve lies, and you're being lied to," she spoke softly, close to Rosa, looking at her eyes.

"Look here, Maria, if you're going to tell me something about my husband, please don't. It wouldn't change things and . . ." Rosa shrugged her shoulders and started to walk away.

"No, God, no. I don't mean your husband."

"Lucia?" she turned around and approached the woman once more.

"I went to the market yesterday, and there were these two women saying that your daughter was a hypocrite and like that. The two witches said that with the excuse of studying and all that what she's really doing is having an affair with her teacher," her last words were almost inaudible; compassion made her put her hands on Rosa's shoulders.

"Listen, you've no right to tell me those lies," Rosa looked down and moved away.

"Don't get angry, Rosa; let me go on. Before telling you, I wanted to make sure, and I waited for your daughter after school. I saw her kiss the teacher as she left his house." Rosa grew pale; she could not believe it. "Even worse, I saw nobody else leave the house, and I stayed around until after Lucia had gotten home. I don't even want to think of the things Lucia must be being taught alone with that man. I decided to tell you because you're a good woman, you work very hard, and don't deserve what your daughter is doing—I mean—that's a crying shame."

"If what you tell me is true, you've done me a great favor, and I really appreciate it," Rosa took Maria's hands and pressed them gratefully.

"Never mind. May God be with you."

Juan always stayed at the cafe and came home for dinner late at night. Lucia and Rosa had to wait for him, anyway because he did not like to sit at the table by himself. It was while they waited that Lucia usually read, and Rosa sewed or folded the laundry. Then, mother and daughter talked.

"Lucia, child, stop reading for a moment. There's something I have to tell you." Both her voice and her expression were solemn.

The girl paid no attention to her mother's request and kept on reading.

"Lucia." This time she softly took the book away from her and, with her hand on the girl's chin, forced her to look up. "Today I heard something that has made me very sad." She said it without recrimination.

"I know what you want. Behind all those stories, what you really want is for me to quit school. What do you want me to do? Go out in the fields every morning? That's what you would like, isn't it?" Lucia walked around her mother and shouted defensively. "I know it; you've never liked me. When I was little, you didn't want me to go to the nuns' school; then you didn't want me to go into the convent, and now you don't want me to go back to the teacher's house."

"Lucia, how did you know what I wanted to say?" Rosa could not help the tears that ran down her cheeks.

"I heard you talking to that busybody down the block," Lucia looked around aimlessly, unable to face her mother directly.

"I don't want you to get hurt. I do want you to learn; maybe you can go somewhere else."

"What would you like me to be, an illiterate bumpkin like you?"

"Lucia, I'm your mother!" Rosa's voice was almost imperceptible, full of pain.

"I don't want my hands to be like yours, rough, with callouses, filthy. I'll be a lady, like my father says."

"Lucia, I only want the best for you. You're my daughter. In my family and in your father's, women have always been decent. That's why it hurts me to hear people talk about you." Rosa's mild recrimination did not soften Lucia's attitude.

"I'll do as I want. If you have nothing better to say, you'd better shut up, mother. That gossip makes me sick." She walked away, trying to avoid her mother's eyes.

Chapter 40

"I'm glad you're here, Jose. I was waiting for you," Gerardo Santiesteban underlined with his smile his evident pleasure in sharing some news with Jose Garach.

"For me, Don Gerardo? Am I late?" Jose, not quite twenty-one, still had that mischievous air about him that made others grin.

"No, not at all; it's still early. It's just that I wanted to talk to you before the customers begin to arrive; it's difficult to find the time when the store is full."

"Well, what's on your mind?" he said leaning against the all too familiar counter.

"How long has it been since you started working for me?" Gerardo began reminiscing, his blue eyes filled with kindness.

"If my memory serves me right, it was about 1919, six months or so after I arrived from Spain," Jose scratched his head chuckling over the memory of the awkward, twelve-year old, scrawny version of himself years before.

"You were just a boy; your nose hardly reached up to the counter, and you had to step on a box to wait on the customers," Gerardo smiled.

"It was generous of you to let me stay. I was too young for those things."

"My wife always told me to take you home to spend the night; I've watched you grow into a man, as it were; I believe I know you well, and you're like me, dependable and hardworking. There's this store on San Anselmo and Salvador; it went bankrupt because the owner didn't take good care of it. I was thinking that maybe we could be partners and buy it between the two of us. You'd look after it and gradually you could be on your own."

"Don Gerardo! I don't know what to say, honest! It's a great honor that you, one of the smartest and nicest persons I've ever met, should ask me to be your partner; I want you to know that." Jose walked to the other end of the counter and shook the old man's hand with the warmth of his excitement over the newly revealed plans.

"Well, young man, think about it; it's an important decision," Gerardo warned.

"If you think the store has the right potential, there's nothing else to talk about; I've got the money," he answered touching his pockets as if he had it all there.

"It's settled then. We'll talk some more later on." Gerardo evidently had good feelings about this new venture, and an enthusiastic handshake closed the deal.

The prospect of becoming a store owner seemed like a dream to Jose. For six months he had been looking in vain for the right opportunity. To have Don Gerardo come and make an offer like that to him was the luckiest break of his life. Elated, he sublimated all his energies into a mock fist fight behind the counter—complete with uppercuts and fancy footwork—blissfully ignorant of the three customers watching him with curiosity.

"What's the matter with you, Jose? Who are you fighting?" a fat lady finally asked him.

"Oh, I'm sorry. I didn't realize you all were here . . . I mean, I did not know you were looking at me," he answered blushing.

"Are you going to become a boxer, boy?"

"Well, I really like it a lot. I've got all the tackle to practice with, up there on the flat roof."

"You're really good at it, you know? I'm sure that if you put your mind to it, you could make the major leagues."

"That's baseball, ma'am," he smiled. "Anyway, what can I do for you today?"

Jose waited on the talkative woman as fast as he could. He wanted her to go quickly; his head was beginning to spin with all that prattle.

Don Gerardo and the travelers arrived in the afternoon, just as the day seemed to be asking for a rest. An automobile stopped in front of the store. Jose dried his hands on the apron and scrutinized the vehicle to make sure that it actually was they. With the high incidence of terrorism in Havana those days, one had to make sure who was riding in strange cars.

It was Don Gerardo and his wife. A thin girl stepped out from the car followed by her mother and a small boy. Milagros called out to Jose and waved at him. She had grown and looked much healthier. She ran towards the counter and gave the young clerk her hands to help her jump over and kiss him hello.

"Have you seen my son?" Doña Joaquina asked.

"How old is he?"

"He's four. Rafael, come here." The boy, too serious for his age, joined them. "This gentleman is Jose; he works for your father."

"Watch what you say! We're partners now!" Gerardo added.

"Well, congratulations! May it be for the best. Well, let's go home no. Come, Milagros, leave Jose alone; you've got to help me unpack."

"No, please. Let me stay here with dad and Jose, please, mother, please."

"Come, child, I'm going home with you, too," her father said.

The girl kissed the young clerk and did as her father asked.

Jose watched the family get into the car and drive away. So absorbed was he in his own thoughts that he did not notice the man sitting by the counter having a beer and watching them intently.

"Listen, is your last name Garach?" The man spoke in a whisper. "Is your last name Garach?" he repeated.

"Yes, may I help you?"

"I asked you if your last name is Garach."

"I answered yes."

"Do you have a brother called Andres who works at a bookstore on Infanta Street?"

"Yes, sir. Has anything happened to him?"

"No, not yet, but something serious could happen to him if he isn't careful and leaves us alone."

"What did Andres do to you?"

"They plot against the government in that bookstore. You tell him that Spaniards should look after Spanish affairs. Cuba's got more than plenty with the Cubans."

"There must be some sort of mistake, sir. My brother is a very peaceful person; he doesn't like to get involved in politics or any of that."

The man gave him a sly look as he tasted the last sip of beer.

"You tell him, because one of these days they're liable to find him in some ditch, his head blown off."

Jose knew that they very well could.

Chapter 41

Carolina, Lucas' wife, at times hoped that when her baby was born, and if Lucas let her, of course, she could have a girl come help her with the chores around the house, to do the laundry and things that each day of her pregnancy became harder to accomplish. However, Lucas was well known for his thrifty spirit and both Carolina and her mother doubted he would yield to having a maid, even if only temporarily.

"Oh, mother, you exaggerate things; he's good and kind. He wants to raise capital, and we have to do without certain things," Carolina faithfully defended her husband, "but the maid and a house to live in are an absolute must, and I'm sure Lucas won't mind. Do you suppose we could ask Cachita to come?"

Carolina was embroidering a baby blanket. She stopped, rested the blanket on her lap, and looked at her mother.

"No, Cachita's got enough problems of her own to be minding somebody else's."

"Cachita? Problems?"

"And big ones, too. I bumped into her the other day downtown. I hadn't seen her since before you were married. She's looking real pretty; well, you know, she was always very cute. She looks older now, but she's pregnant and looking better than ever."

"I'm so happy for her! Whom did she marry?"

"That's the problem; she isn't married. She has a lover, the poor thing. She didn't boast about it; on the contrary, she was very embarrassed, but you know how much she likes me, and she couldn't lie to me."

"The poor thing; she was always so nice and kind."

"And that's not all. This baby she's expecting is not the first one; she already has a four-year-old son," the woman confided, almost whispering.

"Expecting again? From the same man?" Carolina's could not hide her obvious disdain.

"It seems she's been with this man for some time now. She was as affectionate as ever; she sent her love to all you girls and asked me to tell you that she's never forgotten you and your sisters and especially you, Carolina, especially you."

It would be years before Carolina would find out the truth.

Chapter 42

After her conversation with her mother regarding her love affair with the teacher, Lucia was careful to hide it from the town's watchful eyes. Rosa told her husband but Juan, blind believer of his daughter's virtue, had called her a liar and had closed the issue.

One Thursday, early in 1931, the small living room, dining room, and kitchen of the humble Garach home seemed smaller than usual to Lucia. She paced the room from wall to wall as if wishing to draw geometric designs with her feet on the dirt floor. First, she walked the width of the room, then she paced it up and down. She only interrupted her mechanical wanderings to look out the window anxiously and take deep breaths, as if that were the last thing she would do in this world. Her mother talked to her, and she nodded or uttered simple syllables, almost without parting her lips. Yes, she was studying to be a teacher. No, she would never actually teach but instead manage the family business, when the boys returned from America. No, she barely remembered her brothers; they had all left when she was too little.

"Well, child, I'm sure you know more about books and things than I do. I don't know very much about managing and numbers and the like because all I've done in my life is work; I'm glad you're heading in a different direction."

The girl didn't quite understand what her mother meant; she shrugged her shoulders and resumed her nervous pacing, sighing deeply every time she looked out the window.

"What's wrong, Lucia?" Rosa finally asked.

"It's Professor Gomez. He went out of town and is due back today. I can't stand all this waiting."

"Don't be impatient. He went to see his parents, didn't he? Who knows? Child, I never imagined you liked school that much."

"Look, mother, a man's standing by the door! I don't know who he is!" the girl exclaimed as she peered through the window.

Rosa looked out; it was a rather slim, very well dressed young man.

"He's from the city; people from Benicarlo don't dress like that. Who could it be? I'm sure he comes from Madrid. Maybe he's looking for an address, and he's not coming here." The knock on the door dissipated the women's doubts.

"Holy Madonna de l'Avella! He's coming here! I'm not dressed. Lucia, go open the door while I put on a clean apron."

"Good afternoon, miss. I'm looking for Mrs. Rosa Garach. Does she live here?" the young stranger asked with a smile.

"Yes, sir. Wait a moment, please. Mother! Someone's looking for you," she called out. "The gentleman asked for you."

"Ask him to come in, child."

"Please, come in, sir."

"Rosa Garach, at your service," she said, straightening out the white apron with one hand and taking the other to the knot of her braids which, through the years, seemed never to have moved from its place on the back of her head.

"Don't you know me?" Jose almost added "mother," but seeing that Rosa did not recognize him, he only smiled.

"Your face seems familiar, but I can't quite place it." Rosa looked at him intensely, examining his features, trying to recall his face.

"I met you years ago, when you lived in Tirig."

"What's your name?" she asked confused.

"Juan Jose Garach, at your service," he replied ceremoniously.

"Holy Madonna de l'Avella! Why didn't I recognize you before?" El Morellano's wife put her hands to her head and collapsed.

Jose rushed to raise his mother from the floor and sat her on one of the chairs nearby. Then, stroking her cheeks softly to help her come to, he repeated: "Come, come, mother; don't get sick now that I've come to see you. Open your eyes, mother, please. My God, Lucia, I should've let you all know I was coming. I shouldn't have surprised her like this; maybe it won't be good for her."

Rosa opened her eyes slowly.

"You know? I've met many mothers, but none have eyes as pretty as yours."

"Sweet talker!" she said.

"Are you feeling better now?"

"Yes, it's going away. When did you arrive? Did you come alone? Why didn't you send word?"

"I got to Benicarlo a while ago. I asked for you, and they told me how to get here. I thought of letting you know I was coming, but then I decided to surprise you."

"Have you come to stay?"

"Just one month, that's all. I own a store in Cuba, you know? I just bought it, and I have to go back to it."

"And your brothers, how are they? Lucas' wife, Carolina—isn't that her name?—how is she? When will the baby be born?"

"It was born before I left. It's a girl. They called her Carolina, after her mother."

"She's fine. I don't know about baby stuff; she looks just like . . . like all other babies!"

"A granddaughter! I'm a grandmother already. I can't believe it and not because I'm not old enough; you can see how worn out I am."

"Come now, mother; you're looking better than ever."

"You haven't changed, son," she said with a smile, looking tenderly into his eyes, "you've been gone for so many years that sometimes I thought I had only dreamed having had you and your brothers. It seemed as though the time I had you with me had been nothing but a dream that just ended one day." Suddenly, she felt an overwhelming urge to hold her son in her arms. "Come, here, son, let me hold you. Maybe being here with you is another dream, and I don't want it to end before I kiss you."

"Don't worry, mother. I won't leave for several days. I've come from Cuba to see you, and I want to be with you as much as possible. You'll see what a nice time we'll have together, you'll see. Right, Lucia?"

The girl watched her mother and brother with mistrust, hating her mother for not having treated her with the same affection. Lucia was not intelligent enough to realize that she had never given Rosa an opportunity to show her love.

Juan felt ashamed when his son went looking for him at the cafe. He had imagined that when his children returned, they would find him at the farm, working, ploughing the fields, active, useful. Of course, it would have been like that if they had let him know in advance, but Pepet had come without warning and had found him at the last place he wanted to be found. But Jose did not seem to mind, and he spent the evening with his father, telling, step by step, what the four brothers were doing in America.

"Will you ever return to Spain? Would you come back as we planned once? Are you back to stay?" Juan could not contain the eagerness this, his most vehement desire, inspired.

"No, I am never coming back." Jose wished his father hadn't asked, but he had to answer him truthfully. "It isn't that I want to be the one to break the family dreams, but I don't like Spain's political future, and I can't exchange what took me so much to earn for something uncertain." He shook his head softly, looking for the proper words.

"But, son," Juan tried to interrupt.

"As a matter of fact, father, this evening, in the cafe, didn't you hear those boys talking? That's communism. Everybody, the Church included, is in for a shock in Spain, especially those who own business and property."

"I don't think it'll come to that."

"Well, I do. This is my country; here I would have to fight for my people. Cuba is no political paradise, mind you, but I'm not forced to do anything. I don't have to join the army, I don't have to fight. I can live in peace, building up a capital with no one to bother me, do you know what I mean?"

"If that's the way you think, son, you're old enough to know what's good for you. I've lived in Spain my entire life, and I'm telling you nothing's going to happen here. Spain is entering a new era and, at any rate, it's our country. Abroad you'll always be a foreigner, right?" Juan asked with ill-concealed disappointment. "What do your brothers think of this?"

"Fermin and Lucas still think the way you do. It won't be this year, but next year, or the year after, you'll have them back here with you; wait and see. As I said, Lucas owns all by himself one of the best grocery stores in El Cerro; Fermin bought one in Luyano some three years ago, and he's doing quite well. Whenever they're ready to sell, they'll get a fortune for the stores."

"If it is like that, then things aren't all that bad," he thought out loud, "our family will have roots here and there, in two different continents. If things should go bad on either side, all they'll have to do is cross the ocean."

On the other side of that ocean, it was a totally different story.

Chapter 40

"Cachita, open, open quick; this is Andres." The banging of his fists against the wooden door underscored the urging in the young man's voice. "What's taking you so long? Open quick, Cachita."

A light came on, and children's voices let Andres know that they had heard him inside the room. A few minutes went by and then Lucas, half dressed, opened the door.

"Shit, Andres, what the hell are you doing here so late at night?" It wasn't a very warm welcome; Lucas didn't even ask him to come in. Andres squeezed into the room through the half-open door.

"Now, Lucas, don't get upset. I came because there was nothing else I could do. Otherwise . . . Hi, Cachita," he said when he saw the woman putting on a robe and holding in her arms a baby boy who cried loudly.

"And if I may ask, why did you come here?"

"Look, I can't tell you too much, but they were plotting an attempt on the life of this bigwig at the Palace, and they arrested the man who was going to do it."

"So? What have you got to do with all that?"

"Well, the thing is that it was all planned at the bookstore where I work, and I need to drop out of sight for a few days until this thing blows over. You know what I mean?"

"Shit, Andres, why do you get yourself into these problems? You've fucked up my evening, and these days I hardly get a chance to be with Cachita."

"It's a matter of life or death. They're tracking me down. They know that you all are my brothers. Jose hasn't come back from Spain yet; I can go to his store, but they'd bomb it. I can't go to your store or your house either; Fermin would be in danger too if I asked him to hide me. They know all my friends. Cachita is all I have left. What do you say, Cachita, can I stay here for a few days till this thing blows over?"

"Sure thing. No need to ask; this is your house. And you can keep an eye on the kids while I go out, 'cuz with these two kids I don't even have time to breathe. Juanito is a big boy already, but all Albertico does is cry, eat, and sleep."

"Sure, go ahead and tell him it's all right," Lucas yelled angrily. "If I could hardly come here before, now it'll be impossible. Because I don't suppose that with this guy here you're thinking of . . ." Cachita did not let him finish. With a warm kiss, she made Lucas forget his anger.

"Don't you get mad, honey; you know you're king in this room. Look this business can even be good for us," she said persuasively. "When you come, we'll go to Domitila's place. I told you she's landed this fine job as a cook in Miramar, and her room is empty. She keeps it because she wants to have a place to come back to in case they bug her too much at work."

"And Jesusito? What will you do with him?"

"Jesusito is gone with her. They're teaching him to be a gardener, and they even pay him a small salary. Don't you see what I mean? We take off, and Andres takes care of the children for us."

"Well, that wouldn't be so bad then, "Lucas admitted relieved.

"Listen, don't you think this will be forever; in a week or so I'll get out of here," Andres warned.

"So, you know, Lucas; see how you can manage to get away from your wife a couple of times this week. It'll be like our honeymoon, sort of." Cachita was always the same. She still had the restless and alluring nature that had trapped Lucas almost seven years before.

Chapter 44

Jose's visit coincided with a worsening in Lucia's disposition. She flatly refused to help Rosa with the chores; hers was an absolute indifference, totally impervious to interruptions or recommendations. Her only wish seemed to be to wait in vain by the window. One morning when Lucia and her father were alone in the house, the mystery at last came unravelled.

"Wait, father, please. I'll die if I don't talk to you right now."

"Don't say that, child. What could be so serious as to make you talk of dying?"

"Father, the teacher hasn't come back."

"Maybe he found something better back where he came from. We'll find another teacher, a better one maybe; I'm sure we will. Besides, you'll be leaving for Valencia soon, what do we need the teacher for?"

"He promised he'd marry me!" she said as she began to weep.

"What? That egghead for a son-in-law? The kid will never make a businessman, I know. You deserve a man, not a boy, Lucia."

"No, father. I want him; it's got to be him; it can't be anybody else." The anxiety and sorrow pent up for weeks were finally welling up.

"Come, come. Don't cry over that, child. It isn't worth it."

"Listen, father," she said trying to control her emotions, "do you remember when mother told you . . ."

"Yes, but that was taken care of," he interrupted, "it was nothing more than the gossip of some envious witches in town."

"Forgive me, father, forgive me!"

"What do you mean?" Juan sprang to his feet and looked at his daughter in disbelief. "Why should I forgive you?" his voice sounded of controlled fury, yet it was but a shadow of the wrath his daughter's suggestion produced.

"It was true."

"And you dare tell me like that, so impudently?" Juan had never shown his anger to his daughter, but that afternoon his rage reached the flashing point. He struck the girl violently, time and again, until Lucia fell to the floor.

"Please, don't hit me any more, father. I'm expecting . . . his child!" she wept. "Do you see now why he's got to come back?"

"Get up, Lucia. How do you know that?"

"I know it the same way all women know. I've skipped my period; I've skipped it twice already. I'm sure; I don't know what to do father. Oh, please, help me!"

"If what you say is true, there's only one thing to do."

A noise by the door signalled Jose's presence.

"I'm sorry, father. I should've knocked before coming in; excuse me!"

"Come in, son, it's all right. What happened? Did you forget something?"

"No, nothing like that. It's just that I wanted to talk to you alone, and I thought that if the two of us walked over to the farm, I could tell you what I have in mind."

"Fine. I could use some fresh air now. Lucia and I," he said staring accusingly at the girl who lowered her head in shame, "will continue our conversation some other time."

Father and son left the house and headed slowly towards the farm. Jose did not know how to broach the subject. It was about the farm, how much it had cost, and how much was still owed on it. Juan's forehead beaded with perspiration as he told his son of his ups and downs with the property. Four years before they had had a poor harvest. They had lost money, he lost interest, and Rosa had taken over the planting. That was the year the harvest didn't yield enough to meet all the payments, and he had to mortgage part of the farm. There were two debts, totalling some thirty-four thousand *pesetas*.

"Father, I've brought enough money with me to pay off both debts."

"Do you realize what you're saying, son?"

"With the rate of exchange, I have plenty, and it won't hurt me; you can rest assured. Here, here's all of it in an envelope." Juan counted the money quickly and noticed that there was more than the total owed on the farm. "That's my second request. With what's left left over, I'd like to buy a fare for Cuba."

"Yours?"

"No. I want you to sign some papers and give your permission for mother to go to Cuba with me. I haven't said anything to her yet; I wanted to talk to you first. What do you say?"

Juan had not expected any of the three pieces of news he had received that afternoon. He stood still in the middle of the street, looking gravely at the envelope with the money.

"So be it, son. I'll sign whatever papers you want me to," he finally said. "You can take your mother to Cuba with you; that's settled." Nothing but the right reasons could have made Juan agree.

Chapter 45

Rosa was deeply moved by Jose's wish to take her with him. She was overjoyed at the thought of seeing her four Garach boys together. She had dreamed of that reunion so many times! But it could not be. It did not make any difference that Juan had said she could go; she, Rosa Garach, could not accept. Lucia was still a girl, she needed her mother; she could not stay all by herself. She would not leave her behind for anything or anybody; she was grateful to her son, though.

"What won't you leave for anything or anybody?" Juan overheard her answer as he came in.

"My daughter Lucia. Pepet has asked me to go to Cuba with him to see the boys. I told him it couldn't be; the girl is too young to be without her mother for no good reason."

"That again! The girl is a woman already, and she doesn't need anybody. You'll go with Jose; you'll go and that's final. Don't try to contradict me; the question is settled."

That was the way things were always decided in the Garach household. Juan banged on the table, and the matter was closed. The last word was always his and no other opinion, however reasonable, was ever important.

At times, Rosa thought she would go mad; her heart would beat with hope one minute, only to disappear the next under a wave of anguish. Like a sinner who tries to cover his guilt, she would conceal her joy; then, she would hang her white apron to dry with its hem wet with tears. The night before her departure, Juan returned home alone. He had left early in the afternoon with Lucia. He explained he had taken the girl to stay with some friends. He wanted to spare her the pain of saying good-bye to her mother. Rosa complained; she told Juan it would be worse not to see the girl. She should know; but women were not entitled to their views, at least, that was El Morellano's law. Jose, visibly upset, looked at his father; he did not think he was treating his mother fairly. He did not express his opinion lest he spoil the trip he had planned with so much love.

"Enjoy your trip, Rosa. This will be the first time and the last you'll travel alone," her husband warned her as he kissed her on the forehead.

"You've got a smart son who knows how to do things, that's the only reason I'm letting you go away. Good-bye, Pepet; thank you for your help, son. Good luck to you on your new business. Say hello to your Don Gerardo, and be sure to thank him for me for having been so good to you. I'm very proud of you, my son."

As soon as the locomotive bound for Barcelona disappeared from sight that summer of 1930, Juan rushed in the opposite direction, across town, anxious to hear from his daughter. Lucia had stayed with a midwife, so they could "fix her well," as her father had instructed.

"Anything, anything at all. That baby must not be born; my daughter cannot dishonor the family; a Garach can't stand for that. Anything at all, except, of course, endangering my girl's life," he hastened to add.

"These things are done every day. If the girl is healthy and she's not too far advanced, everything will be all right."

Under that condition, Juan had left his frightened and confused daughter in the woman's house. Rosa was not too far from Benicarlo when the child was wrested from Lucia's womb. When Juan arrived, his daughter was asleep, pale and restless.

"Everything went all right, Juan; it couldn't have been better. Your girl was brave, and she's now resting in the bedroom."

"May I come in?"

"Yes, go in, but you must leave her with me another couple of days, until she's finally recovered. That's part of my services, and it's included in the price you'll pay me."

"I trust you'll be discreet; this would've been useless if the whole town knew that . . ."

"You need not worry as far as I'm concerned. Now, the neighbors . . . that's a different story."

"I see," Juan could not quite tell what about the woman revolted him so; he tried to put it out of his mind and went in to see his daughter.

"Lucia, open your eyes; it's me, Juan, your father. How do you feel?"

"Father, you came!" She was ready to cry. "It was horrible what she did to me! If I had only known! I would've never . . . I loved him, father; I loved him and my baby," she confessed weakly.

"And mother. Did she come with you? Did you finally tell her?"

"Yes, I did tell her," he lied. "But your mother isn't here; she left with your brother this morning."

"You told mother, and she left?"

"That was the only way, Lucia, the only way."

"No, father, go and get her, please. Ask her to come; tell her I want to see her, and I need her," Lucia sobbed.

"She won't come, child. She's gone to America with Jose; when she comes back, you won't even remember any of this."

"But I want to see her; I need to see her right away," her loud cries were heard in the living room, and the woman came in to ask Juan to leave; he shouldn't upset the girl. Juan did as he was told. He did not know how wrong he had been in letting Rosa leave for Cuba without telling her what would happen to Lucia.

Chapter 46

Andres had been hiding in Cachita's room when Fermin arrived one day with a telegram from Jose. The message wasn't clear; he wanted everybody at the pier when the ship put into Havana harbor; everybody: Fermin, Lucas, Carolina, the girl, and Andres. He had a big surprise for all of them.

"Would it be safe for you to come out?" Fermin asked him after reading the telegram.

"I think so. Things have calmed down. Cachita asked a few questions and found out that the police killed the boy they had taken in because he wouldn't rat on his friends. He didn't tell them anything. I was planning to leave tomorrow, but I'll stay another day, just in case."

"You're right. I'll come and get you here; it'll be in the afternoon. Is that all right?"

Cachita listened attentively; she was sitting on the bed, holding Alberto in her arms. Sometimes she was content just being Lucas' mistress; others, however, she felt neglected, especially when she could not partake of family get togethers. Andres, the more observant of the two, realized what was on the girl's mind and tried to cheer her up.

"Don't worry, Cachita; don't be sorry you can't go to the pier with us. Jose is quite a joker; I'm sure he's just bringing a fellow Valencian with him, and he would like us to meet him. Maybe it's nothing important."

"Maybe he's coming back married; those things could be embarrassing, and you wouldn't have a good time. Don't be sad," Fermin added.

"No, it ain't that. I ain't sad," she smiled again. "It's just that I ain't got no family, you know? All I've got is my two kids and you all. But the problem is that you're family and, at the same time, you ain't. What can I say? I guess I'd better get used to it, 'cuz this problem of mine ain't got no solution," she sighed.

"Don't worry. Neither you nor your children will ever be alone. We're your family too, right Andres?" Fermin, always the tactful diplomat, tried to keep everybody satisfied. "You'll never be alone; your sons are our nephews, right?"

"That's right, Cachita. You can always rely on us."

After considerable insistence, Fermin was able to persuade all the Garachs to go to the pier to see Pepet's surprise. Andres and Fermin went together; Lucas and his wife met them by the docks. They did not have to wait long for the bow of the *Marques de Comillas* to cross in front of Morro Castle. The Garachs vied for positions from where they could see the ship and discover Jose's surprise before the passengers came ashore.

"He's the one on the corner!" shouted Fermin.

"No, he's the one towards the center!" said Andres, pointing at someone on the ship.

"I think you're all mistaken," said Carolina. "Jose is that one waving at us, don't you see him? He's dressed his white suit. Isn't that him?"

"Carolina is right; look at him. It's him, it's him!"

"He's got a lady to his left and a girl on his right."

"Could she be his wife?"

"They don't seem together; they're too far apart," Carolina noted again.

"Maybe the girl is shy on account of us being here and all."

"Look at the lady to his left. I'd swear she looks like mother," Andres commented.

"It can't be; mother alone? Father would never allow it."

"Well, I also think she looks like mother," Fermin said. "Look, she seems to be waving at us; Jose's talking to her now."

"It can't be her," Lucas said.

"I was the last one to see her, and I'm telling you that's her, that's Rosa Garach," Andres insisted.

"Look, they're waving at us. It's mother! It's mother!" Andres and Fermin shouted, overcome with joy; Jose's surprise was most unexpected.

"Mother!"

"Mother!" The two of them called out together.

"I'm so happy, Lucas. Lina and I will get to meet your mother at last! *Abuelita* Rosa is here, Lina; there she is!" Carolina waved her handkerchief as a welcome sign. Lucas was the quietest in the group.

"We'll see now when and how she decides to go back," he said sourly.

"Lucas! How can you say such a thing? She's your mother!"

The wharf was alive with excitement, as several dozen people welcomed friends and relatives. The waiting Garachs could see Rosa drying her tears.

"Your Cuba is a lovely place, son; lovely," she said.

There were moments that afternoon when Rosa thought she would not be able to stand so much joy. Never before had she enjoyed life so freely; she told her sons that so much happiness seemed sinful to her, and they all laughed at her quaint motion.

Chapter 47

In 1931 Cuba was living through turbulent times. President Machado, like a tailor's apprentice, tried to patch things up here and there, but his regime was too worn out, and no patches could prevent its eventual tearing. The Cuban people expressed their rebelliousness in many ways, and a change of rulers was imminent.

With the exception of Andres, the Garach family was not part of the political activities. But the eldest brother, under the influence of the atmosphere at the Caribe bookstore, was an active participant in the opposition. So far, nobody had pointed a finger at him, but he became more involved with every passing day, and there was no telling what the future might hold in store.

"Look, let me tell you," Fermin warned him, "I don't like what's happening here. There's too much political turmoil, and what's coming after this will be terrible. I can tell."

"It's the same all over the world. It's the dictatorships, the rulers who want to stay in power, they're the ones spoiling everything. That's why you've got to hit them and hit them hard."

"You know I don't like to poke into your business, but you're letting those people lead you by the nose, and you'll regret it."

"Look, Fermin, as soon as I came here, I adopted Cuba as my own. I knew immediately that I could stay and build my future here. I can't live here and not feel the country's problems; I can't do what I don't think is right just because I fear for my life. I'm not like that; I'm just not like that at all."

"You're a year older than me, and I'm not going to force you to see things my way. But, as far as I'm concerned, all this will catch me far, very far away. Before the year's out, all of us will be back home."

"Not all; Jose told me he's not leaving, and neither am I."

"Well, that's what you say now, but you'll see how, when you see us living in Spain like royalty, you too will make up your mind and come to Benicarlo. I'm sure."

"All right, but I'd rather stay. I've grown used to Cuba; I don't think I can be yanked away that easily. What's Lucas got to say about all this?"

"Lucas agrees with me. He also plans to leave with his family before the end of the year."

"What's he planning to do about Cachita?"

"I don't know how he's going to handle that problem. Time will tell, I guess. We'll see."

Chapter 48

No one could deny that, even at age sixty, Juan Garach controlled the destinies of virtually the entire family. Following Rosa's departure, and as soon as he was able to arrange it, he sent Lucia to Valencia to finish her studies. That year's crop did not seem very promising, and he had barely harvested it when he left for Santander and took passage on a ship bound for Cuba. He had to gather his flock and bring it back to Spain; it was a fact that, unless he used his influence, he might never see them together again in Spain.

Jose was able to free himself from his father's orders. He stated unequivocally that he would stay in the island and bear the consequences of his decision. Andres was not planning to return to Spain either. However, Fermin and even Lucas, the rebel, agreed to their father's suggestions. Soon after his arrival, the old man began to set goals and give orders.

Carolina did not hear the news until after Lucas had already found a buyer for his business. The young woman hoped that she would find help or advice in Rosa, but it was useless; Lucas' decision was final.

Between Fermin and Lucas, the Garachs were able to put together a rather sizable sum. The certainty that this time they would really do great things seemed to rejuvenate Juan. The other two would come as soon as they realized that life for them would be better in Spain. The nature of Spaniards did not go well with Cuban customs, Juan often told his family. His sons—the eldest and the youngest—had not realized it yet.

"Look, man, I've got to talk to you now, I mean right now. Either you come with me, or I'll raise hell; it's your choice. And you'd better decide quick because, *caramba,* I'm getting real nervous."

Lucas never lost his calm demeanor, regardless of how complex or unforseen a situation might be. When he saw Cachita standing in front of him, in the threshold of his home, holding one of their sons by the hand and the other in her arms, Lucas cursed himself for not having set the trip for a few days earlier.

"Easy, Cachita; my wife and my daughter are inside; shut up, please; don't spoil everything." Lucas thought that perhaps it would have been better to tell Cachita the truth in time, but then, it was too late for regrets.

"Either you come back to my room right now, or else I'm kicking all of you out of here. You just don't do what you were fixing to do to Cachita Montero."

"I'll go; go on, and I'll go right away."

"You good for nothing bum! If you're not there in half an hour, I'm coming back. And I won't be whispering then; I'll be screaming at the top of my lungs right here, in front of your house; so now you know."

"Believe me, Cachita; I'll be right over. Be quiet now. My father and my wife are inside, and they could hear you."

"Lucas, who's at the door?" Carolina's voice made him turn pale.

"Half an hour!" a furious Cachita warned him.

It had been Andres who had broken the news of the trip to her. The eldest Garach was again involved in political trouble, and once more had gone to Cachita for help. No one had told him that the trip was supposed to be a secret, and he mentioned it to the girl in passing.

Cachita gave herself no time to reflect. Driven by a desperate impulse, she took her two sons and set out to kill Lucas. But, by the time she reached his house, she had calmed down. Walking silently, the rhythmic breating she felt next to her chest and the soft warmth of her oldest son's hand made her think things over.

Cachita Montero had to keep her head. Her children's future—whether or not they would have to beg from door to door—depended on the tactics she used.

Be patient, Cachita Montero. Don't let yourself get carried away and do something you'll regret later; keep your cool. The problem here is money, and Lucas has always paid for the room and given you money for food. You need a place to stay and money for the children's school. You'll hustle the food; you'll do whatever has to be done; you'll be a maid, you'll wash, iron, or find something else. Lucas's got to leave the room and the children's school all paid for. Either he gives you what you ask, or you'll give him the granddaddy of all scandals right in front of his house. You bet he knows what's good for him. "As if I didn't know him," she muttered to herself.

When Carolina asked Lucas who had knocked at the door, he told her it had been a beggar and her two sons. He got dressed in a hurry and left almost without saying good-bye. He told his wife there were a few last minute details he had to take care of.

"Damn it, Cachita, you really scared me this morning. What's the matter with you?"

"I'm going to scare the shit out of you, you good for nothing liar, unless you do right by me and your sons. I'm telling you; I'm ready to do anything," she wanted to sound convincing.

"Who told you I was leaving?"

"Forget it, *sinverguenza*. I know how to keep a secret for a friend. It was someone much more decent than you. I'm telling you no more."

"I was going to tell you, but I didn't do it before because I didn't want to hurt you. I was going to tell you today; you've got to believe me, Cachita, for Christ's sake."

"Bastard, that's what you are. And a liar, too. You didn't want to hurt me, did you? You were fixing to leave me with the two kids and not a single penny. I like the way you take care of things! If you don't want this whole city to find out that you've been my lover for six years, and that you had a son by me the day before you married your wife, you'd better get your pocket ready, sonny. They can say I'm a bitch or anything they want; I don't give a damn. But I'm no fool, no sir."

"How can you think that, Cachita? I love you more than anything in this world!" He tried to hold her by the shoulders to make her more vulnerable.

"Get away from me, you liar! You'll never lay hands on me again! You're nothin' but a fuckin' two-faced liar." She writhed away.

"Well, so that you know who I really am, look what I had ready for you." He reached into his pocket, took out an envelope and handed it to her. She opened it, and when she saw its contents, she made a mocking face and took out two hundred-dollar bills.

"This won't last long, buster. By the time you get back to wherever it is you came from, Juanito, Alberto and me will be walking up and down the Malecon with a tin can, begging for food. I think we've got to have ourselves a serious talk, you're takin' me for a fuckin' fool."

"What do you want?" Lucas asked sitting down.

"Look, there's two things we need." She flung the money he had just given her at his feet. "We need a place to live where we don't have to pay no rent, and the kids have got to go to school."

"Well, that's what public schools are for . . ."

"No way, man! Juanito and Alberto have got to go to the Marist Brothers."

"You're crazy; I can't afford that."

"Well, you'd better can. This very day we go over to the school, and we ask how much it is for the kids to go up to sixth grade. If they get that far, I'll be satisfied. Besides, we go over to the notary, and you have to sign your home over to me."

"You're asking too much, Cachita. I can't give you all of that."

"Haven't I given you enough? Think it over. I know you're leaving the day after tomorrow. If you don't bring a receipt from the school and take me to the notary public to fix the deal with the house, you'd better get ready, buster, *por estas*," she ratified her determination crossing her thumb and index fingers and kissing them , then continued, "I swear to you, everybody in this town will be reading in *La Marina*: MISTRESS KILLS MAN, WIFE, AND CHILD. 'Cuz that's what I aim to do, and I don't care if they put me in jail or take me to the nuthouse. Look," she stabbed her chest with her index finger, "you made a fool of me, I don't deny that. Now, you or anybody else won't make fools of my kids. I'll see to that. Don't you think that they'll be gardeners at some big mansion, like Jesusito. No, sir. They may have dark skin like me, but I'll do whatever has to be done so they can be gentlemen. They won't be hired help in some rich folks' home. I'll do whatever has to be done . . . Well, no need to say any more. I'll do whatever has to be done, and don't you forget it."

The way Cachita put it, that morning Lucas tore out of her room in the tenement house *como un volador de a peso* . . . real fast.

Chapter 49

Andres needed to see Jose immediately, and as soon as Lucas was gone, Cachita left in a hurry to get him. Jose and the three employees who at that time worked at the grocery store were in constant activity. Cachita's arrival created a stir among the men milling about the store. The girl had not really done herself up, but she was striking all the same.

"Holy Mother of God!" said one of the men when he saw her walk into the store.

"Don't miss this, guys. Take a look over there at that sweet thing. Shit! Would you look at that pair of legs? Shit!"

"Jose, Jose, don't miss this. Maybe we haven't got what she's looking for. Quick guys, she's leaving!"

"Well, you can look all you want, but don't you give me less than what I'm paying for. I may be old and fat, but I'm a good customer," one of the women protested.

"Don't you get like that, Cristina. You know you always buy from me almost at cost."

"All right, Jose, sonny, all right. But don't you get all shook up with this pretty girl!" the lady smiled good naturedly.

When Cachita heard the woman call Jose by his name, she walked over to him.

"You're Jose Garach, right?" eyebrows like question marks, lips half-open in an honest smile, Jose had just seen Cachita Montero at her best.

"Well!" one of the employees exclaimed. "It's Jose she wants after all!"

"May I help you?" Jose seemed undisturbed.

"I'm Cachita." Her name needed no further introduction.

"Is anything the matter with Lucas or the children?" he answered softly to disguise his concern.

"No. It's Andres," she placed both elbows on the counter, and pretended to be flirting as she whispered.

"Andres?"

"Yes. Look, I can't talk to you here. May I come in?" she said pointing with her finger inside the store.

Jose opened the counter and went with Cachita to the back of the store. Rosa was sitting in a rocking chair mending socks.

"Andres is hiding in my room. He sent me to tell you that he's got to see you right away; it's very urgent. He can't come out of my room, that's why he couldn't come himself," she moved her hand up and down quickly, as if underlining the urgency of the situation.

Cachita didn't have to say any more. Jose took off his apron and followed her out of the store.

Andres would not have made Jose leave his business if it had not been a matter of life or death. But this time he had really gotten himself into serious trouble. Before his brother had a chance to start explaining his situation, Jose looked suspiciously at the young woman. Cachita had just put one of the boys to bed and was straightening the room.

"Don't worry; we can trust her. She's Cachita; we're among family. There's no need to worry."

"¡Recollons!" Jose had never met his brother's illegitimate family.

"Well, have you read the newspapers?" Andres' usual nonchalance had turned to worry.

"Yes, why?" Jose seemed puzzled.

"Did you read about Vazquez Bello's murder?"

"They shot him, didn't they? That's what I heard in the store. Yes, yes; I know more or less what happened. They killed him in Marianao, didn't they?" Afraid of what Andres would say next, Jose sat at the other end of Cachita's bed.

"They shot him on Country Club Drive. I was one of the people who killed him." With his arms on his knees, Andres let his head drop and looked down as if no more explanation of his troubles was needed.

"Andres! Why do you get mixed up in these fine messes?"

"This is not the time for questions; you know how I feel. They've got us all checked out. Yesterday they planted a bomb at the bookstore; the owner was inside, and I got away by pure chance. One of our people found out what they were going to do and sent word to me at home to go into hiding or else . . ."

"And then?" Jose ran his hand through his hair and began treading the small room nervously.

"Well, I can't get out of here. They'll kill me the minute they spot me. I'm very conspicuous; this arm and this damn leg single me out, and I've got to disappear until this thing blows over."

"Shit, Andres, why did you have to get mixed up in this right now, now that mother's here? They're leaving in two days, you know."

"The plan was foolproof," he argued. "It wasn't Vazquez Bello we were after. All the bigshots were supposed to go to his funeral, at the family plot in Colon Cemetery. Once everybody was there, we were going to blow up everything sky high. All the charges and everything had already been set through the sewage system. It couldn't fail; it was very carefully planned. Many brains got together to figure it out; it was supposed to have gone like clockwork."

"But it fucked up," Jose replied, ill-humored.

"The family decided to bury him in Santa Clara instead. Somebody let the cat out of the bag; they found out about us, and they've been running us in one by one. Some turn up dead at home, others washed ashore on Malecon. They know everything about us. It's just a matter of hunting us down." Andres took his good hand to his neck in a quick and graphic movement.

"And now what?"

"You've got to find a way to get me out of the country."

"Where?" Jose opened his eyes, amazed at his brother's request.

"Well, I've got to go back to Spain; it'll be easy for me to go back. You'll have to get me aboard the ship where mother and father are leaving the day after tomorrow."

"Have you got a passport?"

"Yes, here it is. But there's one problem; if they check the passenger list and find my name . . ."

"Then, what are we going to do?" Jose was panicking.

"You'll buy the ticket under your name. You give me your passport, and I'll take it from there."

"And what will I do without a passport if there's a revolution or something?"

"After a few days, go to the embassy and tell them you've lost it."

"Very well, Andres; I'll do it. But don't you come looking for me again if you get mixed up in more police trouble."

"It'll be the last time. If I can get out of this problem alive, this will be the end of my career as a revolutionary."

"Have you got any money?"

"Not on me. You'll have to lend me some."

"How do you plan to get on board? You can't do it in broad daylight, when everybody can see you . . ."

"Well, I'll have to think about that. Right now, go and take care of the ticket; the rest . . ."

A knock on the door alerted everybody in the room, including the children. Cachita peeked outside and saw a black car and two men waiting.

"Who is it?" she asked softly, almost in a whisper.

"This is the police. Open up, ma'am, we have to ask you a few questions."

Quickly, the girl took charge of the situation. She told Juanito to take off his shoes and to pretend to be asleep in his bed. The boy was fascinated by the whole thing; he remembered a story about cops and robbers Jesusito had told him once.

"Andres, hide!" she hesitated and looked around the room, trying to find a convenient place. "Here, inside the wardrobe. Jose, take off your clothes."

"I beg your pardon?"

Cachita took off her blouse leaving it carelessly on the bed enough to throw Jose into a state of confusion and amazement. In seconds, she unzipped her skirt let it fall on the floor walking right over it. When she was only wearing a slip and bra, she kicked off her shoes and ruffled her hair.

"I told you to take off everything, man!" She helped him strip down to his shorts and got him into bed, under the sheets. Before opening the door, she scattered hers and Jose's clothes around the room. Barefoot, clad only in a revealing slip and bra, her hair about her face, she addressed the man outside with disarming candor.

"Listen," she said leaning provocatively against the door, and showing more than necessary pretending not to realize it. "This visit of yours don't help my business none. I'm tellin' you, people can't even make a livin' in peace."

"Who lives in there with you?"

"I've got two kids; one's six; the other's two."

"Is there anybody else in the room now?"

"Well, if you were somebody else, I'd tell you to stick your nose into your business. But since you're a cop, and a good-looking one too, I'll tell you that I'm with a . . . customer. Listen, just between you and me, I want no hassle with the law."

"How long has he been here?"

"Oh, he just got here a while ago. So, I was busy last night, and I had given this guy an appointment for the morning. But, look, man, you come in and search all you want, but do it quickly 'cuz the next one is coming soon, and I've got to take a break between clients or else . . ."

"What's the name of the man you've got in there?"

"See, he always tells me his name is Garcia, but just between you and me, I think it's a fake name," she replied in a mysterious tone of voice. The policeman opened the door ajar and stepped inside the room. Jose, in bed, was shaking like a leaf, unwittingly acting out his part to perfection.

"Listen, what's your name?"

"Pepe Garcia."

"Listen, honey, don't spread it around," Cachita interrupted. "Maybe the poor guy's married, and you'll get him into trouble. Look, why don't you drop by again in a little while, after I'm done. I'll make you some coffee, and we'll talk, I swear. But right now, you've caught me at the wrong time. See? I haven't got nobody hiding in here but that poor son-of-a-bitch in bed, and he comes here for a little lovin', that's all," she said pointedly, smiling at the visitor.

"Hey . . . what's your name?"

"Cachita Montero, for whenever you want anything," she said straightening up his tie and winking her eye.

"Look, Cachita," he started to say again, trying to keep his composure. "They told us that a strange man had come here, and we came to check out this story. Be careful you don't let anyone inside your place who's got problems with the police."

"It must have been that old witch in number ten; she's not doing so hot in business, you know. It's envy, man; there are people who can't stand to see one like this," she said as she moved both hands tightly over her breasts, waist, and hips, "so . . . well off."

"Well, thank you, and sorry for the interruption, Pepe."

"Never mind, man. Hey, listen," she stepped outside the room and shouted unabashedly at him. "You know where you can find me whenever you feel like it."

When the automobile pulled away, Cachita went inside, closed the door and dressed quickly. Neither Andres nor Jose stirred until she whispered to them:

"You can come out now, guys. Would you like me to make you some coffee?" Again Cachita had managed to do the unexpected.

Chapter 50

Lucas was not as frightened by Cachita's threats as the girl had hoped. He knew full well that precisely because she loved the children, Cachita would not do anything rash. However, in order to avoid difficulties of this type, he decided to grant her part of her wishes; after all, he had not lived with her for just a couple of days. Besides, she had given him his only two sons, and indications were that Carolina would not be able to have any more children. When the time finally came, he would have a big business, an international business perhaps, he would need a man he could trust to help him, a man who would look after his interests. Who could be better than his own sons? Yes, for his sake, as well as for that of the children, he had to pay for their studies. He liked Cachita's ambition; the girl had a good head on her shoulders; no one could deny that.

Andres could not leave the girl's room. Following the police visit, a man had been posted on the corner to keep an eye on all the comings and goings in the block. Jose, however, was able to carry out his brother's instructions to the letter and had returned on the following day with the ship's fare and his passport.

"Look, Andres, I can't come back. You're leaving, but I'm staying, and I can't get involved. You've got everything you need to get away without problems. Once the ship sails, and you leave Cuba behind, you won't have to worry any more. With Lucas and Fermin on board, everything will be all right. The difficult part is going to be for you to get on board."

"Don't you have any idea how I can do it unnoticed?"

"Gerardo knows this sailor, Francisco, who's from his same home town. He works on the ship where father and the others are leaving, the *Marques de Comillas*."

"Did you talk to him?"

"Gerardo did."

"You told him? Shit, Jose, if someone finds out, it could cost me my life."

"There was no other way, Andres. Shut up now and let me explain. That guy, Francisco, is blond, not too tall, with blue eyes and wears a uniform. After dark, at eleven o'clock, he'll be waiting for you at the Alameda de Paula. We've paid him to help you out. He'll take you on board the ship and will hide you until you can come out."

"And how can I get to the Alameda de Paula?"

"I don't know that. You've got until nightfall to figure out a way." Andres sat down and held his head in his hands. The possibility of failure obsessed him.

"Don't worry, Andres. There's time. We'll think of something. I'll help you," Cachita said.

"Andres, let me hug you and wish you good luck. I hope to see you again soon." Jose stood up and approached his brother.

"Machado won't last too long in power. I'll come back as soon as he's gone."

"I hope so."

Jose left the room quickly. Andres and Cachita remained silent and not a word was spoken until Alberto began to cry in his cradle demanding attention.

"It's all right, Cachita. I'll pick him up; I've gotten used to it. The kid takes my mind off my problems. Since I do nothing but think, it's a welcome relief."

"Look, Andres, one of Domitila's nephews is a cab driver; he's a very nice man. I've never heard anybody say anything bad about him. Maybe you . . ."

"Don't get mixed up in this. You've helped me enough already."

"It's no trouble, man; if it could harm me in any way, I wouldn't even mention it. What I can do is go see Domitila over in Miramar. It's real fast by bus."

"What would you tell her then? Remember that the more people who know about this, the worse it is."

"I'll tell her to give me her nephew's phone number and that's it. And then, I'll call him and tell him to wait for you in some alley not too far from here. You go with him and that's the end of the story."

"Whereabouts around here?"

"It can be any place, as long as it isn't right in front of this room, 'cuz we've got that cop on the lookout. You can go out the window and on to the next block."

"Will I fit through the window?" Andres asked.

"If you don't, we'll cut a chunk off you; how about that?"

"And then what?"

"You climb up to the roof, jump to the next building, and take off with him. You tell him where he's supposed to go and not a word more. Since it's me who'll be calling him, he'll think you're my lover or something. See? There's no problem, man."

"You're worth your weight in gold, Cachita. My brother would have been wise to have married you."

"That's what I kept telling him, but here I am; single, with two kids and not a penny to my name."

"Didn't Lucas leave you anything?"

"I talked to him the day before yesterday, and I really let him have it, but he hasn't shown his face here again. I told him I was going to kill him and his whole family, to see if he'd get scared and give me a break, but that brother of yours is as hard as nails."

"I swear to you that, for as long as I live, you and your children will have everything you need."

"Thank you, Andres, but I'd like to hear that from him." The young woman remembered her eldest son sitting next to her, listening to the conversation and told him: "Go play outside, Juan, honey. Keep an eye on that bad guy who wants to pick up Andres, and if you see him move, come right back and let us know." The boy left to carry out his mission. "I don't like Juan to hear these these things; he's a big boy. He understands everything and gets worried."

The night was far clearer than Andres had hoped for; several tenants were still out of their rooms, visiting each other in the central patio of the old, run down building. Cachita's window opened onto an alley between her tenement building and the next house. Juanito went out first; both he and his mother helped Andres squeeze through the narrow opening.

The boy behaved very well that night. Holding his uncle by the hand, he went up to the roof, and then to the next block. There they came down to the street where, fortunately and very prompt, Domitila's nephew was waiting.

"So long, boss," Juan said in a very low voice.

"Good luck, Juan."

"Will you be back soon?"

"Who knows? Be good to your mother."

"Yes, sir," and he snapped to attention, the same way he had seen it done at the movies.

"Call me uncle, Juan; I'm your uncle. Didn't you know?"

"My uncle?"

"Yes, son," Andres ran his good hand affectionately through the boy's thick hair and got inside the taxi that awaited him across the street.

In the afternoon of the following day, a stranger knocked at Cachita's door. He had an envelope and a key in his hand.

"Cachita Montero?"

"In person," she smiled. The man did not seem to be a policeman, but her heart sank thinking that they may be coming to arrest her or to tell her that Andres was dead.

"Look, a gentleman sends you this. He asked me to give it to you right away."

"Do I owe you anything?"

"No, ma'am; I've already been taken care of."

"Well, hang on. Here's a nickle, go and buy yourself a cup of coffee. You really scared the hell out of me; I thought it was someone else."

"Thank you. So long."

The piece of paper shook in her hands as though moved by fears of its own. It read:

> The house is still in my name, but you can move in within two days. If they ask you, you're the new tenant and that's it.
>
> Juan can start at the Marist Brothers in September; there's still time to see about Alberto.

There was no signature.

PART V

Don't ask me how, but I could feel the silence when I arrived at the house in Benicarlo. The dirt floor was dry and dusty; the walls were damp and quiet. Perhaps it was Lucia's absence or my having arrived a different person because indeed I was, and I just couldn't understand why.

I was fifty-six years old then, and I'm ninety-four now. The years have shown me what my change was all about. You see, when I was twenty, I married him. I went from my father's hands to his and never had the chance to see myself as a person separate from either of them. Juan's control of my life was absolute. He dictated almost my every move, when I would have my children, when I would feed them, where I would work, how I would mother them. He ruled my sleep and waking hours with a force that was typically his.

Then, one day, a son I hardly recognized took me away from Juan's domain. My son, a man I never knew, for the first time gave me a glimpse of freedom making me realize that I liked being alone; I found joy precisely in being away from Juan.

I saw I could sew, do the wash or cook without giving reasons or taking orders. I think it was then that I really learned to think, and found great peace in being with my own thoughts. When Juan arrived and interrupted my inner harmony, I wanted to run the other way. That night, I cried and asked God to forgive what I thought were sinful thoughts. How naive I was then, even at fifty-six. For thirty more years, I failed to admit my longing for independence.

Chapter 51

By the end of 1936, little was left of the enthusiasm and renewed vigor that Juan Garach had gained from his visit to Cuba in 1931. Jose had been right. The war in Spain did break out, and it became a fierce struggle that left Spaniard pitted against Spaniard for many decades, but the Garachs were not cut out to be patriots.

Andres was the exception; whenever he found a cause in which he could firmly believe, he would follow it and be capable of any sacrifice on its behalf. However, his Cuban experience had taught him the results of direct involvement in political affairs; thus, the Spanish Civil War failed to touch him in any appreciable way. Early in 1935, before the war broke out, Andres sold his share in the business to his brothers and left Spain; he said it was for the last time.

One night, in July of that same year, Carolina and Rosa waited longer than usual for their husbands and for Fermin. They were late in coming because several friends had dropped by to tell them that, finally, Spain was at war with itself.

"We have to think very carefully about what we're going to do," said Lucas as he came in.

"You see, mother? I told you something serious had happened; I knew it," Carolina said, alarmed.

"Calm down; let's see what they've got to say."

"The situation is not as serious as you see it, Lucas. Probably it's just an uprising, and it won't last long. Let's keep our eyes open and see how things evolve over the next few months."

"What do you think, father?"

"I agree with Fermin. We live in a relatively small town. The trouble won't be so big as to reach us here. It's possible that everything will be over in a few months. There'll be no reason then to undo all that we have accomplished over these last few years."

"I'm afraid of what may happen to us, especially to the two of us. We're both thirty-four years old, and that's the right age for a soldier. If this should go on, we won't be able to stay and work here; they'll make us fight, and that can't be."

Rosa and Carolina exchanged concerned glances. Seldom had the future looked more somber.

"Let's see what happens," Juan said at the end of the conversation. "Maybe we're fretting over a rumor. We'll have to keep a close eye on things."

Rosa knew little or nothing about governments and wars, but she did know her husband quite well. When she saw him staying in bed late, several days in a row, his head under the sheets, she realized the true situation of the country.

"Is anything wrong, Juan?"

"Leave me alone, woman. I'm not sick. I need to rest; I've got some important things to decide; let me be."

Rosa kept quiet, but she could not stop worrying. Had it not been for little Lina, the Garach household would have fallen prey to the same sadnesss that had engulfed the other homes in town. Every day Carolina cursed the moment she had allowed them to convince her to move to Spain. Fermin and Lucas went about their business in an obvious state of shock. The situation grew more desperate by the minute; Juan did not leave his bed for a week, and when Rosa gazed down upon the dirt floor of the house, she could imagine her sons, in uniform, dead.

Juan chose the day of his daughter's arrival in Benicarlo to gather his entire family around the table and talk to them.

"I also have something to tell you," he began ceremoniously. "Lucia, child, I'm sorry that we have to welcome you like this. We should be celebrating your graduation; you've accomplished something no other Garach ever did. But what I have to say to all of you can't wait any longer." Visibly upset, Juan put both arms on the table and prepared to explain his position. Reason and emotion struggled within him; reason spoke, but emotion regretted each and every word he said.

"I must admit that I was wrong. I mean, I made a mistake in bringing you here to Spain, in making you sell all your property and in asking you to return."

"No, no; that's not so, father," Fermin protested. "We came of our own free will and not because you ordered us. If things have not come out all right, it's not your fault; it's circumstances."

"Well, circumstances or no circumstances, the point is that we have failed. Jose was right. We have to find the way for you to go away, to leave Spain. *All* of you. The situation is serious. We shall all go, including Lucia, including your mother and me."

Rosa could not recall Juan ever having spoken so sincerely, or having admitted a mistake so readily.

"There are many important people in big cities, where the problems of war are greater. They'll want to come and live out the war in a small town like this. We may lose money in the process, but we must get rid of the business. You'll need the money to get started again in Cuba."

"There's this man, Sanchez, who came over from Madrid last week. I think he's interested in buying us out."

"Do you know where he lives?"

"No, but he comes by every day."

"You talk to him tomorrow. We've got to do something as soon as possible. Fermin and you must leave right away. You're young and single. You have a choice; you can either join the army or go abroad. I want you to go abroad."

"It won't be easy," Fermin pointed out.

"You can't leave the country legally. Lorenzo, Concha's husband, will be able to help us out."

"Lorenzo?" both brothers asked at once.

"He's a railroad engineer, and I know he'll help you both get across the French border."

"And what about us, Lucas, what will we do?" Carolina became very nervous at the mention of a separation.

"You, the girl, and Lucia will follow later, and finally Rosa and myself," Juan said.

"Well thought out, father; well thought out," Lucas granted.

With an age-old "Holy Madonna de l'Avella" on her lips, Rosa got up from the table and began to serve dinner. All the others, except Juan, remained glued to their seats. Even the girl, in her own childish way, stayed quiet and serious.

"I won't have dinner here tonight. I'll be at the cafe if you need me," Juan said. Taking his jacket, he headed out the door.

He didn't go to the cafe. As soon as he left the house, he changed his mind and, walking in the opposite direction, walked all the way down Avenida del Mar until he reached the Mediterranean. There, he sat on some rocks by the wayside and let the cool sea breeze clear up his thoughts.

They haven't realized it, Juan, but you've given up everything you worked for your entire life. Dreams you nurtured in your soul since your first child was born; the ideas you instilled into them; everything has been brought down by war, by a war you don't even understand. You've never been lucky, Juan. You left La Morellana and time and again you had to change direction because things didn't work the way you wanted them. You consoled yourself then with the thought that they would leave and come back with enough money to open up a business. "When we open the business!" you used to dream. There would be no more failures after that. Look at yourself now, Juan. "Juan Garach & Sons." You've done well; your sons have worked hard, yet everything is gone. All you can do is flee and start all over again. Easier said than done; start all over again at sixty-five years of age. Juan Garach, for the last time you have to start all over again.

He almost saw the sun come up from the rock where he had been sitting all night. The same thoughts preyed upon his mind. He had the premonition that, if he stayed there, he would sooner or later discover that it was all a horrible nightmare. He would then be able to shake the gloom from his head and return home once again strong and ready for a new day. The first light of dawn hurt his eyes and his mind. The idea that had so cruelly tortured him through the night had been no dream. Convinced at last, he struggled to his feet. Standing before the sea, he let the wind and the cold of the morning dry out his tears.

Chapter 52

"Juanito, honey, you're gonna fall flat on the floor when you see who's coming." Cachita and her sons, Juan, eleven, and Alberto, almost six, were in the front porch of the house where Carolina had once lived. The woman was wearing a white dress and fanned herself vigorously with a wicker fan.

"Who is it, mama?"

"Look, can't you see that man walking over there?" She stood next to the boy and pointed at the sidewalk on the other side of the street.

"That's my uncle, mom!"

"Shush, boy. Who told you such a thing? It must have been Domitila; she's a real busybody. I don't care how good a friend she is!"

Andres had almost reached the porch and Cachita did not give him a chance to surprise her as he had wished to do.

"Andres, hey, Andres, how're you doin'?"

"Cachita! I figured you lived here. Imagine. I went to your room on Tulipan Street, and they told me you had moved away years ago. The woman on number five told me; remember her? She's still there."

"Yes, yes. I found out about this house after you had left, that's why I couldn't tell you. Come, come here and meet the boys; they've really grown. Look, this here is my son Juan."

"Hi, uncle!"

"There you go again with that 'uncle' bit. Show some respect, boy!"

"And this here's Albertico." The child shook Andres' hand ceremoniously.

"Albertico Montero, sir . . . uncle." Since he had been born after Lucas' marriage to Carolina, the child was not Lucas' legitimate son.

"How did you wind up here, Cachita? Lucas used to live here before he went back to Spain. I think he owned this house."

"Juanito, Alberto, why don't you two guys go to the store and bring me one pound of coffee so I can make some for Andres. Juanito, tell the grocer I'll pay him for it tomorrow on my way to work." Both children left and Cachita brought Andres up to date on everything that had happened since his departure.

"And there you have it, Andres. This way we at least have a roof over our heads and Juan goes to a good school, which is what I wanted. But now . . .

"Are you working?"

"Yeah. Do you remember Domitila?"

"The woman who used to be your neighbor? The one who had a grandson who was a gardener?"

"Man, some memory you've got!" she exclaimed. "Right. The poor old lady is going blind. I don't know what it is, but it isn't contagious. The long and short of it is that they fired her 'cuz she confused the gentleman of the house with the driver; it was awful. When they fired her, she came and told me. At that time, I sure could use a job; with the baby and all that, I hadn't worked for some time. I asked Domitila to come and stay here with the children while I went to Miramar to work as a cook. She said it was okay and here we are, not doing so bad after all."

"Where is she now?"

"Today she went to Luyano to spend the day with Jesusito's family. Do you remember him?"

"I sure do! The night Juan was born, he came to get us."

"Well, he's quite a gardener, and he married a girl who was the maid next door."

"And what's the matter now?"

"Well, Andres, my job pays enough for food, clothing, you know? Every day expenses and the like. But we just don't have enough to spend on Alberto's tuition, school uniforms, books, and all that. I feel so sorry for the poor boy! He's just a kid, and he can't understand these things. That good for nothing bum of your brother . . . Sorry, but it's the truth. He's never cared for his sons, and they are his," she stressed, "his alone."

"I know, Cachita. Lucas doesn't think things out. But, look, you don't have to worry about Albertico's education. I'll take care of that."

"No, I can't accept that. That would be too much. Why should you spend your hard-earned money on my son?"

"Look, you saved my life once. I owe it to you. Besides, the boy is my nephew, and I have a right, don't I?" Andres smiled.

"It's his father who should take care of that. He sang the blues and now he's got to pay his dues, right?"

"Well, but I'm a Garach too, so everything stays in the family."

"I always said to myself, 'Cachita, you should have fallen in love with Andres. There's a nice, honest guy.' But, man, there's no thinking straight when it comes to love. If Lucas came back now and told me two or three sweet things, I couldn't say no to him. Would you believe me if I told you that I haven't been with another man since he left?"

"Yes, Cachita, I'd believe you."

"I'm a . . . a fool, to put it nicely, but I'm still in love with him. Besides, he gave Juan his name and all . . . Look, let's drop the subject of Lucas. I get all mushy when I start thinking of him, and a mushy Cachita ain't no Cachita. Come into the kitchen; the kids are coming back with the coffee, and I'll make you some."

Cachita's involvement with the Garach clan was destined not to ever end.

Chapter 53

One of Andres' old friends who had survived the terrorism of Machado's regime got him a job at the Nuevo Horizonte bookstore. Andres did as his friend suggested, and he began to work the following week. He deposited in a bank the savings he had brought from Spain, and solemnly promised himself not to rest until he had his own bookstore. His job afforded him ample opportunity to read.

Shortly after having started to work at Nuevo Horizonte, Andres met Norma Recio, a law student at the University of Havana. Until the moment when Norma asked him for a book one afternoon, Andres had never been truly interested in any particular woman.

"Good afternoon, may I help you?" Andres said.

"Maybe it was good yesterday; today . . ." She closed her dripping umbrella and smiled, amused. "If I had waited any longer you'd have seen me paddle my way in here in a canoe!"

"I'm sorry, Miss. I was just trying to see if you needed any help."

"It's all right, Mr. . . . ."

"Garach. Andres Garach."

"It's all right, Mr. Garach. This just isn't my day. I've missed two buses; I left my umbrella at home and had to borrow this one to avoid a prolonged stay in the hospital; I also left my purse at home with all my money. I only had the fare for the bus in my pocket. Still I told myself I would come and pick the books I want. I think you can set them aside for me, and I'll pay for them later."

"If it's money you're worried about, don't. How much do you need? I'll lend you some." Norma was not only beautiful; unlike other women he had met, she didn't seem to notice his handicap.

"Impossible! You don't even know me? What If I never show up again?"

"We would meet some place else, and you would be embarrassed to death," Andres replied. "Besides, don't think I'm going to make it all that easy for you. We close in an hour. You can wait for me, and I'll take you home. You don't have any money for the bus anyway. That would also give me a chance to know you better. What books are you looking for?"

The girl pulled out a crumpled piece of paper from her pocket and opened it up. The paper had gotten wet, and the ink had run.

"See what I told you? This isn't my day; I shouldn't have gotten out of bed this morning. I can't understand a thing written here . . . It's so frustrating!"

Andres' experience in the book business and a few hints from Norma helped them decipher the titles of the books Norma wanted.

"What did you say your name was?" she asked as Andres wrapped the books for her.

"Garach."

"That's funny. There was a big to-do in my family over a boy by that same name. Garach." She stared at him. "No, but it couldn't have been you; it would be too much of a coincidence."

"What was it all about?"

"A cousin of mine who used to be a seamstress in Old Havana was almost engaged to this man named Garach. They were ready to get married, and she had already bought her wedding gown when one good day he told her he had to go back to Spain. She wanted to go too, but married, of course."

"And?"

"He flatly refused. He broke the engagement and left her."

"What happened to your cousin?"

"She was so upset, the silly thing, she became a nun."

"Rather drastic, isn't she?"

"She was never too bright. Hey, do you have any brothers?"

"Yes, but look; one is a Don Juan—he has more women than he can handle. The other is really a saint, totally incapable of doing anything like that. The third one lives only for his work; he lives in El Cerro and owns a grocery store there."

"What's the Don Juan's name?"

"Lucas."

"No, that's not the one."

"What was your cousin's boyfriend's name?"

"Fermin Garach," she answered. Andres opened his eyes and Norma realized she had hit the bullseye. "The hard worker or the saint?"

"The saint," Andres replied amazed.

They looked at each other and began to laugh.

"Look, Norma, why don't you wait for me until we close?"

"I don't know what to say, honest . . . with a Don Juan for a brother and another one who's a saint, like Fermin . . ."

"I'm different," he said, so earnestly that the girl decided not to tease him.

"All right. I'll go and get good and drenched. I'll be back in an hour. Since I'm already soaking wet, the best I can do is enjoy the rain."

Chapter 54

Juan stayed in Benicarlo through the early part of nineteen thirty-seven, hoping to be able to sell the business and leave Spain quickly. The sale of the store was not as quick as he had hoped, and the young men had to flee before their parents. Lucia, Fermin, Lucas, Carolina, and the girl were taken to Concha and Lorenzo's house in the City of Valencia. With Lorenzo's help, they would cross the French border and take a ship to America.

Back in Cuba, it was unusual for Andres and Jose Garach not to see each other in months. For the moment, they did not know the whereabouts of their parents, brothers, and sister; their letters went unanswered. Andres and Jose imagined them hiding in some unknown place, trying to escape from the war.

"How about you getting married?" Jose intended to tease his brother. He didn't know that Andres had a definite answer for him.

"Don't you or Fermin plan to start a family?"

"Fermin almost did a couple of years ago."

"What?"

Andres told Jose the story of their brother's courtship of the seamstress who entered the convent. The two laughed and wondered why Fermin had kept his romance a secret.

"Who could have imagined it?"

"How did you find out?"

"That's something else I wanted to tell you," Andres added shyly.

"You have a girl." Andres nodded. "Congratulations! Who is she? How did you meet her?"

"Her name is Norma Recio. I met her when she came to buy some books at the bookstore. That was two months ago; we've already been dating seven weeks, once a week because she's a college girl."

"I knew she was your type. What's she studying?"

"She's a law student."

"Well, I guess this is the night for secrets," Jose smiled.

"Do you have a girl, too?"

"Her name is Milagros."

"How long have you known her?"

"Around ten years."

"Why have you waited so long? How come you never told us?"

"I had to wait for her to grow up. Ten years ago, Milagros was exactly ten. She's Don Gerardo's daughter."

"Is it serious?"

"For me it is, but she doesn't know anything yet."

"And what are you waiting for?"

"I want to buy Don Gerardo's share in my store. I don't want him to think that I'm courting his daughter so he can give me his part in the business as a wedding present. Know what I mean?"

"What if the girl falls for somebody else?"

"Can't happen! I keep close tabs on her! They live right in the back of this store. I make all the deliveries myself, and I look at her in a way that she must know I love her."

"Pepet, you're almost thirty years old, and you talk as if you were still a kid."

"Like hell I do! I'm serious, Andres. In two years, no more than that, you'll have a new sister-in-law."

"You'd better talk to her or to her father, if you don't want somebody else to beat you to the altar."

"No way, I tell you. Everybody in the neighborhood knows that girl is mine. They even tell me that her mother calls me 'the farmer's dog.'"

"Why does she call you that?"

"It's an old Spanish proverb. It says that the farmer's dog doesn't eat and won't let anyone else eat either," he said raising his eyebrows and laughing at the woman's words.

Chapter 55

Juan Garach was beside himself with worry; a month had gone by, and he had not heard from his sons. He waited for them to let him know when he could leave Benicarlo. However, El Morellano's patience was running short.

"We can't put up with this any longer, Rosa," he said one morning to her over breakfast. "The boys haven't written to us; we haven't heard from Lorenzo; we've got to do something."

"It's up to you, Juan; you've always been the one who makes the decisions in this household," she answered, trying to conceal the sinking feeling in her heart.

"We can't stay much longer in Benicarlo. We've got to go some place where we'll be safe. The war grows worse by the day, and this town by the sea is not the best place."

"I don't know where you plan to go. If the boys haven't written to us, that means that they haven't been able to get away. What would we do, an old couple, moving along some God-forsaken road, hiding here and there?"

"We won't be on any God-forsaken road; we're going back to the *masia*."

Rosa wanted to cry when she heard her husband's decision. To go back to her starting point would draw her away from her children even more. But it was he who had to decide; it was he who had the last word, and it was her duty to follow. Duty bound and helpless she returned to La Morellana. It had taken her half a lifetime to realize why women don't write. If they did, sometime it would be a man's turn to follow.

Chapter 56

La Morellana was full of family, friends and strangers together trying to find some solace from the turmoil of the Spanish Civil War.
During those days Juan was in a worse mood than usual. It was not strange for the *masia* to be enveloped in a gloomy silence; Juan would hardly ever smile.

"Listen, Rosa," Candido, who was hiding with them, finally said one day with a concerned frown, "something's the matter with Juan. I don't know what it is, but he hasn't been himself lately. Haven't you noticed?"

"Juan's a very strange man; one never knows with him."

"It's been like this since we arrived," Candido insisted. "Do you remember that night? I began to notice it then. He didn't want to get up; he didn't offer to be with me. He, Juan, my lifelong friend! Something's the matter with him."

"I've asked him so many times!" Rosa sighed, "And he always tells me to leave him alone, not to bother him. What else can we do?"

"We'll have to ask him today; this can't go on. He's got to tell us something; it's the only way we'll be able to help him."

"He'll get angry; I know it."

"Well, after dinner, when the two of you go up to the bedroom, I'll go up, and we'll find out just what is the matter."

Rosa was smoothing the sheets, and Juan was taking off his *espardenas* when Candido knocked at the door and went inside the bedroom.

"Listen, Juan, I'd like to have a word with you. Do you suppose we could talk now?"

"Go outside, Rosa; these things aren't for women."

"No, Juan. I want Rosa to stay with us. What I have to say actually comes from the both of us because we've talked about it already. Well, we want to know what's wrong with you. Why the sour faces and the quick temper. You've always been a tough man, Juan, but I've never seen you like this."

Juan wiped his forehead with the back of his hand.

"Nothing's wrong with me," he replied curtly, "I'm just tired; that's all. What do you want from me?"

"We want to know the truth, because something's going on here and we don't know what it is. We're living as if we were one big family, Juan. You cannot go on behaving like this, not letting us know what the matter is."

"*¡Recollons!* Nothing's the matter, I'm telling you. I guess it's just that I'm getting old, the war . . . I don't know."

"You can curse all you want and get angry; I don't care. When we got here, you used to help us. You assigned the hours and told us what we had to so we could all live together in peace. And now it's you who isn't doing his share. That's not like Juan, El Morellano. I've known you for fifty years, Juan. You may fool others, but you aren't fooling me. I want you to tell me what's wrong with you."

"I'm sure it's this woman who's got all those funny notions. That's what she always does. That's all she's ever done, Christ, she's only trying to make me miserable."

"Shut up, Juan, it isn't that at all!" Candido shouted back at him. Rosa did not cry, but she felt ashamed, belittled to have Candido hear the torrent of insults that Juan continued to heap on her.

"You're getting away from the subject," the barber went on, "and I'm prepared to stay here for as long as it takes. You can rant and rave all you want. Rosa and me intend to find out tonight what it is that's been eating you—and us—up for over a month."

Candido's firmness succeeded in silencing Juan. Rosa had never seen him cry. When she saw her husband sobbing, she hurt inside like when he had shouted obscene curses at God. She could get close to him, put her hand on his shoulder. Her mind played tricks on her at times; Juan broke down, and she remembered Caliqueno the donkey, and Juan's words as he helped her get off from the animal a day after they were married: "Everything you see from here is ours." So many things had happened since then! She blinked several times, but all she could see was that vigorous, blond young man who loosened her braids and told her he wanted to see her hair. The man before her, however, pushed her aside violently.

"Get away from me, *recollons*, get away from me!" he yelled at the top of his lungs.

Candido leaned against the door to make sure that nobody else would come into the room. The situation had become far more tense than he had anticipated. Rosa stood next to him, lifeless, silent, her blue eyes brimming with tears.

"Calm down, Juan; nobody meant to offend you. You don't have to get like that. What we want is for this thing, whatever it is, to go away, for you to be yourself again."

"How can I be myself again? I'm sick," he finally admitted.

"What's the problem? What do you feel?"

"I can't pee; that's what's wrong with me. Could you imagine anything worse? When I can urinate a little, *collons*, the pain almost kills me. It's got to be something bad, Candido, it's got to be. I had never had anything like this ever happen to me. If a man doesn't get rid of his wastes, he dies. Don't you think I know that?"

"There's always a cure for everything. Let me see if among the pills I brought with me I can find something that'll help you. If not, we'll go to Tirig and even to Castellon if need be. Do you think we're going to let you die? I'm sure it's nothing serious, and in no time you'll be fit as a fiddle again."

"The worst," he admitted more calmly in a softer voice, "the worst part about it is that I can't die yet. I just can't. You know what I mean? I haven't done yet what I have to do. Why is it that I can never see anything of mine finished? Candido, my entire life, since you've known me, I've been trying to do something. I want to be somebody, someone like you, Candido; people admire you, they look up to you."

"What are you complaining about? They admire you too. You're Juan, El Morellano. You even were the mayor of Tirig once. What are you complaining about?"

"But I haven't finished, you see? Alone, I wasn't able to do much, but with my children I almost made it. They were going to make it; in fact, they almost made it. You didn't see us, but together we almost made it. The other two would have come too, I know it, but the war forced us to cut it short. I can't die now; I've got to see them make it. They will all come back, and we'll open up the store again. Don't you understand, Candido? I can't die, but this damn pain won't go away. It's as if somebody were telling me: 'Hang on; you haven't got much time left. Do whatever you have to do because your time's up.' That's what's really got me upset. I can't bear the idea of dying and not being able to finish what we started together." Suddenly, he put his hand to his chin, as if regretting having said what he had just finished saying. He sat on the bed, silent. Rosa didn't dare move closer to him.

"Wait here; I'll be back with my bag of pills. We'll find something; we'll measure your urine. Maybe it's just your imagination. If in a week we'll see; if there's not much we can do, we'll go to Tirig. Don't worry, Juan; it'll be all right. Have you ever known your friend Candido to let you down?"

But Candido's pills were useless. Juan never got up from the bed after that conversation. His silence was the most disturbing aspect of his behavior. He would only break it to insult and verbally abuse his wife. Rosa continued to look after him despite it all; she prayed that, in fact, it was a temporary illness and that her husband could see his children one last time. That was the least she wished for herself, and she wished her husband no less.

"Look, Rosa, I'm going to have to go to Tirig. Juan's not improving, and we'll have to do something about it. I'll ask for the doctor, and if he's left town, I'll find another."

"Couldn't we take him? Maybe it'll be quicker that way . . ."

"Impossible. He's too weak, and what he told us is true, he can't pass any urine, he just can't."

"He is in pain . . ."

"You think so?

"I know so."

"And why doesn't he speak? Why doesn't he yell or say something?"

"Could you get word to the boys?"

"You forget there is a war going on."

"You're right. It's better not to say anthing. You're a good friend; the best. May the Holy Virgin guide your steps and bring you back soon. Thank you, Candido, thank you."

The barber left so early the following morning that nobody saw him leave the *masia*. The place was even quieter than usual, perhaps as a sign of respect for the sick man. The barber had been gone four nights when El Morellano, almost out of breath, called his wife.

"Rosa, Rosa, I know you're there. Come here a minute."

The woman obeyed in silence.

"Come where I can see you, Rosa." Juan was pale; he had not shaved for days. He was still heavy, but he gave the impression of being hollow, bereft of energy. "Rosa, I want you to write to the boys and tell them to come back. Tell them to return; ask them not to leave this unfinished. Tell them to come back, Rosa."

"Don't think about that now, Juan. Don't talk."

"I'm thirsty; give me some water." Juan Garach's skin was pale, with a yellow tinge. His eyes, devoid then even of desperation, were framed by profoundly dark circles.

"Candido said for you to drink as little as possible until he came back, but wait, I'll go and wet a cloth. I'll wet your lips with it, and that ought to quench your thirst . . ." Rosa spoke softly, with a kindness she thought she could never again express to her husband.

"Rosa," the sick man stretched out his hand and opened it.

When she looked at the hand, she remembered that they were in the same place where that hand had first loved her, then, had first struck her. When the pain from that blow went away, it took along some of her devotion for her husband. In spite of the sad memory, Rosa took his hand apprehensively, and he tried to squeeze it faintly.

"Wait, Juan," she said trembling, "I'll go get you that wet cloth. You'll feel better, you'll see." His hand was left empty, dangling from the bed, devoid of the energy of life.

She left the room to get the cloth and returned in a few minutes. When she touched his lips, Rosa realized that the water was no longer needed. Juan El Morellano was dead. She set the cloth aside, closed his eyes, and made the sign of the cross over his chest. She stayed with him a few seconds before letting the others know; she wanted to pray, but all she could do was look at him. She also wanted to cry, but to her surprise discovered that she had no tears left. She wished for a deep sorrow, as when her father died or when she went to her mother-in-law's funeral or when Juan took Lucia away from her or forbade Andres to go to school. But she could neither cry nor feel sorrow. Despite herself and against her will, Rosa Garach felt a deep sense of peace.

Chapter 57

"Don't get upset, Lucas; there's no reason for it. She's your sister, your youngest sister. What she wants is not impossible: she wants to go to college to finish her career or to get a license to teach here. I really don't know about such things, but it's something like that."

"And does she figure we're going to support her all that time? That you'll be washing her clothes and taking care of her? What about our daughter? What about the house? It's too much for you. What Lucia's got to do is get herself a man who'd marry her and support her."

"I don't mind helping her out. She's your sister, Lucas; be patient. Remember your parents, and don't get like that." Carolina tried to tame him with her usual kindness, but her efforts were useless.

"I've just opened up a store, and have little money to spare. This girl's got to find a way to live elsewhere, because I don't intend to support her, you hear me? I don't intend to have her stay here longer than a month. So, you talk to her; we'll try to find a place for her to go."

"Don't be like that," Carolina pleaded, "we're not all that many; four can live just as easily as three on the same income. It's not a big difference, my dear."

"Listen, don't you get started. You women solve everything with sweet talk, but I don't fall for that."

Carolina heard the front door close and decided to say no more to prevent the situation from getting worse. Lucas, however, went on: "Tomorrow I'll talk to this Catalan woman who rents rooms, and we'll have Lucia move in with her. I've already got plenty of women to take care of, and the last thing I need is a kid sister."

Carolina did not understand the references to "plenty of women," but Lucas was right. After his wife's arrival, he had stopped his daily visits to Cachita. However, the two months he had spent with her before Carolina's return had bound him again to his lover, and he had no option but to pay for his younger son's education.

"Be quiet; Lucia just came in, and she may hear you."

"She'll have to know sooner or later. Things cannot go on the way they are, Carolina. Sometimes I get the impression that you think money grows on trees. Well, it doesn't, let me tell you; I've got to sweat hard for it!"

"You're not being reasonable, Lucas. Quiet, I hear steps."

"May I come in?" It wasn't Lucia but Andres who knocked at the kitchen door. Lucia and Norma were behind him, but they did not say a word as they came in; they could see the time was not right for pleasantries. Where Lucas was concerned, they all knew that was not at all unusual. "Hi, how's it going?"

"Well, here I am, Andres, cooking. Have you all had lunch?" she asked, trying to change the subject.

"Yes, we had something on the way over. We come from the university," Andres said, steering the conversation towards the topic he had in mind.

"Hi, Carolina," Norma said. "You just keep on working and don't mind us. We're leaving soon."

"Listen, Lucas, we just came from the university," Lucia said.

"We went and they told us that for her degree to be valid in Cuba, she would have to take some courses for a year. It isn't really expensive, but I cannot afford it all by myself. With Lucia living here, it would only be tuition and the books we would have to pay for, and I thought that among the four of us perhaps we could help her."

Carolina shuddered by the sink, afraid of the answer her husband would give to such a proposal. She knew that Lucas would never agree to help Lucia the way she so badly needed; Carolina realized he had the power to do so, but felt he would not. She caressed the dishes with the sponge and soapy water trying to understand why a woman would want as much as Lucia seemed to want; she also asked herself why some other women, like herself, for instance, were only taught a narrow road to self fulfillment.

"As a matter of fact, I was just telling Carolina that Lucia is going to have to find someplace else to go; we just haven't got enough room for her," her husband's voice interrupted her thoughts.

"How's that, Lucas?"

"I don't like to beat around the bush; we all have to pitch in to get Lucia a room somewhere. You can count me in for that; now, studying and things like that, that's not for women. What does Lucia want to know so much for? You tell me. We never got past the fourth grade at Don Poli's, and here you have us."

"But father always wanted me to finish my university studies," Lucia complained.

"What you should do is get married and stop wasting time. Women belong at home, with a husband, and for that you don't need university degrees."

"I don't agree, Lucas," Andres argued. "Lucia should not live by herself in somebody else's house; after all, she's got brothers."

Carolina dared nod her head approvingly.

"If you don't like my idea, why don't you take her with you?"

"Lucas, you must understand that I'm single, I live alone; it wouldn't be right for Lucia to live with me."

"Get married, then."

"We plan to get married in three years, when Norma finishes law school."

"Listen, Andres, I honestly couldn't care less when you plan to get married or whether you live alone or not. Lucia will go and live at Lolita's, the Catalan woman who rents rooms. She's not a bad woman, and I'll pay my share of the rent. I won't give a cent for studying. Is that clear? Don't you all talk to me about college; I'm just getting started on my business, and I haven't got time or money to spare."

"Father would have wanted it otherwise, Lucas. I know it. He always helped me to get an education," Lucia refused to give up hope.

"Then you'd better wait for father to come from Spain, and he'll help you. And you'd better change the subject or get the hell out; don't talk to me any more about the university."

"Wouldn't you care for a cup of coffee?" Carolina hoped the argument would not go any further.

Andres thought of Cachita, looked at Carolina, and wondered why those two women, so kind and compassionate, had decided to join their lives to a selfish brute like Lucas. Norma was visibly uncomfortable too; she stood impatiently by her fiance until she could bear it no longer and begged him to leave.

"Andres, I've got an exam to study for. Could we possibly leave?"

"Of course. Don't worry, Lucia; maybe when Jose gets back we'll be able to do something."

"Jose," Lucas muttered. "That's another nut. He's been in France eight months already, and he still thinks he's going to bring Fermin back. Really! Sometimes I wonder if there are any brains at all in the

Garach family." Lucas Garach had an excellent business mind, but very little heart.

Chapter 58

"I knew it; I just knew it. I knew that what this poor girl needed was a husband. Poor thing! She does the groceries for me, you know, Lucas? But you can see she's bored; she doesn't have anything to do. She spends the rest of the day lying in bed in her room, reading. Even before you told me, I already knew that the girl needs to get married."

"She doesn't have to get married today or tomorrow," Lucas explained, "but Lucia is not a forceful woman. On her own, she'll never be able to find a husband. You know, she's quite an expense for us, and we all think that the sooner we can get rid of her, the better," he lied.

"Leave it to me. The owners of the grocery store across the street are two boys from Asturias. You can see they are well bred; they're brothers, Jesus and Miguel. Jesus is already married, but Miguel is the oldest, and he's still single. If I were a few years younger, I wouldn't think twice: that man would be mine and nobody else's, but the kid is only in his late thirties, too young for me," she said.

Lolita kept her word: Before the week was out, she had a confidential talk with Miguel Suco. Of course, she was no busybody, but she had been buying her groceries at his store for years, and she couldn't help but notice that he was alone. Well, it so happened that there was this very pretty girl rooming at her house who would be just right for him. Was she decent? He'd be hard put to find a finer girl. From Valencia. Her family, the best. She's got several brothers, all of them grown men already employed. They wouldn't be a burden on him. What could he lose by checking the girl out . . .

Everything was arranged. Miguel would observe the girl when she came to the store to buy groceries for Lolita and on Saturday he would go to the boarding house for dinner. Lolita would see to it that he sat next to her; Miguel Suco could not hope to do better than Lucia Garach.

Lucia's only hope was that her father would solve everything. But she would have to wait until he arrived in Cuba or until the war ended in Spain, and he could send for her. Until Miguel entered her life, Lucia had known no man other than her teacher at Benicarlo. Whenever a boy showed any interest in her, Lucia invariably hastened to end the relationship; she tried to do the same with Miguel, but other interests were at play then; it was not easy to set him aside.

When Lolita announced that she would introduce her to a very good looking young man, Lucia replied that she did not have the slightest interest in meeting anyone, and that she intended to go to bed immediately after dinner. Lolita insisted, and the girl had to give in.

"It's a real pleasure, Miss Garach. I've often seen you when you go to my store, but you're so quiet I didn't even know your name."

"I'll leave you two to talk now; I've got to see about dinner. See how all the guests are streaming into the dining room? Dinner will be served in a minute." Large gatherings and romantic meetings excited Lolita the way liquor did others. Smiling and red-cheeked, she went into the kitchen.

"Have you been in Cuba long? Lolita tells me you're from Valencia."

"I arrived a few months ago."

"Did you come to stay?"

"I don't know. I came because of the war. My parents are still in Spain. I'll know for sure when they come. I'm a student," she said, as though that made her different from everybody else.

"Really? That's nice. What are you studying?"

"I want to be a teacher."

"If you'd like some practice, I have two nephews who are about ready to go to school. They're home, pestering my sister-in-law."

"I'd love it! If your sister-in-law doesn't mind, of course." Lucia's features softened, she looked at Miguel with a trusting glance. He had succeeded in reawakening her interest.

"Why don't you pay us a visit some time?"

On the following day the plans were finalized. Both parties liked the idea very much.

"What do you think of the girl?" Miguel asked his brother once Lucia had left.

"Well, Miguel, she's all right. She'll keep the boys busy and will take some of the pressure off my wife. Having to cook for all our clerks, she barely has any time left for—"

"I'm asking what you think of her as a woman," Miguel insisted.

"Nothing to write home about. She's pretty, yes, but very quiet. She barely talks!"

"Do you see anything seriously wrong with her?"

"One can never tell about those things the first time around, but I guess I didn't see anything basically wrong with her," he answered hesitantly. "She's not my type, of course, but then again I'm married, and I don't have to worry about such things. Why do you ask?"

"See? She's going to be my wife, and I wanted to have your opinion before making a firm decision."

"I don't know what you see in her, Miguel," Jesus objected, "I don't know what's gotten into you. Are you in love with the girl?" Miguel smiled pensively while his brother talked.

"Love has nothing to do with this whole business of marriage." He looked at his brother in the eyes. "It's the right moment, that's all. I am almost turning forty. She's single, decent, and she's here ready to marry at my asking. Love is bound to come later." That is the closest Miguel Suco came to ever falling in love.

Chapter 59

On the night the telegram arrived all four brothers gathered at Jose's store, and they shared memories of their father in a spontaneous memorial service. Jose received the news of Juan's death one and a half years after it happened. "Juan Garach died at La Morellana," the telegram said. Rosa had not been able to get word to her children before then; the war had kept her at La Morellana. In the spring of 1939, when they returned to Tirig, the first thing she did was to inform her sons of their father's death. Nobody dared touch the problem the news had created for them: who would tell Lucia?

"Do you remember how he used to put me down all the time when I was a kid? After I grew up he changed. I'd say he even loved me," Andres commented.

"He was very demanding."

"Those who are born without courage would have been better off not having been born. He always said the same thing. He had absolute trust in us," Lucas added.

"Who's going to tell Lucia?" Carolina wanted to know.

"I don't know why the fuss. She'll be told, and that's that. Lucas, as always, could not hide his dismal lack of sensitivity for other people's feelings.

"Our sister was always very close to father; he really got along with her well," Fermin remarked.

"She's looking forward to father's and mother's arrival; she's really excited about it now that she knows the war's over. I don't know how she'll react," Carolina said.

"Now, you know that if there's one thing father didn't do right in his life, was the way he brought up Lucia. She's totally useless! Instead of all those university airs, she'd be better off knowing how to cook and wash. Hell!"

"Don't get upset, Lucas. It's not her fault. Besides, she's a good girl. I heard that there's a man who has taken an interest in her. What do you all know about that?"

"Yes, he has," Jose added. "Lucia told me he has already asked her which one of us he should see about marriage."

"And what has the idiot told him?"

"She said she could not think about marriage until after father gets here, and she's finished at the university."

"The shithead!"

"Shut up, Lucas. We've got to see how we can solve this problem."

"How can we solve it? Real easy; she's got to get married, that's how. Then, it'll be her husband who'll have to worry about her. We've got to convince her to get married."

"I don't want to be involved in those things," Fermin announced.

"You may think I'm cruel, but, let's face it: each one of us has got his own business and Lucia's nothing more than a burden. The girl's twenty-six years old, for Pete's sake! She's got to get her feet on the ground and stop daydreaming. A woman's future lies in marriage and nowhere else."

"Who's going to tell her?"

"I think a woman would be better for that," Andres worried about his sister's possible reaction. "Could you do it, Carolina?"

"Don't you get Carolina involved in this. This is a Garach problem and one of us . . ."

"Lucas," she interrupted, "Andres has asked me a question, and I do think it's me who should answer it."

"You shut up; you're my wife." But Lucas' harsh order failed to impress Carolina this time.

"You are my husband, but I happen to think that Andres is right. I lived with Lucia several years; I think I can talk to her as if I were her sister or even her mother. I can't believe you've turned so calloused you'd be opposed to something as harmless as this."

Lucas was not sure he knew the meaning of the word *calloused* and did not want to acknowledge his ignorance before his brothers.

"Oh, well, do as you please," he said finally Carolina's gentle disposition proved to be a perfect match.

Chapter 60

Lucia had not yet returned from her classes when Carolina arrived at Lolita's place. Lucas' wife had spent the night up, thinking of how to break the news to her sister-in-law. Juan's death had definitely changed everything.

Lucia was surprised to see her brother's wife waiting for her at the boarding house, but did not suspect anything. She greeted her affectionately and went up to her room. It was a small bedroom, and a photograph of Juan El Morellano hung from the wall. Carolina gulped when she saw it.

"I've heard that the uncle of those boys you teach has his eyes on you, I mean, that he's in love with you, kind of."

"Yes, that's what they say, but I don't pay attention. Those things are better left alone." Lucia shruggged her shoulders and tried to put her room in order.

"Have you stopped to think he might be a good man, Lucia? Maybe he's just right for you." Carolina looked at her intently in an unsuccessful effort to make eye contactwith her sister-in-law.

"No, Carolina; I have no intentions of getting married yet. When father and mother get here, I want to finish school; that's what I really want. I'm not the type that likes to cook and wash; I want to be a teacher. But you know that; I don't want to bother you with old stories."

"That's precisely what I wanted to talk to you about, Lucia. Come, sit next to me." Once she did, Carolina took the young woman's hands.

"What?"

"About your parents." Carolina looked down hoping to find some courage to say the rest. "It's your father, Lucia." Carolina watched the girl, her facial muscles tense, her eyes grimacing in tearless crying. "Your father's dead. We got the news yesterday." Lucia did not answer; she did not change her expression or cry. She looked at Carolina with lifeless eyes. "Those things can't be helped. My father died when I was still a girl, and my mother had to bring up all of us."

Carolina did not want to say any more. Anything else would have been empty prattle. She walked up to the girl and put her arm over her shoulders. Lucia did not flinch.

"My father was the only one who really loved me," she finally sighed after a long pause.

"Your mother loves you, Lucia. I love you, we all love you. Don't talk like that. You're a fortunate girl, after all. God has sent you a good man, honest and hardworking, who wants to marry you."

"I don't love him; I don't want to marry him."

"Think it over. Believe me, I've been thinking about this all night long, and this man—what is his name?"

"Miguel."

"Miguel is good for you. Sometimes marriage comes first and then love. Have you talked to him about your plans? He might even want to help you go to college and do all those things you want to do. Good men like him, like your brothers, don't come by easily. There are certain opportunities in life one can't pass up. You should think things out."

"Do you suppose Miguel would be willing to let me go to college?"

"I don't know him, but I don't think it would be unfair for you to ask him. It's your only way. Then, when your mother comes, you could bring her into a happy home and have children."

"No, Carolina; no children, no children." Lucia wept for the first time that afternoon. "I couldn't face it; it frightens me."

"Come, come; don't be upset now. You've got to look to the future with confidence. Your father's dead, but I'm sure he's with you in spirit. He'll help you, you'll see. Look, I want you to come home with me and spend a few days with us."

"Lucas won't like it."

"Lucas won't be home. He told me today he's got to go to Santiago de Cuba with that gentleman from the business. You'll stay with me until he comes back, and then you can do what you want."

On the following morning, Miguel went to see Lucia at her brother's house.

"Carolina, Carolina," she called out, frightened. "Here he comes!"

"Who's coming? Why are you so pale?"

"It's Miguel, Miguel Suco. He's across the street, headed this way. What do I do now? I'm sure he heard about father and that's why he's coming. What do I do now, Carolina?"

"Come, have a sip of water and calm down." Someone knocked at the door. "You were right; here he is. Look at me, Lucia, and listen to what I'm going to tell you. Let him speak first and then you explain to him the same thing you've explained to me so many times. See how he reacts to it, and then answer him whatever you think is best for you. Don't throw away your future, Lucia; sometimes things seem worse than they actually are. If he's the way you've described him to me, you will be happy with him." Neither of them understood that the 1930s was no time for a woman to plan out her life carefully.

Chapter 61

Candido took Rosa to Barcelona to board the ship that would carry her to Cuba. The answer to the telegram which told of Juan's death had been a letter from Jose in which he announced his impending marriage and asked his mother to go to Cuba at once. The barber saw to everything and stayed with her until she was in her cabin, ready for the voyage.

"Well, Rosita, I don't think you'll be needing anything else until your children come to pick you up at the pier in Cuba." Candido smiled at his longtime friend.

"How could I ever thank you, Candido?" Rosa's honest, caring expression had not changed through the years. Her hair pulled back in a bun lacked the luster of before, but her eyes were just as vivacious and warm as ever.

"You don't have to thank me."

"You forget the many times you've helped me. I'm going away today, but I'll never forget all that you've done for me." There were no tears left in Rosa's eyes, but her heart beat faster, foreboding the last goodbye between two good friends.

"You won't really go away. We have many years of common memories, Balbina, Juan, you and me . . . You may go to Cuba, but . . . look what you've done . . . I'm crying."

"I won't be able to write to you all. I still don't know how. I'll ask Lucia to do it for me, maybe she will."

"We'll write to you. Don't look so solemn, Rosa, we aren't about to die. God bless you. You are . . .you've always been an angel. God will repay you in a few days when you are with your children and your granddaughter once more. It'll be beautiful, Rosita, you'll see, you won't even have time to remember us," Candido burst out laughing.

They fell silent. Candido and Rosa held each other, and their silence spoke eloquently.

"Good-bye, Rosita; may God bless you." He pulled himself away from the woman and began to walk down the hall, turning around at times to wave a final farewell. "Don't tell the boys you saw me cry; I don't want them to laugh at their godfather!"

Rosa closed her cabin door and greeted the unknown with a deep sigh. There was a mirror behind the door. She looked at herself in it and wondered if she was the same woman who had been born in Cati, the daughter of Fermin and Andrea; the same girl that Juan El Morellano had met when he went to town to sell some sheep. The *masia*, Vicenta, Zacarias, Don Poli, Tirig, Charco Street, it all seemed so very far just then.

By the time Rosa arrived in Cuba, late in nineteen thirty-nine, Andres and Fermin were the only Garachs still single. In September Lucia had accepted Miguel's proposal and married him. Jose and Milagros got married in November.

It was Lucia who had the entire family worried. Before they were married, Miguel had agreed that the girl should finish her studies. His unexpected agreement made Lucia regain the hopes crashed by Juan's death.

But Miguel changed after the wedding. When Lucia brought up the subject of going back to college, her husband told her that she had plenty to do around the house to worry about such things.

She began to wither, little by little. First she would spend long hours sitting on a chair and looking out the window; when people talked to her, she seemed not to hear them. Carolina found her in bed one afternoon. Sick? No, just tired and sad. Another day, Lolita, the Catalan woman, found her crying and calling for her father incessantly. Miguel tried to console her, but it was to no avail. When he left, Lucia got out through a window and began to run. She was dressed in a nightgown. Some neighbors who saw her called Miguel and then Lucas, who took her to the Covadonga clinic. One week before Rosa's arrival, she was released from the hospital, thinner and more dispirited and dejected than ever.

Chapter 62

A tugboat nudged the huge liner towards its berth. The passengers watched the maneuver on deck, as they said good-bye to their recently made friends on board. Rosa Garach had had to wait almost sixty years before being able to enjoy fourteen days of her life on her own. She had left back in Spain that fear to speak, to move, that had ruled her entire life. She had recovered, to her amazement, the joy of waking up in the morning not knowing what was in store for her, or of smiling and talking freely, not worrying about someone else's disapproval. No, she dared not tell anyone, but as much as she wanted to hold her children close to her, she did not wish for her newly found independence to come to an end as the ship entered Havana harbor. But it did.

The Cuban sun shone with passion that afternoon of Rosa's arrival. The tugboats greeted her transatlantic liner while the deep horn welcomed the beginning of a new life for Rosa. She could not understand why everyone smiled and let her pass when they saw her. She imagined people saw in her an old woman in need of help, and she could not stop and tell them that she felt younger than she had in a long time.

Fermin, Andres, and Jose fought like children for Rosa's first kiss; they had seen her at the same time she saw them. She was wearing black, in mourning for their father's death, but she had cut her hair and looked younger than ususal.

Her sons were so immersed in their fight to see who kissed their mother first that she embraced Milagros.

"Of course, I recognized you! I'm so happy to see you again! I met you when you were still a little girl, long before Jose and you ever thought of getting married."

"Just a moment, madam; your son would like to see you," Jose said teasingly.

"Carolina, is this the girl? Holy Madonna de l'Avella! She's grown so much I could hardly recognize her. Milagritos was about her age when I saw her last. Look at her now!"

"And soon to be a mother, unless my arithmetic fails me," added Jose.

The kisses and embraces were not over yet when Rosa, looking about surprised, finally asked: "Where's Lucia? Where's my girl?"

All lowered their heads, not knowing how to broach the subject. Milagros was the first to react. She took her mother-in-law by the arm and started to walk.

"She had to stay home, Rosa. We're all going there now. It'll be a few minutes by car. Did I tell you that your son Jose bought himself a car? Come, I'll show it to you."

"Is she expecting?" Rosa asked, thinking of Lucia.

"No, it isn't that. Don't worry, it's nothing serious."

Nothing made the unfortunate woman smile during the ride. She was not amused by Jose's poor driving techniques or by the fact that they were sitting like "canned sardines" in the back seat, as Milagros put it.

After half an hour and quite a few lurches and sudden stops by Jose, the car came to a definite stop and Milagros announced that they had arrived. Rosa got off the automobile almost shaking.

A young, clumsy-looking girl opened the door and asked them to come in. She did not smile or show them any courtesy; she barely informed them that Lucia was in her bedroom and disappeared into the kitchen. Rosa walked slowly. Unconsciously, she smoothed her skirt on the spot where her apron would have normally rested and reached up behind her head, where her braids had been not too long before. Milagros opened the bedroom door and amidst the darkness and the shadows that poured out, they could see Lucia, motionless, her hands folded across her chest. The room smelled of camphor and disinfectants, but it was the sight of her daughter that really impressed Rosa. Lucia was pale and lifeless amidst the white sheets. The others could be heard talking. Miguel's voice was welcoming them and asking for his mother-in-law. Rosa ignored everything but her daughter and sat on the edge of the bed, softly caressing the young woman's cold forehead and hands.

"Lucia, darling, Lucia, *hija*, wake up; it's your mother. I just arrived." Her voice trembled.

Lucia opened her eyes but closed them again. She reopened them and looked around the room, startled, as if looking for something.

"Mother," she muttered looking at her and making no attempt to hold or kiss her. Instead, she turned her head the other way. One of the girl's hands came to rest on her mother's knees, and Rosa held it tenderly.

"I was dreaming of you, Mother," she said at last. "I could see you clearly. You walked through the door, just as you did now, but father was with you. In my dream, everything they've told me was just a dream, and when I woke up, I saw father next to you."

"It wasn't a dream, darling. Father died, but you mustn't think any more about it. You father's been dead over a year."

"You don't know, mother, how many times I've thought that when I saw you, it would all turn out to be a mistake, a nightmare. Something told me my father was coming back."

Rosa looked at her, not quite knowing what to do or what to say. Milagros slipped out of the room, leaving the two of them alone. They were together for a long time. Rosa stroked her daughter's hand with all her tenderness; Lucia just cried silently. A bond that was some twenty years too late had finally been formed.

Chapter 63

Rosa always liked to spend several days at each of her children's home around the birthday of her grandchildren. The day before Lina's fourteenth birthday, Rosa arrived at her son's home. Lucas had left; he would not be back in time for the small family gathering Carolina had planned, but he had bought the girl a big gift to make up for his absence.

"You see, mother, how improved Lucia is, and how well she's feeling?" Carolina's blue eyes glanced distractedly out the window as she was talking to her mother-in-law in the dining room waiting for her daughter to come home from school

"Yes, but she was really sick, Carolina, really sick." Rosa was mending socks, so she spoke with her face down, looking up once in a while at her daughter-in-law.

"Well, it looks as if the treatment has done her a lot of good." Carolina's gentle manners and innate kindness inspired peace.

"Yes, she's better, but all she does is lock herself up in her room and spends most of the time sleeping. Lucia had an awful temper when she was a girl, and I thought she was going to turn out different. I don't know," she admitted, shrugging her shoulders, "so many things happen that I don't understand. Well, at least I have to thank the Virgin for giving her back her health; I was afraid she would be sick with nerves forever, *Mare de Deu!*" she exclaimed making the sign of the cross to ward off any unexpected misfortune.

"Wait, mother, there's someone knocking at the door. It can't be Lina; it's still too early. Let's see who it is."

Rosa could not see from her seat who was at the door when Carolina opened and said "Good afternoon."

"Yes, I'm Carolina. Yes. I'm Mrs. Garach. You didn't recognize me you say? Have you seen me before? Wait, wait; your face does look very familiar. I've seen you before. You? You worked at my house? What house? Before I was married? Cachita! Cachita Montero! Well, this is quite a surprise. Come on in, Cachita, come in! I'm so happy to see you! please do come in." Carolina locked arms with Cachita Montero and so led her inside her home. One's white skin contrasted the other's caramel complexion. One's composure clashed with the other's vivaciousness.

Cachita Montero had changed, and that was why Carolina had not recognized her initially. Many signs were still present of what had been a most beautiful woman in her time and class, but she looked weathered. She was dressed plainly and had a puzzled expression on her face. She went into the house toying nervously with her pocketbook; she was obviously distressed. The presence of Lucas' wife belittled her; she wanted to turn around and run from the house or to think up an excuse for the true reason for her visit, but only the truth made any sense at that time.

"Come in, please; make yourself at home. Cachita, I'd like you to meet my mother-in-law. Mother, this is Cachita Montero. She used to work at my mother's house when I was still single. It's been, what? . . . almost twenty years since I last saw you. How have you been?" Carolina asked her to sit down. Cachita was on the verge of tears; fortunately, however, a surge of internal energy transfigured her and gave her the strength she needed.

"Well, Miss Carolina, all right, getting along," Cachita just could not sit down.

"Tell me, do you have any children? Are you married?" Carolina was obviously pleased to see her old servant and friend.

"Yes. I have two boys. Well, I guess you could say the're grown men already. They're taller than me." And she motioned with her hand above the head, indicating how tall they were. "Now, as to being married, no, I'm not. I live with my sons and with an old lady who's been very good to me. Yes sir, since my aunt died—may she rest in peace—she's been like a mother to me. I work a lot, ma'am. I'm a cook at one of those big mansions in Miramar. Today is Monday, my day off, and that's why I've come to see you," she added apologetically.

"But sit down, dear," Carolina said affectionately. "I'm so happy to see you again, Cachita. You were like family to us. You're really looking fine; you even talk differently."

"Well, something is bound to rub off on you after working so many years in Miramar, Miss Carolina," she smiled for the first time since her arrival.

Suddenly, neither woman knew what else to say.

"I've got a very beautiful daughter. You'll meet her; she's just about due home from school," Carolina said at last.

"Look, Miss Carolina, I'd like to talk to you. To you alone, no offense to the lady. She's very nice and kind, but I don't know her, and what I came here to tell you is for you only." Rosa started to get up, but her daughter-in-law intervened.

"This lady is as if she were my own mother. You can tell me whatever you wish in front of her; I keep no secrets from her. Anything you tell me won't go beyond this room; is anything the matter with you? Are you sick?" In her eyes there was sincere concern.

"No, it isn't anything like that at all, ma'am, St. Barbara be praised. Look, it's just that the time has come that I can do no more; I can't stand injustices. I don't know whether I've done right or wrong in knocking at your door and bothering the two of you, but . . ."

"Now, Cachita, be more explicit, because I can't understand you. What injustices are you talking about? What's wrong with you, dear?"

"It's my son, Miss Carolina. He's a fine boy, he is. He's almost twenty and a high school graduate." Her pride and satisfaction in speaking of her son made her smile for the first time.

"Then things can't be all that bad. There's no need for you to get so upset."

"Yes it is. You know, he went to school at the Marist Brothers on a scholarship. They really loved him there, and one of the brothers tried to help him get into the university. He couldn't get a scholarship, I don't rightly know why. But it so happens that this brother had some contacts in the United States, at an American college. My son was admitted there. The brother made a few phone calls, sent my Juanito's transcript and three months ago they answered him and told him he had been admitted on a full scholarship."

"My God, Cachita, this is great. What could possibly worry you with a son like that?"

"Miss Carolina, he can't go—he has no money to pay for his living expenses over there. And I don't think it's fair he should have to let an opportunity like this pass by just because I, on a cook's salary, can't help him. You see? I've got another boy to take care of."

"And how can I help you?"

"Miss Carolina," she sobbed, "you can't imagine how it hurts me to have to tell you these things because you are a good woman. Here you are, trying to cheer me up and holding my hand when you should kick me out of your house."

"Heavens, Cachita! Why would I do such a thing?"

"Juancito, my son, is a Garach too, like your daughter, like my son Alberto. They all have the same father. Many years ago, your husband was with me. And I was stupid enough not to show him the door, which is what he deserved."

Rosa was growing red in the face and seemed about to explode.

"Do you know what you're saying?" Carolina, ever calm and controlled, asked softly.

"I swear to you, Miss Carolina. And if it had not been for that no good husband of yours, I would've never told you, but my son's got to get ahead in life. It isn't his fault that I made a mistake and that his father doesn't want to have anything to do with him."

"Have you told Lucas any of this?"

"He won't let me. I call him at his office, I've even gone there, but nobody helps me, nobody wants to tell me where he is. Juanito has even waited outside for him and nothing. He doesn't want to see me and he doesn't want to see him either."

"Are you sure that your son is my husband's child?" Carolina let go of Cachita's hand and began to pace the living room.

"Look, Miss Carolina, I brought along my son's birth certificate. His name is Juan Garach." Rosa shuddered when she heard her husband's name. "He acknowledged him and gave him his name. I was able to get that much out of him. Things were different back then," she said wistfully, "but now and with all his businesses there's no way to get to him."

The woman took the paper Cachita offered, read it, gave it back to her, and resumed her pacing.

"Does you son have to be at that college by a set date?" Carolina closed her eyes for seconds at a time; the unexpected news had truly shaken her.

"The thirtieth. It expires at the end of the month. If he's not there by then, he'll lose everything."

"Tell him to go and see his father a week from today. You've got to give time for him to come back and for me to talk to him. You son shall have the money he needs, I promise you that. You're right; it isn't fair. Although I would've preferred to leave your relationship with my husband as a mere rumor, which is all it was for me before, I don't blame you for coming here. I would probably have done the same thing if it had been my daughter. Now, I'm going to ask you for something in exchange for this favor you ask of me," she stood in front of Cachita looking directly in her eyes. This transformed Carolina was determined and strong; she had lost some of her kindness but was filled with a profound sense of fairness.

"Anything you say, Miss Carolina."

"You must never again see my husband or have intimate relations with him. Hear me well, Cachita, you must never see my husband on personal terms again."

"That's the way it's already been for some years," Cachita confessed with a strange mixture of pride and regret.

"If he comes looking for you, kick him out of your house. I wouldn't want Carolina, my daughter, to find out about this side of her father's life, I wouldn't want her to feel ashamed of him; at least not until she's old enough to understand these things."

"I swear to you, believe me; I swear to you that he will never again enter my house," and as if to stress her oath even more, she kissed the cross she formed with her thumb and her index finger, falling to her knees before Carolina.

"Get up," Carolina warned. "You don't need to do that. I wouldn't like my daughter to come in and see you like that."

The girl's voice relieved the tense situation that existed in the living room. Carolina helped Cachita to her feet and went to open the door for her daughter. The girl hugged her mother.

"How was your day in school today, Lina?"

"Oh, Mom, Marisol will be fifteen in a few months, and she told me they're going to give her a big party at—" She fell silent when she saw her mother had company.

"Come, darling, you can tell me all about that later. Right now I'd like you to meet a dear friend of mine, from the days I was still single, long before you were born. Cachita," she said in her usual affectionate way, "this is my daughter Carolina. Carolina, I'd like you to meet Cachita Montero."

It would take a lifetime for Cachita to forget that moment.

Chapter 64

"Smile!" The photographer stepped aside from the camera and repeated: "Smile! ¡Sonrían! Listen, little girl, look at me and smile. Come on, the one with the nicest smile will get a lollipop, how's that? You're also in on the game, *Abuelita.* One doesn't turn seventy-five every day, and we should leave a nice memento of this for posterity. Now, freeze!"

The Garach family smiled together. They were celebrating their mother's birthday, and as she smiled from the center of the photograph, Rosa wondered why the photographer insisted so much that she smile. That's all she had done since sunrise. Seventy-five years old! Five children and six grandchildren! She never tired of counting her blessings. And just as the light flashed in her eyes, she remembered she had eight, not six, grandchildren. Two were missing, the sons of that poor woman she had met at Lucas' house long before. One of those boys was the only one of her grandsons to be called after her husband: Juan Garach. She would have liked to meet them, especially today.

"Now, one with just the sons and the daughter. Right, like that, all seated on the sofa, the way they were before. All the daughters and the son-in-law, please move aside. The grandchildren too!" The photographer was not a very patient man, and large groups like this one made him sweat for every penny he earned. "Not you, honey. Little girl, I'm telling you to move aside and leave your uncles and your grandmother alone. Hey, kid, move it!"

Natalia, Jose's youngest daughter, was about six years old. Her eyes were big and round, and they looked at the photographer as if she had not understood a single word he had said.

"Does this girl speak Spanish?" he asked in frustration, wiping the perspiration off his forehead and neck. He was trying, unsuccessfully, to attract somebody's attention. "Ay, that coffee!" he sighed reacting to the pungent smell of freshly brewed Cuban coffee. "Can someone get me a cup?" he begged.

"Pssst! Natalia, get out of there. If your mother sees you . . ." Another girl, slightly older than Natalia, was calling her. "*Pssst!*

Natalia!" Their olive colored skin and big brown were proof of their Mediterranean descent although they had never seen La Morellana.

"Who's this girl's mother?" Even those who were to be in the photograph paid no attention to him. Finally, Jose realized what was happening; there was a little in his daughter of the mischievous little boy who roamed the streets in Tirig.

"Milagros, Milagros; get our daughter out of here; she refuses to obey the photographer," Jose yelled to his wife understanding quite well the girl's temperament.

"Natalia!" her mother called. "You come here right now unless you want me to pull you out by the ears. Natalia!" The girl did as she was asked and gave the photographer a mean look as she walked away.

"Carolina, look at *Abuelita*. She looks so happy!" Milagros remarked once her daughter had complied with her command.

"This is a big day for her. She's been ironing that dress since she got up this morning at the crack of dawn. Yesterday I took her to the beauty parlor and you should've seen her getting her nails done for the first time in her life!"

"Juan Andres!" Norma's voice boomed. She was Andres' wife and was concerned that their son might provoke a catastrophe. "Get away! If you knock down this man's camera he won't be able to take any more pictures tonight." The boy was on all fours, trying to crawl through the tripod's legs taking advantage of the man's absence. He had gone to tilt Lucia's head to the right angle.

The family had already had dinner and was now feasting intermitently on dozens of *pastelitos de guayaba* and *dulces de almendras* which were spread on the dining room table. They had unanimously decided to have the party at Lucas and Carolina's house, which was the most spacious. Lucas could not conceal his pride; he had recently moved to Miramar, a fashionable, high-class Havana neighborhood, and this was the right opportunity to show off his new home.

"Leave the girl alone!" Milagros jumped up when she saw Juan Andres, Andres' son, pulling on her daughter's ponytail. "She's the youngest. Pepe, Pepito, son, go out to the garden and take care of your sister. Will you do that for me, please? I don't know where this girl gets her energy from; she's always doing something. I'm glad she's starting school in September. She's going to first grade, you know, Asuncion," Milagros said to Fermin's wife.

"Rosi's not like that at all; she's very quiet. Look at her, sitting over there. I don't want her to go outside; it's damp, and she might catch another cold. I already told her that if she came down with a sore throat, I'd have to clean out the back of her throat with methylene blue, and she's terrified of the very name of it." Asuncion had married Fermin eight years before, and Rosi was born exactly nine months after the wedding. By that time the whole family knew that Asuncion did not really know how to make shirts. The inheritance had never come through either.

"What school is Rosi going to?"

"It's a neighborhood school, not far from home. It isn't bad, and it's convenient."

"Asuncion, you shouldn't skimp on your daughter's education. That girl should go to a school where she can learn English."

"It can't be, Milagros; all those schools are very far away, and Rosi would never stand the long bus ride. Maybe later when she's older. Anyway, why should she learn English? We only speak Spanish in Cuba; it would be useless."

The photographer's voice was heard again.

"Now, each of the families, one by one. The gentleman who owns the house first. Mr. Garach . . ." The four brothers turned around at once; the poor man was ready to give up. "No! I mean, Mr. Lucas Garach. Come, please, and bring your wife and family. We'll take these photographs outside; it's cooler," he said, fanning himself desperately with a sheet of paper.

Carolina went to find her daughter, and the three of them followed the photographer to the spot he chose. Lina, as her mother still called her, was twenty-six years old and her father's child in many ways. She had gone off to college in the United States and had returned six years later.

"¡*Abuelita, Abuelita!* A telegram! There's a man with a telegram at the door!"

"Bring it here, Miguelito," Andres said. "I bet it's from Candido and Balbina; they never forget your birthday, mother."

Andres kissed the old lady and helped her get up to go where Milagros and Asuncion were talking. The group had broken up; they were talking in pairs while the children ran among the grown-ups and the maid—another sign of progress by the Garachs of Miramar—did her best to take the coffee and pastries all around the room.

"Mama!" Natalia ran into the living room from the garden. "Rosi says *Abuelita* doesn't love me. Well, she says she loves me a little, but she loves her and Miguelito more." The girl clung to her mother's knees, whimpering. Milagros cut short her conversation with Asuncion and bent over to see what was the matter with her daughter.

"Let's see what's happening to my girl; she's crying like when she was a baby." Natalia hugged her mother, who smiled as she wiped off her tears. Actually, a combination of sleep and exhaustion was more responsible for her crying than Rosi's comments. "What happened, darling? Stop crying and tell me."

"Rosi told me that *Abuelita* doesn't love me, that she loves her better and that that's the reason why she spends more time at her house than at mine. She says that's why her name is Rosi, like *Abuelita*, and mine is Nataliaaaaa," she continued to cry.

"Don't get like that, Natalia. Go on, kiss your *Abuelita*, and you'll see how she hugs and kisses you back. Go on, go on," she said. Nudged by her mother, Natalia walked up to Rosa.

"*Abuelita*," Milagros called out loud enough for her mother-in-law to hear her and notice the little girl on the way.

"Come, Natalia, come with me. Come, and they'll take our picture together," Rosa said. Natalia did not have to be asked twice. When she realized they were asking her to pose with her grandmother, she ran to the old lady and hugged her, all the while flashing a victorious smile at Rosi. Then, it was Rosi's turn to cry. Everyone in the living room began to laugh when Rosa had to hold the two girls. Juan Andres, who did not want to be left out, began to pout.

"Paco, Paco; come quick! Take a picture of them like this; it's so cute!" Carolina shouted to the photographer. Paco came in panting; he looked as though he had been working for a year without any break at all. He was exhausted. But he was able to catch Rosa as she bent down, holding her three youngest grandchildren. While her two cousins were crying, Natalia continued to smile.

"Children are a lot of fun! There's no controlling their reactions; they do things so naturally, one can't help but laugh. Isn't that right, Lucas?"

"I've never liked children very much, Andres; they're a real pain sometimes. I'm glad that mine is already a grown woman."

"And the others are grown men," Andres added.

"Yes, I know; they too," Lucas repeated, giving his brother an icy stare. "How's Alberto doing? Juan works with me, and I see him every day, but I haven't seen Alberto in ages."

"If you drop by my bookstore you can see him whenever you like. He's been working with me for several years now. He's a smart boy; I'm very fortunate in having him to help me."

"What does he do there?" Lucas was curious.

"He and I take care of the business. He knows a lot; he's always reading and wants to be on top of things. In my business, that's what counts."

"Have you heard from Cachita?"

"Norma and I have been by to see her once in a while. She's doing fine. Her sons love her very much. Alberto lives with her and doesn't let her work any more."

"Juan's a real smart cookie. That boy has some future ahead of him," Lucas said proudly. "He works hard and does things right. I couldn't do without him at the warehouse."

"I heard he got married," Andres asked in a low voice, afraid that someone else might be listening.

"Yes, he married a girl from a nice family. He got married in the United States, while he was going to school over there."

"Tell him to come by and see me some time; he used to love me very much when he was a boy. Will you tell him that for me?"

Rosa was across the living room rocking her granddaughter to sleep. From her vantage point she saw Andres calling Milagros over. As she looked at her eldest son, she remembered the many times she had been told he was useless, that he would never be good at anything. If Juan could see him now! A hard-working man, the owner of his own business; happily married and the father of a fine boy.

"Sing, *Abuelita*, sing to me," Natalia begged her, opening one of her eyes. "I go to sleep better that way."

"I want to talk to you about Norma, Milagros," Andres explained to his sister-in-law making sure that they were not being overheard.

"What's wrong?"

"There's nothing wrong with her; at least not with her health if that's what you're thinking. The problem is that she's getting herself into certain things that I don't like at all."

"What kind of things do you mean?"

"Political things. There's no reasoning with her. I have asked her to drop all that; if not for my sake, then at least for the boy's."

"But, what is she actually doing?"

"Well, let me tell you. You know she's a professor at the university. She loves her students, and they adore her. Some of those closest to her are plotting against Batista. They plant bombs and do as they please. I've hid several of them at home. Right now we have a box full of explosives in our house," Andres said with alarm.

"And what would you want me to do?" asked Milagros confused.

"I want you to talk to her and make her realize that this is all a big mistake. If they catch us, we'll wind up in jail or with a bullet in the head, dumped by a trash can. She pays no attention to me or to her parents. I want you to talk to her when the time is right, and see if she quits doing these things. I'm afraid something may happen to her. I'm tired of telling Norma, but she won't listen to me. Since you're a woman, and about her same age, maybe you'll be able to get through to her."

"We'll see what she says. I promise you I'll talk to her, but I can't promise that it'll do any good. I'll talk to her as soon as I get a chance; I'll call her tomorrow morning."

Jose interrupted the conversation to ask his wife to say good-bye; it was getting late, and they had to get back home. One by one, the Garachs gathered their families and thanked their hosts for their hospitality. Carolina saw each family to the garden gate and asked her sisters-in-law to take with them some of the food left over from the party.

Rosa was by the gate, waving good-bye to all her children. She went back towards the house, where she watched the headlights of the last car disappear around the corner. Rosa breathed in deeply the scent of the Cuban night that lay before her. Lina and her father went inside the house at once; Carolina waited for her mother-in-law by the steps leading up to the front porch. Rosa returned to the house slowly; she felt as though her soul had broken into many fragments, scattered about by the warm Caribbean breeze that enveloped her. Her shoes glistened by the light of the lamp post next to the door. The stockings that

Asuncion—or was it Milagros?—had given her some years back, discreetly covered the varicose veins that had invaded her legs. Her hair, more grey than black, graciously lined her face. The dress—fine dark blue with a lace collar—was impeccable and made her quite distant from the peasant from Tirig that ironed her family's clothes and baked their bread until very late at night. Filled with hope, as always, she looked up to the sky. The stars were out, and she smiled; the stars, wherever they might be, were always an inspiration and a source of strength for her.

"Come, mother, let's go in. It's damp, and we don't want to wake up tomorrow with a cold or a sore throat."

"I'm coming; I'm coming."

As she began to climb the steps, Carolina climbed down and held her by the arm to help her up.

"Thank you, Carolina; you're always so kind to me."

"Now, now, you deserve it; you're the best looking seventy-five-year-old mother I've ever seen."

Once inside the house, Rosa began to pick up the plates and glasses that were scattered all over the living room.

"What are you doing?"

"Carolina, we have to pick up all these things from the party so that the house will be tidy and neat in the morning."

"Oh, no, we don't. You come with me. That is what Rita and Zoila are here for. It's past eleven, and you have to go to bed and have a good night's sleep."

She let Carolina lead her to her bedroom. Instinctively she reached with one hand for the braids that no longer existed; with the other, she tried to smooth an apron that was no longer needed. No one realized that Rosa's seventy-fifth birthday marked the end of an era for most of the Garachs, including Rosa herself.

PART VI

I had weathered more than one storm in my lifetime, but I did not fully understand what troubled my children as the nineteen fifties drew to a close. I had already seen so much that I worried little, certain that no evil could last forever. Nevertheless, television brought out what I had never seen in the other troubles which Cuba had experienced before. For one, the cries of paredon were growing more frequent and alarming.

I wondered what the people asked for when they repeated that word over and over again. Miguelito told me, I remember. He said that the people asked that those who opposed the revolution be shot by a firing squad. This was not the only thing that the Revolution did. They showed the men in jail right before the television cameras. It was so that people could see what happened to those who plotted against the government.

I could not help feeling sorry for the families of those poor people, so I often found myself muttering, May the Holy Madonna de l'Avella protect them . . . and protect us! I heard everyone say that as long as we didn't get involved in politics, everything would be all right. But that was nonsense next to the destruction that I saw the Revolution leave in its path.

I could not understand then why Andres and Norma went on unexplained trips so often; I couldn't see the connection between them and Jose, who had begun to find business far away from Cuba. I found it odd that Lucas would want to get passports for me and all his family. Everyone seemed to be going in different directions, and I felt foolish wanting to ask them to stop. The Garach family seemed to me to be doomed to wonder like gypsies. I did not realize at the time the strength of dictators; the push of injustice. I wondered what made so many people so devoted to Fidel Castro, and I remember once confiding to the stars that I saw a devilish shine in his eyes when he spoke. The stars didn't tell; neither did I, and the unavoidable became history.

Chapter 65

Miguelito could not start college on time because the country's political situation forced the University of Havana to close. He told his parents that he wanted to go to college abroad, but it was no use. His father said no, and Miguel Suco was stubborn. The boy appealed to his mother and received the same answer as always; his father knew what was best for him, and if he obeyed him, everything would be all right.

In his short life, young Miguel Suco had lived in what he often described to himself as premature death. His parents provided food, clothing and shelter but were never ready to show him the beauty that life can offer primarily because they saw little beauty in life themselves. Miguelito had gone to the best school in Havana; nothing had been spared for his education, but it was there, at the expensive prep school that he learned to experience misery and disappointment. Most of his friends belonged to Havana's most exclusive social clubs. They went to parties, drove cars and travelled. Although Lucia's family could have afforded such pleasures, Miguel, the father, thought them superficial and unimportant. As the fifties drew to a close and the sixties began, Miguelito's friends, upon graduating from high school, left for prominent colleges in the United States, just like Miguelito's first cousin, Jose's son, Pepe, had done the year before.

"Frivolous and unnecessary," Miguel had commented when he heard of Pepe's departure. "There are good universities right here in Cuba," had been his verdict. He would not even allow himself to be convinced by his son's pleas.

Lucia, with an insensitive spirit calloused by years of tranquilizers, never connected with her son's feelings and supported her husband, thus nourishing even more Miguelito's resentment and bitterness.

Rosa did not understand why her daughter refused to intervene on the boy's behalf, but it was not for her to give an opinion; she could neither read nor write, they usually reminded her, and, besides, at her children's homes, she had to listen and say as little as possible. When she saw the cavalier manner in which Lucia dismissed the matter that so worried Miguelito, she went to the wash sink to finish washing some garments left over from the previous day. Talking to herself where nobody could hear her, she thought of a plan.

Late that night, Rosa sat by her chest of drawers. She opened the last drawer and pulled out a small bundle of yellowed newspaper pages. Miguel and Lucia had retired for the evening; the hallway connecting the bedrooms was indirectly lit by the dim light from Rosa's night lamp and Miguelito's reading lamp on his desk.

"Miguelito, son, are you asleep?" Rosa's voice and her gentle rap on her grandson's bedroom door were barely audible.

"Who is it?" he asked from the inside.

"It's me, *Abuelita* Rosa; may I come in?"

"Yes, come in, *Abuelita*." There was something very tender about the old lady in her pink flannel sleeping gown, her hair under a hairnet, her blue eyes sparkling with life.

"Look at what I've brought you," she said as she untied the bundle she held in her hands. "This may help you some. Come, look." She peeled off the newspaper pages one by one. As she smiled, the wrinkles around her eyes became more numerous. "You know that your uncles always give me some money on my birthday, on Mother's Day, and all. I always thought it'd be better to save it for a rainy day. Here, it's yours," she said, placing everything on the desk. "It's yours to go away and study. Take it, go to school at that place where your cousin is. Count it. According to my count, there is twenty times one hundred *pesos*. I don't know how much that school costs, but this is a start, don't you think?" Proudly, she finished untying the bundle and showed her grandson her entire fortune, the bills neatly arranged in groups of one hundred dollars, wrapped in pieces of cloth and reeking of perfumed soap.

The boy looked at his grandmother in disbelief. She was glowing; no one could have denied that she had just accomplished one of the worthiest feats of her seventy-eight years. Neither knew what else to say. It was Rosa who broke the silence.

"Well! count them again; I may be mistaken, and there may not be as much as I've told you," she insisted trying to rescue her grandson from his own reality.

Chapter 66

Norma, Andres's wife, looked pale and hesitant as she walked into her husband's bookstore. She had the feeling that she was to blame for what had just happened; she feared it might adversely affect her family. Andres Garach was happy to see her, but realized immediately that something was wrong. He led his wife to the office he and Alberto, Lucas' illegitimate son by Cachita Montero, shared on the second floor. Norma looked guilty when she sat across from her husband.

The boy? He was at school. They had come after he had left. Polito Cruz, two professors and five other persons. All of them apparently very decent and reputable people, the best one could expect to find, but all of them really involved in counterrevolutionary activities. They thought the situation was very serious; they claimed Fidel was a communist. The agrarian reform was just the beginning of worse things to come.

"What do they want?" Andres interrupted.

"The first thing is to gather weapons; that's why they came."

"Norma, that's very risky, it's not like hiding some kid at home. Weapons haven't got legs to run; if they should find them, that'll be the end of us."

"I know it, Andres, and that's why I want this to be our joint decision," she replied excitedly, lighting a cigarette.

This type of problem had dogged Andres throughout his life: first, the struggle during Machado's reign, then the hiding of revoultionaries during Batista's years. This, however, was far more delicate; Castro's surveillance of the Cuban people was growing more strict by the day. Norma answered that they had to help for precisely that reason: the olive green regime could not be allowed to root itself in power. Andres realized the impotence of the counterrevolutionary movement quicker than his wife; he could never make her understand the truth.

"Darling, we should stay out of this for our son's sake," Andres feared what could happen if they joined the counter-revolution. What will happen if anything should go wrong? Fidel won't last long; Cubans like the good life too much to go for his revolutionary committees and all those absurd ideas. Cubans like to talk, express their opinions, criticize the government; they won't allow themselves to be ruled by just one man, regardless of how charismatic he may be."

"They're only asking us for our house in Tarara to stock the weapons there. They wouldn't have anything to do with our apartment; we wouldn't be directly involved."

"Norma, we've got to be careful. If it should come to our having to leave the country, we shouldn't do anything that might jeopardize our going away."

"How could we possibly go to a foreign country after having failed to defend that which is ours? We've got to keep this damned man from extending his network of informers across the island. They're talking about taking children away from their parents; there are so many horrible rumors going around that I don't know how to say no to these people."

"Well, all right, we'll do it, on the condition that you don't refuse to get our passports so we can leave the country if we have to."

"Perhaps, if everyone cooperates, we won't have to take such a drastic step. A united front could fight anything . . . maybe . . ."

She seemed calmer; she leaned over to Andres and held his hand.

"Thank you, love. I'll do as you say; I'll apply for our passports today, to please you. But we won't have to use them, you'll see; we won't have to leave Cuba. This whole thing will end as quickly as it began."

Norma was about to kiss her husband when the door opened; it was Alberto. His face told them that something was wrong.

"I'm sorry, Andres, I'm sorry, Norma." The Garach couple looked at his startled face; the young man closed the door behind him and twisted his mouth.

"What is it?" Andres asked.

"There's a man from State Security out there; he's looking for you, and he says it's urgent."

Chapter 67

At Jose and Milagros' home, early in nineteen sixty, Rosa immediately sensed the anxiety that hung over the household when she went to spend some time with them. She found Milagros crying every time she went to look for her. There was a sense of journey, of going far, of leaving everything behind. No one spoke to her directly, but she sensed the end of stability and permanence.

"*¡Abuelita!* How could you think such a thing? How could you believe you're in the way?" Milagros, always frank and expressive, cared deeply for the old woman who stood before her.

"You're not acting like you always have; something is going on here. Jose looks worried; I've seen you moping around the house, sighing a lot. You don't have to tell me what it is if you don't want to, but I thought that if I left, you and Jose could solve your problem by yourselves."

"You're something else, *Abuelita*." Despite her many worries, Milagros could not help laughing at her mother-in-law's idea. "In a way, you're right. We've got problems, plenty of them. I'm sorry I can't continue to hide them from you now that you've come to stay with us for a while, but how can I help it if—" The smile she had struggled so hard to achieve gave way to tears. Rosa let out her customary deep sigh. At times like this, she was at a loss for words; she put her arm over Milagros' shoulders and allowed her to weep freely. When she saw her daughter-in-law regaining her composure, she got up into the kitchen to get her a glass of water.

"Where are you going, *Abuelita?* Stay, stay with me, please. Don't go away now; I want to talk to you."

"It's better for you not to talk about things that cause you grief."

Milagros ran to the bathroom to wash her face while Rosa headed for the kitchen to help Migdalia, the cook, finish lunch.

"Milagros," Jose shouted from the door, "where are you? Come here; I'm leaving right away! Pack my suitcase, my plane's taking off at three."

Without any further explanations, he went into his bedroom and began to undress to take a shower.

"You're leaving? Where to?" Milagros looked tired; she had not slept well and spoke as if she expected the worse to happen any minute.

"Guatemala. We've had a stroke of luck. This Guatemalan gentleman came into the office asking for equipment for a chain of supermarkets that belongs to him and his brothers."

"And what does all of that mean?"

"It means that we may have to spend some time in Guatemala. It's a large order; there may be others after it, and maybe we'll be able to get away from this place."

"Leave Cuba?"

"Look, Milagros," he answered, "it's time to go."

"Oh, Jose, you don't know how worried I am!"

"I haven't got time to talk about that now. Pack my suitcase while I take a shower; I've got to go."

"This won't be forever, will it?"

"I don't know yet for sure, but I hope so. Cuba's headed for trouble. I've heard rumors that the government intends to confiscate all businesses and private property. So far it's only rumors, but what would happen if it turned out to be true?"

"Listen, Pepe wrote today. He's sick."

"That was something else I wanted to talk to you about. Fermin told me something this morning about the military draft. They're going to call young men to the army, and those kids of Pepe's age will be the first to go. It's going to be a mess! Call him and tell him he's not to come back to Cuba, not even for the summer. Tell him to stay put; we'll keep on sending him money, but he's not to come back under any circumstances."

"Jose, he says he threw up blood!"

"He's just saying that to scare you so you'll tell him to come home. Don't you pay any attention to him. Tell him to stay put." He banged the bathroom door and ended the conversation, causing the already troubled Milagros to become even more alarmed.

Sitting on the bed, with her hands on her head as her expression of desperation, she was truly at her wit's end. *Military draft, blood, Guatemala, confiscation:* The words danced in her head like objects in the hands of a circus juggler. She leaned back for a second to collect her thoughts, and then got up to pack her husband's suitcase. When she was done packing, she looked for a bottle of cologne, poured some on her hand, and rubbed the back of her neck. The cold made her feel better, but an uneasy feeling in the pit of her stomach told her she wouldn't be able to eat for a week. She could barely believe her eyes when she saw Jose step out from the bathroom, a towel wrapped around his waist, singing "Granada" at the top of his lungs. How could he be in a singing mood at such a time?

"What will Natalia and I do?" she asked.

"First thing, apply for your passport and an American visa; we'll see what happens."

"Jose, do you really think we'll have to leave Cuba?"

"Honestly, I don't know, but it's always good to have everything ready just in case. But the first thing you must do now is tell Pepe not to come home for Easter. Tell him not to move from New York until I tell him to; agreed?"

Milagros nodded. When her husband closed his suitcase, she ran to ask her mother-in-law to go with them to the airport. The three of them got in the car and arrived at the airport in plenty of time for Jose to check in. He kissed them both and asked them to return home at once. They were not to say a word to anyone about Jose's trip or their conversation; not even their closest friends were to know.

The steering wheel seemed colder and harder than usual to Milagros, maybe she was losing strength. It was hard to tell. When she stopped the car, she would step suddenly on the pedal, causing the vehicle to jerk forward. Rosa could not hide her worry over Milagros' unusually nervous behavior and her own fear upon perceiving that the life the Garachs knew in Cuba had begun to crumble.

Chapter 68

Six o'clock was the official closing time for Lucas Garach and Company. The warehouse, a fortress of a building, three stories high, was empty, and the fifty delivery trucks bearing the sign LUCAS GARACH AND SON on the side were parked outside until the following morning. This, Lucas used to tell his son Juan, was the most important moment of the day; they planned new strategies, took stock of what had been accomplished, and decided where to start on the following day.

Lucas and Juan had a lot in common. Lucas, dressed in a an elegant linen suit, was very much in charge. His body had rounded and lost its muscular build, but his intelligent eyes had the same, perhaps more of the, sparkle of incessant creative thought that made him invent ways of making money where, for others, none existed. Juan was a star salesman for his father's company. He had been fortunate to have the Garach fine features and blonde hair. His mulatto ancestry was not evident in him as it was in his brother Alberto; however, Juan possessed Cachita's electrifying energy, her talent for making a friend of her worst enemy, her capacity to disarm the negative and inspire the positive. The between Lucas and Juan relationship was unique. They understood each other well and always thought along the same lines. Everyone of their employees knew that, more than just partners, they were in fact father and son. In the presence of others, his son called Lucas simply "Lucas."

For them, too, the political situation was rather confusing. The time had come to decide whether they would invest more capital in Cuba or open branches abroad to guarantee their future. When the government began to restrict the movement of money going out of Cuba, father and son began to worry.

"I think I have good news today," Juan told his father. "Blanca's father has found a way to help us exchange *pesos* for dollars."

"Let's hear it, the time couldn't be better," Lucas whispered. The office was quiet; everyone had gone home, yet in Cuba of the 1960s there was an everlasting fear that the walls could hear and then talk, to the government, of course.

"It's this guy, a certain Fernandez, who was a bigwig in the Batista administration. He fled last year when his people got the boot. He took most of his money with him, but his parents stayed behind. He would like to have them join him in the United States, but he's afraid they won't stand the cold weather. So, he prefers that they stay here until the political situation changes; after all, nobody thinks Castro is going to last more than a few months."

"Fine, but what about us?"

"I'm coming to that; if we give fifteen thousand *pesos* to Fernandez's folks here in Cuba, he'll give us ten thousand dollars through my father-in-law in New York."

"But that isn't an even trade!"

"Lucas, that can't be helped right now. What we have to worry about is not going under, if the situation should get worse here in Cuba. Besides, if it is a false alarm and things go all right over here, we'll have a branch of the business in New York City; ten thousand dollars is all it takes to start. There's no way this can go sour."

"I see what you mean, but you would have to start the subsidiary; I can't speak English."

"Don't worry. It might seem right now that we're going to lose five thousand dollars, but we'll have established ourselves abroad in a city like New York!"

Lucas was silent for a few minutes. He knew that during uncertain times, one had to make quick decisions. The risk had to be taken. He crossed his hands under his chin and leaned back in his swivel chair. He waited for everything to fall in place in his head; he needed a clear idea of how things would fit together.

"All right, we'll do it. But we'll only invest fifteen thousand. If the problems here turn out to be a tempest in a teapot, we won't have to move any more funds."

"I'll let my father-in-law know. I'll go to New York in person to close the deal. Well, if things were to get bad here in Cuba, you'll have to move to New York with me, won't you?"

"I was just thinking about that. If things should go from bad to worse in Cuba, we'll just have to look for a way to invest more in the New York branch."

"And how do you intend to do that?"

"Oh, I'll think of something, don't you worry," he answered. "I'll think of something." Juan looked at him intrigued; he knew his father well, and he was sure that the old man was several steps ahead of him already.

"What are you thinking?"

"Well, I'll be honest with you; I've had a fabulous idea. If things go wrong in Cuba, we have a piece of property in Spain that we can sell and we'll have more than enough to continue the business in New York. Besides, if I go to Spain, I'll be able to make new contacts, get in touch with the companies we already represent, it'll be an excellent opportunity to bring in new products. The more I think about it, the more I like the idea."

"What property are you talking about?"

"My father's farm. It's fully paid for. Nobody works it, nobody lives in it. If we sell it, we'll be all set."

"But that farm isn't yours, it's your mother's, isn't it? For as long as she lives, it's hers; right?"

"We will have to see about that," Lucas said, his eyes fixed on tomorrow. "When the time comes, we'll see whose farm it really is. Women don't think enough to own land and know what to do with it," his tone was so confident that Juan thought it best to end the conversation there.

Chapter 69

Whenever the telephone rang, Milagros had to control her emotions. She could not help fearing the worst, and the ringing—probably an innocent call from her mother or one of her sisters-in-law—had become a constant threat. It could be Pepito, sick in some hospital; or Jose, asking her to join him in Guatemala. That Thursday, early in May, the call made her go urgently to her daughter's school.

Beards and olive-green fatigues were beginning to get on her nerves. If those men were only in the army barracks and the police stations, it they went out to apprehend a political enemy, then it would not be so bad. But they seemed to multiply like evil thoughts. Every time she went out, she saw six, twelve, hundreds of them! For God's sake! Olive green, black boots, submachine guns. One, two, three, four. One, two, three, four. She was already across the Almendares Bridge, and she could still see them marching around the park, across from her house on Cruz del Padre. One, two, three, four. Young boys kept step single file, making believe they were real soldiers; on their shoulders they carried broomsticks which dreamed of becoming rifles. One, two, three, four. Where had the ice cream man and the peanut vendor gone? Maybe they now were chairmen of some "neighborhood committee." The "one, two, three, four" echoed heavily and sadly in her mind and in her heart. What were Cubans made of that they could change their national image so rapidly? At least they had kept their sense of humor, though. She could not help a smile as she remembered the many jokes Cuban wits had spun on the subject of the martial fervor that seemed to be sweeping the island.

Uno, dos, tres y cuatro,
Comiendo mierda
y gastando zapatos.
Cuatro, tres, dos, uno,
Suena un tiro y
no queda ninguno.

Milagros' heart started beating rapidly once again when she finally caught a glimpse of her daughter's school, the Ursulines of Miramar, surrounded by gun-toting militiamen. Mother Loreta, the school principal, had personally phoned all the parents and asked them to come and get their daughters. With no previous warning, a militia squad had surrounded the building, and five or six militiamen had gone in to search the school. They had received information claiming that the nuns were sheltering counterrevolutionaries who had engaged in terrorist activities.

The school seemed to be involved in a war; two military trucks were parked in front of the main door, and a string of militiamen in olive-green fatigues surrounded the block. Milagros parked on the first spot she found and took her place last in the long line of parents waiting by the door. No one spoke; there were no words of complaint or protest. The parents went into the building one by one. As they came out with their daughters, their relieved expressions contrasted sharply with the worried looks of those still waiting outside.

Finally, it was her turn. Of course, there would be school on Monday. Naturally, there was no reason at all for the suspicions. The principal apologized; Milagros nodded her head. She would have agreed to anything then as long as they gave her back her daughter and her niece. Yes, Natalia and Rosi Garach, yes; they were cousins. One was in fourth grade and the other in fifth. The militiamen standing by the door held his machine gun under the arm and lit up a cigarette.

"Rosa Garach, Natalia Garach," a voice boomed over the PA system.

Milagros had tried to conceal her deep concern, but when she saw the girls walking down the hall towards her, she let go a heartfelt "Thank God!"

"Forget God, lady," the militiaman with the cigarette barked. This time he held the gun with both hands. "Thank Fidel. If it hadn't been for him, your daughter would've stayed in there three days maybe." He laughed aloud mockingly.

Milagros controlled herself; somehow she overcame the repugnance she felt towards his yellow smile and olive green, pungent smell.

The girls, unaware of the seriousness of the situation, laughed happily. For them the commotion just meant a day off from school and no homework to turn in tomorrow.

"Aunt Milagros, I wish you could've seen Mother Corazon when they searched her. They even took off her hat and everything." Both girls laughed. "She's so ugly! I don't know if they expected to find one of the thieves in there."

"They are not thieves, Rosi," Milagros explained.

"And they're going to shoot them," Natalia said boasting of her exclusive information. "The one with the pistol told me."

"They all had weapons, silly," Rosi objected, "and they were not pistols; they were rifles and machine-guns."

"Mom, tell Rosi to shut up; the militiamen told me, not her. I saw he had a pistol."

"You're a fool, Natalia. I can see you're only in fourth grade," Rosi retorted putting on an air of superiority.

"So what? You're in fifth grade and I'll be in fifth too, next year," and without ending her sentence, the younger girl kicked her cousin in the leg and turned the back seat of the car into a battlefield.

Milagros was forced to interrupt her thoughts, stop the car and put an end to the fight. Rosi moved to the front seat while Natalia decided to take a nap. Milagros' heart beat out of control as she reflected on what could have happened. Havana was full of stories of children plucked from their parents' side and taken to Russia. She felt the onset of a nervous twitch in her face just thinking of Natalia or Rosi becoming one of them.

Chapter 70

Shortly after Rosa's seventy-fifth birthday, Fermin Garach decided to give up the grocery store, his backroom home, and Rosi's neighborhood school. Prodded by Milagros and Jose, Fermin began to work as bill collector for his brother's refrigeration firm. They moved to a two-bedroom apartment on Johnson Street and agreed to send Rosi to the Ursulines of Miramar, the same school Natalia attended. Those changes for the better, as they had called them, were similar to a change of skin that still felt tight. The suggestion Milagros offered them when she arrived from the school with both girls seemed totally unwarranted to them.

"Listen, Milagros, don't get carried away by this kind of thing. Could I get you a glass of water?" Asuncion, Fermin's wife, was weary of any more sudden changes.

"Asuncion, I'm telling you: I didn't like what I saw today, not a bit. Not only what I saw today but what we're seeing every day."

"Wait, let me get you a glass of water," she repeated.

"Fine, Asuncion, bring me the water, but don't change the subject, please; this is very important. Look, the government is going from bad to worse. This thing that happened in school today . . . if you had seen that scum with guns; just as if it were some barracks, only that it happened to be a school for girls. Do you know what that means?"

"It must be some temporary measure; they're getting started in politics, after all, and they've got to have some way to ensure order."

"Aren't you afraid they may take your daughter to one of those farms or to some school you may not like at all?"

"I think you listen too much to rumors. Nothing like that's going to happen. You'll see, Milagros: Soon there'll be fewer and fewer militiamen, and things will return to normal. Don't you agree, Fermin?"

"Asuncion is right; come, Milagros, sit down. Have your glass of water, and you'll feel better."

"Just listen to what I have to tell you. Jose's told me that I must join him in Guatemala by the beginning of August. We'll stay there until this thing blows over. Because I'm sure it'll be a temporary political problem. But, nevertheless, I think you ought to apply for Rosi's passport and let her come with us."

"God Almighty!" Asuncion exclaimed, "I can't let Rosi go. Milagros, do you realize what you're saying?"

"When this is over, we'll come back. If, on the other hand, things get worse, and you have to get out of Cuba, it'll be easier to do it without Rosi."

Fermin and Asuncion stared at her in disbelief; they could not understand what she was trying to say. He got up from the table and wiped his forehead with a handkerchief. Asuncion joined her hands as if in prayer. She was silent but kept moving her head sideways, rejecting her sister-in-law's proposal. Their reaction was such that Milagros thought she might have hurt their feelings.

"Please, don't take it like that," she said.

"Milagros, the girl is everything we've got; we wouldn't know what to do if we didn't have her," Fermin was on the verge of tears.

"This will blow over; you yourself said so," Asuncion insisted. "If things were to get too bad, we just won't go out of the house."

"Maybe all three could come with us; I don't know. It's just that I wouldn't want anything to happen to Rosi."

"Don't worry; I don't think it's as bad as you think, you'll see. Besides, what would we do in another country?" Fermin's countenance grew somber as he asked this question. "No, Milagros; no way, we belong here, together."

Three consecutive knocks seemed to echo his last words. Fermin stopped talking, but the knocks persisted. Milagros, alarmed, got up from her chair. Fermin sat on a rocking chair, and Asuncion went to open the door.

"Heavens!" Norma exclaimed when she saw the gloomy faces that watched her from the living room. "Is this some sort of a wake! What's the matter? Is anyone sick?" She did not know whether to laugh or feel sorry for them. She walked in, holding Juan Andres by the hand, and waited for somebody to say something to break the awkward silence.

"Please, Norma, sit down. Juan Andres, honey, come; the girls are playing in the bedroom; come and play with your cousins. The boy left with his Aunt Asuncion, and his mother remained with Milagros and Fermin in the living room.

"What's the matter with you?"

"Norma, did you hear about what happened at the Ursulines?"

"That's the school the girls go to, isn't it?"

"They searched the school; the place was crawling with militiamen. They were saying the nuns had some counterrevolutionaries hidden there."

"Those things are a shame, but that's the kind of terror under which we're living."

"That's right; we've jumped from the frying pan into the flames, as the saying goes."

"Don't worry too much, Milagros. Just between you and me, the government can't last too long. It has to collapse; it's inevitable."

"That's the way I see it too," Fermin interjected. "As soon as they start taking things away from the people, this whole thing is going to blow up."

"It may blow up even before that."

"You think so?"

"Look, Milagros, this smells of communism, and that's an ideology that doesn't suit the Cuban temperament too well. There's bound to be a popular revolt, an uprising."

"Aren't you going to get the papers ready for the boy and for you and Andres? I mean, just in case things get really nasty."

"I have applied for our passports, but I know we won't have to leave. Things will happen that will prevent that. I know for a fact."

"Exactly what I was telling her, Norma. See, Milagros? There's really no reason for you to worry."

"What does Andres say about all this?"

"We agree: This can't go on past December."

"I don't know much about these things, but what happened today scared me; I don't mind telling you. There are too many soldiers, militiamen, or whatever; it'll take an army to defeat them."

"Are you finally going to go to Guatemala with Jose?"

"Early in August."

"When are you coming back?"

"I guess for Christmas."

"By the time you return, it'll all be over." Norma sounded very sure of herself. "I'm sure I'll be saying then: 'See? I told you so.'" Milagros, unconvinced, shook her head.

Chapter 71

"Enough is enough. What we're doing is crazy," Alberto Montero, Cachita's younger son, was determined to put an end to his Uncle Andres' counterrevolutionary activities. "Anything could happen. They could find out about him. Him? Us! He's had me bringing books into the room all night long. We haven't got any more space for them, but he pretends to keep on bringing them up here and stashing them in the corners, anywhere, as long as they're out of the way down there. Just one person, just one, that smells something, and we're done for. Through! Thirty years or the firing squad. A fine way to go! Well, shit, no way, not me! I think I've gone as far as I intend to."

The windows that normally allowed light from the outside into the basement had been boarded up, so that the flickering light of the candle could not be seen from the outside. After all, how much light did one need to take books out of boxes and fill them again with machine guns?

The young man came to a stop and looked at his uncle. Sitting on one of the crates that had already been filled with guns and ammunition, Andres Garach was carefully taking textbooks out of other boxes and placing them on the floor. Alberto could not understand why he did not seem nervous. Perspiration glistened on his forehead and balding head; his left arm hung next to his body while the right one moved incessantly. His hands, seemingly unaware of the lethal instruments they were handling moved calmly, with precision, arranging weapons and ammunition in the right places. Alberto could not express his dissatisfaction; he did not understand himself why he wanted to speak out. He looked at the wet forehead and the sparse hair, as brightly white then as it had been shiny blond once; he saw the lame arm, the daring hands, and remembered that that man had been his father when his natural father had shirked his duty. He climbed down the last few steps, picked up some books, and began to go upstairs again. Andres looked at him briefly, and Alberto could hear a silent "thank you."

In spite of the stifling heat, the metal surface of each of the guns seemed piercingly cold. Andres imagined that was the beginning of the invisible thread that linked them to death. It was absurd, but each rifle made him think of Norma and Juan Andres. He was risking his life for them and also increasing the danger to their lives. Would it have been better not to have gotten involved? He looked at the weapons lying flat on the bottom of the crate; for a moment he could have sworn they were dead bodies, indifferent to the fears the sweaty man next to them felt over his wife and son.

He stopped. Again he touched the guns. This time they seemed to burn him. However, neither heat nor cold kept him from placing that gun and many more into the box, until it was full. Then he quickly sealed it. It was no great physical exertion, but he felt drained, out of breath, as if the candle on the corner had burned up all the oxygen in the basement.

"It is our duty to help, Andres. We have a son, and we want him to grow up in a country free from foreign doctrines and tyrants. We have to join hands with others like ourselves and fight. If we don't do it, we won't triumph, and the revolution will swallow us. Soon, it won't let us move. We have a moral duty to cooperate; if we don't, we won't even be able to begin figuring out how much we will lose."

Norma's voice made him impervious to the wilting coldness of the weapons, to the possibility of death, to fear. He moved the crate to the side and began to fill up another. He would have liked to know with certainty that others, who also longed for a free country, were also risking everything to attain their goal.

Alberto's steps interrupted his cogitations. The young man was also perspiring profusely, but he had decided not to leave his uncle alone.

"Many more to go yet, Andres?" There was no hint of reproach.

The old man shook his head negatively. Heavy firing could be heard far away. They could tell when one side was shooting, when the other returned the fire, and when all fired at once, as if they finally agreed on something.

"I wish those out there were fireworks," Alberto said ironically. "Let's wind up; tonight we'll have to sleep on the floor or on top of the desk. If we go out, they'll shoot us full of holes into the hereafter."

It was a pity Cubans couldn't understand each other. It seemed that the island had become too small for both sides.

Chapter 72

The box looked sturdy enough. Besides, it had the exact dimensions of the statue of Our Lady of Charity which for years had presided over Jose and Milagros' living room. Joaquina, Milagros' mother, bought the box because she thought it would be good to give it to her daughter the day before her departure. They had said farewell to each other several times in the past, but that afternoon's turned into a rather solemn good-bye. Milagros unwrapped the wooden box. No explanations were needed. She lifted the lid and looked at her mother, who shifted her eyes up to the image.

"Don't leave the Virgin behind, Milagros, take her with you wherever you go."

"Mother! You talk as if we were going to Siberia. Guatemala isn't all that far away, you know?" But hard as she tried, Milagros could not conceal her anguish.

Rosa Garach looked at the two women from an easy chair. She had thought it her duty to be with Milagros until she left and for more than two weeks she had helped her pack an entire household into a few suitcases.

"*Abuelita*, could you hand me the Virgin, please?" Rosa walked up to the mantelpiece and devoutly held the statue in her hands. "Don't look so sad; I'll be back soon, you'll see. This is like a vacation. When we gather here for supper on Christmas Eve, you'll tell me I was right."

"Milagros, dear, it's hard for me to understand these things. I'm old, and one of these days . . . Who knows what can happen. That's why it's so difficult to smile when the family goes far away. I've been through so many farewells!"

"*Abuelita*, please! Don't say those things! You can ask Norma; everything will be over by December. Everybody who knows anything at all about politics will tell you the same thing," she said in a whisper. At times a comment like that was the cause of a formidable interrogation.

"Look, Rosa, what you and I need is a little music. Why don't you come home with me? I'll play the piano. Come, there's nobody home now, and we'll be all right," Milagros' mother did her best to make Rosa Garach forget her worrisome present.

"Go on, *Abuelita*. When I'm done putting away these last few things, I'll go over and then the two of us will come back home together."

After combing her hair and putting on a clean apron, Rosa took Joaquina by the arm, and the two ladies walked out of the house. Neither of them spoke; had they, they would have realized that both wondered if they would ever see their children again, if the family would ever be together as before. Milagros watched them go down the steps and walk the short distance between her house and her parents'. She looked beyond and let her eyes roam through the park across the street; every bench, every palm tree became special. The park somehow looked different by the light of a setting sun and under the prospect of a long absence. Milagros Santiesteban de Garach attempted to imprint upon her mind those sights that were real then and would become a memory early the next day.

Natalia's age kept her from understanding the somber expression on her mother's face the morning they left. She also wondered why her grandmothers had left so early for church and had refused to say goodbye. She had never been on an airplane before, and that in itself made the day special. The children in the neighborhood admired her because of it and had made her promise to write and tell them everything she had seen.

Gerardo, Milagros' father, and Uncle Fermin arrived to take them to the airport. The girl went quickly down the stairs; her grandfather followed her and got on the front seat of the car. Milagros was the last one in; she wanted to take one last look at every window in the house before saying good-bye with the inevitable loud bang on the front door.

"Mom, hurry; we don't want to miss the plane!" she shouted excitedly.

Natalia's childish enthusiasm made the trip to Rancho Boyeros Airport tolerable for Milagros. As the car turned the corner onto Santa Catalina Street, the girl caught a glimpse of her two grandmothers coming out of the church. She almost jumped out of the car window shouting and waving. Her loud good-byes forced the two ladies to make use of their handkerchiefs.

"Bye, *Abuelitas!* Mother," she asked as the car pulled away, "why are they crying?"

Milagros could not answer; she held her daughter's hand and asked her to sit down and be still until they arrived at the airport. She asked too much. Milagros was weary and quiet, a marked contrast with the girls effervescence. Natalia continued to fidget and ask all sorts of questions. Fermin drove his small Fiat with caution as the usual trucks full of militiamen and ammunition passed them on the streets and highways. Gerardo Santiesteban, his family's pillar of strength, wondered if he could stand long enough to saying goodby to her daughter in an honorable manner.

"God bless you, my child," the old man managed to say when a voice announced a final call for the passengers to board the plane. Fermin said nothing but wiped the perspiration off his forehead with a handkerchief and wondered if anyone had ever sweat tears.

"What's the matter, mother?" Natalia saw her mother looking back repeatedly: her grandfather and uncle waved them good-bye. Don't you want to go? Is something bad going to happen to us? Aren't we going to see Papa?"

"Natalia, you're too young still to realize it, but today we're leaving our country. Some day you'll understand."

From that day on, they had to learn to do without.

Chapter 73

It was a time of loss for Rosa Garach. Standing in front of the church that morning in August when her granddaughter Natalia waved goodbye from the passing car, Rosa could not imagine that a month later would find her with a torn heart, at the foot of the stairs that led to her son Andres' apartment. Juan Andres' hadn't had a chance to say goodbye like Natalia; he had just screamed: "*Abuelita*, don't let them take me away, please!" She ran; she cried for help, but damn her age, damn her slow legs, damn her little strength, for if the strength of the soul mattered, she would have followed that car and not let the man that looked like Juan Garach take her grandson away.

Juan, Juan Garach. The man did look like Juan. Juan and his crazy obsession to make money and to triumph had taken her four boys away from her; her soul had been torn then too, torn to the point where it hurt to cry every day, but then she used to think of Lucas' pride, Fermin's determination, and Jose's smile . . . This time it was different; she had no pleasant thoughts to appease her; she only heard Juan Andres' panic over and over again: "*Abuelita*, don't let them take me away, please!" Rosa could not remember how she got from Andres' building to Lucia's house that night; someone told her she went into shock. That had certainly never happened to Rosa Garach any more. Into shock.

The physical pain had become lighter when she felt herself part of her world once more, but she could not stop hearing the boy's screams as her laced shoes, wrinkled and colorless, resounded with clockwork precision against the tile floor at Lucia and Miguel's house. The rocking chair enabled her to rest without interrupting the constant movement she craved. She needed that continuous activity so that by nightfall her body would beg her for a rest. But even then, she had spent many nights with her eyes wide open staring into the darkness. Lack of sleep frightened her. Did that happen to those who were about to die? It had been years since she had last been able to cry; after Juan Andres' disappearance, she could no longer smile. Her feet beat tirelessly against the tile floor.

She needed the rocking chair's constant motion especially that afternoon when Lucas insisted that she leave Cuba with him and his family.

"I don't think so, Lucas; no. I can't leave Cuba now; your brother, your nephew, your sister-in-law are missing. How could I go away without making sure that they're alive and well. What if they need us?" Rosa protested.

"Mother, don't be obstinate. I don't like to be hard on you, but it is possible that Andres may be dead. And only God knows where Norma and their son may be," Lucas paced the room with a cold stare in his eyes.

"It can't be," she shook her head. "A mother knows when her child is dead. Andres is alive; he may need me. I can't go now."

"Soon they'll start clamping down on people who want to leave the country, I know it. If that happens, you will be trapped here, with no way out."

"You're dreaming, Lucas," Miguel commented sourly.

"Mother, please, listen to me. Come to Spain with us." Lucas Garach did not tolerate interruption.

"I'm needed here. What would I do back in Spain?"

"Away from danger one will be able to do more," he realized that a softer tone perhaps could convince her. "I'm sure. Maybe we'd be able to find out where Andres is. In Cuba, people don't want to talk any more. One says the wrong word to the wrong person and winds up behind bars."

Miguelito listened attentively from the other end of the couch. Everyone talked about leaving Cuba; everyone but his father, that is. Why couldn't he understand that Cuba was no longer the same? If only he could flee to Spain! He still had the two thousand *pesos* Rosa had given him. There were good universities in Spain!

"Uncle Lucas . . ." Everyone looked at him.

"Yes, Miguelito."

"Look, I was just thinking that if *Abuelita* doesn't want to go, maybe I could take her place."

"What do you mean?"

"I mean that if you already bought her ticket and everything, maybe I could use it . . . I'll pay you for it. I'd do anything you want me to, if you help me get out of here."

"Miguelito!" his father exclaimed, shocked. "How dare you!" Rosa looked shaken.

"Look, Miguel, leaving Cuba is not as simple as that. You need a passport, a visa . . ."

"I have a passport, Uncle Lucas," he replied.

"What?" Miguel was thoroughly confused. "Look, Lucas, don't pay any attention to the boy. I don't know where he got this notion from, but this is my house, and I have the last word. Nobody is leaving; nobody except Rosa if she wants to. That's her decision."

Rosa Garach realized that she was confronting a new problem and continued to scrutinize Miguel's, Miguelito's, and Lucas' faces, one by one, trying to find the right answer.

"Besides, Miguelito," Lucas pointed out lamely, "whatever little money I manage to take out of Cuba will have to last us until I can get my business going again, and that's going to be difficult. *Abuelita* is different; she's an old woman. You'll have to talk to your father and find another solution."

Her grandson's evident frustration and humiliation made Rosa see things more clearly. She stopped the rocking chair and looked at Lucas.

"Listen," she trembled and her voice was weak, "I'll do as you ask, Lucas, but on one condition. Miguelito has to come with me. If you can arrange things for him to come along; we'll both be ready whenever you say. I will just not go alone." Rosa became firm for the first time.

"Miguelito won't go!" roared Lucia's husband. "I won't allow it; I forbid it!"

"Look, father. I'm almost twenty years old, and I don't depend on you any longer. I make my own decisions now. If my uncle says it's all right, I'm leaving. You will never boss me around again. You don't own me; I don't like this life of denial. I want to live far away from both of you. I hate everything about this life, the darkness, the stillness, the silence . . ." Then, he brought his hands to cover his ears, and Rosa perfectly understood her grandson's personal agony.

Miguel jumped up from his seat and raised his right arm tempted to strike his son. The young man got up from the sofa and looked at his father eye-to-eye, letting out in his stare all the bitterness that had been building up for years.

Miguel lowered his arm, turned around and locked himself up in his bedroom. The confrontation between father and son was over.

"Well, mother, if that's the only way you'll go, I'll have to see what we can do. Miguelito, let me have your passport. I'll let you know as soon as I have some news," Lucas said.

Rosa would have been grateful if somebody had explained to her what was actually happening. *Communism, expropriation, reform, firing squad:* What relation existed between those strange words and her shattered family? The world must indeed be a very big place for all the Garachs to be so far apart. Where were Juan Andres, Norma, and Andres? Lucas had told her that communism was an idea, and that it was responsible for everything. How could an idea move so many people? Communism had to be a very powerful person who was able to entrap people; he was also responsible for her return to Spain. It was too much power for just one man! Just too much power.

Chapter 74

Friday, October 14. INDUSTRIES AND BUSINESSES EXPRO-
PRIATED.

"Hello? Fermin? This is Gerardo." Milagros' father had grown
close to the only Garach brother thought to have stayed behind in Cuba.
"Yes, yes I saw the announcement. No, there's no list, no. What? Well,
I thought maybe we had been spared this time, it's not a large business
and, after all, neither Jose nor my sons have openly opposed the government. You saw it?" Suddenly, he had to sit down. He was pale; the
muscles on his temple were tense. "What paper? Hey? Well, maybe the
communist party is up to its old tricks again. Tell me, does it show the
name? The list is in the back? Please, read it, yes." The old man's
shoulder fell and seemed to fuse with the chair. "What? You saw it on
page eleven?" All hope left him. "What does it actually say? I see. It's
in the 'Construction' section. 'Bar and Cafeteria Equipment, Inc.' It
doesn't say Garach or Santiesteban; could it be another company?" he
asked shyly. "You don't think so. Well, I guess we'll have to go there
and find out for sure. Are you ready? If I could ride with you instead
of taking the bus, I'd get there first; ahead of the boys you know.
Maybe there's still something we can do."

It was a very personal matter to Gerardo Santiesteban, the retired
grocer who had handed over his savings ten years before to his three
sons to start a business with Jose Garach, his son-in-law. The unimag-
inable was happening. He wished to tell the sun not to be so hasty that
particular morning, to linger for a couple of hours more on the horizon,
to give him time to go to the office and make sure that the company
which had been expropriated—according to the official organ of the
Communist Party—was not his children's but another's.

He closed the door silently and saw Fermin's car turning the corner. Gerardo walked to the car as fast as his old legs could take him; the
ride to the office had never seemed longer to him. Diez de Octubre
Avenue, Jesus del Monte Road, President Menocal Avenue. Far away,
he saw Carlos III Avenue, coming back to life after a restful night.
There were men and women walking hurriedly along the streets, hold-

ing newspapers in their hands. There was no avoiding it, all of Havana would know that the business had been confiscated.

They turned left on Estrella Street, one ahead of Carlos III, and parked in the first free spot they could find.

"Fermin, isn't that my son's car?"

"Yes, Gerardo, but don't worry. Rafael is smart, and he'll know how to take care of things."

"We'll see." Fermin could not help feeling alarmed when that man, whom he had always regarded as a tower of strength, answered him in a faint, hesitant voice.

Rafael was arguing with three of the firm's mechanics by the main door of the "Santiesteban & Garach, Bar and Cafeteria Equipment" building.

"Look here, Santiesteban, you, your father, your brothers, and your brother-in-law might as well hand over the keys and get out. This company isn't yours any longer." Guerrero, who was the spokesman for the threesome, disturbed Rafael Santiesteban; the man took obvious pleasure in what he was doing.

"Listen, Guerrero, we always treated you well. You've got no right to talk to us like that," he replied.

"The keys, man. You haven't got anything else to do here; go away. The revolution has given me my rights. Didn't you read the papers today? This business doesn't belong to you any more; it belongs to the people, and we're the people."

"Listen, friend, for your information, it was my sons and my son-in-law who built up the business, and don't you forget it. It is theirs. What the hell do you think you're doing?" Gerardo's voice regained its strength; the old man would have liked to have been twenty years younger so that he could have punched that scoundrel in the mouth.

"Shut up, dad. We won't solve anything that way."

"Well, well, what have we got here? The old man is itching for a fight, ain't he?"

"Guerrero, mind what you say to my father." It was a fierce, desperate warning.

"Gerardo," Fermin pleaded, "there's nothing else for us to do here; let's go."

The argument was taking place on the sidewalk. The leader and his two cohorts barred the way to the door, emphasizing their newly acquired authority. The old man—his jaws clenched, a stony look on his face—did not budge. He looked at the name engraved on the terrazo floor: "Santiesteban & Garach, Bar and Cafeteria Equipment, Inc." It would be a while before that could be erased.

"Look, man, I can't be here all day; I've a company to run," Guerrero shouted, "give me the keys. You too, boss," he added looking mockingly at the old man.

The bystanders, already more than ten, followed the controversy with interest. They seemed ready to clap or whistle anytime someone in the group said anything. Rafael walked around the three men and headed for the door. The spectators waited for a reaction, but nobody moved, nobody said a word. It was not only his silence and the impassive look on his face that made the others remain silent; his motions had a certain compelling majesty that awed his former employees.

"Where are you going?" Guerrero said at last.

"You aren't going to keep me from opening the door one last time before handing the keys to you, are you, Ramon?"

What began as a semi-official act degenerated into a show. The old man had his eyes glued to the sign on the floor; Guerrero and his revolutionary friends did not know what to do. Rafael pulled out his keychain, chose the right key, bent over and inserted it into the keyhole. Only the noise of the cars could be heard, jockeying for position on Ayesteran Avenue; no one spoke. The key turned once, twice. Rafael straightened up slowly to push the door. It seemed stuck. Finally, it opened. Gerardo lifted up his eyes and saw his son calmly prying the key loose from the keychain.

"Have you got your key with you, dad?"

The old man followed his son's example and handed his keys over with feigned indifference. Attempting to efface the
solemnity of the occasion, Guerrero tightened his belt and called out:

"Let's get to work, guys. Come on, let's go in. This business belongs to the people of Cuba now, and we're the people."

"May we go up?" Rafael interrupted.

"Sure! You can go up and down the stairs all you want, but you're not going into any of the offices. Nothing in there belongs to you any more."

"My college diploma? The photographs?"

"I'll bring them to you. And be sure to tell your brothers that they have to come and bring us their keys unless they want the police to pay them a visit. And tell your brother-in-law . . ."

"He's in Guatemala."

"Better that way. Fermin, ain't you coming? You're one of us."

Fermin Garach blushed, embarrassed and angry over such a thought.

"Look, Guerrero, leave me out of this, you hear?"

"Hey, watch it, man. You've either got to be with the revolution or against it."

"I'm simply neutral," he answered without a trace of irony. "Come, Gerardo, let's go home. There's nothing for us to do here."

The old man did not move.

"Go with Fermin, Dad. I'll drop by to see you later on."

That afternoon, and for many years afterwards, whenever he thought of that moment, Gerardo saw himself as a coward. One had to fight hard; if all one hundred and four expropriated firms had challenged the order, things would have been different. His entire capital, the fruit of forty years of hard work, hauling heavy sacs full of rice, beans and flour on his back, of working eighteen hours a day, of good management, of thrift. He had given all of it to his three sons to open up a business. One night, one man's decision put an end to it all.

A few minutes later, Fermin had to call for help. Gerardo said nothing, but his body rebelled and collapsed with a thud on the floor sign which bore his last name.

Chapter 75

"¡*Abuelita, Abuelita!* Come here, somebody's looking for you," her grandson called out.

Her spirit lacked the strength to shudder, but she shook so violently she thought she would have to lie down. And yet, she amazed herself by walking to the living room from where her grandson called her. There was a woman, standing by the window, looking out as if afraid of something.

"Good morning," Rosa greeted the stranger, unable to recognize the weathered face and the black eyes that still retained some of their old fire.

"Mrs. Garach," the woman said, "don't you remember me?"

"Sit down, please." Cachita was moved by the old lady's kind voice. "Yes, your face looks familiar, but I can't quite place you. Well, what can I do for you?"

"I'm Cachita Montero, don't you remember? I met you many years ago at Miss Carolina's house."

"Is it you?"

"Yes, ma'am, yes," she admitted, "but don't worry, I wouldn't have recognized myself either. The years don't go by for nothing."

"Cachita?"

"Yes, Mrs. Garach, I was . . . I am the mother of two of your grandsons, Juan and Alberto."

"Yes, I'm sorry. I didn't realize it. I'm very upset and at my age, faces, even memories, are hard to recall. It's quite a coincidence that, after so many years, you should've come to see me today, of all days, when I'm going away."

"I know it, that's why I came. I asked a neighbor of yours, you know? Nowadays everybody knows everything in this country. Well, at any rate, when she told me you were leaving today, I said to myself, 'Cachita, you've got to go real early and talk to Mrs. Garach.' What I have to tell you will bring you some happiness."

"Happiness?" Her eyes trembled with curiosity.

"I bring you word from Andres."

"He's alive."

"Yes, ma'am, and he's fine. He's worried, but he's fine."

"Where is he?"

"Hiding out. The government is looking for him. He was able to escape the ambush, but since they took his wife prisoner, they are looking for him."

"Norma?"

"Yes, ma'am. Normita, such a good woman, a fine lady, she's in jail, sentenced to twenty years. It was a summary trial in Las Villas. She was lucky, though. They could have had her shot!"

"In jail?"

"It's horrible, yes, I know. They took a big chance. This was not the time to smuggle arms; these creeps have got their eyes peeled. The thing that really gets me is how much they enjoy themselves when they catch somebody and send him to jail or to the firing squad."

"And the boy? What about Juan Andres?"

"That's what's got Andres climbing the walls, Mrs. Garach."

"What's Andres going to do?"

"For the time being, and with Saint Barbara's help, he'll have to remain in hiding; eventually, he'll have to escape. We all will have to escape. He asked me to tell you not to be frightened, that nothing's going to happen to him. 'Tell my mother I ask God to bless her,' he told me to tell you," Cachita added carefully pronouncing each word. "He wants you to take care of yourself; he hopes to see you soon, and he says for you to pray to the Holy Madonna de . . ."

"The Holy Madonna de l'Avella."

"Right."

"The poor boy."

"Don't worry, Mrs. Garach, you're too fine a lady to get upset."

"I won't forget what you've done for us, Cachita."

"Look, I've got to go; a snitch may see me here and put two and two together."

"Come, you can use the back door. Come with me."

Rosa Garach walked across the dining room and the kitchen and unlocked the back door; Cachita followed.

"I wish you the very best, Mrs. Garach. Where are you going? Miami?"

"No, back to Spain."

They looked at each other. Cachita would have liked to hold her in her arms. Rosa put her hands on the woman's shoulders and kissed her on the forehead.

"May God bless you and your sons."

They heard the living room door open. Lucas' voice pierced the silence with a shout of "Mother!" The two women looked at each other again, and they embraced one another. Cachita could not keep her eyes from welling up as she pulled herself away.

"Go, Mrs. Garach, go. Your son's calling you."

So Cachita Montero left, with a feeling that they would meet again.

Chapter 76

The transition from gardener to manager of a recently expropriated soap factory was not exactly Jesus Garcia's life-long dream; however, the new position had seen to the most pressing needs of Domitila's grandson and his family. That is why he donned the olive-green fatigues, drilled with the militia, and had more "This is your home, Fidel" signs on his front lawn than any other house in the neighborhood.

The house! Even that he owed to the Maximum Leader! It was so easy to forget the twenty years that he, his wife, and their eight children had lived in a tenement building in El Cerro, especially now that they had a bathroom all their own, a gas range, and three bedrooms with enough room for the whole family.

It had not been for want of trying, but Barbarita, his wife, had had to quit her job after their third child, when it became impossible to find a baby-sitter. "Learn to do something useful, Jesus; get yourself a job in a factory, drive a truck, do something to get us out of this mess." Barbarita always told him the same thing. But it was hard to leave a place where they already knew and liked him, where the lady of the house gave him candies and hand-me-down clothes for the children. They were not well off, but they could have been worse off. Domitila had been right when she had told him: "It's better to have a bird in the hand than one hundred in the bush." Jesusito clung to his job in Miramar and to his humble room in El Cerro, putting up with the crying of children and Barbarita's never ending complaints.

January the first, 1959, took Jesusito by surprise. He had always stayed out of the political turmoil that regularly swept Cuba. The reality of what was happening struck home on the following morning, when a relative of the owners of the house gathered the household servants and informed them that by the end of the week they would have to seek employment elsewhere. And so, there he was, forty-one years old, eight children to provide for, his job as a gardener over because the family had decided to stay permanently in the United States. A friend pointed out to him that it was very likely that the family sympathized with Batista and when Castro came to power, they could not return. "Fuck Castro, then!" he had shouted in anger.

Late in February, one of Barbarita's nephews came down from the Sierra Maestra wearing several decorations that attested to his courage and his sacrifices for the cause of the revolution. It was about then that Jesus Garcia and his family had begun to go under; the grocer told them that their credit was no longer any good, not even for half a pound of beans; it would not be too long before the landlord had them evicted. Jesusito lost weight; even if there had been enough to eat, his worries had made him lose his appetite. Barbarita, on the other hand, had shouted herself hoarse, heaping abuses on her husband and even threatening to commit suicide.

The revolution, which had initially been the cause of their despair, also rescued them from their predicament. Thanks to his wife's nephew, Jesusito worked for a year and a half at the Armed Forces Bureau of Investigations. After an earth-shattering indictment he returned in El Vedado, he was promoted to manager of an expropriated factory and earned the admiration of his large clan when he announced that they would be moving to a house in Santos Suarez. Barbarita moved into the new house with no apparent suicidal inclinations and feeling—as she herself put it—"quite a lady."

It was only because of his great affection for Cachita that the former gardener agreed to hide Andres Garach in his house, ignoring Barbarita's warnings.

"You listen to me, Jesus Garcia; in your whole fuckin' life you've never seen it so good. If you go now and spoil everything just because Cachita asked you to do something for a friend of hers, I swear to you that I'm going to go crazy, and you're going to have your head blown off!"

"Sometimes you just can't say no. Cachita is like a sister to me, you know that. My grandmother, Domitila, lived with her." Jesus shook his head, stoically withstanding his wife's objections.

"As if Domitila hadn't washed plenty of sheets for her and her kids. It's Cachita who owes her the favors."

"Those are things I remember since I was a kid. Cachita was a young girl, and I was just a boy; we were as poor as country mice. Whenever she smiled at me or asked me to share a Coke with her I felt so happy . . . Shit, Barbarita, those things are important too, aren't they?

Now she's asking me to stash away her brother-in-law; how can I say no to her?"

"Cut it out; I happen to know Cachita never married that rich guy."

"Hey, don't you give me that holier-than-thou bit. I could say a few things about you, you know? . . . Besides, that man was really good to her. Andres and his wife visited her often and gave her the money for Albertico's tuition. He may be a counterrevolutionary, but he's all right by me. You'd better shut up and see to it that they don't find out he's here, because Andres is staying here until I give the word."

Cachita took Andres to the house in Santos Suarez late one Wednesday night. Jesus let Alberto's car into the garage, the fugitive stepped out and, without uttering a single word, mother and son drove away quickly. Andres' room was at the rear of the house and had been previously used as a utility room.

"If I can escape this, I'll owe you my life," Andres had told him; he had gotten older since the last time Jesus had seen him. Exhaustion, sorrow, and the inexorable weight of his years made him look like a broken man.

"We're human, right? I'll help you today, you'll help me out tomorrow; that's how it goes," he said closing the door, so that no one could overhear their conversation. "I don't know how comfortable you'll be here, but you'll be better off than in jail, I know that. The thing is that I've got eight kids. Two of them are away; six live at home. None of them know about you. We're revolutionaries, you know, and, well . . . I'm sure you understand that the kids can't understand the difference between a counterrevolutionary and a good man. They only know that Fidel is great."

"I know."

"I'll come to see you once a day, more or less at this time. You can pee and do everything else into this pot, and when I come to bring you your food, I'll empty it. Don't make any noise and don't look out the window; if anybody sees you and wants to hurt us, we'll all wind up in jail."

"Don't worry. May I smoke?" Andres asked, getting his cigarettes and matches.

"I'd rather you didn't." Jesus' voice was firm.

"All right."

"Have you got any children?"

"Yes, one."

"Then you know what I mean. One of the kids may smell the smoke and start asking questions; we don't want that to happen, right?"

"As you say, Jesus. You must excuse me. I've been through a lot for two weeks, and I don't know any more whether I'm coming or going; I've hardly slept at all; you must excuse me."

"Why are they looking for you?"

"We were taking supplies and ammunitions to the fighters in the Escambray Mountains. It happened there."

"Damn it! You were the ones who got caught on the ninth?"

"Right. I got away. I'd be better off, I guess, if I were in jail with my wife, but I escaped because of my son."

"Your wife is in jail?"

"They grabbed her that night, yes. There were four of us. We decided that, because of my handicap, I should stay in the car."

"Where were you?"

"In Manacas," he replied, crushed. "My wife and the other couple left to meet the rebels. They took too long; they had been gone for over an hour when I first heard shots. It was dark, only the moonlight to guide me. I began to look around, and then I saw several militiamen hurrying in my direction; there weren't too many of them. They didn't see me at first; then I heard one of them say: 'We bagged them all!' We can read all about it in tomorrow's paper."

"Shit!" he exclaimed.

"I realized then that everything had failed, although I didn't understand what the militiaman meant. I wanted to get off the car and see if there was anything I could do for Norma, but the slightest noise would've brought a whole swarm of militiamen down on me. Besides, I can't even run on a flat floor, so you can imagine what it would've been like in the bush country."

"What did you do?"

"A few minutes later, one of them realized that there was a car, my car, off the road. It was a clear night, and they saw me as plainly as I saw them. Well, I turned on the engine. I was thinking of my son, I swear to you; otherwise I would've never abandoned my wife." Andres' pained expression impressed Jesusito.

"Come, get a hold of yourself. Things look desperate sometimes and then . . ."

"I hit the accelerator so hard, I think I killed one of them. He was standing right in the middle of the road. I drove till I got on the Central Highway and kept on going until I ran out of gas. I started to walk, then, until a truck driver picked me up and gave me a ride. He dropped me off near Cachita's place."

"Where is your son?"

"It seems they took the boy away somewhere. Cachita sent a friend to find out, and she told her that our apartment is empty; they took everything out."

"There's no stopping this revolution!" Jesus' voice sounded proud and ashamed at the same time.

Gradually, a strange friendship developed between the two men. Jesus would regularly open the door to Andres' hideout. First he would take out the trash; then they would sit down and talk for a few minutes.

"What day is today?" Andres asked.

"November 29. You've been here almost a month."

"Have you talked to Cachita?"

"Yes, she still doesn't know anything about your son. But, I'm sure he'll turn up one of these days," he paused for a second and added, "she's ready to leave the country. Cachita's turning into a *gusana*," he said using the name coined to refer to anyone who opposed Fidel and wished to leave the country.

"Shit, Jesusito, why are you involved in all of this? Do you agree with the government?"

"Well, yes, I do," he hesitated.

"You're really risking an awful lot by hiding me here. Have you realized that?"

"I know it, but sometimes you've got to do things like these for your friends, you know. Cachita asked me and . . ." he scratched his head looking for the right words.

"Isn't all of this against the revolution, your revolution?"

"I don't know, Andres. You don't hurt anybody by being here. It's hard to explain. What I do know is that I have a large family, and that if the revolution helps me feed my children, then I'm for the revolution. I don't know what Fidel's trying to do, but he's given me all you can see. I had nothing and no way of getting nothing. I've got to be thankful to Fidel and the revolution. The country is better off too. Everything's distributed evenly now."

"But, what about the people who've been shot by the firing squads, the political prisoners, the lack of freedom?" Andres objected.

"There were dead people and political prisoners under Batista too. They are people who go against the leader and force him to do things to them. If they went along, they'd have plenty of everything, like me."

"I don't mean to offend you, Jesus, please understand that, but don't you feel the lack of freedom, the stifling control?"

"I don't know what you mean by freedom. Freedom," he repeated slowly. "To me that means being able to do the things you want to. I've got more freedom now than ever before to give the children the things they need and to keep my wife happy. Do you know what it is to know that my son Jesusito is going to go to college? Now, for me that's freedom. He's a smart kid, and he'll be able to do something with his God-given talent. Two years ago, I would've had to take him along to learn about gardens and plants, and he would have become somebody's gardener. Now, some day, he'll be a professor, an engineer, maybe even a doctor. Dr. Jesus Garcia, it has a nice ring to it, doesn't it? I know nothing about political ideals, but I can tell you a few things about freedom. Before, there wasn't much I could do; now, there's a whole lot of things I can do. I never had so much freedom. Never."

So said Jesus Garcia, a true child of the Revolution.

PART VII

The Valencian sun flooded my mind with many long forgotten sen-
sations. Whenever it was a bright day at the farm in Benicarlo, I felt
the dirt between my fingers, my nails digging into the ground the way
that I, so many years before, had when I fought for survival. I heard the
wind move my fields of corn and felt the leaves caress my skin with the
scorching sun above us. I felt the weight of the shovel I carried on my
shoulder to dig ditches to water the crops; I smelled the wet fields and
felt the cold rainwater washing down my worries as it saturated my
mind and my clothes. I recreated things that had been and were no
longer there. The years seemed not to have passed, and without clos-
ing my eyes, I saw Fermin and Andres helping me with the vegetable
garden, Lucia walking with me to the wash fountain. It felt as though
Pepet would come out from behind a corner, his pockets full of peanuts;
Lucas would be out of town with his father. Juan, Juan Garach, my
mind's sight of him was fainter than all the others; his was the only
memory of those days which did not make me smile.

But the Garachs, as only I remembered them, were no more. God
only knew where communism had thrown my children, and there was
always Carolina's voice asking me, "Mother, do you feel all right?" to
bring me back to reality when she saw me leaning my head over my
arm as I held to the rock fence that bordered one side of the vegetable
garden. It was nothing, really. Maybe the sun was too hot that day or I
was too old. I used to think those were things that happened to people
when they were close to death. I was old by then, I supposed life was
over for me. Time proved me wrong.

Chapter 77

Together in the loneliness of the farm, both Rosa and Carolina had achieved a closer relationship than ever before. Carolina wrote Rosa's letters for her; Rosa lightened Carolina's load with the housework.

They had advised Miguelito to be patient, to persevere and to study hard. But Madrid was too cold, the university professors too unfair, money not enough, and in 1963 the disappointed young man decided to go to Miami to join his Aunt Milagros.

"He's better off with her. He'll probably live with Milagros and her family and then he won't be so lonely," Carolina said reassuringly.

"May the Holy Madonna de l'Avella hear you, Carolina, but that country's got such a long name. It's not like Spain or Cuba; the U–ni–ted States." She pronounced each syllable slowly.

"It's just a place like any other, mother. Well, everything is cleaner, better organized, that's true. Lina and her husband live there, and they're happy. As soon as Lucas gets done with the paperwork for the sale of the farm, the three of us will move there too."

Several months earlier, after having made a few improvements to the farm that increased its value, Lucas found a buyer for it. Rosa did not understand the details, but her son took her with him and explained everything as best he could.

"You know more about these things than I, son," she said, awed by so many deeds and signatures. "I wanted to tell you, though, that this money should be for those children of mine who need it the most. I'd like to . . ."

Of course, that went without saying. The farm was Rosa's and the money was hers too. Until she made up her mind, the *pesetas* would be deposited in a bank. She signed the documents carefully: R-O-S-A G-A-R-A-C-H. If only that money could help her find out where Juan Andres was.

She went to her bedroom and opened her purse to look at the family picture she had carried with her for the past five years. It was such a handsome family! She would gladly give everything up for the chance to see them together again. Andres, Fermin, Jose, Lucas, Lucia, Norma, Asuncion, Milagros . . .

"Holy Madonna de l'Avella," she prayed in silence, "grant me that I may see all of them again, even if it is in that country with the big name where everything is so clean."

"The United States," she said out loud. "Even if it's there, Holy Madonna!" The rest was a matter of a Virgin, listening to an old mother's wishes.

Chapter 78

"Yes, this is Lucas. I'm glad you called, Jose, but I can't do anything about this situation you're describing," Lucas spoke standing up, walking as far as the telephone cord would take him. "If Fermin asked you to try to help him leave Cuba, we've got to do it right away. Listen, but those people don't really know what they want. Now they want to leave, eight years after we did. Why didn't they leave then? . . . Yes, yes; I know. Indecision, the hope that everything would be over soon . . . Of course, we can't say no to them now . . . Sign an affidavit?" As if Jose could see him, Lucas shook his head violently. "Count me out. I can't assume any more responsibility. What would I do with so many people depending on me? What's Miguelito got to say about it? At least he ought to be responsible for his folks . . . Oh, so now he says he wants nothing to do with his folks." His expression spelled "I knew it," but he didn't say as much. "The guy's a bum . . . Yes, Jose, I know you're right, but as I told you, count me out. I've got enough with the old lady . . . Yes, her. I can't take care of four more people; I think that's your job . . . Well, man, do what you think is best; fortunately, they didn't write to me; they wrote to you, and I don't have much to do with it. Of course, he's my brother too, but that doesn't mean that I've got to give them any guarantees. It's four old people, Jose; if they get sick . . . You know what medical expenses are like in this country . . ." He shook his head once more. "No, no; I don't like to beat around the bush. Let Lucia and Miguel straighten things out with their son; you take care of Fermin and his family, and I'll look after the old lady. Okay? Yes, yes; everybody's fine. Carolina's down with the flu. It's very cold up here; you know what New York is like. Well, good luck; I hope everything comes out all right. Bye. Say hello to Milagros for me."

Rosa Garach had not been able to tell anyone that she did not like New York City. Carolina wrote her letters for her, and it would have upset her to know that her mother-in-law was unhappy. Lucas, too busy to talk, would have misunderstood her.

One evening she thought she would drown in her loneliness and her thoughts. It had been snowing fiercely for over a month, and everyone had agreed that the grandmother would be safer if she stayed inside the house. She could bear it no longer; when her son, her daughter-in-law, Lina and her husband went to sleep, Rosa bundled herself up in the warmest clothes she could find, went downstairs and out to the garden. There, in the summer, she found the scent of Carolina's roses; in winter, it smelled icy white.

At last! She took a deep breath, as though she had not breathed for a month. She began to walk along the sidewalk in front of the house and looked up to the sky, hoping to see the stars. She would have confessed to the stars that in such a modern city there was no wash fountain, not even a public wash fountain, and that there was no room to hang her wash to air. The stars would have understood how hurt she was at being forbidden by Lina to enter the kitchen because once she had burned some milk she had tried to boil. God would understand her frustration because she still could not sign her name. She looked, but she could not find a single star to which she could trust her confusion. New York lights dared to hide God's stars!

The shoes she wore were not the right type to contend with the ice that covered the cement sidewalk; she was near the door when she skidded, fell down, and felt the bite of pain on her left ankle.

"How's that ankle doing, *Abuelita*?" Ricardo, Lina's husband asked her every evening. If he only knew that she had fractured it because of the stars!

Lucas did not tell Rosa about the stragglers' plans to leave Cuba and come to the United States. The news was lost in the monumental bridge that spanned the distance between the warehouse and the Garach's Long Island home. Carolina and Rosa found out through a letter from Lucia. They would soon be on their way. Perhaps it would take a while, but, why would communism want to keep them? At last they were going to Miami. Miami!

"Carolina, is that place too far from here?"

"No, mother, not at all. It's two hours away by plane."

"Ah, children!" Rosa sighed. "Will I be able to see them when they arrive? Tell me the truth, Carolina, will I?"

"Of course, mother; of course."

"I love you all very much, my dear, but they'll need me more over there. Lucia's got her son, but Fermin . . . it's my duty to be with them and help them. Don't you think?"

"As you say, mother."

"I'll get the money from the farm, and we'll buy a small house to live with Fermin and Asuncion and Rosi."

"For sure," Carolina enjoyed seeing the shimmer of wishful hopes in Rosa's blue eyes. "I want you to rest for a while; you get too excited when you get letters, and we talk about these things; you must rest after so much excitement. Will you promise that you'll sleep at least for an hour? It's only a week before they take the cast off your ankle, now that's something to dream about."

"I'll do as you say, child."

Carolina drew the curtains to keep the light from shining on Rosa's bed. The old lady made herself comfortable between the sheets. She had lived through so many bitter moments in all her years! Yet, one joyous instant was enough to erase all the sad memories. Almost all, that is, for she looked at Juan Andres' picture on her nightstand.

"Holy Madonna!" she whispered. "This child must be a man by now. I wonder where he is?" Juan Andres' whereabouts still remained a mystery.

Chapter 79

There stands a tower in Miami, overlooking the bay, that is unlike any other. Today, it is a monument to art deco architecture and an homage to freedom. In the sixties it was the headquarters of the relief service that helped solve the desolate plight of the Cuban exiles. Its rooms saw Cubans find jobs, get free groceries and get relocated to find better opportunities in far corners of the United States. When Fermin and his family left Freedom House in Miami, Jose was waiting to take them home where all the others, including Rosa Garach and Lucas, were expecting them.

"Eighteen thirty-one, 'sausgooest' Seventeenth Terrace."

"Terraz, Fermin; you spell it Terrace, but it's pronounced Terraz."

"Very well," Rosi's father made a quick note of this first English lesson, "Terraz. You know now, Rosi, learn to say things right from the beginning. Listen to your Uncle Jose."

"What does Terraz mean?"

"It's something like a street, Rosi."

"Is *Abuelita* coming to Miami?"

"She arrived today; she's waiting for you at home."

When the headlights of Jose's Plymouth flooded the living room at eighteen thirty-one, family ties were renewed on the lawn in front of the house. Natalia was the first one to see them and ran outside to greet them. Milagros was in the kitchen and came out drying her hands with a dish towel. Rosa got up from her seat. Lucas thought the excitement too much and never admitted that his heart too was beating faster.

"*¡Abuelita!*"

"Mother!"

"Son!"

"Rosi!"

"Aunt Milagros!"

All the names were repeated in unending succession, until the demonstrations of affection were exhausted. Rosa wished for wings instead of arms, to gather under them all her Garachs and hold them close to her.

The lights on the house next door went on in alarm. That section of the Southwest was not used to such commotion.

"My Lord, let's get inside; Americans are not used to these shouts, and they call the police," Milagros said leading them inside the house.

Friends and relatives came to congratulate the newly arrived Garachs. They wished them well with some small gifts that would help them get started again. In the middle of the living room there were sheets, pillowcases, a coffee pot, an iron, a cutlery set, and a toaster; Fermin had more than five hundred dollars cash in his pocket.

"People have been so kind!" Asuncion exclaimed.

"It's always the same over here; family and friends help a lot," Milagros told her as she handed her the dishes to dry. When we first got here nobody had anything and people had to share things. I know families who used the same iron, the same pressure cooker, and they managed like that. Somebody would use it on Monday, somebody else on Tuesday, and so on."

"You don't say!"

"Churches of all denominations helped by distributing food and household items. Thank God we never needed any of that, but I know people who used to dress as if they were going to a costume party. Imagine: The shirt came from the Methodists; the pants from the Baptists; the hat from the Second Church of Christ, Reformed."

"What's that?"

"It's a religion. Over here there are religions with very unusual names."

"Approved by the Pope?"

"No, Asuncion; they are Protestant religions."

"My God!" she exclaimed piously, making the sign of the cross.

"We have this friend who got a hat at one of these church charities. One day, he took his wife grocery shopping on Flagler Street, a street where there are a lot of businesses. Now, pay attention, Manolo, our friend, was dressed in such a way that when he took off his hat to scratch his head, a gentleman who was passing by tossed a coin into it thinking he was a beggar." Both Milagros and Asuncion laughed.

In the living room, Natalia and Rosi listened to their parents, uncles, and aunts talking. Rosa was delighted, but she was sleepy too. She couldn't understand many of the things her children were saying.

"Fermin, you've got to be ready to do whatever comes your way. There are no social classes over here; everybody works and makes an honest living," Lucas advised.

"Don't worry about that; I'm prepared to do whatever comes along."

"I've already talked to someone about a job for you at a cafeteria on Eighth Street," Jose told him.

"And Rosi," Lucas added, "has the right age to go work in a factory. Even at the minimum wage, the three of you will be able to manage on your own."

"What's a factory?" Rosi asked her cousin.

"I'll explain it to you later, Rosi."

"Lucas is right; besides, there's the Refugee Center, that'll help you with doctors and medicines." Fermin was dazzled by so much advice. He took out a handkerchief and dried the perspiration off his forehead.

"Actually . . . Asuncion and I want the girl to study, so that she can have a good future. We're prepared to do anything to help her."

"Studying is for rich people; now you've got to see how you can get enough to eat," Lucas insisted.

"That's right. That's right," Fermin realized that Lucas and he did not see eye to eye on many things and pretended to agree to close the subject.

"I'm leaving," Lucas said suddenly, "it's very late, and I'm flying back to New York tomorrow."

"If you don't mind sleeping in the living room, Lucas, you're welcome to stay and spend the night," Milagros offered.

"No, don't worry, Milagros; thank you. You've got enough already as it is. I'll go to a motel near the airport so that tomorrow I won't have to get up so early. See you later, mother," he said as he kissed Rosa on the forehead, "sleep well."

"You know, son," she added, "about that bank book. I need the money from the sale of the farm," she hesitated for a minute, "to help your brother and you sister, you see."

"That money is safe with me, mother," he chuckled. "You're old. You are fine here with Jose. You won't need anything. Women shouldn't handle money, anyway. We'll talk again when I come back."

Jose took Lucas to the motel, and Milagros tackled the job of distributing the sleeping space in the house. Rosi would, of course, sleep in Natalia's room; Asuncion and Fermin in the sewing room; Jose would sleep in the Florida room. and Rosa would sleep with Milagros in the master bedroom. The house had two bathrooms; Rosa went into one, and Asuncion used the other. Milagros turned off almost all the lights and sat down in the living room with the two teen-agers to await their turn.

"Rosi, Natalia and I have gotten you a few things that may come in handy, and we've kept them for you here. Look, here you are."

"If you need anything, just let us know; we're about the same size, and although I'm a bit taller, there isn't that much difference. What's mine is yours also, Rosi. Listen, don't pay attention to crazy Uncle Lucas; he thinks he can boss people around, and he doesn't really know what he's talking about."

"Natalia! How dare you talk like that about your uncle?"

"It's true, mother. Do you know what he told Uncle Fermin?"

"What?"

"That Rosi's got to go work in a factory."

"What do people do in a factory?"

"They sew, cut thread, and fill boxes with clothes. Everything. That's not for you dear. Natalia is right; don't pay attention to Uncle Lucas. The important thing is for you to study."

"That's what I'd like to do," she admitted shyly.

"You'll see, you'll go to college in September."

"College?"

"Yes, Rosi, a place where you go for the first two years of university studies."

"I don't know too much English."

"You'll make it. On Sunday we'll look for a part-time job for you, and then you'll begin school."

The bathroom door creaked, announcing that *Abuelita* was done. Milagros smiled when she saw her mother-in-law in her pink sleeping gown.

"My, my. Doesn't she look dashing? Look, *Abuelita*, this is our bedroom. You choose the side of the bed you like the best, and I'll sleep on the other."

"But, Milagros, let me sleep somewhere else. Let Jose rest in his bed."

"Jose will sleep somewhere else; besides, who's the most important person around here?" Persuaded by her daughter-in-law, Rosa stayed in the room. Milagros turned off the lights and closed the door. "Good night, *Abuelita*."

Asuncion came out of the bathroom, and Rosi went in.

"Go, Natalia; go to the bathroom."

"You go first, mom."

"Don't you intend to go to bed?"

"I've got this song in my head, and I want to play it on the piano and jot it down before I forget it."

"But, dear, can't you see it's one o'clock and everybody is going to sleep?"

"C'mon, mom; just a while longer."

"Well, until I come out of the bathroom but not one more minute."

Little by little all the noises died down. Rosi went back into the living room and saw her cousin sitting by the piano.

"What are you doing?"

"Sssshhh. Be quiet or I'll lose my concentration. I'm composing a melody." Rosi smiled and tiptoed to her room; the bathroom door creaked once again.

"Natalia!" Milagros called out in a whisper. "That's enough. Go on, go to bed."

"A little while longer, mom."

"Tomorrow you do what you want, but it's too late now; you're going to wake up your *Abuelita*—the whole family."

"Aunt Milagros!"

"Good night, Rosi, dear."

"Why is this room so cold?"

"Your cousin doesn't like the hot weather and turns the air conditioner on really high. She says she prefers to cover herself with blankets.

"Blankets in July?"

"Yes, here they are."

The notes from Natalia's piano could barely be heard, soft and remote as night whimpers. Milagros came out again to remind her daughter that it was very late. She saw her bent over the piano, jotting down the notes, and decided to leave her alone. Quietly, she opened the bedroom door, but Rosa was not sleeping. She had drawn the curtains and was looking out the window, mesmerized, unaware of her daughter-in-law's presence.

"*Abuelita*. What are you doing? I thought you were already asleep." Apparently it was very difficult for everyone in the Garach family to fall asleep that evening.

"I didn't hear you come in, child."

"Did you hear a noise outside? Are you afraid?"

She could not say that. When she looked out the window at the sky, she saw she had found the stars.

Chapter 80

Miguelito arrived on Saturday, four days after his parents. He came alone, bringing with him only a long list of reasons why he had been unable to come earlier. Such was Miguel and Lucia's joy, that they did not give him a chance to excuse his behavior or explain his delay. It did not matter. The important thing was that they were together again, and that he had come to get them. Lucia and Miguel really wanted to make up for lost time with Miguelito. Nine years before, their farewell notes had been harsh and dissonant. The couple wanted to give what they had never given before: love.

Rosa Garach was an old woman, but she was no fool. Besides, lately she was forced to understand things by merely looking at people since many spoke in a tongue and even at a speed which were not her own. After the initial moments of happiness, she observed her grandson's attitude and felt uncomfortable. The joy Miguel expressed was never present in his son's eyes. Lucia had sat next to the young man and tried to take him by the arm, but Miguelito got away from his mother and sat on an easy chair by himself, conveniently removed from his parents. Something was definitely wrong. The young man, full of rancor had not forgotten the bitterness that had driven him away from Miguel and Lucia.

"C'mon, *Abuelita*, let's go inside; it's very hot out here." Milagros begged Rosa as the couple and their son headed for the automobile.

"What's going to happen here?" the old woman wondered outloud.

"Don't worry; we'll just have to wait and see. Maybe when he spends some time with them, he'll treat them better."

"Holy Madonna de l'Avella, help my daughter," she sighed when Miguelito, Lucia, and Miguel got inside the car and drove off.

On the morning following his son's visit, old Miguel had neither laughter nor loving words to remember from the previous day. Still in bed, he prayed with his eyes closed. His prayers helped him overcome the emptiness, but it was difficult for him not to think, for he was very much aware that the cupboards of his new apartment were bare, and that there was only a pitcher of water in the refrigerator.

"Lucia," he called out, "where are you?"

"In the living room."

"So early?"

"It's cooler over here," she lied.

"What time is it?"

"I don't know; maybe around seven."

What did time matter? She was still trying to understand what had happened the day before. The light coming through the naked windows cried out to her: "You're alone; you're hungry." Lucia refused to listen. Her son was not a bad boy. After the part about "everybody's got to fend for himself," the conversation had turned less tense, but Lucia could not hear the explanations that Miguelito gave her. The words which her son had uttered with demolishing impact, danced before her eyes for the rest of the afternoon.

They tried to look for an apartment. Twice she kept herself from asking him: "Take me home, son; I don't feel well." Their home was . . . was it ninety miles away? But that was no longer theirs. Finally, they found a place. It was on a two-way traffic street, where trees and cars vied for first place. She did not understand why they called it Coral Way, the coral road, as Miguelito told them.

The address was 1874 Coral Way, first apartment upstairs to the left. They went back to Milagros', gathered their few belongings and some household items they had been given, and then were unceremoniously dropped at their new place. The whirlwind came to an end as Miguelito closed the door and silence engulfed them. Lucia and her husband did not look at each other after that; each one went into a different room as if in fleeing from each other, they could escape their own truth. She made the bed while he looked out the window and saw the automobiles rushing down Coral Way. They undressed to go to bed and, even before the birds and the sun had finished their song, they closed their eyes and pretended to sleep.

"Did you sleep well, Lucia?"

"Yes, I did," she lied again.

"Don't worry. He's not a bad boy; it's just that he's not used to having us around" he said as if he had heard her thoughts instead of her words. "Are you feeling all right?"

"The apartment is very comfortable, isn't it?"

"Are you hungry?" He was in the living room and, for the first time since the night before, she looked at him.

"A little. What are we going to do?"

"We have money, look; we've got quite a bit left over after paying one month's rent and one month's security."

"Did you see any grocery stores around here?"

"Why don't we go out and get a bite to eat somewhere?"

"Remember what they said at Milagros' house; over here they mug anyone for money. Miguel," she hesitated.

"Yes?"

"Why don't we go back to Cuba? I was thinking, if we went back right away, wouldn't they give us our home and pension again?"

"That's no longer ours, Lucia. We gave everything up to come here."

"What are we going to do here without Miguelito? I never imagined we'd be alone. If I had known . . ."

The sentence was never finished and, before they were able to continue, a knock on the door returned to them part of the hope they had lost the day before. Miguel ran into the bedroom to put on a shirt. Lucia combed her hair in the bathroom.

"It must be him, Miguel. The boy must have thought things over and is coming back to see us. Maybe he's even going to take us with him."

"Open up, Lucia; we don't want him to think we're still in bed. He might leave if we don't answer."

"Coming, coming!: She was smiling as she unbolted the three locks.

"Hi, dear."

A pair of piercing blue eyes inundated with love and maternal insight looked at Lucia; those eyes knew what was happening just by a glance. It was Rosa, the old woman with the apron, still unable to read or write, but wise in human feelings. She took her daughter's hand and entered the apartment slowly. Milagros followed close behind holding a tray with some coffee and buttered bread.

Chapter 81

Make it touch me. God, make the light touch me. Don't let it stay up there like it did yesterday: first in front; then to the side; then behind, but up there. It's eight meters, God. Or maybe four. Tell it to come down. You can do everything; tell it to come down and touch me. I can't lift up my head any more. I've got a thread for a neck and if I look up, I know it'll break and then, what will I do? A headless body, supported by other bodies, trembling, warm, wet bodies like mine. So, ask the light to come down and touch me and bring me, with its long arm, a piece of the sky from where it comes, so that I know that I'm still alive.

I haven't lifted my arms for centuries; they're stuck to my body and to other bodies; and my hands . . . are they still mine? I don't feel them any more. I look up, and I see nothing but a wall, a coarse wall. I'm a tall woman, and all I see is a carpet of heads, God, between my body and the wall. Those in front of me cry or look up and call You, God; yesterday I counted twenty-eight of them. Then, I felt the touch of a hairy body reminding me that I still had legs. One cord stroked my ankle; then another; it was a tickling sensation. Someone behind me managed to say feebly: "Rats!" and I shivered, because I felt no fear or revolt. Could I have lost so much? Is it that I can no longer feel? "Rats!" They repeated it many times and those three hundred bodies wanted to move but couldn't, for there were three-hundred of us, God. I was able to count twenty-eight, but there were more beyond the reach of my eyes. Three hundred bodies crying with sweat, urine, and blood. I felt tears slide down my thighs, plough furrows along my legs and finally hit the hairy warmth nestled on my feet. I could feel my body weeping, but I could smell the crying of my fellow inmates, piercing what was left of my body. And yet, it didn't hurt, God; it didn't hurt because it bound me to the others as much as the pressure of our bodies against one another; we were sisters, joined in a common womb of coarse, colorless walls; a womb eight meters—or is it four?—high, with a breath of light that doesn't reach me, God, that doesn't reach me.

I heard a complaint that soon filled up the cell: "Doc-tor, Doc-tor." The sisters in the other ward needed medical assistance and were asking for it in desperate screams: "Doc-tor!" I wanted to protest too, to join the others, but I remembered my son, God, when he used to pretend he was a doctor and would come with his plastic stethoscope trying to listen to my heart and assuring me that he had heard it beating in the middle of my chest. I don't think he was lying, God; my heart would've gone wherever he would have ordered it to go. "Doc-tor, Doc-tor." That's what my baby would say, God, the son they've stolen from me, just like they've stolen my life. Don't believe them if they prove to You that I still breathe, because they've taken away most of my life on the tips of their sharp bayonets or the butts of their rifles. They've taken away my life, God; I've left pieces of it on the dark floors of the cells. Now, the rat gnawing at my ankle is sucking at my remains, drop by drop. What life is left in me is as fragile as the thread I feel holding my head up.

"We'll be home tomorrow." Do you remember, God? That's what I told Andres before I left. He had a premonition and that was why he looked at me so insistently and asked me: "Why are we doing this?" Could they have murdered him, God? I dream I see him for an instant, and I ask him: "Do you understand why I did it?" He never answers. Could he have died without understanding my reasons? It would be even worse if he were still alive and thought the whole thing useless or absurd . . .

Why does someone always sing in jail? An old Spanish song comes from the corner to the right, and I could swear that the tune cools off the bodies next to me. Somebody's moving; my support has left me for a fraction of a second. My legs give way. The rat has fled, imagining itself crushed by the weight of my body. Silly animal. If it had realized that I'm only a bag of bones it would have laughed. My sisters prop me up and keep my head above the sea of bodies. Didn't I tell You that we were really sisters?

You haven't listened to me, God, and You're taking the light away. I don't blame You for that. I know it's your duty, and that the rest of the world depends on it. But they don't know when You take the light away, the room around me shrinks to nothingness, until my eyes are empty, and I can't even see the forehead of the woman who jabs at my chest with her frail body.

Someone has just announced that they're coming to let us out. They hear keys and footsteps. Of course, when the eyes become empty in the darkness, the ears capture even things beyond their reach. Do You know that I'm afraid to leave this place? I'm afraid, although I've been on my feet for more than twenty-four hours, talking to You. Remember, I've already seen Your light twice from here.

I hear keys. Will we be able to move away from one another when they open the door? Listen to them cry. Is it joy, or could it be that they're as frightened as I am? The human mass we were until a moment ago grows less compact; we return to our condition of separate beings; one by one they must be filing out from the cell. Now it's my turn. My legs don't respond. God, tell them to move. They've been still for so long that . . . God, please make them do it. Being left alone here would be a far worse torture than being locked up with all the others. It's sad not to feel a human heartbeat close by; that's at least some consolation.

Thank you, God. Was it You or was it the woman next to me, who grabbed my arm and led me out of the cell?

Guanajay! The alarming news spreads like wildfire. That's what they were plotting, to take us to Guanajay, the prison where even the female guards take advantage of the inmates and abuse them in the most intimate ways. The news spreads: Guanajay! In silent agreement we lock our arms and forge a chain of human steel; remember, God, I don't have much strength left. Guanajay. We are all out in the yard now, our arms interlocked, and they're trying to force us inside a truck. Is it You who's given me strength? For I'm holding fast, God, and though my legs think they're going to collapse by themselves, they hold me up. The hands I thought would never again belong to me are mine once more, God, and they hold on to Your arms, or are they my sisters'?

In spite of kicks and blows with the butts of their rifles, we resist, and no one remembers the smell of sweat, blood and urine, or the tickling contact of the rats. We endure it and, their designs foiled, they hurt us madly with violent jets of water that come—damned darkness!—from I don't know where. We fall to the floor, and they curse us because they can't pry us apart; gradually we become a chain of laughter. Laughter, God! Was it your idea?

I have been among the first to fall. I sink my cheeks in one of the huge puddles and laugh even louder. How delightful the feeling of water on my lips, on my legs! Suddenly, I sense that my son is alive and thinking of me! Was it You, God, who chose the night to shed some light on me? I've felt, God, that Juan Andres is safe; I also felt that Andres understands.

Chapter 82

Almost a century of events failed to exhaust Rosa's stamina and will to live. She felt certain that death played hide and seek with her, and was always looking for some sign of its proximity. The word death assailed her during the still of the night. Then, she would ask herself: "¿*Plegaré?* Will I make it?" And there would always be a star that, with a twinkle of light, would reassure her. Then she could go to sleep in peace and dream with her eyes still open that Juan Andes was coming back, that Norma was getting out of jail, and that Lucas would let her have the money from the sale of the farm to buy a house for Lucia and Fermin.

They could not give her a party for her ninetieth birthday because Carolina died suddenly; a diabetic coma, Milagros told her.

"A diabetic coma," she repeated.

"Yes, *Abuelita*; it's something that gets in your blood and kills you," Natalia explained slowly, with kindness.

"So young! Carolina was only sixty-seven!" Rosa complained sadly.

Rosa didn't eat for two days. It surely was sinful to eat after such profound sorrow. On the third day she broke her fast, and two days later she began to dream again. *Diabetic coma* joined *communism* among the most painful words in her vocabulary.

"Come, *Abuelita*; it's time for dinner. You know how hungry people get in this house around seven o'clock," Natalia tried to lighten up her grandmother's somber mood.

Milagros went into the kitchen and began to call her family one by one, by name, the way she did every night.

"Dad! Jose! Come, dinner is served."

Gerardo was usually in the back yard at that time; Cuba and the Revolution were very far away.

"Natalia! Mother!"

Between six-thirty and seven in the evening, the house on Seventeen "Terraz" was in full motion. Jose sat at one end of the table, Gerardo at the other. Natalia and Rosa between the table and the wall; Joaquina and her daughter, across from them, closest to the kitchen.

"Natalia, go to your room and get dressed. I don't like you to come to the table in your pajamas," Jose complained.

"I came home dead tired from a full day at the university. It's too hot, dad. Please, let me stay like this. We're all family anyway," Natalia's arguments usually prevailed.

"All right. But let this be the last time. Tomorrow, no pajamas."

"All right. Can I help you, mother?"

"No, don't get up. There's no room in this kitchen for so many people. *Abuelita*, please, sit next to Natalia," Milagros suggested.

It was the same problem every day. Rosa had to get across to reach her side of the table. She shrank when she had to go past Gerardo, much to the merriment of the rest of the group.

"Please, don Gerardo, you go first," as if her words were not enough, she even bowed to him.

"Rosa, I insist, you go first, please."

"Come, *Abuelita*, sit down or you food is going to get cold."

The old lady lowered her eyes and sat at her usual place.

"Milagros, listen. Do you know who called today?"

"I'm sorry, *Abuelita* Joaquina; mom, do you suppose you could finish my white skirt for next week?"

"Yes, Natalia; it will be ready this Friday. Who called, mother?"

"Miguelito, your nephew."

"On a Wednesday? Is he here in Miami?"

"I think so. He wanted to talk to Jose; he said someone was after him."

"After him?"

"Yes, some government agency; the one that's in charge of investigations."

"The FBI?"

"No, I don't think so. But it's something like that."

"The CIA?" Natalia asked.

"Right!"

"That boy's got bats in the belfry," Gerardo commented.

"Dad, please!" Milagros motioned discreetly, pointing at Rosa. "She shouldn't hear such things."

"Maybe it was some practical joker, mother. Did you recognize his voice?"

"It sounded like him, and he kept asking for his uncle."

"Well, he'll call back if it's important. Let's change the subject," Milagros warned. "*Abuelita* may be a little deaf, but she's no fool . . ."

"Hey, Gerardo, did you see the potatoes I brought home? I bought them for a customer. I had never seen potatoes as big as those. They are Iago potatoes and look . . . They are this big," Jose added, stretching out his hands to show the size of the potatoes.

"And where did that guy Iago get such big potatoes?"

"My customer's name isn't Iago."

"Who's Iago, dad?"

"You ought to know that, Natalia. That's the place where they grow the best potatoes in the country." The girl, her grandfather, and her mother looked at one another confused.

"Do you mean Idaho?"

"Whatever. They grow these real big potatoes in that place."

"You've been in this country so many years and still you haven't learned how to pronounce things right. It's 'Idao'."

"No, grandpa, it's pronounced Ida*ho*. In English, the 'h' is not mute, as in Spanish. It sounds like out 'j'."

"See, Jose? Just like I told you," the old man insisted.

The evening meal always ended with a peaceful argument over a wide range of subjects: the foreign policy of the United States, civil rights for blacks, or the special sale at the neighborhood supermarket. That Wednesday, however, the doorbell interrupted the conversation.

"See what I mean, Natalia? Go to your room; somebody could see you in those pajamas!" Jose objected.

"Who could it be at this time? Jose, you open the door; my hands are wet. People shouldn't make social calls on weekdays; tonight I had planned to finish Natalia's skirt and . . ."

"Miguelito! This sure is a coincidence! Joaquina was just telling us that some nut called saying things about the CIA. She thought it might have been you; the voice sounded like yours. When did you come to Miami? On a Wednesday? That's odd." Milagros felt a sense of foreboding when she heard her nephew's name.

"It was me, uncle. No, I'm not a nut; it's the truth," the young man explained in the living room. "I called because it's true. I owe the bank a lot of money, and they want to kill me."

"Don't talk nonsense, kid. In this country, they don't kill people because they owe money."

"They'll kill me, I know. I left Orlando because I realized that they were pumping poisonous gas through the air conditioning ducts and they were going to kill the three of us: Susana, the baby, and me. Now, as soon as we got here, they've got this guy tailing us. You've got to help me, uncle, you've got to help me."

Milagros signaled her husband not to answer. Jose got up and walked over to his desk to light up a cigar.

"Miguelito, where are Susana and the baby now?"

"They are at her parents!" His hair was wet from copious perspiration; he looked wan and pale, with dark rings around his eyes.

"Son, are you sleeping well?"

"No, Aunt Milagros; I can't afford to sleep. I have to be on the lookout. If I let my guard down, they'll find me and . . ."

"Look, why don't you and I take a look outside?" Milagros felt a chill run up her spine as she got up. "There's nobody there, see? What happens is that you haven't had a good rest in days, and that's made you nervous."

"No, I saw them, I tell you. It's the CIA. They've got me surrounded. They're liable to bomb this place."

"Jose, come here."

"What's the matter?" This type of situation always put him in a bad mood.

"Let's take Miguelito to Susana's parents'; he needs to rest. You go with him in his car, and I'll drive ours."

"They'll find me, Aunt Milagros, they will. If I go back, they'll grab me."

"Nothing will happen to you with us; you'll see," she answered patiently, leading him by the arm.

Rosa looked at them from her chair in the dining room. Suddenly, the food seemed to have disagreed with her. She did not understand why Jose and Milagros had gone out with Miguelito. Natalia, who had heard the door close, came out of her room and immediately noticed the change in her grandmother's attitude.

"Is anything the matter?"

"You have no idea how terrible it is not to know, Natalia! Your mother and father went out with Miguelito."

"Where did they go?"

"I don't know. He was swearing a lot; he looked at me but didn't see me. He said somebody was after him."

"Who?"

"I didn't understand."

"We'll find out when mom gets back. Why don't you come and watch the soap opera with *Abuelita* Joaquina and me?"

"Miguelito's sick; he didn't look well."

"Don't say that, *Abuelita*. We don't know for sure yet. Maybe he's tired or had a fight with his wife or something. Come, *Abuelita*, the program is about to start."

"Remember, Natalia, that your father doesn't like me to watch television so late. He'll be angry when he gets back."

"Don't pay any attention to him. Come, you should get your mind off things and get rid of that long face." She took her by the arm and Rosa, with a sigh, followed her granddaughter.

Two hours later, Milagros breathed in relief when she saw Natalia huddled up in an easy chair, watching television with both her grandmothers. "Guard her, please, Lord. Protect my son too. Heal Lucia's son, please." Jose just slammed the door.

"Who is it?" Natalia asked, reaching up from her chair.

"It's us; don't be alarmed."

"I don't know why I watch these dumb soap operas," Natalia mumbled.

"Hey, it isn't all that bad and besides, it's the only way we get to see your face. Otherwise you wouldn't come out at all; all you ever do is study. You have to have some fun too!" Something in Jose's voice echoed of Juan Garach.

"Even dad's here watching tonight's episode," Milagros said, looking at Gerardo. "Well, what happened? Did I miss something exciting?"

She sat next to her daughter; and Jose went inside the kitchen for a glass of water. He was still upset; he would have preferred to have gone to bed right away, but he saw his mother in the group and called out to her:

"Hey, mother, what are you doing still up at eleven o'clock at night?" Everybody fell silent; only the television set continued to be heard. "Haven't I told you a hundred times that you should go to bed by ten?"

Rosa stopped smiling and looked at her son.

"Come, let's go to bed," he said, taking her by the arm as if to assert his authority. Rosa got up. The others were watching her, and the old lady was obviously embarrassed.

"Listen, dad, leave *Abuelita* alone, will you? She's having a good time," Natalia said firmly.

"Your *Abuelita* will do as I say," he ordered. Natalia got up and dared to walk over to her *Abuelita* and speak again.

"Look, *Abuelita* is over ninety years old, and she can do as she pleases, including the time she goes to bed."

"Natalia, how dare you?"

"*Abuelita*, are you sleepy yet?" the girl ignored her father's command.

"Child, don't ask for trouble."

"If you're not sleepy, come, sit down here where I was; it's more comfortable than the chair you had." She held the old lady by the arm, pulled her away from Jose and helped her sit down again.

The rest of the family appeared to be holding its breath. It took all of Jose's self-control to keep him from striking the impudent young woman. He flung to the floor the glass he was holding in his hand and went into his bedroom, slamming the door behind him.

"Natalia, how dare you contradict your father like that?" Sometimes Milagros wished her daughter were not so impulsive.

"Mom, you know I can't stand injustice. Dad seems to be under the impression that *Abuelita*'s a slave or has lost the ability to make her own decisions. I can't stand that attitude; he's got to learn to treat her like a person."

"Well, do you or don't you want me to tell you what happened in tonight's episode?" Joaquina asked her daughter.

Natalia's reaction made Rosa wonder what would El Morellano have done with a character like her granddaughter.

Chapter 83

East of Twenty-Seventh Avenue, Eighth Street had a flavor all its own. It smelled of Cuban coffee, roast pork and fried plantains. It tasted of mango, coconut water and *pastelitos de guayaba*. It sounded of Celia Cruz and Benny Moré, of crackling dominoes and *piropos*—loud compliments to pretty girls—on every corner. It felt of tight dresses, rhythmically swaying hips and the warmth of its inhabitants who in the 1970s were mostly Cubans. By five o'clock in the afternoon, Fermin was in charge of the counter at a coffee shop on Eighth Street. His behavior was ample proof that no happier man existed, now that he had a steady job. Finally, at midnight, the last customer was gone. The sidewalks were empty. Fermin closed the counter facing the street and saw Rosi waiting for him across the street in the old Ford.

"Hi, honey. Been waiting long? I'm sorry. Today was my first day, and I lost track of time. It won't happen again, I promise."

"Oh, it's all right, dad. Actually, I'm glad. I had a chance to rest. When I get home now, I'll have to study for a test I have tomorrow."

"You're doing fine, love, aren't you?" The young woman answered with a happy smile.

"I can't complain, although this first semester at the University of Miami has been tough."

"When you graduate, you'll be glad you made the effort."

"I wish you couldn've seen what happened to me in school today; it was really odd. I was studying in the library, and this boy came to talk to me."

"Did he get fresh with you," he asked upset.

"Oh no; nothing like that. A real good-looking boy, but it was the strangest thing."

"What do you mean?"

"First, he walked up to me, and he asked me my name. He looked like a decent enough guy, so I told him. When he found out my name was Garach, he looked at me as if he were impressed. I told him I'm Cuban, and we talked for a while."

"You shouldn't talk to strangers like that. One never knows, and if he turns out to be a bum, he can give you a scare."

"Don't worry, dad; nothing can happen in the library."

"What did he tell you?"

"He told me about himself; he's an economics major. We have a lot of things in common; he also misses Cuba a lot."

"Please, honey, not that again."

"No, don't worry. I miss Cuba, but it isn't like I'm ready to get on the first plane back. For the first time since I arrived in Miami, I've shared that feeling with somebody," she said. "But, listen, that's not the best part of the story."

"Did he get fresh with you? Tell me the truth, Rosi. If anybody lays a finger on you, I'll . . ."

"Calm down. Do you suppose that if he had done something to me I'd be here talking like this?"

"So?"

"Nothing. Marcos . . ."

"What's his name?"

"Marcos Uriarte. He fled to the United States and sought asylum here."

"Did he come over in a boat?"

"No, he asked for asylum first in Canada."

"From Cuba?"

"No, he was on his way back from Russia."

"Rosi, you'd better watch what you say to this man. He may be a spy, and they may deport us or take away the money we get from the Refugee Center. You'd better be very careful, honey."

"No, dad, he's not a spy. But, look, when I told him my name, he asked me if I had any brothers. I told him I didn't and then he asked me if I had any cousins. When I asked him why so many questions, he told me that he had had a friend in the Soviet Union with that same last name."

"In Russia? A Garach in Russia?"

"You want to know his name?"

"Come now, Rosi, don't tease me like that. Who is it?"

"Juan Andres."

Chapter 84

On the morning after Miguelito's attempted suicide, Rosa saw the sun rise and light up the entire area she saw from her window. She hadn't put on her nightgown or gone to bed; her place was next to her daughter Lucia. They had refused to take her to the hospital because she was too old, and the hospital may frighten her. The least she thought she could do was to spend the night up, praying by the telephone.

She had answered the call the night before. It seemed like her daughter's voice, but Lucia asked most urgently for Jose. Then, they talked about Miguelito and pills. His son did not answer the questions and went out with Milagros in great haste.

Yes, she knew her grandson was ill; Natalia had told her. The boy had taken a bottle of sleeping pills; that's why he looked dead. It was to be expected; when the nerves are not all right—well, one never knows. No, that night she could not watch television or sit down to chat like other nights; her grandson might be dying in some hospital. She felt much more comfortable sitting in the dark, by the window, saying Hail Marys to the Madonna de l'Avella, and hoping that the Mother of God would soon hear her prayers.

Milagros found her the following morning, her head leaning against the windowsill and the rosary lying on the floor.

"Wake up, *Abuelita*," she said, patting her softly on the back.

"Milagros!" Life filled Rosa's blue eyes once more.

"Are you all right?" Milagros asked, rubbing the old lady's back.

"Yes, I was praying, and I must've dozed off," she apologized, straightening out her hair and smoothing out the marks of unrest on her apron.

"Have you had breakfast yet?"

"No, I don't want anything. How's Miguelito? How's Lucia?"

"He's out of danger. We talked to the doctors, and they have to keep hin in the hospital under observation to see if he'll get over it."

"Will he be all right?"

"Probably, if he reacts well to his treatment. What about you? Have you slept at all?"

"I've been thinking all night, Milagros, and I believe I should get a house and move."

"Move? A house."

"I should go and live with Lucia."

"With Lucia? There's no room there. Miguelito sleeps in the living room; the only other place is that small Florida room."

"Right; that's why we need a house. I'm certain; it is my duty to her. Milagros, I want you to call Lucas and tell him that I want him to buy me a house with the money from the farm."

"*Abuelita*, you know how hard that's going to be."

"My daughter needs it. That farm belonged to her father, that money should go to those who need it most. We could all live in that house; Lucas promised, and so far he hasn't come through."

"You need to be comfortable. But I really don't know how we can get Lucas to agree."

"I never had any comforts until I was an old woman. All my life I was cold in winter, hot in the summer; my life has had quite a few sorrows. Haven't you noticed that I can't cry any more? She's my daughter, she needs me. I must do what I want at least this once."

Rosa Garach became thoughtful for a few moments and asked:

"Milagros, do you know Cachita Montero?"

"Cachita?" of course Milagros knew.

"Yes, the mother of Lucas' boys. That woman who helped hide Andres. Do you know her? Do you know if she came from Cuba too?"

"Well, *Abuelita*, you know how things are. With Juan working with Lucas and all, I don't know exactly where she lives, but it wouldn't be difficult to find out."

"Call her for me, and tell her I want to see her quickly."

Milagros did not dare pry into the old woman's reasons for wanting to see Cachita so suddenly.

When Milagros left the room, Rosa searched in one of her drawers until she found an old, worn notebook. It was the same one in which Juan Andres had taught her how to write her name, and every page had years of Rosa Garach written neatly. The first were unintelligible, slowly the letters became round, smoothly joined to one another and clear. She had never learned to read, but she had finally learned to sign her name and perhaps today her lifetime effort would prove worthwhile.

Milagros came through with Cachita Montero's telephone number, and the following day the woman was in to see her. *Abuelita* Rosa was up to something, Milagros could tell. What was surprising was that in all the years that she had known the old woman, Milagros had never seen her more focused or determined. Cachita came at midday, when Natalia was at school, Gerardo and Jose were at work, and only Milagros and her mother tended to the house. *Abuelita* Rosa was grateful that Milagros and Joaquina had left on an errand.

It was early September; a rain shower had cooled the otherwise warm breeze that filtered through the living room blinds. Cachita sat at one end of the sofa and Rosa at another. Rosa looked at her hands, parched and neatly folded, covered with the scent of soap of over seventy years of washing.

"I'm glad you're here, Cachita. At first, I wasn't even sure you had come from Cuba."

"Oh, yes, abuelita. I came after my second son, Alberto, left the island. I escaped by boat, the Vodoo, with Polito Cruz, one of Norma's frieds. It must have been . . ." She closed her eyes thoughtfully. "About six years ago."

"I am old, Cachita; may I call you *Cachita*?" her eyes for the first time glanced directly at her.

"I call you *Abuelita*, don't I?" The old woman smiled.

"You know, I don't know much about things, about business, about money. There is something that I need to do, and I need help."

"I hope I know enough to help you, but if I do . . ."

"My son Lucas, a few years ago, sold my husband's farm in Spain," she began. "It wasn't worth a fortune, but he received good money for it. That much I know." Rosa hesitated in an effort to find the right words in her still peasant mind. "I have never had anything that was mine. When my husband was alive, he gave the orders and made every decision. I could never express my views or my needs. That's how my children, one by one, left my home, that's how I spent years without really knowing where they were, because my husband throughout my life with him said that women don't need to write."

Cachita, whose nature was impulsive and expressive, moved closer to the old woman and instinctively took both her hands in her own.

"When my husband died, I came to my children, and they were the ones who took over. Never again did I have a home of my own, all of them, God bless them, treated me well, but none of them knew that there were certain things I wanted to do." She paused. "I am over ninety now, I've even stopped counting years, but I need to do one last thing for my daughter, and that's why I need your help."

"Where do we begin?"

"This will mean going behind Lucas' back, for if he were to find out, then it would truly be impossible."

"I have done well going behind Lucas' back before," Cachita smiled.

"I could tell. That's why I called you. I need to get the money for the farm."

"Your money," Cachita added to dispel any guilt from the old woman's mind.

"Lucas has a bank account in his name and mine, and that's where he keeps it."

"Could he have spent it already? Maybe he put it in the business."

"I saw it before we came to Miami, about a year ago."

"Could he have it here, in Miami?"

"I don't know, but if you could find that bank book . . ."

"We could go to the bank, and we could withdraw the money."

"I don't know what that is, but we could take the money to buy a house for Lucia, so I could help them. They're the poorest ones."

"Are you sure the account is under your name?"

"It has my name second, Lucas showed me; I know it says Rosa Garach."

"If we go to the bank, can you sign your name?"

"Juan Garach always said that women don't need to write. I knew he was wrong, so Rosa Garach is all I have ever written for the past seventy years." She looked at her hands and stretched her fingers. "I think I could do it at the bank, don't you?"

Chapter 85

Lucas enjoyed celebrations; that's why, every year, on the day of the company's anniversary, he took all his employees to an elaborate dinner, to note their success. Cachita knew, and she waited for that day in mid-September.

She had kept her promise to Carolina and had never spoken again to Lucas Garach, but she was close to her son Juan, and when there was a need, she went to his office to see him. That is why it wasn't strange for the guard to see the woman come through the door.

"How are you doing, Emilio?" Cachita was at her Sunday best with her light pink linen dress and her high heels, and the security guard would have never guessed her humble origins.

"You look well, Doña Cachita." He smiled. "But you know that Don Juan has gone to the big party."

"Oh, yes, Emilio, I know, but Juan asked me to get something for him, that's why I'm here."

Emilio himself unlocked the door and let her in. When she eluded his supervision, Cachita Montero went straight to Lucas' office.

Cachita aimed first for the desk drawers, but had no luck. They were full of old correspondence and memos. It took her some time to find a section and the end of the bottom drawer of the cabinet labeled "Passports."

"This is the private stuff," Cachita muttered to herself.

She took the file and placed it on top of his desk. She could not help but look up at the picture of Carolina and her daughter which he kept next to the telephone. Cachita stretched out her hand and with the tips of her fingers caressed Carolina's image. How could one care so much for another who had been one's enemy? Nah! it did not matter any more. Carolina was no longer alive, and there was nothing left of Cachita's story with Lucas, except Juan and Alberto, of course. Nervously, she searched the file. There were Carolina's old passport; next to it was Rosa's. She took Rosa's just in case and put it in her pocket. There were Lucas' citizenship certificate, his passport . . . Bank books were next. *Lucas Garach,* read one. *Lucas Garach,* again, read another. There were two cancelled books. Cachita's fingers sped through the file. There, at the end, was one that read Lucas Garach and Rosa Garach. It was old, opened in 1970; no withdrawals: *$47,200.00.* Cachita banged lightly on the desk as a sign of victory. She put the bank book in her other pocket and sped out of the office, forgetting to place the file back in its place.

Chapter 86

Celebration or no celebration, Lucas never went home from any kind of meeting or activity without returning to the office to set his agenda for the following day. In his seventies, he still kept the same spirit that had helped him start anew so many times. Late that night, he greeted Emilio, the old guard by the door.

"Everything quiet all afternoon?"

"Not bad for a Friday, sir. Had to turn a few people away, but they said they would come back Monday."

Lucas nodded and proceeded to his office. The light was on. He had to get after that new secretary. Great capitals were built from small sacrifices. Watching electricity consumption was one of them. It was inexcusable to leave his light on uselessly through the day. He sat at his desk, closed his eyes, and rested for a few seconds. It was when he opened his eyes that the file labeled "Passports" opened on his desk, caught his attention. He hadn't had any need for that file for days. He wasn't planning to travel. He sprung from his chair and walked around the desk for some more clues. Someone had been searching through his things that afternoon. There was nothing of real value there; he kept his money, deeds, really important matters in the box on the wall, in the closet between his and Juan's office, but someone had been through his desk that afternoon. Curious and angry, he dashed to Emilio to investigate the matter further.

"Emilio, exactly who was here today?"

The old guard could sense urgency in Lucas' voice, so he turned to the sign-in sheet.

"Well, sir. There wasn't much going on, like I said. The exterminator was here; two packages were delivered. I think that was it . . . Oh, and Mrs. Montero came to get something for Mr. Juan. You know, Mr. Juan's mother? She came. She's been here before, though. That's why I let her in. She went to Mr. Juan's office to get something. She left rather fast, I would say."

Lucas approached the man to see for himself Cachita's name on the list. Cachita Montero. Now, what had that woman come to get from Juan's office?

"Thank you, Emilio," he said putting the list down and heading back to the main office.

"Anything wrong, sir?"

Lucas had no time to answer. Oblivious to the guard, he walked as quickly as his legs could carry him to Juan's office, which was next to his.

Chapter 87

Cachita would have rather waited for Saturday morning before taking Rosa to the bank, but she changed her mind when she remembered that she hadn't put things back in order at Lucas' office. That old Valencian had a way of reading people's minds; it would not be long before he realized what she and Rosa were planning to do. One didn't have to be too creative to imagine his fury. Cachita had never seen anyone contradict Lucas' wishes, and it pleased her to think that this meek, old woman, who had seldom carried out her wishes could, this once, get her way.

"Is Miss Rosa at home, please?" Cachita could not recognize the voice who answered, but she had to get through to Rosa and let her know that she was ready to pick her up to go to the bank.

"Well, yes. Who's calling?"

"It's Cachita Montero. Juan's mother," she added.

"Hi, Mrs. Montero. This is Natalia Garach." The young woman's voice seemed to recognize Cachita's relationship to the Garach family. "*Abuelita* will be right with you."

"Alloy . . ." Rosa Garach was as foreign to telephone language as she could have been to computers, but she tried to say the customary "hellos" the same as everyone else.

"*Abuelita* Rosa, it's Cachita. I have it."

"The money?"

"No, not yet. I have your bank book. Now, we must go to the bank and close the account, so you can get the money."

"When, tomorrow?"

"I'm afraid it has to be today. Lucas, your son, is bound to find out about this soon and could try to stop you."

"What will I have to do?"

"I have your passport. Bring your green card. You will have to sign a slip of paper asking the bank to close your account and give you your money."

"*Cha!*" Indeed she was about to do something extraordinary. "Sign my name?"

"Yes. I'll pick you up in about fifteen minutes, *Abuelita* Rosa." Because she felt the old woman's voice tremble, she had to ask something before saying good-bye," The time has come for you to sign."

"Yes, I know," she said, although she was not very sure at all that her hand could remain still long enough to do it. She did not want to confess to Cachita that she had never had to sign her name officially before.

She hung up the telephone and rushed to her room in the converted garage. She had to sign her name; she *had* to sign her name. Women need to write! Rosa untied the string that held her apron in place and got her purse and her sweater ready for her journey. She took a clean handkerchief, wet it in cologne, immediately, she went to her drawer to find the book that had accompanied her seventy years and had seen Rosa Garach turn from a scribble to legible letters. So much kindness linked to this book. It had been Socorro, and Candido and Balbina. Don Poli had done his share; then for years she had signed her name alone. Her grandchildren had helped her next, Miguelito and Rosi, Natalia and . . . Juan Andres. If that money could bring him back, she would give it all up. She had to sign her name. She brought a chair next to her dresser drawer, opened the book at the last page and tried to steady her grip on the pencil. R-O-S-A G-A-R-A-C-H. R-O-S-A G-A-R-A-C-H. Natalia's hand on her shoulders suddenly scared her.

"Women need to write!" she uttered incoherently.

"*Abuelita*, what are you saying? It's almost dinner time, let's go."

"Not tonight, Natalia. Tell your mother I have to go out for a while."

"Alone?" Natalia had never seen her go out on her own.

"No, Cachita Montero is picking me up. She'll bring me back."

"*¡Abuelita!*" the young woman smiled, for suddenly, at that very moment, her grandmother had gained individual stature, and had become alive. "That's great, *Abuelita*. Where are you going? The movies?"

"No, Natalia. I have to go and do what I think is right."

Cachita had arrived; they could hear the hum of her car's motor. Rosa wanted to go meet her, so Natalia helped her grandmother up the short steps, out the door, and to Cachita's car outside. Never had *Abuelita* Rosa seemed so persevering; never had Natalia seen her take her purse with such firmness or walk with more determination.

When she walked inside the house, the telephone rang, and Natalia ran to answer it.

"Hi, Uncle Lucas . . . Yes, she was here up to a minute ago, but she had to go out . . . Yes, out . . . No, she went out with a friend of the family . . . No, she didn't go to the doctor. I don't know where she went, just out . . . " Lucas would not hang up until his niece told him who had come to pick up Rosa. "Well, if you really want to know, it was Cachita Montero." Natalia thought it odd that Uncle Lucas had hung up the telephone without saying goodbye.

Chapter 88

Cachita knew Lucas Garach. Years had passed since she had last spoken to him, but she knew Lucas, forever the businessman, Lucas, never to be contradicted, Lucas, always looking out for himself first, Lucas. She knew he would smell their plan, guess their moves, and somehow find them. She feared for the frail soul that was sitting next to her. On that woman's shoulders lay a lifetime of doing what others thought best, obeying what others ordered. A will that had been crushed for a lifetime had suddenly been given a chance to breathe. Cachita was concerned and nervous. Rosa had become confident and only prayed. They were already inside when Rosa asked:

"Will the bank close soon?" Rosa knew little of bank procedure.

"They will lock the doors in about fifteen minutes, but we are already in, so it's fine. They'll take care of us regardless."

"Mrs. Garach," a bank officer called, and Cachita led her to his desk. "What can we do for you this evening?" Rosa looked helpless.

"It's this account," Cachita began, giving the officer the bank book. "Mrs. Garach wants to withdraw some money, but since it is a sizable amount, she could not do it with the teller."

"I'm sure we can help you with that," the officer smiled at the old woman, "does she have identification?"

"Give him your green card, *Abuelita*," Cachita ordered softly, handing over the passport.

"How much do you want to withdraw?"

"She wants forty-six thousand, six-hundred and eighty," Cachita explained, "she needs a cashier's check made out to her name."

The bank officer was somewhat surprised by the large withdrawal but did his best not to look amazed.

"That will leave twenty dollars in the account," he commented. "This is an old account, may I ask if suddenly you are not pleased with our bank's services?"

"Very much so, sir," Cachita answered affably, "but you see, the lady here, is buying herself her first house."

There was no signature of Rosa on record at the bank, but her signature matched the one on her passport. Her picture proved that she was who she claimed to be. The account was clearly under her name, and the bank had no reason to deny her withdrawal. Rosa would have rather seen the cash, she thought it would take at least two envelopes to carry all the money, but all she got was a piece of paper, a check, they claimed that was good for the whole amount.

"It's a check to your name, *Abuelita*." Cachita explained as they stood up; then, she added softly, "Now, we go to the bank across the street which is open until seven-thirty, and we'll open an account with this money."

"Another account? Can't we keep this at home?"

"I wouldn't want you to lose it, or get robbed or something. This will be an account under your name and someone else's, but you will have full control."

"I could get it when we find a house," she clarified.

When they opened the front door of the bank, they saw Lucas getting out of his car. That *cabron* had to catch up to them, Cachita thought. She ran her hand through the old lady's elbow to look Rosa's purse between their hips.

"Hold on to me, *Abuelita*. We're facing a battle," she muttered softly. Rosa did not know they were at war until she saw her son Lucas.

"What are you doing here with my mother?" he almost screamed, unable to control his rage.

"Come off it and start again, 'cause I don't allow anyone to use that tone of voice with me any more," she said without even stopping to look him. She felt the hand of the old woman at her side unexpectedly freeze inside her own.

"What have you done to my mother?" he whispered, grabbing Cachita by the other arm and forcing her to stop walking. Rosa did not know what to do.

"Listen, buster, I should be the one asking you a few questions. So mind your own business and get lost," Cachita intended to proceed to her car, but Lucas would not let go.

"I'll have you prosecuted for extortion. You are trying to get the money off the old woman, and you won't," he threatened.

"As usual, you got it all wrong," she said facing him. In an instant, she saw in his eyes the time, years back, when she had to do the same thing. If destiny had made her confront this man once, and she had gotten her way, there was no way that she would let go of victory now.

"Your mother wanted the money you never wanted to give her, and I showed her how she could get it herself. She just did, so butt out and let us go."

"I know what's best for her; she'll squander it and will have nothing left in a month," he complained.

"Lucas Garach, you only know what's best for you, you old and stupid miser. Your mother is a person who can think for herself and who should do what she wants," Cachita argued.

"She is just an old woman. I'll have you arrested; that's what I'll do. You conned my mother into doing this."

Cachita stood still between Lucas and his mother. The years had given her manners, but there was still some of that daring, poor girl whom life had forced to look out for herself and her children. She took Lucas' shirt in a tight grip in the front and pulled him close.

"You selfish asshole, if you so much as talk to the police, if you so much as come close to your mother to take away what is really hers, I'll go to the newspapers and show them a side of Lucas Garach that few people know. It will be enough to have the public stop buying your beans, so lay off and let us go. We women still have a lot to do," Cachita remembered Lucas' fear of defacing his public image; she had used that against him once, and he had tried it again hoping it would have the same impact.

Lucas straightened up his shirt, regained his composure and, ignoring Cachita, reached for his mother's other arm.

"Not now, Lucas, not now," his mother said firmly. "We have things to finish, let go." Rosa and Cachita had reached Cachita's car. The old woman got in with the help of Cachita while Lucas just stood baffled, watching them.

Chapter 89

"*Abuelita* wants to buy a house."

The first to know was Milagros.

"A house?" Everybody echoed the words in disbelief.

"Yes, *Abuelita* is going to buy a house for Aunt Lucia."

"My, but where do you get that from, child?"

"She told me, just now, when I drove her over to Aunt Lucia's."

"Where did she get—"

"The money?" Milagros nodded. "She has it now; she took it from Uncle Lucas."

"Is this true? I have never seen anyone take anything from Lucas Garach. I can't imagine how she . . . Cachita," she added, convinced.

Milagros didn't say more. She remembered the day when *Abuelita* had asked to speak to Cachita. Cachita, street-wise Cachita, must have helped *Abuelita*.

"A house?" Jose echoed the words just like everyone else. "Where did she get the money?"

"It's her own; she took it from Lucas." Milagros was proud of the feat even though she had had nothing to do with it.

The girls were the most cooperative. In their free time, they launched a search for a house for *Abuelita*. Rosi and Natalia drove block after block, looking for a place that would be appropriate. Three bedrooms, small lot, old but liveable, not more than forty-five thousand.

It was Cachita who found it. Thirty-fourth Street and Thirty-fourth Avenue, Southwest.

"It's a duplex, *Abuelita*. Hadn't you ever thought of those?"

"Duplex?" *Abuelita* had much to learn.

"It's two houses in one. Three bedrooms, two baths in the back, two bedrooms, one bath in the front," Cachita explained.

"One entrance?"

"No, two. One for each."

"One kitchen?"

"No, two . . . and two laundries, many closets. Two porches, one for each, to sit in the afternoons," Cachita smiled with pleasure over *Abuelita* Rosa's expression.

"Cha!" was all the old woman could say.

Abuelita Rosa, Lucia, Natalia, Rosi, and Cachita were the first ones to see it. The walls needed painting, the bathrooms, some cleaning. New paper to line the kitchen cabinets could do the trick there. Lucia began making plans. Where her gait had been slow and hesitant ever since she arrived from Cuba, *Abuelita* Rosa noticed that her daughter waltzed through the house they were inspecting.

"How much do they want for this?"

"Fifty-seven thousand," Cachita answered.

"Oh no, we don't have enough. We could never . . ."

"Listen to me, *Abuelita*. Fermin and his family could live the front part; you wanted him to be part of this too, right?" Rosa nodded. "He could pay a hundred and fifty per month to the bank that would give you the extra money you will need. In fifteen years, it will all be paid for. In the meantime, you would all be able to enjoy it."

"Even if we don't have all the money right now?"

"The bank will certainly lend what you need," Cachita assured her.

Cachita spoke to the owner, and she was able to lower the price to fifty. The owner financed ten thousand, so no bank intervention was necessary. *Abuelita* never quite understood the details of the transaction, but she trusted Cachita. That night she dreamed she was sitting in the front porch of the house watching all her children and grandchildren coming to visit her. Anyone watching her sleep would have seen her smile.

With her main plan well under way, Rosa Garach had one more thing to do. She needed help for this too, so she set on a quest to ask one of her children or grandchildren to teach her to read and write. It was during breakfast at the old apartment, that she finally managed to make her request known.

"Lucia, do you think you could teach me to read and write? Knowing how to sign my name is one thing, but I want to be able to read letters and write to my children who are away." She was thinking of Andres in Guatemala.

Lucia smiled faintly thinking how hard she had tried to become a teacher, to be able to do precisely what her mother was asking her now, to teach others how to read, write, and learn. She smiled and nodded. Mother and daughter embraced like they had not done for many years.

Lucia and Miguel, usually somber and depressed because of their son's sad predicament, also become alive at the prospect of a new home. Maybe Miguelito could be discharged from the hospital in time to join them. He could enjoy his own room; he could take walks around the neighborhood. That would certainly speed his recovery. There was mild joy and hope, lots of hope in that household.

The closing was set for November 17, Miguelito's birthday; that had to be a good omen, Rosa thought. The house had been inspected. The few repairs that had to be made were completed, so it was just a matter or preparing and signing the documents. The house would belong to Lucia and Fermin; Rosa wanted it written that they would be able to stay there for as long as they or their husband, wife, and children lived. In the years to come, when they all had died, the house would belong to Rosi and Juan Andres.

Thus, Rosa dreamed of things that could be.

Chapter 90

"Andres, listen, it's me Milagros . . . yes, Milagros, I'm calling from Miami . . . What did you say? Talk louder; I can hardly hear you." Milagros got up from her seat and continued to talk standing up as if being on her feet brought her closer to her brother-in-law. "I'm calling because you are going to have to come . . . Yes, it's—No, it's not about your son. No, it's not about Norma, either. No, we are celebrating *Abuelita*'s birthday, June 10. Yes, it's a Saturday. Listen, I'm telling you a month before so that you can make all the arrangements."

Rosa Garach had a lot to celebrate for her ninety-fifth birthday. She thanked her Holy Madonna de l'Avella every morning when she saw the leaves sparkle in the sunlight outside her kitchen window. She had woken up early that morning in May to fix fried tomatoes and onions for her son-in-law. The doorbell rang, and she walked quickly to get it.

"Natalia, my, it's early for you to be up and running!" she exclaimed, embracing her granddaughter.

"*Abuelita*, I brought you a fresh loaf of bread. I just wanted to come and talk to you before going to the University." The young woman, more than a head taller than Rosa Garach, smiled and looked around. "Is everyone still asleep?"

"Cha! You've grown, child. I have to look up to see your face," *Abuelita* Rosa exclaimed, "You know, I hear people say that old people shrink in size, and I guess it must be true. I remember when I thought I was a tall woman, and now I have to look up to see your eyes."

"How is Aunt Lucia?"

"Your aunt was up until late last night, embroidering some pillow-cases for this lady whose daughter is getting married. You know she is doing this embroidery, and she goes to a school to help the small children twice a week."

"Does she like it?"

"I've never seen her so active. She sleeps only at night and by eight-thirty, she is up and ready to face the world."

"Good morning, Natalia," Miguelito entered the room and greeted his cousin. "Good morning, *Abuelita*."

He had recuperated most of the color and weight he had lost after two months at a mental hospital. When his parents went to pick him up, three weeks before, he agreed to come home with them, and soon after his arrival, Miguelito had found a way to make a modest living.

"How is your business coming along, Miguel?" Natalia asked.

"We're just starting," he explained, "my father and I, that is. He is like the manager, and I do the work."

"What exactly do you do?"

"Well, I build those toys that people buy from the store in boxes. People either bring them here, or I go to their back yards and build everything from bicycles to swing sets."

"That's a clever idea," she commented, pleased at her cousin's unusual enthusiasm, "What made you think of doing this?"

"It was father's idea, really. Then, I bought the shed in the back, and got it ready for the job, with my old tools and all . . . There are two people coming today at ten, I have to get ready." He kissed Natalia good-bye and went out the back door.

"One of the miracles that I've seen happen in these past few weeks is Miguelito's transformation," Abuelita was radiant. "He is much more communicative, and somehow has gotten to understand his parents. They have changed their attitude too, I have to admit. Miguel even places an add in the neighborhood newspaper to advertise Miguelito's services, and people call all the time."

"What a change, *Abuelita!*"

"I know I have shrunk in size," she observed, smoothing her apron, "But I have never felt so tall. I thought my family was falling . . ."

"But you helped them up."

"God helped me do it. If only we could get Norma out of prison and find Juan Andres. I know God will help us to do that too. But look at me, I'll be ninety-five next month; I'm getting old . . ."

"Rosi went to a rally for relatives of political prisoners in Miami, and they're talking about freeing them all at once."

"Communism is letting them go?"

"Yes, we just have to be patient and wait." Natalia saw some reading books on the coffee table and picked them up. "Aren't these the reading books I brought you?"

"I've been using them too. Since we moved into this house, even before. Your aunt is teaching me, and I'm doing so well that I can read newspaper headlines." She paused. "That's one of the things I told you about feeling tall. I had never learned to do that before."

"If you could be where you wanted, would you rather be in Tirig, back in Spain or here?"

"You see Natalia, it is nice to live a long life, because one gets to see one's children grow, and the grandchildren born and grow, and great-grandchildren, but it is also sad because one also sees one's friends die, so there is no one any more who likes to do the same things we do, or likes to eat the same things we like. Then, one has to change, and one has to move and one has to be where one's family is."

Chapter 91

"Did you talk to Uncle Andres, mother?"

"Yes, I did, and he promised to come. He will be here June 9 and get ready for the next day." Natalia sighed with relief.

"Now there's only Uncle Lucas. You know he hasn't visited *Abuelita* for the past six months?"

"That's right, since she bought the house. It's a sad thing, but he is still angry over it, and he refuses to budge."

"We need Uncle Lucas, Uncle Andres, Aunt Norma, and Juan Andres," Rosi said going over the party list.

"You're really asking for too much, Rosi. Uncle Andres is coming, but who is going to get Uncle Lucas to come? Who knows anything about Juan Andres?" Natalia was less of a dreamer and more pragmatic than Rosi.

"You're such a realist, Natalia. Plus you think you know everything. I have been able to find out that Juan Andres is alive." Rosi waited to see her cousin's expression.

"You've got to be joking. Who told you this?"

"C'mon, girls, don't kid around with that. It's something really sad that has happened in our family, and we can't joke with this."

"I'm not joking, Aunt Milagros, I tell you. I know for a fact he's alive."

"Okay, Rosi, now you sit down and tell us how you managed this one." Natalia sat closer to her cousin so as not to miss a word.

"You know that I have this friend from the university . . ."

"Sure, friend?" her cousin interrupted sarcastically.

"Well, you either let me finish, or you'll never find out how come I know this."

"Leave her alone, Natalia," Milagros, always the mediator, interceded for her niece.

"Marcos, my friend, lived and studied in the Soviet Union for ten years."

"I bet he's a communist."

"And I bet you're wrong because you haven't even spoken to him once."

"Don't fight, girls! Does your friend Marcos know anything about Juan Andres?" Milagros asked in disbelief.

"He knows he met a young man, a little younger than he, whose name was Juan Andres Garach."

"In the Soviet Union?"

"Yes, in Kiev, which is where he went to school. Marcos told me a long time ago, and I asked him to write and find out if the boy he met is there still."

"Marcos can write back? I thought he defected?"

"He did. In Canada, but he can still write back."

"And?"

"The friend answered with Juan Andres' address. He is still going to school in Kiev. He is studying engineering at the University."

"My God," Milagros exclaimed.

"Amazing story, right?" Rosi was pleased with her shocker. "Well, I wrote to him then, and asked him to write to us and gave him *Abuelita*'s address, and asked him to write to her."

"Heavens, child, your *Abuelita* can't read."

"That's what you think! Are your ready for another shocker?" Natalia offered. "*Abuelita* is already reading newspaper headlines, and she is not stopping her lessons. If Juan Andres writes legibly, she'll be able to read his letter, and you know what?" Natalia approached Rosi and embraced her warmly. "Nothing in this world would please *Abuelita* more, Rosi. You've done a super job."

Milagros was ready to cry watching her niece and her daughter, but Natalia was not one to brood over emotion, and immediately snapped back. "Now, how do we do this? Do we tell Uncle Andres when he comes?"

"No," Milagros was quick to react. "We don't even know if this is going to happen or not, so let's wait."

"Now, if we could just get Uncle Lucas to come," said Rosi.

"You leave our Uncle Lucas to me. He can't say no."

"What about Cachita? She's done so much for *Abuelita*, should we include her?"

"I don't see why we should exclude her from *Abuelita*'s birthday celebration. As far as I'm concerned, she should be coming too. She's been a member of our family for so long. It's time we proved it."

"Well, Natalia," Rosi announced, "I guess Cachita is yours too. You call her and make her come."

Natalia who was playing with a napkin, rolled up into a ball and threw it at her cousin. Rosi, falsely enraged by such a move, grabbed a napkin herself, crumpled it into a ball and threw it back. The two young women, turned children, began running around the dining room table, throwing paper balls back and forth and laughing wildly.

"Girls, girls, *formalidad*, please. Now, when are you two going to grow up? Look at this mess! You are almost university graduates and are behaving like . . ." That's when Milagros decided to join the fun and start throwing paper balls.

The Saturday after Mother's Day, Natalia and Rosi went to visit Cachita Montero. Cachita had always wanted to be surrounded by a lot of land, so time and circumstances had placed her far from the little room in El Cerro where she had borne her two children. Cachita lived in what Miamians called "horse country," a section to the west of Miami where lots are at least an acre, and where amidst huge mansions lay smaller estates-turned-nurseries. Cachita's home was one of these.

The two young women drove down the entrance where they saw an old station wagon parked.

"We're in the right place. That's her car," Natalia said.

"How do you know?"

"I saw it when Cachita picked up *Abuelita*. It must have been the day she took her to the bank. Boy, what guts."

"What do you mean?" Rosi understood English well, but still, some expressions baffled her.

"Courage, I guess," she said, picking up her purse and getting out of the car. "Had Uncle Lucas known, he would have had her executed. It was just one gutsy person against another."

"Her *guts* won, you could say, right?"

Natalia wasn't sure you could really say it like that, but Rosi was right. Their thoughts drifted, however, for within seconds a Cachita, much different from what they had seen before, appeared before them with her arms loaded with plants.

"Well, look who's here. Why didn't you call me, so I could have cooked something for you, girls? What pleasure to see you!" Cachita put down her orchids, took off her gardening gloves and approached Rosi and Natalia to welcome them with a kiss as if it were customary for the girls to visit her. In fact, this was the first time either of them had seen Cachita at home.

"Don't worry about it, we're just here for a little while," Natalia's attention had drifted to the beautiful flowers Cachita was holding in her hands. "What do you call these? They are truly beautiful."

"Oh, they're epidendrums. I learned to grow them when I worked for a lady who had a passion for orchids," she said putting on her gloves again and picking up her plants. "Now, I grow them as a business, and quite a good business it is too. Come, let's take this to the nursery, and then we can go inside the house and have a *cafecito*."

No one spoke again until they were seated in Cachita's porch where, faithful to her Cuban tradition, she kept four huge Cuban rocking chairs. "This is where I rock my nervous thoughts to rest every evening." Natalia liked the thought of rocking nervous thoughts to rest.

"Cachita, we are here to talk about *Abuelita*'s birthday."

"Oh, yes, the tenth of June, I know. I never told her, but I prayed for her on that day, ever since I knew that was her day."

"And when was this?" Rosi had not finished asking when Natalia had inconspicuously kicked her in the ankle. She had warned Rosi against asking Cachita any embarrassing questions, but you could leave it up to Rosi to . . .

"Oh, that was years and years ago, before you girls were even born," Cachita smiled.

"Well, we're celebrating *Abuelita*'s birthday big time. Cake, paella, a professional photographer even is coming to take pictures. Uncle Andres is coming from Guatemala . . ."

"Oh, Andres!" Cachita exclaimed, "I would really like to see him."

"Yes, he's coming just for the occasion, and . . ."

"We'll like you to come too," Rosi blurted out, "if you don't mind, that is."

Cachita looked down, silent for the first time since the two cousins had first arrived. She rocked her rocking chair slowly, making the wooden board beneath her creak cheerfully. To calm her nervous thoughts, Natalia imagined. With both her hands, Cachita, who usually made no show of emotion, wiped tears on the edge of her eyes.

"I'm sorry, girls, but I . . ." she remained quiet in search of words for a few seconds and then continued, "It's hard for me to say no, because I have wanted to be part of your family a whole lifetime, but . . ."

"You have been, Cachita," Natalia objected, "You helped Uncle Andres, not once but many times, right?"

"Oh, he deserved my help because he was good to me and to my children," Cachita said looking up earnestly.

"Had it not been for you, Rosi added, "*Abuelita* would not have bought the house where we live."

"That's right," Natalia echoed. By then all three of them were rocking away their nervous thoughts.

"A long time ago, when I needed help badly for one of my children," Cachita confessed, "I was so desperate that I went to your Aunt Carolina, may she be in God's care. She promised to help but she asked for one condition."

"That you not see our Uncle Lucas," Natalia added.

"You knew?"

"No, I imagined."

"Well, that's right. I've kept my promise. To this day, I have never seen your Uncle Lucas again." Suddenly she smiled. "Except that day at the bank some months ago, when I am sure he wishes he hadn't seen me." She raised her eyebrows and smiled mischievously.

"But will you come?" Natalia insisted.

"No, I plan to keep my promise until Cachita Montero is no longer, but," she added thoughtfully, "I would like for you girls to do me a favor."

The two young women stopped rocking and looked at Cachita intently.

"Invite Juan and Alberto and their families," Cachita asked. "You know, I never had a family to offer them. They could never join the Garach family as they were growing up because of who they were. Lucas has accepted them and all; I know they're grown men, but they have never met *la Abuelita*, and they have never felt part of a family, your family."

Natalia and Rosi stood up to embrace her. Lucas and Alberto had just become part of the Garach family.

Chapter 92

Andres Garach had not returned to Miami in five years. He had made Guatemala his home and enjoyed the loneliness and the distance that separated him from Cuba and his painful memories. Norma's imprisonment and Juan Andres' disappearance had taken the life out of Andres' eyes and the joy from his heart. He had lived a lifetime surmounting odds: his physical handicap, his father's animosity, poverty. Those obstacles were small challenges compared to the uncertainty he woke up to every morning since Norma had been captured in Manacas by Castro's militia. Miami was, for Andres, an arm of Cuba, so even at the airport, he felt the reality of his own tragedy pounding in his head in a way he had not felt for years. Two young women approached him as he left customs.

"Uncle Andres, it's us," his niece came up to him and embraced him warmly. "I'm Natalia, don't you remember me?" she asked looking at him.

"My how you've—"

"Don't tell me that I've grown, because I haven't." She smiled, a little worried over being the tallest in the whole family.

"I don't mean grown, I mean more . . . like a woman."

"I know what you mean, it's the university graduate in me, it's showing," she said jokingly as she took his arm and led him to the parking lot. "I graduate next year, you know."

Rosi immediately caught up with them and took her uncle's other arm. He looked at her, startled, unable to recognize who she was.

"It's Rosi, your other niece," she explained.

He stopped walking and looked at her closely, perhaps trying to find in her eyes some part of his life that had left him behind.

"You look so much like my sister, like your father. I would have recognized you anywhere." The way he ran his hand across her forehead and down her hair, it was easy to tell he saw a little of Juan Andres in her too. He recovered quickly from the gust of emotion. "Your parents, where are they? When am I going to see them?"

"You'll never believe what *Abuelita* did, Uncle," Natalia began. The story continued as they rode out of Miami International Airport, down Thirty-seventh Avenue, and straight to *Abuelita*'s duplex. News of Rosa's feat had not reached Guatemala City, but it was enough for Andres to forget his misery and smile like he had not done in years.

"She took it just like that?"

"She did," Rosi said proudly.

"But someone must have taken her to the bank, who told her she could do it?"

"Cachita Montero, do you remember who she is?"

"Ah, Cachita," he said longingly. "It seems like that woman came to earth to get people out of tight spots."

"What do you mean?"

"Well, she got me out of many difficult situations."

"Back in Cuba?"

"Years ago," he added.

"Listen, Uncle," Natalia interrupted, "the important thing is that today is *Abuelita*'s party, and all the Garachs have to gather at her house this afternoon."

"Does she know?"

"She has no idea. We have to keep it that way too," Rosi said. "The hard part will be getting Uncle Lucas to come."

"Has anyone told him?"

"Really, no one has had the courage to," Natalia confessed. "Since *Abuelita* took the money, he has been really angry and upset. He could not accept that *Abuelita*, and not he, had her way."

"So what are you going to do?"

Natalia turned at her grandmother's driveway in time to answer her uncle's question. "We will have to trick him somehow, I guess," Natalia shrugged her shoulders. "Well, this is it! This is *Abuelita*'s new home."

"My goodness! This is really, really, really nice." Looking at Rosi, he added, "Does she know I'm coming? She is pretty old for surprises, you know."

"Mother told her you were coming to visit, so she's expecting you any day now," Natalia said.

Andres, who used to be the tallest of the Garachs, had stooped to time. His limp was hardly noticeable, but the weight of circumstances was heavy on his shoulders. He carried his suitcase walking slowly to the front door of his mother's home. Rosi ran ahead of him and raised her index finger to her lips to ask him to be quiet; she had the keys to

Rosa's home, and wanted to open the door quietly. The key turned twice while Andres peeked through the window and saw his mother sitting in the dining room table, with Lucia at her side.

"She's there," Andres whispered, "and so is Lucia. What are they doing?"

"This is *Abuelita*'s time to take her lesson."

"Lesson?"

"Yes, Aunt Lucia is teaching her to read and write," Rosi smiled as the door opened noiselessly. Lucia looked up; Rosa Garach turned her head. They were not expecting anyone just yet, and were curious about the noise at the door. "It's us, Natalia and me," Rosi announced, "and we have a visitor."

Lucia immediately recognized her brother and looked up. Rosa Garach squinted at the sight in front of her. The glare from the sun outside only revealed the silhouette of a young woman and an old man; she could not distinguish the face. He had not seen Rosa Garach in ten years and, at times, thought he would not see her ever again. Often when he closed his eyes he could picture her always at the wash fountain in Tirig, with her wash basket on her hip, her apron wet with wash water or maybe tears, her braid tied back, her blue eyes, almost imperceptible, squinting—just like now—at the brightness of the Valencian sun.

"Rosi, is that you?" she asked.

"Yes, *Abuelita*, I have brought you a surprise," she said slowly.

"Surprise? What could surprise an old woman like me?" she commented, smiling. She put her hand over her eyes to see better, but could not tell who it was until Andres began to walk.

"Andres?" The strength left her voice, and she had to sit down.

Andres Garach quickly reached his mother and knelt by her side to hug her.

"Yes, it's me, mother." As he looked at her, tears slid down his cheeks. "You are as beautiful as ever, you smell of soap, and you look so good!" His words never expressed the happiness he felt with her by his side.

She hugged him tightly and caressed his shoulders, maybe to make sure that he was really there.

"My son, my eldest son!" Rosa Garach trembled next to him. "My eyes lost all their tears long ago. Since then, I haven't cried, but how wonderful that my heart still has room for happiness."

"How long since I last saw you?" Fermin said, coming into the room, visibly moved by his brother's arrival.

"Almost ten years."

"We were so near each other, and you never let me know. I would've taken things to you," Fermin complained to his brother.

"It would have been too much of a risk, Fermin. Remember that if Castro's militia had found out, they would have killed us both. Then what would have happened to the world." Andres tried to smile to hide a deep sigh.

"Have you heard any news about Aunt Norma?"

"Natalia," Rosi interrupted, "those things are best not talked about. We don't want to make Uncle Andres sad."

"No, Rosi, I haven't forgotten your aunt and cousin. They're always in my mind and if there's such a thing as mental telepathy, they must know it too." He turned to Natalia. "No, I've had no news. But as they say: 'no news is good news.' If anything had happened to her, I wouldn've known already, I'm sure."

"How could you get out of Cuba, Uncle? Weren't they looking for you?"

"I hid for three years not too far from where you used to live."

"Who lived there?"

"A good man. He helped me because he was a friend of a friend of the family," Andres explained.

"Why were you hiding for so long? Why didn't you leave earlier?"

"At that time I still hoped to find out the whereabouts of your cousin, Juan Andres. I had several opportunities to get away, but I asked the man who was hiding me to let me stay."

"And?" The Garachs made a circle around Andres.

"Wait, Uncle Andres, don't say anything until I get back." Natalia jumped from her seat and ran to the bedroom.

"Don't worry, Uncle Andres," Rosi explained when she saw her uncle's curious glance, "Natalia probably went to get some paper and pencil. She has this odd habit of writing everything down."

In a few minutes, Natalia returned with paper and pencil, ready to listen to her uncle's story.

"I decided to leave the country when I realized that there was nothing I could do for my family as long as I was cooped up in that small room."

"What did you do then?"

"First, I talked to the man who was hiding me. Everything depended on him. If he hadn't helped me . . ."

"Was he a counterrevolutionary?"

"No, Natalia; he was a *fidelista*, but a fine man all the same. Thanks to him I'm alive today. It's a hard thing to believe, but I think he was sad when I told him I had decided to leave. We had become such good friends. I don't think I'll ever forget him."

"Then he was the one who arranged for you to get on a boat."

"Well, not exactly. Jesusito was a foreman at a factory in Havana. In 1967 they sent him to Mantanzas to learn some new techniques. While in Mantanzas, he also learned that some workers were making plans to leave the country illegally. They thought they would go to jail for sure when Jesus found out their plans, but he promised not to say anything if they agreed to help me."

"Did they?"

"They had no choice. There were three young men and a fourth one who was a draft deserter and was hiding in a garbage dump in Mantanzas. That was the place Jesusito took me."

"How long did you stay there?"

"About ten days. The plan was to steal a fishing boat from the Yumuri River. The guy who thought of it must've been crazy; none of them knew a thing about boats or sailing. Besides, it was December, and the seas were rough."

"Wouldn't it have been easier to leave from the coast?"

"Not in this case. The coast was more heavily patrolled than the river; the idea of escaping from the river was so crazy they didn't imagine anybody would try it." Andres paused for a few seconds and then went on. "One of them went to get us at the dump on December 27, the other two were already at the river. We were all wearing dark clothes."

"Of course! To blend into the darkness!" Natalia interrupted excitedly.

"Natalia, let your uncle go on."

"Three of us were going down one side of the river, the other two were going down the other. The three of us got into a row boat and made our way downstream. The other two cut the lines of a forty-five-foot boat and set it adrift. We had to row to get to it. All of that had to be done before getting to the big bend of the river where there were always many militiamen. Finally, we got on board the boat, broke the padlock, and hid in the cabin. The two who stayed on deck were posing as soldiers. We made it into Matanzas Bay without being detected, but then a heavy storm broke out. Instead of bearing towards the left, where the customs office was, we put the helm to the right, trying to get out to sea. They turned on the searchlights then and located us. We thought they were going to catch us, but the waves were so high they hid us from the searchlights. The storm grew worse by the minute; the boat was being thrown against walls of water."

"Who was the pilot?"

"That guy I told you had concocted the whole scheme and knew nothing about boats."

"It was crazy!"

"Weren't you scared to death?"

"Not really. The situation was pretty serious, but the boat was full of foodstuffs we hadn't seen in years. We decided that if they were going to catch us, at least we'd have full stomachs. We spent the night eating and watching the lighthouses on the coast. In the morning it was cold, and our 'leader' decided to turn off the engines to give them a rest. We had cut the engines when all of a sudden two Cuban coast-guard cutters appeared over the horizon. We tried to start the engines again, but the damn things didn't want to work."

"That was bad luck! What did you do then, Uncle?"

"You'll see. If we had been able to get the engine to start again, they would've picked us up on radar, but since we couldn't start the motor, we were able to escape. By seven o'clock that night we spotted the lights of Marathon Key, in Florida."

"Thank God!" Milagros sighed, relieved.

"The worst part was that they wanted to send us back to Cuba. They said we had stolen a boat, and that was piracy. Luckily, they found out that Norma and the father of one of the boys were in prison, and that helped us."

"Uncle, what does Yumuri mean?"

"This girl never gets tired of asking questions!" he smiled. "That's the name they gave the river and its valley. According to legend, that was the name of an Indian who preferred to throw
himself in the river and die rather than submit to the Spaniards."

"Something like what you did, right, Uncle? Only that you came out of the river alive," the girl added. Everyone was silent for a few seconds. "Well, people, I have to go now, I'll be back later on today, but I have to do things." She winked at Rosi.

"Oh, Rosi, somebody called you from ASCUPP. They said they had to get in touch with you today," Lucia said.

"ASCUPP?" Rosi's eyes opened wide even though she tried to look natural.

"What a weird name, Rosi—ASCUPP?"

Rosi smiled and rushed to the door to close it behind her cousin. "You are so tactless that I could cut you up into little pieces, *caramba!* Why did you have to go around repeating that ASCUPP business?" Rosi became really angry at Natalia.

"What in the world is ASCUPP?"

Rosi pressed her lips together. "ASCUPP, for your information, is the Association for Cuban Political Prisoners."

Chapter 93

"Lucas Garach, please." As soon as Natalia got to her house, she called her uncle to put her plan into action. "Uncle Lucas? It's me, Natalia. Listen, uncle, I have this problem and perhaps you can help. This friend of mine, his father, owns a grocery store. He wants to order the products you represent, but he wants to meet you and talk to you. I told . . . Yes, it's here in the city. Well, I told him that I would introduce you myself, and . . . Well, I was thinking of this afternoon, you know, late, after work and all? You will? You can? You don't know how grateful I am for this, Uncle Lucas. It's a good friend, and I really want to serve his father . . . I can pick you up if you want . . . At six? Six-thirty? That's perfect, Uncle. See you then."

Natalia breathed a sigh of relief when she hung up the receiver.

Back on Thirty-fourth Street, everything was being prepared at Fermin's house, right in front of Rosa's. Andres had kept Rosa and Lucia occupied all afternoon, so Asuncion and Rosi had time to get some of the food ready and set up the apartment for the party. The table was ready with its best tablecloth; Asuncion was in the kitchen while Rosi was dusting the coffee table and the frames holding pictures of almost every family member living and dead.

"Mother, tell me, when was this?" she asked holding up a picture of a heavy set man dressed in black, his wife sitting next to him, four boys surrounding them, and a baby in the wife's lap.

"That's *Abuelita* and the whole family the day your father left home for the first time."

"Amazing how they all changed, although Uncle Jose does have the same face, and Uncle Lucas has the same . . . the same look in him, like one who is going to own the world."

"I guess it was all clear then that he was going to be wealthy and successful," Asuncion observed.

"Aunt Lucia was so cuddly. All of them had such serious faces, though," Rosi was thinking out loud, "and everyone is wearing black."

"They must have been either mourning for someone or black must have been the fashionable color for pictures back then," the telephone interrupted Asuncion's comment, and since she was closer, she answered it. *"Diga.* Yes, this is the home of Rosi Garach . . . Wait a moment, she will be right with you." With her hand on the receiver, Asuncion came closer to the living room. "It's those people from ASCUPP again. They called you this morning."

Rosi raised her eyebrows and smiled. She was the only family member who had been in touch with the Association of Cuban Political Prisoners on behalf of her Aunt Norma, of course. No other family member had had hope. Aunt Norma's family had refused to leave the island thinking that they would be more useful to Norma herself there. Uncle Andres thought every effort was surely useless. Rosi had hope and knew that pressure from Cuban exiles and from the world community would one day convince Castro that political prisoners were not adequate propaganda for his regime.

"Yes, this is Rosi Garach . . . Oh, hello, Luis . . . Yes, I remember what you said, but, . . . I wasn't expecting it so soon . . . You think that perhaps by next month? . . . Well, this is something her husband has to hear, and he has just arrived in Miami this morning. Yes, give me your number, and I'll go see him right now and have him call you."

Rosi placed the receiver on her chest as she recovered from her amazement at the news.

"They had word from reputable sources now, and they even have a list of the first group. Aunt Norma is on it!"

Such was Rosi's surprise that for a few minutes she remained sitting, the receiver still in her hands.

"Do you believe them, Rosi?" The uncertainty of their experience had made Asuncion incredulous.

"There have been rumors of freeing the prisoners before, but they never had names. This time it could be for real." She finally hung up the receiver and commented thoughtfully, "Now I don't know how I will tell Uncle Andres."

Chapter 94

Lucas Garach met his niece in the waiting room of Lucas Garach, Inc., the company he had founded in Cuba and had been able to resurrect in the United States. He was the most affluent of the Garach clan; this was evident from his tailor-made suit, the diamond ring he wore on his left hand, and the gold buckle with his initials he had made for his leather belt. He refused to settle to old age, so he hoped his hair dyed a subtle shade of brown and his impeccable clothing gave him a more youthful appearance. In truth, the clothing, the dyes or creams were not enough to cover years of toil and sacrifice, a lifetime of depending on his gut feeling and imagination to concoct business dealings, decisions that, although he refused to admit it, had left him with his own share of sorrows and disappointments.

"Uncle Lucas, my, how nice you look, as usual I might add," Natalia was at her tactful best that afternoon, for with Garach obstinacy, she was determined to take her Uncle Lucas where he had made it clear he did not want to go. She approached him and kissed him on the cheek. "We never get to see much of you any more, Uncle." Natalia took old Lucas by the arm and led him to the car.

They went inside Natalia's car and buckled their seat belts. "Well, now, tell me where we are going and what does your friend's father want to know."

"Now, Uncle, we have to talk quite seriously today, a from niece to uncle type of conversation. We have to talk about something you don't like, I mean." She cleared her voice to be able to continue.

"I don't understand you," Lucas answered confused.

"Well, it's like this. Sometimes we say things or do things we don't mean, and then we get in them so deep, it becomes quite hard to back out." She cleared her throat once more.

"I still don't understand you," Lucas was getting suspicious.

"It's like this. You haven't seen or called *Abuelita* for the past six months, and . . ."

"If you've brought me here to talk to me about your grandmother, you must take me right back to my office, because I have nothing to say on the subject." Lucas' face turned red, and he became quite serious.

"Uncle, you have to listen to me, please," she said softly.

"You have to listen to me young lady. What you have done is a trick, and Lucas Garach will not be tricked." His voice wasn't so soft any more. "Take me back. I order you!"

"Well, right now you are going to listen to me whether you want to or not, because I am not taking you back, you are coming with me." Natalia was driving straight to Rosa's duplex.

"Where?"

"Today is *Abuelita*'s birthday, and we are planning to celebrate."

"Well, go and celebrate; you certainly don't need me for that."

"We most certainly do, and that's why I have gone through all this trouble of lying to you and getting you inside my car," she protested.

"I am not going to see your grandmother. She tricked me too, if you want to know, and nobody tricks Lucas Garach, not even his mother," he said proudly.

"Uncle Lucas I want you to think about something for a few minutes and then answer," she continued ignoring his comment.

"Instead of picking me up, you should have picked up Cachita Montero. I know. I know what she did, and it was downright disloyal," he complained.

"What would you have done if, instead of *Abuelita*, you had been keeping the money for your father? Would you have given it back to him?" Natalia's question suddenly stopped the old man's chatter.

"What do you mean?"

"What I just said. If instead of having kept the money for your mother, you had kept it for your father."

"Well, that would have been different. Father would have known what to do with his money."

"Why your father and not your mother."

"Father had experience. Mother had no experience. She really didn't know what to do with it."

"She asked you for it plenty, and she made her wishes known," Natalia argued.

"Crazy wishes. A house. Now, what is a ninety-year-old woman going to do with a house? She had these impossible dreams."

"What if she had been a ninety-year-old man, possibly grandfather?" Lucas was silent after his niece's comment.

"You are trying to get after me with these woman liberation ideas, and they just don't apply to your grandmother."

"Why, because she's old?"

"Grandmother always had to be led by the hand. She never knew how to do things like this."

"Admit it, Uncle, you could have led her by the hand, and you refused. You wanted to do what you thought best, and she beat you to it." She spoke quickly and didn't give him a chance to react. "She did what was best for her and her children; she had the right. If you could see no further than your own thoughts and didn't pay attention to her wishes, she had no choice but to go around you. She went to someone who she knew could manage what was impossible for her. *Abuelita* was right, and that's how she got her way."

"This is not what was best," he complained again.

"You would not say that if you saw Aunt Lucia's happiness amidst her grief over her sick son. You would not say that if you saw *Abuelita* treasure every inch of land that surrounds her little house. You would not say that if you saw the change it was for Rosi to have a room to study in and stop sleeping in the living room of that rotten old apartment." Natalia took advantage of the fact that her uncle could not answer and continued her speech. "You have to go there with me tonight and celebrate *Abuelita*'s triumph, the only moment of glory she has known in the past ninety-five years. Your presence there is important to her because I am sure she wants you to approve of what she did. She wants you to admit, if not in words in actions, that you could have been wrong in getting upset, and that all is forgiven."

Chapter 95

"*Abuelita, Abuelita,*" Rosi opened the door of her grandmother's house and peeked in. All four of them—*Abuelita*, Miguel, Lucia, and Miguelito—were sitting in the living room, around the television set watching a Spanish soap opera.

"Come in, Rosi, we're only watching television, come, join us," old Rosa offered. She was sitting in a comfortable chair mending socks and stockings with the sewing box by her side.

"I have some things to tell you, *Abuelita*, and since tomorrow is your birthday and all, I think I should tell you now."

"What is it?" Rosa suddenly looked worried. "Anything wrong with your father, your mother . . . you? Has that boy who came from God knows where been treating you well?"

"Everything is fine, *Abuelita*, and I'm sure the news I have will please you a lot."

"News? What news? Are you getting married, child?"

The young woman laughed. "Well, that would certainly be good news, but it's not it." She became serious again. "It's about somebody whom you love very much . . ."

"Ah, child, you know there are many whom I love very much," she answered, confused.

"This one, you haven't seen in a long time," Rosi added.

"Juan Andres," Rosa Garach became quite serious when she mentioned his name.

"*Abuelita*, we have found him," Rosi said gently, afraid that the surprises she had in store for Rosa could be too much for her.

"Alive?" she asked faintly.

"Yes," Rosi took an envelope from her pocket and handed it to her grandmother. "He is living very far away, in the Soviet Union, but he's alive, and he remembers us, and one day, we might even get to see him, I know it." Rosa Garach looked down at her lap.

"Well, open it, *Abuelita*," Rosi said. Rosa Garach looked at the letter closely.

"It's addressed to you."

"Or to you, we have the same name, remember?"

"You read it? Is it really from . . ."

"It came today, and I thought it was for me, so I read it, but it's really for the whole family. There, open it now. Do you want me to read it?"

Rosa Garach shook her head, took the letter out of the envelope, unfolded it, and began to read. Lucia, Miguel, and Miguelito did not dare speak as they watched the old lady scanning the page slowly. Rosa sat up straight, but her hands shook so, that her tired eyes could not make out the message on the page. She stood and walked to the dining room table where the light was stronger, and she set the letter on the table. With her hands holding each other tightly placed at the edge of the table, she began to read. A few minutes later, she looked up at Rosi and the others who were sitting watching her, uncertain if Rosa could actually read and understand the letter.

"*Cha!*" she exclaimed. For the first time in many years, she had to wipe the tears off her face. "I thought I had no tears left," she said sniffling and smiling.

"He is alive; I think he is well," she smiled. "May the Holy Madonna de L'Avella be blessed that on a day like this I have found out that my youngest grandson is alive, *cha!*"

She stood up, walked towards Rosi and embraced her. The rest did not know what to do and applauded smiling.

"Now," Rosi announced as soon as she regained her composure, "You all have to come with me to my house since the surprise does not end here."

"So late? We aren't even dressed to go out," Lucia objected.

"It doesn't matter, Aunt Lucia, it's only us, and besides your dress is fine."

Lucia ran to the bedroom to comb her hair and put on some cologne. Miguelito tucked his shirt inside his pants nervously, and Miguel buttoned the shirt he was wearing over a white T-shirt. Only Rosa Garach, with the letter inside her apron pocket, seemed ready to go.

"Turn off the lights," Lucia warned as she stepped outside to help her mother down the small steps. Miguelito followed in front of Miguel; all of them walked slowly, uncertain as to what was going on. Rosi locked the door and ran quickly to her own front door before the rest of the small group arrived.

Fermin Garach's front door was wrapped in birthday wrapping with ribbons and a bow, just like a present. From the large bow in the middle, hung a card with a message. Rosi smiled when she saw the group look at the door surprised.

"How do you like it, *Abuelita?*" Rosa seemed somewhat confused and smiled. Then Rosi held up the card that was hanging from the bow in the middle. "Now, I'm sure that you can read this on your own, *Abuelita.*" Rosa Garach had not taken her hand out of her pocket for even a minute.

"*Feliz Cumpleaños, Abuelita,*" she read slowly, then smiled as Rosi opened the door and she saw her whole family standing, waiting with glasses of *sidra* held up in the air and singing "Happy Birthday to You." Joaquina was playing the keyboard; Andres, Jose, Milagros, Gerardo, Asuncion, and Fermin, people she did not know, even the neighbors sang loudly. At the farthest end, there was Lucas, her son; Lucas Garach had come and was holding up his glass to toast to her health on her birthday. Rosa nervously struck the palms of her hand together as in a faint clap and did not stop exclaiming "*Cha!*" while her daughter and family, still astounded, joined in the chorus. "*Cha!*" she repeated over and over again. Rosi came from behind and untied the apron to take it off, but before her granddaughter could manage, Rosa Garach rescued Juan Andres' letter from inside the apron pocket and brought it close to her heart.

As soon as the song died down, all the guests slowly approached her to give her a kiss and wish her Happy Birthday. They touched her frail shoulders and back, "Happy Birthday, Rosa." She smiled gratefully; they smiled back. Ninety-five years old, yes, that's how old she was. That she still looked like a young woman of sixty? *Cha!* Now, that could not be true. One of the neighbors gave her flowers, but unable to hold herself back any longer, she walked slowly towards Lucas and took his hand. Her legs seemed to give up, when Lucas led her to the chair right behind them.

"These are Juan and Alberto, mother." She saw Cachita's resemblance and stretched out her hand to caress their faces rather than a formal greeting.

"Now, everyone," Natalia said, "it is time to offer our toast to *Abuelita* on this day," called out Natalia. Instead of having one person propose a long speech, I would like each of you who has something to say, to offer her a special toast on her birthday."

Natalia stood next to Lucas Garach and whispered in his ears while others spoke: "C'mon, Uncle, you must toast her too." Lucas did not give in.

"To my dear neighbor Rosa, whom I see washing, mending, walking about the house putting things in order all day long, from whom I have learned that great effort breeds great rewards," the lady who lived next door was the first to toast.

"Show her it's over; you have to let know that all the bitterness is gone," Natalia whispered again anxiously.

"To my dear mother, whose calm smile through good and bad has always reminded me of the value of being positive," followed Fermin.

"It's your turn now, Uncle Lucas. Say something!" Natalia exclaimed in a frantic whisper.

"To my mother whose love has helped me survive," said Lucia.

"To *Abuelita*," offered Miguelito, "whose presence has given me something to hang on to when I needed it."

Not a word from Lucas.

"To my *Abuelita*," Natalia said, "who has opened her life to me, has shown me where I come from, and has given me lots and lots to write about."

Rosa was radiant. No one knew whether or not she understood everything that was said there that night, but her eyes had a sparkle. Everyone thought the toast was over when Lucas began to speak.

"I know I got my ambition and business sense from my father, but I had never realized before tonight that I received my tenacity and unflagging capacity for work from Rosa Garach. Here's to you, mother, let's all toast to celebrate your long life."

Those present chorused, "To Rosa," and rang together glass to glass. The doorbell! It was the photographer, who had been delayed. Twenty years had passed since her seventy-fifth birthday back in the house in Miramar, but there sat Rosa in the middle of the sofa with Lucas on one side and Andres on the other. Jose and Fermin still filled the next seats on either side, and Lucia stood right behind her mother with her husband and son next to her. Milagros, Asuncion, Rosi, Natalia, Lina and her family, Pepe and his family lined up around them.

The Garach family indeed had grown. The rest of the guests stood in front of them just watching.

"Ready?" The photographer had been patient and was making sure everyone was set for him to shoot.

"One moment, please," Rosa stood up for a moment. "We are not complete yet," she objected. "Juan, Alberto," she called out. "Please, join us with your families," she told them, pointing to the sides of the group where they could stand.

The Garach family was settling into a new present far from la Morellana, Tirig and Valencia, a new present far from La Habana and New York. Rosa felt it was a new present partly created by her and her ever-present dream to take care of the family until the end.

"Smile," the photographer captured the wrinkles of happiness, glow of joy, the strength of togetherness and even the aura of hope that emanated from Juan Andres' letter which Rosa still held tightly in her hand.